DEVIATION

PUSHKIN PRESS

IATION

LUCE D'ERAMO

Translated from the Italian by Anne Milano Appel

Pushkin Press
71–75 Shelton Street
London WC2H 9JQ

Deviation was first published as *Deviazione* in Italy, 1979

This translation first published by Farrar, Straus & Giroux in 2018
First published by Pushkin Press in 2019

9 8 7 6 5 4 3 2 1

ISBN 13: 978-1-78227-388-2

Offset by Tetragon, London
Printed and bound by CPI Group (UK) Ltd, Croydon CRO 4YY

www.pushkinpress.com

CONTENTS

TRANSLATOR'S INTRODUCTION

The novel *Deviation*, by Luce D'Eramo, published by Mondadori in 1979 and reissued by Feltrinelli in 2012, is the story of the author's experiences as a volunteer worker in the Nazi labor camps in Germany during World War II, as well as her attempts to make sense of that "parenthesis" in her life during the decades that followed. Begun several years after her return to Italy in 1945, the book was not completed and published until more than thirty years later. Categorized as fiction, the text may also be viewed as autobiography, narrative nonfiction, a memoir, a testimonial, a Bildungs-roman, and a psychoanalytical probe into the reasons certain of the author's memories were repressed.

Though the events that inspired the novel took place within a relatively short span of time (1944–1945), they played a very prominent, determining role over the ensuing course of the author's life. The biographical facts can be summarized as follows: Luce D'Eramo (née Lucette Mangione) was born in Reims, France. The daughter of Italian parents, she lived in France until the age of fourteen, when her family returned to Italy in 1938. From a bourgeois Fascist family (her father was a government official in the Republic of Salò and her mother had served as a voluntary secretary of the Italian Fascio in Paris), she enrolled in the Faculty of Letters at the Sapienza University of Rome and was a member of GUF (Association of Fascist Students). At age eighteen, rendered uncertain by the collapse of Fascism and her ideals, she left home to volunteer in the German labor camps (Lagers) to disprove what she believed were lies being told about Nazi-Fascism, and to determine the truth firsthand. The encounter changed her, leading to a desire to shed her identity as the privileged daughter of a Fascist bureaucrat; discarding her documents, she voluntarily slipped into a group of deportees being sent to Dachau, from which she escaped in October 1944. These experiences, narrated in the book, culminate with a devastating accident on February 27, 1945, in Mainz: while Luce was helping to rescue the wounded buried under the rubble of a bombed building, a wall collapsed on her, leaving her permanently paralyzed. In 1946 she married Pacifico D'Eramo and they moved to Rome; their son, Marco, was born in 1947. Though the marriage ended in separation years later, Luce went on to make a life for herself and her son, obtaining a doctorate with a thesis on Kant, and earning a living by writing dissertations and tutoring university students and exam candidates.

The autobiographical elements in the novel are plain: the experiences of the protagonist, Lucia (alternately called Lucie, Luzi, or Lùszia), a young Italian girl from a bourgeois Fascist family, retrace those of the author. Confronted with the reality of the labor camps, her journey becomes a harrowing, surreal experience told with great emotional intensity, at once a testament, a cry of alarm, and a tale of self-discovery. In the story, D'Eramo has Lucia say, "Sometimes when you go astray and touch bottom, you finally come out on the other side." With Lucia, D'Eramo revisits a course of development and transformation that was her own, and which involved a shift of consciousness as it looked squarely into the face of evil and horror in the world. Nadia Fusini, in her introduction to Feltrinelli's 2012 edition of *Deviation*, entitled "Resilience, a Virtue," refers to an "abnormality of living" that was certainly known to Luce D'Eramo, in whose difficult times the very ideas of "regulations" and "rules" were subject to perversion and distortion. Those who had to conform to them could not help but "deviate," and in the course of that "deviation" experience the depths of horror wherein all "rectitude" is lost.

The novel's consequent "deviations" result in an account that does not—*cannot*—proceed in a straight line. Bia Sarasini, writing about Luce D'Eramo in the essay "Se scrivere è un viaggio nel tempo,"* points out that, rather than a linear account, *Deviation* is a complex narrative construction of an alteration of awareness, achieved through a display of streams of consciousness and very different linguistic registers—all to accompany the writer and the reader through the abyss and out to the other side. The registers and verb persons change and the chronological order is necessarily shuffled. The story, like the memories themselves, comes out in fits and starts, as a result of a series of repressions and setbacks. At times the narrative voice finds memory less than trustworthy and struggles to get the story straight. In Part IV, she explains: "In fact, nearly a lifetime went by, in which only fragmented memories of the camps and hospitals emerged, and always in very specific circumstances—a forced choice on the part of my consciousness—which cluster around only two periods: the years '53–54 and '60–61." The "specific circumstances" refer to the period when her marriage started to dissolve (1953) and the year she landed in Villa della Pace (1960), a home for the disabled. In both situations she felt trapped. It is not surprising that, confined by a hurtful marital bond, she turned to memories of her earlier, unparalyzed, liberated self:

> That's the context in which I resurrected the buried German experience for the first time. A time when it seemed to me I needed to make a clean break with my present life . . . Unable to run away as I'd done then, held captive by paralysis, by fever, by drugs, by the betrayals, and by my jealousy, what else could I do but look for a less imprisoned version of myself? It was natural for me to recall the escape from Dachau, in October '44 . . .

*Bia Sarasini, "Se scrivere è un viaggio nel tempo," *Il paese delle donne on line—rivista*, April 22, 2017; http://www.womenews.net/se-scrivere-e-un-viaggio-nel-tempo/.

Years later, after a time of living on her own with her young son, she again finds herself in the position of receiving assistance, a role she feels society has forced on her with its insistence on viewing her as an invalid:

> This for me was the ultimate confirmation that my memory block had been linked to the struggle against the social pressures that wanted to confine me to the role of invalid . . . there is always someone who asks, "What! You live alone?" in a mournful voice. "What if you were to fall?" . . .
>
> I'd returned to my proper place, to the role of aid recipient that society had assigned me. At age thirty-five, I found myself back where I started; what's more, loaded with debt . . .

The first chapters of the book, which constitute Part I, "Escape from the Lagers," were written around the same time: "Thomasbräu" in 1953 and "Asylum at Dachau" in 1954. "As Long as the Head Lives," which makes up Part II, "Beneath the Rubble," followed in 1961. It then took a number of years more for "In the Ch 89," which makes up Part III, "First Arrival in the Third Reich"; and Part IV, "The Deviation," to be completed, in 1975 and 1977, respectively. Parts I and II, which cover the experiences in Thomasbräu and Dachau as well as the accident and its aftermath, are narrated in the first person: "In the Dachau concentration camp I was part of the crew assigned to . . . ," and "Until I went to the concentration camp, I wasn't even aware that there was another camp not far away," and "That day I was sure I would die." Part III goes back to when Lucia first arrived in the Lager; though it starts off in the first person, it abruptly shifts to the third: "The first few days, Lucia felt relieved: life in a camp was less harsh than what it was rumored to be."

Why the shift in Part III? Since it was written more than twenty years later than the early chapters, the woman writing at that point in time was no longer the same person, and therefore the girl she sees in some old photos both is and is not her.

> Gradually I had developed a curious image of myself. I thought I'd been a slender girl, with delicate wrists and ankles, who had gone through hell without changing her appearance . . .

If I recalled scenes of anger or terror, I pictured myself as a small, restrained figure amid a mob of frenzied people . . .

But the face that appears in the photograph of a factory badge and on the last fake ID card that was issued to me in Mainz, before the wall collapsed on my back, is a different one: a sturdy face, heavier, not given to dreams . . . there is a willfulness discernible in the downward turn of the tight lips, in the dark eyes staring starkly at the lens.

She distances herself from that girl, referring to herself as *"l'italiana"*: "The girl had a mental image of herself that she had carried with her from Italy and did not see how she had become . . ."

Part IV returns to the first person: "but the sense of estrangement between herself and the other whom she's become grows wider, as though time had hollowed out impassable trenches," Fusini writes. The narrator is determined to bring the disparity between her present self and the earlier girl to light: "There is a fact that I evaded. By so often saying that I had been deported to Dachau, I ended up believing it. But it's not true." In this section the narration becomes more introspective. Explaining why she had formerly repressed certain memories, D'Eramo seems to be trying to make sense of her actions, indeed to question the wisdom of them:

And, constrained by the irrelevance of my paralyzed body, I recognized my limitation in the very air I breathed, measuring the vanity of the rancor that had driven me to join the deportees in Verona, and to escape from Dachau in order to convince my fellow internees that one did not have to bow one's head. And for what? To end up in a wheelchair.

She attempts to clarify why in the hospital, after the accident, her body shattered, she had tried to counteract the damage:

I didn't know where to turn, what with my broken ribs, exposed back, burned skin, split forehead, useless organs, so I poured my whole heart into foolish inanities, as compensation, in the need to matter in some way, futilely, superficially, to endure the blow, to loosen the hold of that body that immobilized me and kept me alive.

In the novel, Lucia's deviations or turning points assume various forms. There is the deviation from an idealized Fascism, with its attendant disillusionment, coupled with the self-doubt that maybe she hasn't really gone over to the other side: "You still don't condemn Fascism," her friend Martine tells her; "you find extenuating circumstances for it as opposed to Nazism." There is the deviation from accepted values by which perversion, in the Lagers, comes to seem normal rather than aberrant. There is the subsequent deviation that leads Lucia to reject her privileged class status and strive to adopt new values of solidarity, identifying with the victims, the *Untermenschen* or subhumans, rather than the masters. There is the deviation by which she loses her fear of those who give orders, realizing that they are not at all superior to those they command; indeed the jailers themselves are subhuman: "If I accused the Nazis of dehumanizing us foreigners, whom should I blame for the dehumanization of the Nazis?" And finally there is the most personal deviation of all, the accident that renders her body broken and useless, forcing her to rely on an agile mind to counter the paralysis of her legs.

D'Eramo's efforts to achieve accuracy and fidelity in order to arrive at the truth about her "deviation"—that of sloughing off the constricting snakeskin of her social class—remain determined, despite the advice offered to her by the writer Elio Vittorini: "You must free yourself from the oppression of memory," she tells us he wrote to her in 1957. Yet memory proves to be fluid: shifting sands that constantly rearrange themselves. As Oliver Sacks writes in *Hallucinations*: "We now know that memories are not fixed or frozen, like Proust's jars of preserves in a larder, but are transformed, disassembled, reassembled, and recategorized with every act of recollection." Because the connection with the past is unstable and volatile, as Fusini suggests, any reconciliation between becoming and being, between past and present, seems impossible. Consequently, *Deviation* resists any ultimate resolution of its series of memories and occurrences. At a certain point the author herself is tempted to give up the attempt to understand why she blocked out certain past events. Her "snake" tells her soothingly:

> "If things are really as you fear, from a compositional point of view you can only rejoice: you don't have to understand the repression—your search fails, and that's that. You even have a nice conclusion: you reveal to the

reader that the story of your deviation was a dream in which your imagination enacted one of the most tenacious (and vain) aspirations of all mortals, the eternal human dream of *correcting the past*."

She admits to being enticed: "It was such a relief to be able to wrap up not only my wartime Germany but my entire complicated life that I almost followed that poetic diversion." In the end, however, she remains resolute: "I won't be like Don Quixote (I thought), who at the end of his life repudiated his knighthood: I was insane, I was insane, he said, now I'm sensible. I've known for some time who I am: a woman who's always told herself imaginary stories . . ."

The metaphor of the snakeskin becomes more prevalent in the latter part of the book. The snake represents the temptation to revert to her origins, to her privileged social status, and to abandon her comrades and their struggle—to abandon her social conscience. At one point the author admits: "I spent half my life playing hide-and-seek with myself." Her wavering and oscillations were there early on, in the Lagers, but the Lucie in the camps hadn't been aware of them:

> I had later become aware of the contradiction, for one thing because my relations with my fellow Lager mates had improved, but this oscillation had existed: I wanted to be a worker, while letting people know who I was, thereby deep down laying the ground for the consideration due to my bourgeois circumstances. The fear I subsequently had of reverting to that temptation—using class privilege to save myself from the fate of vulnerable commoners—and wanting to throw away my papers so as to put myself in a similarly helpless position, is even more understandable. But, in this light, the fact that after Dachau and Thomasbräu I got myself hired at Siemens in Munich, again using my real name, is no longer just the boldness of a nineteen-year-old carried away by her impregnability: it's you popping up again, Mr. Snake, as though I was unconsciously holding on to the possibility of resorting to high places.

Only years later is she able to pinpoint for certain where and when the snake had first tightened its coils around her:

But it was there, in Dachau, that the snake had unquestionably settled in, when Lucia had chosen a solitary path of rebellion, which lasted thirty years . . . She'd fled from Verona but also from Dachau: from her privileged status but also from the fate common to those on the other side, who have no means of getting out, who lack the psychological resources that stemmed from her class and allowed her to address the guards uncaringly.

Ultimately she is able to see the reason for the decades-long repression of her memories:

> . . . deep inside I was secretly aware that it was I who had failed. Simply because the class leap in Dachau had been so extreme, the terror of it so violent, that it drove me to take refuge in oblivion. Actually acknowledging it, however? Never! The lady couldn't admit to her failures, she made others pay for them. The lady understood human frailties so she relativized everything so as not to really side with those beneath her, with whom she declared herself to be so sympathetic. She felt different from the people of her bourgeois class solely because she criticized their *conformist* lifestyle no matter how they were defined (right or left), while continuing in fact—though with her fruitless reservations—to live like them herself.

In the end one can't help but agree with Fusini that *Deviation* is not Wordsworth's "emotion recollected in tranquillity." On the contrary, it is more like a raw expression of what Wordsworth termed the "spontaneous overflow of powerful feelings" that give rise to the emotion that lies at the heart of poetry.* It is this quality that led the writer Goliarda Sapienza, a contemporary of D'Eramo, to describe the narrative voice in *Deviation* as "a nocturnal monologue of a saxophone with brief . . . sunny notes of a clarinet driven to maximum heights of tenderness . . . touching tenuous nerve chords."† Sapienza thought highly of D'Eramo's work, even saying that it

---

*William Wordsworth, "Preface to Lyrical Ballads," in *Prefaces and Prologues*, The Harvard Classics, vol. 39 (New York: P. F. Collier & Son, 1909–14).
†From an unpublished letter dated April 5, 1979; quoted with the kind permission of Sapienza's husband, Angelo Pellegrino.

would "force me to reread [Primo Levi's] *If This Is a Man* and [André Schwarz-Bart's] *The Last of the Just* to prove what I suspect. That is, that Luce's book is the most relevant on that theme, the harshest, most in-depth account of the Nazi experience, the most uncompromising and courageous."[*]

As I read Luce D'Eramo's *Deviation* I found myself thinking of Dante's journey through the abyss. Led by his determined guide, Virgil, the poet is able to climb out of the depths, to finally emerge *a riveder le stelle*,[†] to see again the stars. It strikes me that in *Deviation*, D'Eramo is Dante and Virgil at one and the same time. When Lucia leaves home to go and serve as a volunteer worker at the IG Farben in Frankfurt-Höchst, she effectively enters the gate to Hades, calling to mind the famous inscription LASCIATE OGNI SPERANZA, VOI CH'ENTRATE, "abandon all hope, ye who enter here,"[‡] making Luce-Lucia both the pilgrim journeying through the netherworld (the younger Lucia) and the cicerone (the later woman) leading herself and that earlier girl out to the other side. Since she had literally gone through hell, D'Eramo's passage is transformational.

Anne Milano Appel
July 2017

---

[*]Goliarda Sapienza, *Il vizio di parlare a me stessa* (Turin: Einaudi, 2011), p. 89.
[†]Dante Alighieri, *Divina Commedia*, Inferno XXXIV:139.
[‡]Ibid., Inferno III:9, trans. John Ciardi.

PART 1

ESCAPE FROM THE LAGERS

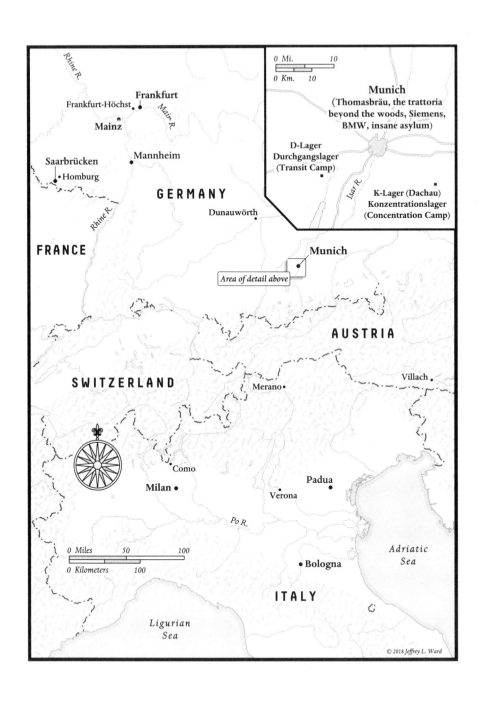

Rhine R.

Frankfurt
Frankfurt-Höchst
Mainz

Main R.

Saarbrücken
Homburg

Mannheim

GERMANY

Dunauwörth

FRANCE

Rhine R.

0 Mi.   10
0 Km.   10

Munich
(Thomasbräu, the trattoria
beyond the woods, Siemens,
BMW, insane asylum)

D-Lager
Durchgangslager
(Transit Camp)

Isar R.

K-Lager (Dachau)
Konzentrationslager
(Concentration Camp)

Munich

Area of detail above

AUSTRIA

SWITZERLAND

Merano

Villach

Como

Milan

Padua
Verona

Po R.

Adriatic
Sea

Bologna

ITALY

Ligurian
Sea

0 Miles   50   100
0 Kilometers   100

© 2018 Jeffrey L. Ward

THOMASBRÄU

Escaping was extraordinarily simple.

In the Dachau concentration camp I was part of the crew assigned to clean out the waste pipes for the metropolis of Munich. Each morning we set out for the city with sticks and scrubbing brushes; they loaded us onto trucks in platoons of twenty people.

Cleaning out sewers is a more varied job than it may appear at first: there are assorted chores involved.

Sometimes you have to lift a metal manhole cover on a sidewalk and lower yourself into the depths below. There's a huge pipe down there with a short, closed neck that protrudes vertically from it. You uncover this neck and jab your stick in, swirling it around to dislodge the amassed feces. You have to scrape and stir them until they slide down again.

At other times we cleaned the toilets and drainpipes in factories and public buildings. Or they took us to the huge drainage conduit where, using the long sticks, we pushed at the encrusted feces from the grated openings and sloshed corrosive acids and water on them; then all that noxious decomposition flowed away rapidly like an infernal torrent. After that we attached scrubbing brushes to our sticks and scoured the walls of the conduit.

But the worst was when they brought us to rural villages to empty the cesspools: out there, there are no sewer pipes. When the black holes fill up, you have to empty them with buckets and eventually climb in yourself. Only then did they give us masks and rubber boots, and we worked covered in shit until we finished.

A lot of people got sick and there were some who died from toxicity.

There were also good days, when the pipes were not blocked by excrement, when the public toilets functioned efficiently and the "grand canal" flowed without obstruction; on those days we were promoted to the grade of manure spreaders, called *Mistbreiter*.

We were sent out to farms. We went behind the stables and, with the pitchforks they gave us, loaded the manure onto wagons. Then we followed the wagons, on foot, to outlying fields. Once we reached our destination, the wagons would stop every ten yards or so and the farmer would dump out a pile of manure that we had to spread around.

I'd sink the pitchfork into the pile and, tensing my muscles, lift with a swift, violent wrench until it emerged with an excessive load of manure; then, as I was about to scatter it around, my muscles would give way, and the fork wavered and tipped its load. So I jabbed the fork in again, trying to pull it out slowly and steadily, but just when I was congratulating myself for how easily I'd lifted it up, I noticed the long, bare prongs draped with only a few strands of dripping manure.

The ideal time to escape was during one of the air raids that would hit while we were at work, without warning, the enemy bombardment sudden enough to surprise the guards, who had a hard time rounding us up.

So that's what I did.

I'd looked into it for some time, cautiously, because the Nazis managed to make us suspicious of one another. The internees do not look favorably upon those who want to escape from the camp, because every runaway doubles the surveillance and results in additional punishments and penalties for those who remain; nor do the prospective escapees ever make themselves known, because they are afraid of being informed on by fellow prisoners unable to endure torture or resist promises of reward.

Under pressure I was able to learn that in the city of Munich, about ten miles away, right near the Labor Bureau, there is a so-called *Durchgangslager*, a transit camp where fugitives hide out while waiting to find a more secure accommodation. The camp is commonly referred to by us as Thomasbräu, after the nearby Thomas brewery. I treasured that reference as if it were a reliable friend whose first name was Thomas and whose last name was Bräu.

At Dachau they told me:

"Kiss the ground and be thankful they didn't throw you into one of their brothels. Nineteen years old, female, what were you expecting . . . freedom in the Third Reich?"

But one afternoon when we'd been transported to Munich, as we were working on the sidewalk sewers in a downtown neighborhood, the siren sounded, immediately followed by explosive thuds; people were fleeing. I flatten myself in a doorway, dash into the next doorway . . . a narrow alley, I squeeze into a niche amid the uproar of the bombs, eyes darting all around me, I throw off the rubber gear. No one is pursuing me. Still running, I reach the station, where I think I'll be safer from any snitches, since no one takes refuge there during bombings.

In the snow, which falls unsteadily, I head for the dead-end sidings where debris piles up, the scraps emerging from the snow to testify to their need, and drawing me to them like sad old friends. I move among the torn-up metal that juts out in twisted hunks and sit behind a shed on a rusty shaft that protrudes sideways from a pile of rubble.

The bombs follow one another compulsively and crash like waves in a stormy sea. I'm not afraid because every boom is my accomplice.

When I see the planes move on to the other side of the city, I get up and go in search of an air-raid shelter, to hide and mix in with the people.

I walk through deserted streets in the dithering snow until I come across the opening of an underground shelter that looks like a subway under construction; I go down the stairs and come out into a long, wide corridor full of pitiable indigents, so it must be a bunker for foreigners. I look at them avidly as if to trace the face of freedom: they have sagging mouths, jaws, and a vague mask of defiance on their faces. No one pays any attention to me.

When the all-clear sounds, I ask an Italian who seems friendly and more welcoming where the Labor Bureau is.

"At this hour?" He looks at his watch.

"What time is it?"

"It's eight o'clock, the Bureau is closed."

"It doesn't matter. Where is it?"

The man picks a crumpled piece of yellow paper off the ground, smooths it out meticulously with his hands, flattening it against the wall, and with a pencil, under the dim glow of a dangling light bulb, sketches a map of the streets I need to take.

Other Italians gather around me.

"Are you Italian?"

"Yes."

"Where are you from?"

"From Rome."

"Interned?"

"Yes."

"For a long time?"

"Yes."

"So, what else is new."

They don't ask me any more questions. They go out of their way to explain to me where I have to go.

One says, "At Sendicatorplatz you can ask." (Later I'll find out that the real name is Sendlinger Tor Platz, which no foreigner has ever been able to pronounce correctly.)

Someone else shrugs. "Don't you understand that she can't ask?"

"Oh!"

They look at me indifferently. I wonder if they can help me? I take a chance:

"Where are you staying?"

"At Siemens. Today is a day off."

"Some day off!" one of them remarks, spitting on the floor. "Stuck in here."

"If you need anything, come on over."

"We're in barrack eighteen, in the first camp."

"But be careful."

They say goodbye. They go away.

I don't know what to do and I hide in a corner. People leave, no German guard appears. The dim light bulbs go out. I wait in the uncertain silence.

I wake up terrified because I fell asleep without meaning to and I'm afraid it's gotten late. I go outside: it's the dead of night. It's still snowing; occasional streetlamps, their glass obscured, cast a mysterious light on the harsh houses, on streets made even more immaculate by the snow.

I walk along following the route on the yellow paper; undisturbed, I wander through streets smoothed over by whiteness, in dazzling solitude, caressed by the snow that lulls me. The Labor Bureau must be here, though I can't make out any Lager, I don't see any barracks, or barbed wire, no guards walking around. Only uniform houses, their white roofs lowered over gray facades like inhospitable visors, continually barring my way.

I'm exhausted from the cold, tired and hungry. A furtive shadow slinks in front of me, sees me, stops, watches me.

It's a blond young man, thin, tense, eyes like two slits. He looks like a foreigner. I wish he'd say something, but he remains silent. Maybe he's waiting for me to speak first. I raise my hand slowly and nod at him. He repeats my gesture. I'd like to call out, but I'm afraid of the sound of my voice in the soft silence. I raise my hand again to motion him over to me.

He approaches, his right hand in his pocket.

"What do you want?" he asks me in French, looking me up and down. His voice is as peaceful as the snow and doesn't disturb anything.

"Are you French?" I ask in turn in his language.

"Yes. And you?"

"I'm Italian, but born and raised in France."

"What are you looking for?"

Suddenly I feel very trustful. "Thomasbräu," I tell him.

A quick smile, affectionate and patronizing, flickers over his gaunt, impassive face.

"Come with me."

He walks briskly, without a sound, on the unspoiled snow, and I can barely keep up.

When we come to a corner, he turns to me: "Hurry up."

"Okay." I nod fervently and move faster; I have the impression that my steps alone are making a terrible racket, while his are muffled.

We arrive in front of a wall. The young Frenchman moves closer and stands facing it.

"Climb on me and scramble over."

I start to climb, but am left awkwardly straddling his back, unable to go any farther.

The boy sighs. "Get down," he says brusquely.

I slide off. He picks me up; I barely have time to marvel at his strength (it comes from freedom, I think joyfully).

"Grab on to the edge of the wall, watch out for the glass shards." I do what he says and cut my hand.

"Put your feet on my shoulders. Now climb over."

A thud and I find myself sitting on the ground, on the other side of the wall. With an agile leap the Frenchman joins me, pulls me up, takes my hand, and pulls me along.

We're in a spacious courtyard, occupied by massive silhouettes of vehicles camouflaged by the snow. On the ground shiny white tracks left by tires trace diamond patterns and arabesques.

The young man stops. "Beautiful," he says, his eyes indicating the tracks: "It looks like they're trying to tell us something." He looks at me and smiles again like he did earlier.

"What's your name?"

"Lucie."

"I'm Louis."

He starts walking again, unhurriedly, lighting a cigarette. I'm worried that someone will pop out from behind a truck, but I don't dare tell him that.

"Is it far?" I ask as we leisurely make our way across the courtyard, as if we were out for a stroll.

"There." He points to a small door that I hadn't noticed in the wall in front of us, which is not actually a wall, but the side of a house without windows.

A pang of dismay stops me dead. "Louis."

"What is it?"

"I was looking for the Thomasbräu Lager."

"I know."

We reach the door. He shoves it open with his hip. He goes in, stamps his feet vigorously to shake off the snow, pulls me inside, and kicks the door shut. He switches the light on.

We're in a clammy corridor full of gobs of spit and dirt; a pipe runs along a wall, bending abruptly into the hall and ending at a thunderous faucet, which noisily spills water into a bucket. The water splashes out onto the floor and races toward the door in rivulets.

Louis grabs the bucket, tosses the water into a corner, sets it upside down.

"Have a seat," he says.

He crouches on his calves in front of me.

"What, don't you like the place?" he asks with mock innocence.

"Oh yes, very much."

"Where did you come from?"

"Dachau."

He gives an admiring whistle. He gathers his thoughts and says, "So then, Thomasbräu is officially the Labor Bureau's transit camp where foreigners stay while awaiting a new job or repatriation, or while waiting for new convoys to be formed because, in case you didn't know it, none of us, not even those sold for free labor, has the right to travel alone."

"Isn't it dangerous there?"

"Dangerous?" He snickers briefly. "Not at all: we're safe there. Who could be better informed than us about searches, rumors concerning escapees or suspects?"

"Aren't there informers?"

"Informers! Don't be silly! The camp also houses those who are really waiting for a decision from the Labor Bureau, there are a lot of them, in fact, and they're constantly shifting, replacing one another: the ones who get a job leave and new ones arrive. New faces all the time! How can the Germans tell the difference between them all? The majority of the new arrivals don't have documents, they're people who've been rounded up in the streets, morons deported by mistake, desperate volunteer workers. If one of us should end up at roll call by mistake, all he has to do is answer confidently to any name, receive a glance in return, and that's that."

"And the new ones keep quiet?"

"What do they know? We sure don't go and own up to them!"

"But at roll call?"

"Not a word! Those people are so scared they're shaking. Don't worry, they don't bother anybody, really: they hole up all day and don't spend their time at Thomasbräu."

"The brewery?"

"Right."

"What about the Germans?"

"Which ones?"

"The ones at the Bureau."

"Who ever sees them? We go there late in the evening when they're at home eating their lard, or in the daytime during office hours, when they're slaving over their stupid paperwork."

"Isn't the brewery owner an informer?"

"Forget about it! Nobody pays him better than we do. It's not worth it to him."

"But where do you get the money?"

Louis stands up, irritated, looking down on me as if to say, Are you done grilling me? Then he says, "Go to sleep, go on."

I stand up too: "Where?"

"In there." With a look he indicates a rickety little door at the end of the hall.

I don't dare move. I'm afraid of being left alone. Just to say something, I ask him, "How come you always keep your hand in your pocket?"

Louis pulls out a revolver.

I stumble over the bucket.

"Where do you come from, anyway?" he says with a tight-lipped smile.

Thin, skinny maybe, but nimble, with something feline about his movements and posture. He's wearing blue coveralls; back straight, head held high on a tense, sturdy neck. He has sharp, pointy features, a little like a weasel; his eyes are small, shifty, changeable, at this moment very dark. His blond hair the color of chestnut wood is unruly in back, his mouth a slit with no lips, his expression guardedly harsh.

He puts the gun back in his pocket and takes his hand out. He seems more conciliatory.

"Force of habit."

"I see," I say (how did he manage to get hold of a weapon?). "I'm sorry," I add.

He studies me. "You're a . . ." he begins, then falls silent. Continuing to stare at me, not turning away, he spits the cigarette stub out of the corner of his mouth like a bullet. "They raised you not to get your hands dirty, right?" he laughs with a quick smirk. I laugh curtly in return. We stare into each other's eyes for a long moment. "Lucky you!" he sighs. He turns abruptly and goes to shut off the faucet: "That water is annoying, isn't it?" He looks at me again and says, "Let's go." He starts toward the rickety door, pushing me ahead of him. He opens the door slowly.

Hidden in shadows, the lumpy profiles of straw mattresses on bunk beds materialize in front of me, and the sweaty stench of humanity in closely packed quarters assails me.

I recognize the world of Dachau. All that effort only to find myself at the same point again.

I stop at the door.

"Are you scared?" he whispers softly.

"Yes."

Louis goes in and disappears among the beds. I hear heavy, raucous breathing intermingling confusedly in the darkness. After a short while he reappears, takes my hand, and leads me through the tight spaces to a corner where two pallets are empty. "Lie down there," he murmurs. He leaves. Someone groans and moves, making the bed creak ominously.

The light from the corridor is turned off. Louis's shadow reappears and he lies down on the mattress next to mine.

He lights a cigarette and in the brief glow of the match the upper bunk can be seen, the eternal baldachin of the Lagers, presumptuous and grotesque in its consumption. Louis slips a blanket out from under his pallet and throws it to me.

"Cover yourself."

"What about you?"

"I'm warm."

"Is this where you sleep?"

"Yeah."

After a while he hands me a bar of chocolate.

"Eat it."

I finger it, because I think it's a joke.

"Thank you."

Slowly I unwrap it from the thin silver paper my touch has forgotten, lingering to savor the delicate sensation.

Meanwhile, more distinct sounds emerge from the oppressive air, muffled laughter, groans, a swelling surge, like a shifting, heaving mass. The wooden timbers themselves seem to be in a frenzy, taking on an insolent nocturnal life of their own.

"Louis."

"Lucie."

"Is this one of *their* brothels?"

"We only screw among ourselves." He waits.

"Men enter freely?"

Louis turns on his side:

"Do you perhaps expect the Nazi gentlemen to be so kind as to provide separate dormitories for men and women?"

"In Dachau . . . ," I start to say.

"There they do, and here they don't," he says, cutting me short. "As it suits them, my dear girl. There they do, because it's easier to monitor them when they're separated, and because abstinence is a punishment. Here they don't, because for a temporary Lager such an arrangement would be too much effort, and because foreigners entering Germany should learn right away that they're nothing but swine." He pauses. "Get it? Inferior races."

"I see."

"You don't copulate over there?" he asks with exaggerated innocence.

"In Dachau?"

"Don't say that name, dummy."

"Some make love, but the men have to sneak in, and are risking their lives."

"What did I tell you?" he laughs. "And you?"

"Me, no."

After a moment, Louis replies, "Too bad," and turns his back.

A big hand moves toward me across the space between me and the other bunk bed. Starts groping the blankets. An arm follows, a hairy face appears.

My throat is dry. I reach out toward Louis. He sits up abruptly.

"What's wrong?" He lights a match. He deals a sharp blow to the fingers that have reached my breast.

The hand retracts like a mechanical device.

"Leave her alone, she's my girl," Louis hisses.

The hairy face vanishes with a grunt.

Louis makes me change places with him and moves over to my pallet. I stare into the shadows. In front of me, in the semi-darkness, on the upper level of the bunk across the way, I gradually make out a jumble of bodies from which tangled arms and legs stick out, stretching and contracting like multiple blind antennae of huge snails. I close my eyes, the rancid smell of the blanket in my nose.

"Squeeze in!" an excited voice yells.

"Don't slump on top of me!" another one pants, out of breath. Teasing, suggestive remarks, rude catcalls then spill out, as if a repressed effusiveness, lying in wait, had been given the green light to emerge. Occasional drowsy voices wearily break their silence.

It's true, escape is merely a superficial remedy; the essentials remain unchanged.

Louis isn't sleeping; he lights a cigarette.

"Don't cry," he whispers. He leans over me. "They're just a bunch of poor bastards."

Having been exposed, I cry even more.

When I wake up, I feel hemmed in: there are people standing up around the beds, chatting, their heads bent forward under the beams of the upper bunks; others are sitting up on top with their legs dangling over; while others still are milling around in the narrow aisles between the beds, backs leaning against the wood frames. Anemic, evasive faces, dark circles under sunken eyes, stick figures made of rotten, measly wood, entrenched filth.

Yet observing those sordid, anxious creatures, I feel like I've been part of this misery, which breathes around me like swamp air on an abandoned daffodil, from time immemorial.

Louis's pallet is empty. There is a package with my name. I take it and unwrap it: in it I find a big piece of bread with two sausages. No one says a word to me. I hide the bundle in my coverall. I go wash up in the corridor, plunging my arms into the bucket and rubbing my face with the bracing water.

The word spreads swiftly like a gust of wind: "Police."

The camp empties. I go outside; to the left of the door, in the courtyard, there's a gate through which they all leave with a show of nonchalance, scattering along the way.

It's raining. The snow has disintegrated into a dreary gray slush.

I walk until I come to a desolate, welcoming cemetery. I go inside; there are no crosses or cypresses. It seems like the old garden of an enchanted castle where everyone has been turned to stone. I stroll along slowly and say a prayer at random: like when I was a little girl and would amuse myself sitting at the window, watching the passersby and mentally reciting the "Angel of God" for figures whom I chose aimlessly, on a whim.

I eat my bread and sausage, savoring them slowly, and spend the day there until, turning quickly, I notice that the shadows are lengthening, reaching out everywhere like absorbent stains, and that the light descending through the latticework of foliage is becoming more and more spidery and tenuous. I race out, bump into a red house starkly exposed on the sidewalk, and return to the camp.

I lie down on my pallet in the darkest corner. The shadows thicken. Louis is nowhere in sight. I'm afraid, what if he doesn't come back? I should try to get some information. But since leaving Dachau I've set myself a goal: to go unnoticed, mix in completely with the crowd.

I don't want to die.

Finally, Louis shows up. I sit up on the mattress. He jerks his head toward the door.

"Come with me."

I follow him happily.

He turns to me and winks: "Let's go get to know Thomasbräu."

In the mist dissolved by the muted red glow of twilight, it seems to me, in my sudden contentment, that the houses with their intermittently illuminated windows are twinkling at me like the befuddled, shiny faces of regulars in a smoke-filled, crowded tavern.

It's as if things were waking up from a hazy languor. Even Louis is different than he was yesterday.

We go into Thomasbräu. A room with solid tables and benches, walls paneled halfway up in wood, dignified deer antlers of various sizes and branches mounted high on the walls, beer steins. A lot of noisy people, foreigners.

To the right is another room with small, intimate tables, white tablecloths and small vases of flowers, swanky customers, a subtle chamber orchestra: the Germans' dining room.

Louis shows me to a seat in the wood-paneled room, next to a couple whom he greets with a quick wave of his right index finger, and sits down beside me.

"Here you are, Lucie. These friends will protect you, since I rarely stay at the camp, so I'm putting you in their hands. They already know who you are."

The woman is young, with a marmoreal complexion, gentle, remote blue eyes, cropped shaggy hair; she's in an advanced state of pregnancy. The man has very dark skin and hair, dark eyes; he's older, with the deep-set wrinkles typical of peasants from the south. He immediately explains to me, in the broken French of emigrants, that the *signora* is Polish, while he is Sicilian.

"I'm Italian too," I say, smiling.

"Oh." He nods soberly. "Good," he says, then proceeds to tell me the story of his companion. "Her husband, a Polish patriot, was shot by the Nazis and she was deported to Germany and placed here to await the delivery. After which they intend to shoot her." He gestures as he talks, but his tone of voice is composed and his hands sometimes pause in midair. "I love her, I want to adopt her child, they won't make a Nazi out of him." His face contracts. He relaxes his jaw: "I want to marry her," he says with a slight bow to his beloved. "She's very intelligent." He smiles at her. "She's already learning a little Italian. I work for a German civilian and I'm trying to find a way out. I have less than two months' time," he says, a gleam of frantic resolution in his eyes. The woman looks at him with patient tenderness. The Sicilian continues:

"Louis told me to watch over you too. So then, always stay close to Dunja, no one will do anything to you."

The woman smiles at me.

Louis looks at his watch.

"I'll leave you now. I have to go."

"Go and don't worry," the Sicilian replies in French, clapping him on the shoulder with a certain respect.

Louis waves goodbye to everyone and without turning around goes away.

At the camp, I lie down next to Dunja.

The days go by without a ripple.

Louis shows up now and then, to take me to the movies. He doesn't talk much. Sometimes I catch him studying me on the sly, but as soon as he sees that I've noticed, he won't look at me again all evening.

The Sicilian man gives me food.

"Thank you. But how can I repay you?"

"Forget it. Louis takes care of everything. All I do is bring it."

"But Louis too, how will I pay him back?"

"Don't worry about it. If he hasn't asked you for it, it means he doesn't want anything."

The side door of the camp opens onto the yard of an ice factory, where the French prisoners of war, who are housed on the upper floors of our building, work.

I've never gone up to their quarters, but they say they have a lot more space than us and many more amenities. They are French soldiers who refused to become civilian workers. I discover that they are doubly well-off because not only are they respected by everyone for practically being heroes of the Resistance, but they also work two steps away from where they live, earn a salary, regularly receive packages from the Red Cross, have proper uniforms that are periodically replaced, also by the Red Cross, and inspire a certain awe in the Germans, on whom they occasionally lavish such unavailable delicacies as coffee and chocolate, which they get in their care packages. Finally, they have all the women they want, between the German girls attracted by the goodies, the strapping military bearing, and the chic French aura, and the women in our camp who look up to them as Prince Charmings, and to whom they resort only in the absence of someone better, and then with a certain arrogant condescension. They do not seem politicized, unlike others I've met before. In fact, on the ground floor, where they rarely set foot, they look down on the banished criminals more so than on the new arrivals. Indeed, they only ever show up here in order to choose some appetizing, compliant girl from among the newcomers.

The ground floor, for its part, liberally returns their contempt, referring to them collectively as the law-abiding ones upstairs.

We are the unlawful ones.

Still, they don't bother anyone and they make it a point of honor never to know anything when the Germans question them about one of us. Finally, when they work the night shift at their factory, they aren't the least interested in our own comings and goings in their yard.

On the other side, our odd camp verges on the courtyard of the Labor Bureau: a rather dirty quad, surrounded by low buildings with dust-covered, frosted glass windows.

Every so often I get in line with the new arrivals at the Bureau to receive, like them, a bowl of soup with two slices of bread, the daily ration the Bureau distributes to those it assists.

But I have another source of personal income.

I go to Thomasbräu with a group. I was commissioned by our bunkmates to sell their cigarettes on the black market to the Germans in the non-pariah room, where there are laundered tablecloths, clean doilies, and vases of flowers on the tables. I get a percentage for this job. I know what to do at a glance, can immediately distinguish the tightfisted Germans, the ones appalled by the boisterous carrying-on in our room, the stern, guarded types, and the more indulgent ones—especially the young people and soldiers who enjoy watching the comings and goings in our ward.

Often I trade the cigarettes for food coupons. Then we eat and sing until the dead of night. Sometimes I sit in a corner and remind myself, "Here I will not do as I did at the K-Lager, in Dachau. Here I will resist. I will hold out until the end. I won't do anything impulsive. I will be one of them, like them, at all times, and that's that."

But as usual, we are out of money and have to leave the waitresses at the Thomasbräu pawns, which later we will not redeem. Stolen stuff.

There is a small humpbacked waitress, a spinster who shows great sympathy for all of us, her chest heaving with compassionate sighs, but she is a very greedy, cunning usurer, with bulging eyes that make her look like a fly.

Most of our time, however, is spent at the camp, where we pass the long hours of the day killing body lice.

We strip and, by the feeble light that filters through the windowpanes, the grayish light from the yard, we search through our clothes, all of us women in the corner, hunting for those repulsive insects; we ball them up between our fingers like children do boogers, and crush them. I have a smooth rock I use for the purpose.

Some are very swollen, gray with pale streaks, their step wobbly due to their big bellies; others have dark spots, some intensely brown; the ugliest, the most sprightly, splatter like worms. There, in the cobwebs of light, in the mud-colored shadows of the large room, those multipedes clinging to the fabric of our clothing and blankets gleam like bronze.

What's more, I've always been quite an expert at this, even at Dachau: at night I wake up to a well-known itch, feel about cautiously, and suddenly pounce on the scurrying insect. Then I toss it on the floor, not bothering to squash it.

I've also discovered that body lice keep you warm.

Louis was right. It's not at all risky living a few yards away from the Labor Bureau. It would appear that our lawlessness here is the natural offspring of the Bureau, and it sometimes seems strange to me that I was surprised at first, as though they were in any way opposed.

Just as incest and adultery thrive in repressive countries with extremely rigid customs, their thousand tentacles protected by a code of silence, undisturbed as long as appearances are preserved, and therefore nurtured by that same intransigence, so we are the most authentic product of the great Nazi machine that manufactures the most obsessive control and discipline in existence, and it is therefore only logical and right for us to be sheltered by its wing.

Armed with this elementary discovery, I wander without misgivings through the area of the Labor Bureau, smiling at my earlier anxieties.

I've also made several visits to the Labor Bureau building itself, to over-hear what was being said about some panicked escapee.

It's a yellow building, the walls flaking, with endless small offices lin-ing interminable corridors, large windows with blank, inert light, lifeless employees sagging behind their desks, and long rows of workers used to being obsequious but somewhat disillusioned by the bloodless imperson-ality of the law. More than anything else, willing to endure it, despite the exhaustion of hours standing in line in front of cramped windows, where the presenting and return of documents that open the way to social assur-ance is purposely complicated and difficult.

Sometimes a German escorted by two SS suddenly storms into the camp during the evening roll call or at some other opportune moment and, after stationing his guards in front of the exits, demands the documents of everyone present.

There have been some fruitful raids. But given the intensity of the crim-inal life going on at our place, the chances of arrest are minimal compared to those anywhere else, and are not worthy of serious consideration.

I come to learn that Louis, in particular, is wanted by the police.

Generally, however, the inspections are harmless. Some Germans burst in, already in a great hurry to get out of this grim, dangerous place.

If I don't have time to hide under a bed, I tag along, preceding them, repeating the unintelligible foreign names that they don't understand, pro-nouncing the syllables clearly. I accompany them back to the door and they routinely forget to ask me for my documents as well.

Louis is an epileptic. During his seizures, his frenzy is treacherous, unexpected. His mouth becomes rigid and his eyes remain wide open, un-moving. He thrashes and kicks in fits and starts, his expression demented, but in him even this rage seems premeditated. I sit with him during the long unconscious periods that follow his seizures, and I'm the only one who does, because he has no friends, except for the Sicilian, who is often absent; I put compresses on his forehead while he looks at me with a yearning, sweet expression, not seeing me.

Sendlinger Tor Platz is a meeting place for foreigners. A large irregular square surrounded by low shops, with a skimpy little park in the middle. There are even benches for *Polen* and *Osten*, that is, for Poles and Russians, and cafés for foreigners, *Osten* included, as the many signs explain. One side of the square is closed off by a wooden pen, the kind in which livestock are crammed during the large regional cattle fairs. I like to wander around in there. This is the foreigners' market, where they officially have the right to trade clothing, tobacco, and stuff to eat.

Foreigners of all nationalities, mostly Slavs, push and shove around ghastly red dresses, green socks, brown handkerchiefs, stale loaves of bread, and moldy packs of tobacco, whose price is sky high. They touch the goods, they shrug.

You think you're living in a silent film because everyone is jostling and gesturing and none of the buyers speak. All you hear is a muted buzzing, as though from a movie camera.

At times you witness a fight, silent at first, which then degenerates into threats from the contenders and incitements from the spectators who egg them on and snicker.

While I roam around idly, I come across Louis. He doesn't look up, doesn't recognize me. He turns away looking irritated. I'm about to call out to him, but he's slipping a roll of marks out of the pocket of a bony man. His expression is preoccupied and slightly tense.

I deliberately pass in front of him again and stop.

"Louis," I say. The money has already disappeared. He raises his eyes without surprise, looks at me sharply, and disappears. I search the crowd, but I can't find him.

I buy a pair of plush clogs with wooden soles for sixteen marks—the fruit of my latest speculations at Thomasbräu—and I have just enough money left over for a pair of panties that make me happiest of all because the rough cloth of my pants chafes my skin. Besides, the overalls that I mended are falling apart and, no matter how many hours I spend patching them, a tear occasionally exposes my skin. And in November it's cold, a cold so intense that I'm always shivering. Though that's the least of my ordeals.

Evening is falling, but I'm so satisfied with my purchases that rather than go back to the camp to look for food, I go into the garage of a repair shop nearby. I feel content: I climb in and out of the trucks, enter the drivers' cabs, jump on the seats, drift from one vehicle to another.

I've just settled into a nice car, landing with a thud on the soft, springy seat, enjoying myself as I put on airs and act like a grande dame, when I freeze. There's a man hiding in there. It's Louis. Actually, he's not hiding, but is quietly stretched out on a seat, smoking, a folded newspaper in his hand. He lights a match, unfazed, smiles at me. Just then I forget about his stealing and in my euphoria I tell him about my purchases. I show him the clogs and he keeps striking matches to consider them.

He looks at me without speaking. He no longer has the ironic manner of the other evening. He is always either very shy with me or abrupt or hesitant, as if he were afraid of doing something wrong, before he finally gets up the nerve and speaks in argot.

He hands me vouchers and money for supper, but as I'm about to take them, I unfortunately remember his theft at Sendlinger Tor Platz.

"Is it a foreigner's money?" I ask him.

"Of course," he says, "I don't steal from our own anymore." He looks at me as if begging me to accept his gift. Suddenly I'm ashamed of my rudeness: What was I thinking! Giving him a lecture! "Thanks." I smile, mortified. "Thank you, Louis."

Then, looking straight ahead—sitting in the shadows, so close to me that I practically brush against him—he tells me that he is the son of Normandy fishermen, that his father died at sea when he was a child. At eight years old he sailed off as a cabin boy and since then he's always been on the water, traveling on the cargo ship of a smuggler from Marseilles; the ship called at the most unexpected shores.

And once, to avoid port customs, they stopped for a long time at a harbor in the French Congo, and he caught malaria. Then, when the ship returned home, they left him ashore with no money, nothing.

"I earned a little, yeah, but I spent it all. Meanwhile, my mother had died from TB. So I went to Paris and looked for another job. I couldn't do much because I can barely read and can hardly write at all. I have no skills. I'm twenty-six years old."

As he speaks, haltingly, he seems like an untamed, wounded animal. I want to squeeze his hand, but I don't dare and I don't move. We fall silent.

"Go and eat," he says finally, "it's late."

"Come on," I say.

"I have things to do."

"Can't you take a break?"

"When I work, I don't think about anything else."

I take his hand, a rough, cracked hand, a hand with chilblains. Louis dismisses me without returning my squeeze. "Go on, go," he says.

I get out of the car and head for camp, shaken, preoccupied by absurd feelings. I now know that I am more drawn to the vagrants at Thomasbräu than to anyone in my earlier, proper life. I'm fearful of the hold such a short time has taken on me, and I feel like my life will never be as genuine and secure as it is now. In my bourgeois way, I know, I'm ashamed of Louis, but just thinking about him I feel a pang, my heart pounding.

I leave the garage; the city throbbing with tiny flickering lights is profiled against the backdrop of a sky in which clouds, like lumps of coal, spread a last flaming glow to the edges. I am suddenly listless, and feel the joy of a short time ago slip down around my feet, like a loose-fitting tunic.

I enter the brewery and slump down on a bench next to my companions.

Three German soldiers come into the room and sit at our table. They've come from the front, you can tell, and maybe they don't know about us or just don't care. They order bread and beer and chew slowly.

We decide to pool the vouchers required for a meal among the three of us and place them on the table, next to the soldiers. They take them without a word. They have no idea how much the vouchers cost us. We start eating again, we even order dessert for them and offer them a cigarette.

They're exhausted, unkempt, their hair is prematurely graying, they don't even talk to one another. In the end they thank us awkwardly. I catch them shooting a vivid glare of resentment at these extravagant, uninhibited foreigners who feed them in their own home. The look of a poor relative.

So I explain to one of them, whispering in his ear, that we're poor bastards with no place to sleep, that we're crammed in like cattle in a stall full of lice.

The soldier looks at me, cowed, then he consults with the others in a low voice. Finally, stumbling over the words, he explains that their houses were destroyed, that they haven't been able to trace their families, and that they spent their whole leave like that, in a fruitless search; his voice is trembling, they don't know where to spend the night. The Soldiers' Home at the station is chock-full and the offices are now closed. Their three questioning pairs of eyes, their three faces marked by unending struggle, their jaws accustomed to a nameless discipline, their calloused, methodical hands all give me an obscure feeling of guilt.

When they've finished, we get up from the table with them and take them to our camp. We give them our best straw pallets, and two women— escaped French partisans—beat and brush the blankets for them.

The next day we see them leave, inconspicuous in their nondescript legality. Dunja even accompanies them for a stretch. The foreigners light cigarettes, frowning, their disoriented dignity stamped in their eyes.

We're almost finished getting dressed when a French girl rushes into the room:

"It's so sunny outside it seems like summer. Today is a great day for an outing. It's Sunday and nobody will ask us for documents."

We all look outside, gauge the sky. It's decided: after excited preparations, the Sicilian gathers us in the entryway with the faucet; there are about a dozen of us, each has procured a chunk of bread, and we leave.

We wander through the city unhurriedly. We amble along the impetuous Isar that twists and turns, its waters absorbing reflections of the sky and some small clouds that lightly float by.

Passersby are smiling. We wander along, dragging our feet on the pavement as though aimless, headed for the dry bed of a tributary.

The sun rises in the sky as we leave the city behind us, and the last houses gleam like little white flashes amid the green.

We skirt the tributary through a stretch of rolling countryside with trim little houses scattered among regular, straight rows of trees.

We climb over the verge and slide down the bank toward the river rocks, which look like homemade loaves of bread arranged on the pale table of the dry riverbed. Rivulets of water flow through them; hopping from one stone to another, laughing, arms outstretched to keep from falling, we reach the other side, which is lower, like an island, and lie down under the trees, in the breezy warmth of the autumn sun, vagrants without a roof and without a care.

We make a ball with a little bit of earth wrapped in a strip of cloth that we tie tightly, and we play. Two or three older ones fashion a game of bocce with smooth stones; the younger guys wrestle. Then we stretch out and smoke. I blow my small white cloud toward a large leaf on a curving branch. The smoke settles over it as though resting on a tray, before vanishing.

"We always go on outings in the summer," a voice says, as if it were true, "such wonderful afternoons, I can't tell you."

Louis appears. He pops out from behind a tree trunk and stands there in front of me. He has two rosebuds in his hand, sets them down beside my feet.

He sits on the ground, not far from me, hugging his knees. I observe him through half-closed eyelids, in the clear, tremulous air that seems to glow with an inner light. With his eyes he's following the movements of those playing bocce.

I sit up. I pick up the rosebuds. Greenhouse flowers. One is like a newborn's skin, with very clear crimson veins, the heart a deep yellow, genteel and languorous. The other has purplish petals with a pastel orange underside fading into a pale pink at the tips.

I am filled with a sense of mellowness, of brimming perfection, of ripeness. The stems are very long, with no leaves, with bright red thorns.

On the way home, I am cheerful and content, the two rosebuds in the buttonhole of my overalls, the stems tapping against my chest with every step; hands in my pocket, I run ahead and sing a pointless, whimsical refrain, having no connection to anything, like my state of mind. I flit from one person to the next, I pass the group, then wait up for it, leaning against a tree, and once again I feel at home, as if I've known my companions forever.

Louis walks far behind with the worried men, staring down at the ground.

The other Italian boys are singing *Lassù sulle montagne tra boschi e valli d'or* . . . up there in the mountains among woods and valleys of gold . . .

I wait for Louis.

"Thank you," I say, falling in step with him. He stops. The others continue on; we remain behind. He takes a small case out of his pocket.

"Here," he says.

I take the case, open it. I find an exquisite little gold watch, a Swiss brand.

"No!" I say, frightened, thinking they'll arrest him, they'll arrest me.

"Because of the money?"

"Not the money!"

"Then why not? Are you afraid of being too indebted to me afterward? Don't be. For me it's nothing."

"That's not it, Louis."

"Wouldn't you like to be dressed nicely, well fed, elegant—in a word, rich?"

"Me?"

"If a man offered you a fortune, would you marry him?"

"If I love a man, I'll marry him even if he's penniless," I say brightly, and looking at him, I realize that Louis has turned violently red. He laughs briefly, as if grunting.

"It's small-minded," he says sarcastically, "to always deprive yourself of everything, to demean yourself."

"What do you care?" I smile at him. But I see he's sulky. "Let's not get ourselves killed, Louis. They mustn't catch you. We can look for work, under false names, until the war ends."

"For you it's the war, not for me. That's why you don't give a damn."

"That's not true!" I shout.

"I know, I know very well," he says under his breath. Then abruptly he grabs back the case, takes out the watch, tosses the case into the river, and slips the watch on my wrist, gently.

I am about to thank him, but he looks up at me, cutting off my words. We return to the camp in silence. Louis says goodbye with a nod: "I'm going."

"At least give me your hand," I say.

His face lights up with a childlike glimmer that instantly becomes amused and ironic. He grips my hand tightly, looking at me almost sternly.

I enter the camp, happy; I don't feel like eating, I just want to hide in a corner to savor my sweet emotions. But the big room is crowded and noisy. I go into the hallway and see the toilet door. I go in, not knowing where else to go, and promptly slip on the feces smeared on the floor; I support myself on the walls, which are also filthy with excrement and obscene graffiti.

Why didn't I ever clean it? After all, I've got lots of experience. The toilet is clogged, no doubt about it.

The alarm sounds, followed immediately by bombs. We are so used to it that only the Labor Bureau's clients run off, the others lie down and wait. And while with every bomb it seems that our hellhole might collapse, I get to work. I've done it so many times for no reason, compelled to, as a captive. Why not do it now, for us?

I get a bucket of water, a bristly slant-edged broom, and scour the walls and floors for who knows how long, uplifted and stirred by a joy, a deep emotion at being alive, by a need for these people who have nothing to grasp at. I feel like a housewife whose children are asleep in the other room and who has no time to lose.

In the end I admire my work and contemplate that toilet as if it were a work of art: the damp walls and gray floor seem benign, the hole in the ground surrounded by four gleaming white tiles looks almost decent. I put away the broom and bucket, I rinse off thoroughly, shut off the faucet, and climb into a bunk. For some time I've preferred the top bunks, because I feel less restricted up there, and can overlook everything from above.

I start jumping around and turning somersaults in the darkness of the blackout, until I go crashing down, together with the pallet and the plank, landing on the bed below, provoking a torrent of abuse from the man occupying it. I run off and hide on another pallet, where I fall asleep at once, dreaming about feces, but not actually feces, it's a plowed field, moist, fertile soil into which I sink as I walk.

An unusual, suspended silence wakes me.

You can't hear a sound, except an ominous roar of engines that seems to well up from all sides, from the depths of the earth, from the sky, from my own body.

"Tonight is going to be bad," a voice whispers.

"That was just a taste."

"Let's go to the shelter."

One by one, careful not to make a sound, as if the slightest noise might cause an explosion, figures emerge from their beds, dress hurriedly. I too begin to panic and get out of bed. We go out stealthily, without even striking a match, holding on to one another. The air outside is even more charged with the roaring that threatens our breathing, ready to crush us. We slip into a small adjacent shelter, where we never go because, when we sense a real danger, we usually run to an underground shelter a hundred yards away.

After some time, people begin talking.

I don't see either Dunja or the Sicilian.

They tell me that, while I was sleeping, Dunja went into premature labor and the Sicilian took her away under the bombs; it was like he'd lost his mind. He kept babbling that the Germans would not get her. It wasn't possible to stop him. No one knows where they went.

"They want the baby so they can make him into a Nazi, but I won't let them have him, even if I have to die for it."

He threw a punch at a Neapolitan who was holding him back and knocked him to the ground, out cold.

"It's not you they're going to shoot," he kept saying, "it's her, it's her, and I did nothing, I wasn't able to."

Some Frenchmen are talking politics. One tells about how before being deported to Germany he wiped out a "nice nest" of "chleux" (Germans)* without ever being discovered. He came here as a volunteer, to perform acts of sabotage. He works outside and sometimes stops by in the evening to see his girlfriend.

"We need to stir up more hatred for the Nazis. Even if it falls on civilians, even if we die, no matter who dies, even if everyone dies. What matters is not letting intolerance for the Nazis ever be extinguished, and if by some absurd chance the Nazis were to be viewed favorably in France, we must see to it that they are understood to be cruel and odious."

---

*The name given by the French to the Germans during the Second World War, replacing the well-known "Boches" of the First World War.

"There's someone from the British service in with us," says one young man after a pause.

"I know."

"That guy benefits twice now, from the airplanes and from dealing."

"Oh, sure, he makes the best deals on these apocalyptic nights."

He nods his head toward me.

"That's his girlfriend."

"Oh." I seem to sense a reluctant respect in the response. To everyone's surprise, the all-clear sounds. We go back out to the open air, discussing the possible route of the bombers. We walk nervously; someone stops, urging silence, and listens intently. It seems that the air still carries the echo of an ominous drone that emerges sporadically, though it can't be pinpointed.

Maybe, anxious over the alarm, I fear insurmountable problems because I don't know what they are and I can't avert them.

I want to work. He won't come with me? I'll go away by myself, I'll present myself as a free worker, I lost my documents in a bombing, the police won't be able to find me, and I'll start over, one of many—without living, feeling, or loving, I'll await the end without intimacy.

I curl up on a pallet, but I can't sleep. I think of Dunja. If she dies, I'll really be alone. My serenity, which I thought belonged to me, came from her.

Louis has no one. No one in his own country, no one anywhere; I don't even know his last name, nor the name of his village in Normandy. If he dies, no one will know that he existed.

A couple of tears roll down my cheeks, and their wet streaks make my skin feel tight.

At dawn, still gripped by an uncontrollable agitation, I get up and go out to the auto repair shop. I look for "our" car. It's empty. On the ground is a branch from a pine tree. I pick it up and lay it down on the seat. The small pinecones without seeds look like little boats floating on waves of green. He'll like it.

I go back to the camp. I lie down. Always the same movements: you pull your legs up and stretch them out one at a time, and fold your arms behind your head. The hours tick away, empty.

Word spreads: Dunja died giving birth.

I found a job, temporary, but still, it's a start. The trattorias sometimes need extra kitchen help and for short periods they'd rather hire undocumented foreigners to avoid having to pay additional taxes and insurance.

The trattoria that hired me is beyond the woods of the antiaircraft artillery. I have to peel vegetables and wash dishes. As for food, no meat of course, but after the place closes there are leftovers of overcooked macaroni, fried sweet semolina balls, boiled potatoes, as well as the remains of meals on the customers' plates. My shift goes from 10:00 a.m. until 1:00 a.m., with a three-hour break in the afternoon.

After lunch I go for a walk in the woods with the restaurant's other girls. It's a mixed, uneven forest, at some points dense with oaks and beech trees, elsewhere sparse with firs and chestnuts.

As soon as there is a semblance of sun, you hear the chirping of invisible birds. Sometimes a squirrel crosses the path, scampers up a tree, and wraps his tail around a branch.

I love those woods and I stop to pick herbs, to study the trees one by one. A chestnut tumbles to the ground, its spines break, its husk splits open, the round, well-formed fruit emerges, smooth and firm.

I too entered the world wearing a spiny outer shell; will I ever be able to shuck the husk of preconceptions under which I was hiding?

Huge, peeled logs are laid out on the ground. The other kitchen girls and I climb on them and compete to see who can run faster on the trunk without losing her balance, or else we play seesaw or chase one another in order to beat the cold. Once, hiding in the bushes, I happened to disturb a couple embracing.

Another time, when I was alone sitting astride a tree trunk—the other girls hadn't come because of the bitter chill—I saw a forester, small and deformed, with a gray, scrunched-up face, brown lips and eyes, and very wide shoulders, spying behind a hedge. He looked like a spider.

He tore through the hedge and shouted: "Halt!"

I glimpsed two young people making love. They quickly composed themselves. Foreigners. You could tell they loved each other. The forester was all worked up: he stamped his feet, croaking that the young man would end up in jail and that he would hold the girl in his hut, there in the forest, while awaiting verification, that is, of whether her papers were in order as a whore. The girl turned frighteningly ashen. The young man bent over the spider in a pleading attitude. Meanwhile, the forester pulled out a revolver. The young man did not get upset: he showed him their work passes, deferentially. It was clear that he was saying that he loved the girl, that he wanted to marry her, that he had been the one to seduce her, that he was solely responsible, that the forester had to let her go because she didn't do that sort of thing for a living.

"Where can we be together," he said loudly, "in my shelter in front of the men, or hers in front of the women?" And so saying he suddenly landed a punch on the forester's mouth, knocking him to the ground, rigid. He then grabbed the girl's hand and dragged her away into the dense woods.

The forester was bleeding, but I was of no mind to help him. I slowly dismounted from my log and went back to the trattoria.

Afterward, for several nights, I dreamed about the forester on the ground, a thin trickle of blood dribbling from his mouth, and a lot of gnomes resembling him crowding around me in the kitchen at Thomasbräu with depraved grins. They told me that there's an Italian roaming around in those woods who, when he sees women come by, opens his pants to attract them, and one day a Czechoslovakian girl from the trattoria could not resist.

Walking through the forest at 1:00 a.m., on my way back to the camp from work, fills me with such terror that afterward I'm left wide-awake on my pallet, numb and delirious, for the rest of the night. I could take the path around the woods, but it's three times as long and leaves me constantly exposed, with the dark wall of trees on one side and open countryside on the other; I feel like I'm walking on the edge of a precipice and am always about to fall.

To cut through the forest instead, all I have to do is strike out firmly, without hesitation. Then I'm not aware of anything. I walk on as if in a nightmare, obsessed by the creaking of branches underfoot, not even daring to breathe, transfixed by the pounding of my heart, proceeding in a straight line, and if I move a fraction of an inch to one side it's as if I were sinking into the void. Until, revived by a breath of fresh air, I make out the silhouettes of the last trees, placid and still, in front of me.

Then I return to my senses. I wake up and heave a long breath. The open air soothes me, like a mother's arms, and I walk along enjoying every step, the thud of my clogs on the ground covered by rotting leaves.

But today, perhaps because I was just fired, and it's the last time, my fear is greater and I just can't face the woods. I'd rather go back to camp by taking the long way around.

I think I hear footsteps beside me, in sync with mine, as if someone were walking side by side with me along the edge of the forest. I don't dare turn my head, I become frantic, I slow my pace, I quicken it, the steps are still synchronized. The gnomes are multiplying.

I look over. Louis's silhouette glides along the trees at my side.

I'm about to call him and run to him but I stop: if it were him, he would speak to me, he would wave to me. Who can it be? My terror grows; I start to run. I glance back briefly and the figure has disappeared.

Back home, at the camp, where everything is quiet, it seems to me that my fear was a hallucination. I'd like to talk about it, tell someone about it, unburden myself, but I sense that as long as I can remain silent and keep others from seeing me hurt or frightened, my secret will be safe.

The next morning, however, I can't resist and, joining a group that's talking about illnesses, I bring up the subject of epilepsy.

They immediately name Louis.

"He can't be cured," says one woman, a prostitute by trade. "He lives the life of a condemned man. He never sleeps—sleeps even less than me!" She laughs, throwing back her head. "He's everywhere, at all times." The way she speaks makes Louis's sudden appearances seem like magic, and it paralyzes me.

"He leads a grueling life," she continues. "You're interested in him, right? I wonder where he is?"

"I don't know, I haven't seen him since the day of the outing."

"I haven't seen him since then myself."

"The Sicilian hasn't come back either," I say.

"Things aren't looking too good for you, huh?" The woman winks at me.

I lie down on the pallet, where I spend the entire day. A squad of Germans shows up, but I don't move from the bed. They look the place over, measure the walls, discuss cleaning everything up. The Labor Bureau's camp will be cleared out and closed and the convoys will go elsewhere. Stores will be housed here, as auxiliary backup during the bombings. I listen as if it didn't concern me. After bustling about at length, they leave. I remain apathetic, not thinking about anything, watching the evening shadows grow heavy in the room.

"Lucie."

I leap up; it's the Sicilian.

"Pietro."

His face is spent.

"Come with me."

I follow him out to the yard. It's raining, it's night, but he doesn't see or hear a thing and he's in no hurry. He sits on the ground under the eaves and I sit beside him. Slowly he begins to speak as if remembering: Louis *was* (past tense).

"Louis was without equal as a burglar, he never backed away even when it came to killing. He hated the Nazis fanatically. He specialized in jewelry shops and warehouses. He was a born criminal. But in recent times he had gone too far. He didn't seem to care anymore. Until they put an enormous price on his head. I went to see for myself. All the local police head-quarters had his photo hanging outside. I warned him. Days ago he gave me this package for you. He opened it again last night to add something. He told me to give it to you when they did him in. He knew very well that they would put an end to him. And still, it didn't stop him. Tonight they caught him, he fired but they hit him, then he killed two of them and they finished him off. 'Give her this money,' he said, 'it's not much, just to tide her over till the war ends.' Do you know he was in awe of you? One night when we were playing cards at Thomasbräu and you came in . . . it was in the early days, how long ago? Two months ago, around two months, the baby should have been born now, now I have money, I too stole, I went with Louis, if she had waited, I just had to fence the jewelry, pay, but I wasn't able to sell the jewels, Louis couldn't either, they found him loaded with diamonds, and what could I do with them? We couldn't sell them, so the money isn't much. He wanted to give you cash, not to cause you any trouble with the jewels. Instead she died, it was her heart, she had a bad heart, I didn't know it, she told me at the end. But she could have been saved if she had waited a little longer to give birth." The Sicilian covers his face with his hands. The tears flow through his fingers. He recovers, gulping, trying to speak calmly: "Where was I? Oh yes, you came in and you didn't see us, and he pointed you out to me: 'That silly fool needs protection too.' He seemed as tightfisted as a Genovese. Drinking, eating, and smoking, always alone. Before you came. Then we became friends. If she were giving birth now, I too have money in my pocket, and diamonds like Louis, and pearls, a pearl necklace to celebrate the birth." The Sicilian covers his face with his hands again. He looks up. "He was a friend. I misjudged him earlier," he says with a smile, "because he never paid women. He risked everything as though possessed. But he didn't steal just for the money. It was an obsession with him to break into an apartment or a shop at night, to come up with a plan, consider all angles, to win. I worked with him a couple of times, he was superb. Plus, he was fair: he divided everything equally. And he didn't steal randomly: he was selective about what he was going to take. But he preferred to work alone. For him, everyone else had no guts."

The Sicilian falls silent. He lights a cigarette, protecting the flame under his jacket. Crying, I tell him about the apparition in the woods.

"If you had called him, maybe he wouldn't have died," he says.

"It wasn't him." I clutch his sleeve. "Please, it wasn't him."

Rome, 1953

ASYLUM AT DACHAU

The transit camp in Dachau is separated from the concentration camp by a long strip of barren wasteland.

The two camps are very similar in their outer appearance, except for one thing: the barbed wire fence enclosing the second camp is charged with high-voltage current.

The surrounding plain is deserted, the weather dismal, the sky itself like a curtain about to roll down and swallow the horizon, so that you feel as if you're in some remote, inaccessible expanse. It's hard to remember that a few kilometers away is a big city.

Until I went to the concentration camp, I wasn't even aware that there was another camp not far away. I only found out about it now.

By escaping, I'd hoped to be able to leave the area, to distance myself from my memories, and instead I find myself back in a place of systematized death, in this transit camp, right in Dachau, a few meters from the K-Lager from which I'd fled with such hope.

The barracks are like ours were, made of wood, low and long.

I crawl under the fence and enter the camp.

Groups of foreigners, mainly French and Italian I think, wander around the barracks chatting among themselves. I stop next to the fence, as if I were thinking and looking for something. Then I walk unhurriedly toward the foreigners, mingling with them and listening idly as though I were one of them.

I have the feeling I'm being watched, spied on, though looking around all I see are distracted, casual glances directed at me. Others approach from nearby groups. They're all wearing civilian outfits, and most are neat and clean, their clothes in fairly good condition. You can instantly tell that they've just arrived in Germany. But they're not the ones who make me uneasy; rather, it's the indifference flaunted by the shabbiest-looking ones with the hardened, worn-out faces. Evidently they've been in Germany for some time and naturally know about the concentration camp. Maybe they can sense that I'm a runaway and, fearing retribution by the Germans, are about to report me. Whatever gave me the idea that I could slip in here of all places. No one has ever done it, I'm sure, and if no one's done it, there must be a reason.

Trying to be as nonchalant as possible, I enter the barrack in front of me, in which some children are sitting on the floor. Typical Russian children. No one looks at me. Even inside, the barracks are like ours, furnished with two-tier double bunks—at our place they were three-tier—with straw mattresses and rough blankets, and a stove in the center.

Women and children are lying five or six to a pallet, while the men are sprawled out or squatting on the floor in silence. Here too most of the people have shaved heads. I try to walk with a straight back and heavy, shuffling steps, like a Slavic girl.

I sit on the floor behind the stove.

I put my kerchief on my head, crossed under the chin and tied behind my head, the Russian way.

"Come on, stop it, you're about as Soviet as I am Chinese," says an Italian who claps me on the shoulder as he slides down to sit beside me behind the stove, in front of the smeared gray window. He's a young man with a shaved head topped by a beret, a scraggly beard on hollow cheeks, black, chipped teeth, and tiny wrinkles around eyes that have an intelligent, frank expression.

"I do not understand," I say in Russian, "*nieponimaio.*"

"Stop it, I'm telling you! Are you afraid of me?" He leans over to whisper in my ear. His breath stinks of alcohol and tobacco both. "I'm a runaway too," he adds.

"*Nieponimaio,*" I repeat.

He looks at me, annoyed.

"If that's how you feel, get by on your own." Seeing my worried expression, he shakes his head: "You're really a novice. Are you afraid of the Russians? Go on! We always feel quite at ease in their barracks."

I'm certainly not about to tell him that if I was pretending to be one of them, it's precisely because I trust the Soviets more than any other people. It's *his* interest that worries me. But intent on not giving myself away, I have to be careful not to show any sign that I understand Italian. He goes on:

"They don't care about us, can't you see? Besides, no one here knows or even imagines that there's a concentration camp nearby. Even those who heard of them before coming to Germany think that this is one of them. They're convinced there can't be anyplace worse than this, so they don't suspect that there can be escapees among them. They're simply counting the days while waiting to be transferred and settled somewhere. And the rest of us fugitives, even if we wanted to, how could we report or harm one another? We have no choice but to help each other! For example, you shouldn't stay in this barrack because it's too close to the kitchens and it's inspected more often—you made a bad choice. I noticed you right away, that one is Italian, you'll see, I said to myself. What do you expect, we recognize each other at first sight, you'll get used to doing it too. But remember, outside the barracks we don't know each other."

He's restless and fidgets as he talks. Finally, he stands up. He's tall and well-built.

"So then, I'll expect you at the toilets tonight, after roll call. Knock twice on the partition. I'll be on the other side, in the men's toilet, and I'll remove a board that we nailed up for urgent talks. I'll explain some things to you, otherwise they'll nab you at the first haul, kid."

He tugs down his beret, which had slipped back, and walks away with his hands in his pockets, strutting. I stay where I am, waiting for the Russians to react to my being there, but as expected no one takes any notice of me. As I sit there waiting for evening, someone outside loudly starts singing the frolicking tune of the Band of Affori:

> Arriva la banda, arriva la banda,
> arriva la banda dei mascalzon
> dei mascalzon dei mascalzon
> col Duce in testa che faceva da caporion,
> eccoli qua, son tutti qua
> camicie nere e federal . . . (the melody swells)

I approach the window on my hands and knees and look outside. The Italian from before is leaning against the doorway of the barracks across the way, staring in my direction. As soon as he sees my frightened eyes, he starts laughing. I back away and rush out of the barrack to hide somewhere else.

"Ruskaia, ruskaia," I hear a girl's voice shout as she runs after me. When she catches up with me she says in French, "I'm talking to you, you know." I stop. She's very young, chubby and childlike, with small, dark, shiny eyes, plump cheeks, jet-black hair, and fair skin.

"I'm Jeanine. Polò told me about you. Polò is my friend. I was just coming to see you."

She walks along the barracks with me and, chatting animatedly, not caring whether I understand her or not, she blurts out at once that she became a woman during the trip thanks to some kind, gentle Germans who gave her everything she could want, then she took up with an Italian friend, a certain Paolo, but a different one, not this one, a pudgy blond. "Would you believe, he kept telling me: thank you, my love." She repeats the words in Italian as if to show me she's not lying. Then she ran off to Munich to follow him but instead he kicked her out, the little bastard. So she came back here and for three months she's been with her new friend who is also named Paolo, but is much better than the other one. First of all he's a sailor, not one of the crew; he was a commander and he knows how to speak. Plus

he wears a beret on his head just like a Frenchman. Actually a real Frenchman is after her, one of us—she winks at me—but she is faithful to her Polò,
except that she goes to an actor on nights when Polò gets drunk, a man
who gives her a lot of money and is so distinguished that leather gloves stick
out of the pocket of his new coat. He's a bit slow, though, not as funny and
clever as Polò is. But she doesn't mind in the least. The man even wants to
marry her, but she doesn't think she should accept, especially since he has
a wife in France. With the money she earns, she buys alcohol for Polò when
she goes to the nearby farm to pick vegetables for the camp; she goes there
with an Italian from the kitchen who is also her friend, but she doesn't let
him put his hands on her, so she can go on taking advantage of him longer.

"Look, there he is."

A smiling, thin little man comes toward us, a farmer who seems to be
walking through bushes, avoiding spiky branches. He greets us with great
civility, an astonished, extravagant expression, invites us to visit him behind
the kitchen and walks away.

"He's a real character—loaded with dough," Jeanine explains.

I observe the comings and goings of the foreigners, trying to distinguish
the escapees. A young man with a round beret pushed back on his head
passes by and greets us with a sly, polite look. I nudge Jeanine.

"Yeah," she says, "he's a student from Gascony, boring as a book. Wait."
She tugs at my arm. "Now look to your left in front of the toilet, that's François, imagine, a student!" She laughs scornfully. "If he sees me he won't
leave me alone, let's go back."

I just have time to catch a glimpse, in the metallic light of dusk, of a
young man, still a boy, elegant, pallid, with a docile look. I glance over at
the toilets as well.

"Are you all French?" I ask.

"And Italian. We're the resourceful ones. But speaking of that"—she
stops abruptly, hands on hips—"how come you speak French?" she says,
laughing.

"I was born there."

"Where? Never mind, it doesn't matter, never give any details about
yourself." She starts walking again. "I want to show you everybody, we're
like a family. We don't readily take in newcomers, but for you we'll make

an exception. We took a liking to you, Polò and I, and we already proposed you to the group. On the whole they agreed; Polò noticed right away that you were afraid, he felt sorry for you, see, and he told the others. Right now we're taking a walk to introduce you, because they haven't seen you yet and they want to get a look at you before they finally accept you. Tonight we'll have their approval, you can be sure, and then you can live happily with us, instead of staying there to rot with the Russians' bedbugs. See that fashion plate? He's an Italian." Eyeing me is a dark young man, tall, slender, well-dressed, slicked-back hair. "That guy stays with us because we found him, but for us he's an outsider. Imagine his scorn for Polò with his tattered clothes and his head shaven like a bowling ball. If it weren't for his decayed teeth, Polò would be a hundred times more gorgeous than that pretty boy, and even the way he is, I wouldn't trade him for that guy—not even for a repatriation order. I don't know his name and I don't want to know it. Now I'm going to show you a French slut, they call her La Scopina, 'the mop,' because of her hair, although she really does a lot of 'mopping' here in the camp, she'll go with a man just for a cigarette. Yet she has a boyfriend who's a coal worker. Just imagine. 'All I ask is one thing, don't betray me,' he told her, 'I won't ever let you lack for anything, not clothes or food or cigarettes. I'll work overtime, I'll give you everything you want. I won't ask you for anything, not even to wash my underwear.'" And here Jeanine doubles over, laughing. "'Just don't betray me.' She swore to him on the two children she'd left in France, wiping away tears, never to deceive him. I'm not lying, you know, I was right on the bed next to them when they made that pact, I saw and heard everything. Instead, with the excuse that she spends half the day mopping up around the men's straw mattresses, she makes love with all of them, 'to keep in practice,' she says, 'in case the cuckold has second thoughts.' As for him, he's a sheep."

Jeanine looks into the doorway of a barrack. "There she is," she says. Under a dull light bulb I see, standing in the middle of the room, an affable, middle-aged woman with reddish hair, a broad impassive face, short torso, and long, skinny legs. The copper-colored hair against the smooth, clear skin of her face is the only thing about her that seems alive.

"What do you want?" she asks Jeanine listlessly. Not answering, Jeanine takes me by the arm and leads me away.

"La Scopina isn't actually one of us, she's working here with the proper papers, but she's convenient for us because she roams around the camp freely and sees a lot of things, and her boyfriend doesn't leave us short of coal." Jeanine seems to be thinking. "Come on," she says, "the only ones left are the French guy who's after me, and Jean de Lille, a cute, young worker; then there's the Moroccan, a real capitalist that one, aside from the fact that his face is covered with smallpox scars. But all three said that they'd seen you. Oh, there's La Pidocchiosa, 'lousy,' the one with the lice. Benito named her that. Benito is the cheese guy, the poor man is furious because at night he always ends up with her again. So sometimes you hear him muttering, 'I'll sleep and that's it, I'll pay you anyway.' I can't tell you how hard the rest of us laugh. And she smokes, she's always smoking, even smokes potato skins rolled up in newspaper. By the way, what's your name? A fake name, though."

"Carla."

"Okay, Carlà. Now we'll go to Benito. He boasts about having been some kind of fearsome partisan in Italy—under the nom de guerre of Benito, imagine! He's a fool—Polò calls him by that name ironically, and Benito is proud of it. Who knows who he thinks he is, he hands out gifts left and right, would you believe, he doesn't eat and slaves away all day to afford it, but meanwhile everyone praises him for his generosity, so he's content."

We skirted the barracks laid out side by side in parallel rows. "Watch out for the barracks that are in the middle, the ones for the volunteers."

I try to get a look inside the volunteers' barracks: they're roomier than the others, they have cots instead of two-level bunks, and the straw pallets are wrapped in checkered cotton mattress covers.

"Remember," Jeanine says, "that we escapees are in barrack fifty-one."

"How are people divided up here?"

"Men in one, women in another, families in a third . . . And the volunteers are kept separate."

As I walk beside Jeanine and follow her words—surrounded by the coming and going of foreigners freely taking a walk, all mingled together, out to breathe the evening air—I sense the invisible camp nearby: there, we were forbidden to even move about and lived holed up in the dark.

We reach the area behind the kitchen, a wooden building longer than the others with a tin roof. Behind the kitchen, against the fence, is a pile of garbage where children are rummaging. We go and wait for Benito there, looking out past the fence as from the rail of a ship. The concentration camp is on the other side.

"Jeanine," I say, "isn't it dangerous here, so close to . . ." I gesture to the plain. "The SS, you know."

"Would a Nazi suspect that we're right here under his nose?" she laughs. "No!"

Benito comes running, hunkers down, unfolds a cloth that he pulls out from under his shirt, and spreads it on his knees. It holds bread, potatoes, and a wedge of cheese.

"Quick," he beckons us, "make everything disappear."

He grabs the food with his bony, gnarled fingers and hands it out swiftly as if he were stealing. Then he stuffs the cloth under his shirt and straightens up, moving uncertainly, with a sly, idiotic expression.

"Now let's beat it," says Jeanine. "I'm tired. Go eat your portion at the toilet and never let anyone see that you have something, otherwise no one will forgive you for it. Bye, Carlà, bye-bye, baby chick, I feel like I'm your mother hen."

She laughs and runs away, disappearing behind the corner of a barrack.

When the guards retire after roll call—they almost seem harmless here, not accompanied by fidgety German shepherds like in the concentration camp—I run to the toilet to meet Paolo.

I knock on the wall.

"I really didn't think you'd come," Paolo says in a low voice. I look for where the words are coming from; behind the last of the eight toilet bowls, down below, I finally spot a gap in the wooden partition, the board pulled off.

"Why did you give me away?" I ask, sitting on the floor and bending over the opening. "I was so content not knowing anyone. You're wrong, you know, to think I'm safer with all of you. In these places you're better off alone, unnoticed, without a name." I speak quickly, gripped by an abrupt terror of becoming attached to other human beings. "So leave me alone, I don't exist."

Paolo doesn't answer, and I wonder whether he heard me.

"Paolo?"

"What?"

"I thought maybe you didn't hear me."

"Isn't that what you want, given that you don't exist?"

"Help me, I'm afraid."

"Of what? I find this dull life so well suited to me that I don't want it to change." Paolo's voice floats up gently.

The door flies open and four girls burst in. Talking fast in a Slavic language, they pull up their skirts and park themselves on the toilets. They look at me sitting on the floor and, nudging one another, stifle a laugh. Then they dash off, leaving the door open to slam in the wind. I get up and close it; then I go back to squatting on the floor beside the partition.

"I loved an Italian girl who was very beautiful," the voice resumes. "She worked at the same factory where we were prisoners. She was a stunning, practical woman who hated the displacements. One day she told me that I was disorganized, argumentative, and indecisive, not the man for her. The next day she was gone, she'd gotten transferred to another city. I escaped in order to find her and ended up here. I took up with Jeanine. Sleeping with her, it doesn't even seem like you're embracing a woman. She has the spirited body of a child, what do you expect, she's sixteen, playful and impish as a cat, plus she knows her way around, every now and then she shows up with tobacco or liquor or bread. 'Imagine, Polò, what a fluke!' she says, laughing. A young girl who makes my life tolerable and lets me be the worm that I am: she accepts me as I am and doesn't go beyond that."

"She's so young!" I sigh.

"Now don't go acting like a great-grandmother, you're young too. How old? Eighteen, right?"

"I'm only nineteen, it's true, but I always forget. Then, when I remember, it's as if I've made a great discovery, and at first I'm somewhat happy because I have so much life ahead of me. But then I quickly turn sad, full of dread about the future, and I wonder how I can live after all this."

I'm practically lying on the floor with my head under the toilet bowl's drainpipe; I can't manage to say anything else and Paolo also falls silent.

"In the camps," his reflective voice then goes on, "the ones who survive are those who retain the moral compass of their lives, there is no middle ground. That's the beauty of it: here you can't lie. Incidentally, where are you from exactly?"

"I knew it. That's what you wanted: for me to talk, to tell you about myself." I raise my head and bang it against the toilet bowl.

"If you close yourself off, you're a goner," the voice says calmly and, after a pause: "Haven't you seen how docilely the deportees die? In a group it's so easy!"

"I know why they die," I reply. "Their real lives ended earlier, so they're throwing away the one they have now, it's hostile to them, like a wall. Not me, I'm keeping mine, the way bears do: don't feel, don't love, just sleep through the cold." I'm choked by hysterical tears. "That's why I didn't want to share anything with you people, but you did it, are you happy now? Look, I've known people who were starving to death but never resigned themselves to eating barley and bedbug soup. What could I do? I ate it. They died and I realized that all of life is that way. They refused to work, even under the whip. They were heroes. For what? What does it mean? They played into the Nazis' hands." I cover my face with my palms.

"You're contradicting yourself," the voice replies softly. "You have a problem with the ones who throw away this life of ours, yet you want to do the same thing."

"No, it's different."

"A bear," he repeats. "Don't feel, don't love."

A silence ensues, then: "Me, I'm enjoying the current situation. Can't you see I'm thriving on it? That I'm devouring it to the last bite?"

"You're the one who wants to die," I murmur.

The door opens again, and, without looking to see who came in, I spring to my feet, scared, pulling down my pants. I sit on the toilet with unspeakable relief, as if I had an ID card in my pocket. When the girls leave, I lie down again with my pants undone so I can make it to the toilet seat more quickly in case of another interruption.

"Paolo?" I whisper.

His voice comes to me: "You're right, *ruskaia*, here I can finally die in peace, very very slowly."

"Why did you call me then?" I rebel again. "Do you want me to give in too, like you?"

"You can see I was drawn to this."

"Never mind drawn to it, I don't believe it, you weren't like that, you wouldn't understand certain things. You say that to convince yourself, so you won't suffer."

"Not so. I've always been falling apart, I've always liked to play the victim of fate and here I found my real element, something to sink my teeth into," he laughs, "and decayed teeth at that!"

"And then you say that *I* act like a great-grandmother. You're the one who acts like an old man. How old are you?"

"Thirty-one."

"What work did you do before?"

"Bosun. Cargo ships."

Another silence, then finally, "If you want to drop dead in peace," I ask him, "why do you try to help others?"

"Who knows, to pass the time. Years of maritime service," he says quietly, "like it or not it stays with you." I hear his breathing: "Maybe it was in the freight containers," he says, beginning to sound upset. "I went crazy. I suffer from claustrophobia, see, it gets you by the throat. You can't help it: you feel strangled. Mother of God, how I hated those containers, and you see the result, right? I associated them with my fate."

"I'm beginning to understand you, you know, you're worse than they are," I say.

"They who?"

"It was terrible . . ."

"Hmm," he breathes beside me.

"If you had seen those women," I say, "they would fight each other like wild animals for a cigarette, a turnip, a man, always the same threats, they'd report one another to the Kapos, the SS, for having insulted Nazism, for having spat on Hitler's portrait, they'd be arrested and . . ." My words come out choked. I make an effort: "Paolo," I confide, "Nazism was their weapon. But you're educated, you've traveled, and it's much worse: you use it as an excuse. You know who you remind me of? There was a German woman among the common criminals, who, at dawn, as we were washing up, would sing a song at the top of her lungs; it's an ordinary parody but, for some reason, it always haunts me when I have hunger cramps." I sing the refrain that in German goes:

> Es geht alles vorüber
> es geht alles vorbei
> mein Mann ist in Russland
> mein Bett ist noch frei.*

The quivering sound of my voice under the toilet's drainpipe singing to a hole in a partition has a strange effect on me and I stop. I feel a confusion, an unreasonable regret, and I blurt out: "I left them. They're there now. I couldn't take it. They've probably been punished because of me." The sobbing suffocates me: "But I didn't want to die, it was stronger than me, you have to believe me."

"I'm convinced the Germans have spotted me, they look the other way so they can keep a closer eye on me and pounce on me at the right time— meanwhile, here I can't do any harm, get it?" There's a grin in his voice.

The toilet's electric light grows dim due to the nighttime blackout, plunging the room into a bleak, dull half-light that hangs over the ungainly white toilet seats.

"It's ten o'clock," Paolo sighs.

"At our camp too, at the same hour."

"It's the first time you've run away, right?"

"The second. This time I've come from a camp in Munich."

"So then you already know that from now on all you'll do is escape. You'll think only about saving your own skin and the hell with all the rest. You'll become less sensitive," he sniggers (which sounds like a groan).

"Instead it's just the opposite. It's always worse for me," I say, still crying.

"Come on, I didn't mean to get you down." His voice cracks: "You shouldn't listen to me, I'm teasing, see, I'm always teasing." Abruptly his

*"All is well / all things pass / my husband is in Russia / my bed is still free."

tone becomes firm: "Enough of that, let's move on to serious matters. You're in trouble. When I approached you this morning behind that stove, you jumped so high, even an idiot would have gotten suspicious. Remember: anyone who jumps at every shadow and looks ready to fight tooth and nail has already denounced herself."

"That's not true. I was composed, I was just keeping to myself."

"Keeping to yourself!" he chuckles. "With eyes that can't stop darting around. That's the mark of a fugitive, what else? Always feeling like you're being hunted."

"So according to you a person should let herself be deceived by the calm of appearances? And thereby neglect even the most elementary precautions?"

"You're quick to leap to the opposite extreme. The point is this: you can't give a shit about the big issues—heroes, significance, weapons, justifications, and whatever else you dragged out! All bullshit. You have to get by however you can, that's the only way you'll see the practical side of things. You have to resist your instinct, my dear girl, the war isn't about to end tomorrow, it will take time, and how! At least several months longer."

"Months?"

"Right, months at least. The winter for sure." He falls silent, then suddenly resumes: "I forgot the best part. I called you here to warn you about an imminent danger to you, but don't panic, it's just a technical danger, so to speak. As soon as the Russians receive their documents, they'll be sent off to perform hard labor somewhere, while maybe thinking they're going to lead a normal life."

The low voice behind the partition laughs with senseless pleasure. "On the day they're transported, the Germans might notice you, so be on your guard: that's when our support can be helpful to you, I would say, essential."

The thought of having to take precautions for the immediate future rouses me.

"Thanks," I say. "I'm sorry, you know, for the way I talked when I came in, I'm just at the end of my rope."

I hear footsteps and men's voices outside. I wait for them to go away, with my eyes closed, woozy. Afterward, I call out.

"Paolo?" No answer. "Paolo? Are you there?" I wait a little longer, then look down: the opening in the partition is gone. I drag myself up; my legs are numb and I feel a little dizzy.

I go out into the frosty December air. I start back to my barrack, lost in thought, skirting the fence to try to make out my old camp in the darkness. But suddenly I stop and crouch down, because lanterns are swaying a few meters away from me and German words can be heard, orders snapped by the SS with detached impatience, which sound to my ears like the cracks of a whip.

They are right in front of the barrack where I sleep: my Russians are being dragged from their beds and lined up in the courtyard. I realize that they are leaving this very night: the barrack door is open and they come out, one at a time, stopped by guards who shine lantern light on their faces as they blink their eyes and show their papers. Vehicles with dim headlights slowly make their way past the fence, stopping in a row in front of the camp entrance. The beams of light pierce the darkness, unhurriedly and insidiously, and I'm afraid of being discovered. If Paolo hadn't arranged to meet me, I would have been captured already. I don't know where to hide. Creeping along the barracks, I slip back into the toilet. From behind the door I listen to the impersonal German voices, the pleading cries of the Russians, the roar of engines, the patter of footsteps.

I preferred the submerged hatred of the concentration camp.

Gradually the sounds fade away and are lost in the night, leaving a wake of muffled moaning, the rustle of clothing, the shuffling of hurried footsteps punctuated by curt peremptory shouts and the thud of imperious military boots.

The toilet door cautiously opens a crack and Jeanine's face appears in the opening, looking around.

"Carlà?"

"I'm over here." I come out from behind the toilets, where I had stretched out and flattened myself against the floor.

"Move, hurry up." She grabs my hand. "Sure, keep to yourself, make me run after you!" she whispers to me, shaking her head. "Do you really think we talk just for the sake of talking?"

"Shut up, please," I implore in a whisper.

"Shut up yourself! After I'm risking my neck for you!" Pulling me by the hand, Jeanine precedes me, creeping along the barracks, then rushing ahead to stop abruptly at every turn. Getting down on all fours, we cross the space between one barrack and another, then we're back on our feet along another row of barracks, again crawling on all fours, who knows how many times, the camp is endless, finally a door opens partway and we slip through into a dark room. As soon as we've entered, someone turns the blue lamp over the stove back on and Jeanine flops down noisily on a pallet.

"We made it!"

"Those bastards make the transfers at night now!" a man's voice says.

"What do you mean, 'now,' they always do," retorts Paolo, standing against the door.

"They try everything to intensify the anxiety here, and drive the rest of us crazy," exclaims the Gascon student, sitting on a straw mattress.

As they talk, Jeanine watches them, hands behind her head, humming a French children's tune:

Malborough s'en va-t-en guerre
mironton mironton mirontaine
*qui sait quand reviendra . . .**

"And if you go and say that," Paolo continues in French, "they'll think you're crazy: What's so criminal about making people travel at night? Force majeure due to the scarcity and overcrowding of trains!" he sneers.

"That's the point: to get on people's nerves while always being on the side of reason," the Gascon student agrees.

Jeanine sits up: "That's enough high-minded politics!" she interrupts. "It's become an obsession."

"She's right," Paolo approves, "we're playing *their* game."

"Even speaking ill of them works in their favor," the Gascon sighs.

"But aren't you overestimating them?" Jeanine snorts, shrugging. "They aren't really all that smart!"

---

*"Malborough is off to war / rat-a-tat, rat-a-tat, rat-a-tat-tat / who knows when he'll return . . ."

A baby frets and a woman's subdued voice consoles him. They are Russian.

The Gascon student comes over to me as I go on standing by the stove: "Sit down, mademoiselle, they told me you speak French quite well." He has a conspiratorial air, like a character in a novel.

"Pretty well."

"The Russians are in their beds," he continues, "you see? They won't bother us, they left a corner in the back for us. Such a hospitable people! Such a lofty sense of live and let live!" And before I can take a breath, he begins a disquisition on the Slavic spirit.

Meanwhile, Jeanine is calling me: "Carlà, come over here by me, hurry up, it's time to call it a night."

The other fugitives would like to approach to question me. A Russian or two leans over to look.

"I can stay and talk with you if this promiscuity is too much for you," the Gascon is telling me.

"Thanks, I'm sleepy," I say, and lie down beside Jeanine, who huddles against the wall.

"Just think," she says, laughing, "we're the only two promising girls in here. We have lots of choices."

"But I'm sleepy, Jeanine."

Jeanine claps her hands: "Okay then! Polò sleeps alone tonight." She laughs delightedly at teasing him. "If anything, I'll leave you for a bit," she adds.

Figures move to the pallets, clamber up in pairs. I spot a woman in her thirties, filthy and unkempt, her hair puffed up like a nest.

"The one with the lice?" I ask Jeanine.

"Right." We laugh like accomplices under the blanket.

Paolo comes over: "I'm going out."

"Do what you like!" Jeanine sulks, and he goes away.

"Where's he going?" I ask.

"To drink."

"But where?"

"He climbs over the fence and comes back at dawn. He does it all the time."

"And they don't catch him?"

"Not him. There are foreigners outside who come around at night to sell alcohol. It's too long a story to tell now. Let's make the most of it and get some sleep." She holds my hand and curls up.

Silence spreads over me like a sheet while, on the various beds, movements and gasps of heavy breathing can be heard, rapacious advances.

"Keep it down a bit, can't you!" Jeanine protests, sitting up abruptly. "You're not alone in here, you know. We have this Italian mademoiselle with us now!" She turns to me quietly: "We have nightlife here!" she confides proudly.

A siren wails, filling the night; it's still wailing as the rumble of planes builds in the oppressive silence and a heavy bombardment begins, seemingly uprooting everything beyond our thin wooden walls. We can't take cover, because in Dachau—in the transit camp as well as in the concentration camp—there are no shelters for foreigners, only for the Germans posted there.

In the darkness the raid precipitates, the frenzy in the beds intensifies, as though everyone is excited by the voracity of the bombs. The door creaks as it's thrown open. The silhouette of a man staggers in the frame.

"It's not him," Jeanine says, irritated.

"Jeanine," the man yells hoarsely, "I'll kill you."

"Ugh, it's François," Jeanine tells me with a trilling laugh. She turns around on the pallet: "He's mad at me. Just because I went with him once, he always wants me. I'm not his!"

The inebriated Frenchman turns on the light. A shiver of fear spreads through the barrack. It's the pale student, still a boy, seen near the toilets during the presentation stroll.

Huddled up, Jeanine shouts, "Turn it off, pig!"

François grabs the poker from the stove and lunges, grinding his teeth: "I'm going to kill you."

Men jump down from the straw mattresses; someone turns off the light. The drunk turns it back on.

A bomb, which seems to rise from the bowels of the earth, as if a lid were lifted up, explodes in a huge burst. After a moment, just in time to make sure that our barrack is still standing, the men rush at François: "Turn it off," they order, fuming with contempt, "they'll see us, you filthy bastard."

The light is turned off, on, off.

The deep rumble seems to recede; a charged silence hangs over everything.

"Pig!" Jeanine's silvery voice enunciates the word clearly and spills into a delicious laugh. The response is a shout, as the drunk rushes in the direction of Jeanine's voice.

The men push him back, swearing at the girl.

"Jeanine!" the raging young man shouts. "Jeanine!" There is an anguished grief in his voice.

Jeanine's words ring out again: "Cuckoo!" and she laughs, drawing more swearing and expletives.

"Cuckoo," she teases, "cuckoo."

"Throw a bucket of water on his head," someone shouts.

"Where is he?"

"Near the stove."

"If anyone moves, he'll be sorry," the boy answers coldly. "I have a knife in my hand." The men stand back.

"Lean a couple of mattresses against the windows and turn on the light."

The light is switched on: François is in front of Jeanine and me, his eyes wild. Jeanine screams, the drunk springs forward, I leap up.

"Give me the knife," I say.

"Leave me alone," he says, coming forward, pointing the knife at me. "Get out of my way."

"Give me the knife," I repeat, moving toward him as well, not taking my eyes off him. He can't be more than eighteen; he looks like a schoolboy. No one around us dares lay a hand on him for fear that he might hurt me. He backs away, pleading.

"I don't want anything from you. Stay out of it." He retreats farther back, among the mattresses.

"Give me the knife, or I'll throw a bucket of water in your face."

"He's a raving wino!" Jeanine jeers, encouraged by my involvement.

When he hears Jeanine's voice, his eyes light up and he emits a kind of painful bellow.

"I have nothing against you." He stares at me. "Get out of my way, I said."

"No." I smile at him.

He moves toward me again. Lunging forward, I try to wrest the knife from him, but he's quicker, and wounds me. I'm holding my left hand against my chest and at first it scares me to see it covered in blood. I press harder. François sees it and, thinking he's stabbed me through the heart, drops the knife and cringes in the corner, looking both frightened and fierce.

Apprehensively I move my hand away from my chest: there's only a superficial cut on my index finger.

"He's a bit player," Jeanine remarks, irritated. At which the drunk, more flushed and menacing than before, comes out of his corner, knocks down the robust young man who was trying to keep him there, picks up the knife still on the floor, and yells, "I'll kill you!" His voice is drowned in a belch.

Meanwhile, I've reached the bucket of water that a Russian woman has been trying to hand me surreptitiously and I grab it. I start to swing it, but François spots me:

"There she is again. What do you want?" He looks at the bucket. "Don't throw the water at me," he pleads, his eyes wide. "Don't throw the water at me," he says, weeping, and comes toward me again with the knife in his hand. "Stop her, I haven't done anything." He looks around, terrified. "Stop her!" Snarling, he suddenly roars: "I'll kill you!" He rushes at me, and quick as a flash I pour the water over him.

He collapses with a convulsive shudder. They undress him, make him lie down. They turn off the light. A growing rumble sucks away every breath before a stunning blow shakes the barrack, pitiably accompanied by the drunk's wails and sobs.

"You shouldn't take risks like that for no reason," the Gascon murmurs to me tonelessly. He flips on his cigarette lighter, and by the glow of the flame, looking into my eyes, he explains that the relationship between my principled act and its base occasion was disproportionate. His eyes verge on green, his features are regular though not exceptional, there's something clammy about them. He tells me that François is a high school student who left home due to disagreements with his parents. Jeanine also ran away from home, chasing after a German soldier-boy's chocolate bar like a horse after a lump of sugar, after which she ended up here, more to avoid working than anything else. Paolo is a petty officer in the navy, a career man, the most intelligent and most mature person in here, but with no real drive.

Meanwhile, I look over at Jeanine, who has placidly gone to sleep. The bombing has moved farther off, its reverberations muffled as they reach us. The Gascon goes on talking without raising or lowering his voice. He is an engineering student, he was rounded up in Paris, but he's from the Pyrenees, "where the trees are very tall," he says, "and the air full of wild scents, the earth damp, savory." He narrows his eyes: "If you only knew how peaceful it is up there, the looming mountains, brief glimpses of sky amid the green . . ."

I realize that I got distracted and I go back to staring at his lips.

"The sunsets are a never-ending rosy pink," he murmurs, "rosy but reserved, know what I mean? Not sudden and brief, like those conflagrations that light up the whole sky for an instant and then die away. It's more like you were seeing it all through water, you follow me? And the air you breathe in is fresh, invigorating to the lungs."

I can't keep my eyes open, sitting on the pallet next to the Gascon student, who in the musty odor of the barrack is breathing in the scents of his land.

The all-clear sounds.

The boy looks at his wristwatch.

"It's three o'clock," he says.

A man sits down next to me: it's the natty young Italian, clean-shaven, hair slicked back, whom Jeanine had called a fashion plate during our presentation walk.

"Signorina, I've been watching you throughout the evening, and I haven't been able to figure out what you think about all this, how you view it."

"This what?"

"This horrible situation, these people! You may speak freely, because they don't understand Italian, and even if they did, do you care? But the Nazis will have to pay for their savage brutality. Only the contempt and rancor that I harbor toward them save me from this motley assemblage."

I remain silent, considering: I just can't feel any disgust.

"I don't think it's so easy to judge," I say at last.

"Are you still able to feel alive in all this chaos?"

"Yes."

"You even feel some interest, maybe!"

"Yes."

"How can you say that? Just look at things objectively for a moment: this monstrousness can't teach anybody anything. And that's only to speak of ourselves! Think of the ones who haven't been here, what can they be expected to gain from it? There is nothing universal about our suffering, there is only paroxysm, inhumanity, triviality. I want to forget it all as soon as possible, erase it all."

I lie down on the pallet next to Jeanine. The elegant Italian gets up and walks away. The Gascon student has fallen asleep sitting up. A man gropes his way among the wooden structures that support the mattresses and wakes Jeanine. They whisper. Jeanine is telling him her adventures, in blunt, coarse language.

"You're really a gamine," the man remarks, amused. But Jeanine seems to pride herself on his enjoyment and goes on to tell him one of her salacious replies to the Germans: "I don't go with them!" she exclaims, full of patriotic ardor. And just as serious and determined, she adds, "At least not until now." She bursts out laughing and asks him what he'd be willing to give her.

The man sits down beside her, lighting a match whose flame illuminates Jeanine. She gives him a mischievous look: "After all, you men are all the same." He's small, well-proportioned, with a clever face and spirited eyes; he explains that, if it's just an occasional thing, he'd pay her a good fee; if, instead, they were to make it a steady thing, then he'd feed her well and show her a good time.

"I'm the one showing you a good time!" Jeanine retorts. She sits up, the negotiations intensify, Jeanine raises her voice, turns up her nose, argues, stamps her foot. Finally, she stands up with a big laugh.

"I don't like you enough," she says, leaning over him. Then she turns toward me: "Oh, Carlà woke up!" she exclaims, then says abruptly to the man: "Go away." Immediately distracted, she goes back to speaking with me. "You're a *nouille*," she says, "but it doesn't matter. I don't fuss over things. However, Polò said to make sure I don't let you go outside. You have to listen to him because he's the group leader."

The man lights a cigarette and goes away

"Did you see that?" Jeanine whispers. "I always say no, sorry, to him, you know, because of Polò. Not for him, since he wouldn't know, but because of people talking—take La Scopina, that one is syphilitic besides. I don't want to make him look bad. But then again Polò is penniless. I'll end up meeting that guy behind the kitchen." She sits up and leans forward: "There she is," she mutters, "why does she always come here to sleep?"

La Scopina stops at the foot of our mattresses, a cigarette in her mouth. She's followed by a man who shines a flashlight on her, the two faces coming into the light: hers pasty, broad, and expressionless, his pockmarked, eyes crawling shamelessly over her body.

"It's the Moroccan capitalist," Jeanine whispers, nudging me.

The two agree on a pair of shoes, which he is holding, for two hours of sex. They disappear into a bed.

"Disgusting!" Jeanine says. "You can't even sleep in peace." She pricks up her ears: "It's raining."

The rain hammers away against the wooden wall behind my head, adding its feverish pounding to the muted jabbering circulating through the unbreathable air of this low-ceilinged room.

The bright light goes on again, and the glare lends everyone's faces a dour, dazed expression.

"It's four o'clock," Jeanine says. "They even waste electricity just to hassle us."

The door opens again and Benito enters sideways, looking around quickly with haunted eyes, a large bundle under his arm. His clothes are clinging to him, soaking wet, making him seem even skinnier and gawkier, hair slicked down over his forehead and ears sticking out. He tiptoes in and shakes the water off himself at the stove. He opens the bundle, which contains copious slices of bread. Fingering them, he shakes his head in distress: "That's all we needed, rain! It had to go and rain right now." He pats the bread with his hand; a slice falls on the floor with a thud, like a stone.

The fugitives, always famished, spot Benito and call out to him from their beds, not bothering to get up:

"There's our savior. Bread for the hungry."

"The great Benito! Bread for the ravenous."

"Over here, bread for the humble."

And he, docile and overwhelmed, dashes here and there, a modest, pleased smile on his lips, waving his hand in denial:

"It's nothing, it's nothing. It's good bread, even though the rain ruined it a little, otherwise the bread is good. Tomorrow, however," he promises with a mysterious expression, "tomorrow, you'll see, I'll bring you some eggs." Winking, he brings his index finger to his mouth: "Leave it to Benito, you'll see!"

"Hooray for Benito."

Jeanine is the only one to get up and go to him. "Poor man," she says, "such a dejected look. You had yourself quite a shower, be careful you don't kick the bucket, my dear little fellow!"

Her attention is attracted by the door slowly opening: a girl is stealthily creeping in and looking around warily. Under a military jacket she's wearing a tattered silk dress. She closes the door, sees that Jeanine is watching, and smiles at her, revealing long, yellow teeth, her lips rimmed with worn-off lipstick. She sits behind the stove, as I had, and talks with Jeanine, looking at her with big myopic bright eyes. Her hair is worn cropped, a boyish cut with bangs, and the long strands on her forehead seem like thready legs incessantly tickling the short, slanting hair of her eyebrows.

A young man plops down next to me with a thump. "You must be the new girl!" he says. "I'm Jean de Lille."

I close my eyes, hoping to sleep, but then I realize that the introduction ritual is continuing despite me. It's a major help for me to know whom I can turn to, so I have to stay awake. Meanwhile, Jean de Lille tells me he was deported as a hostage, but being here is almost worse than being in the labor camps. And he starts explaining the differences that I'm well aware of—though I don't tell him—between the various camps. There are five types: in addition to the transit camps for everybody (*Durchgangslager*), there are the camps for free workers where volunteers are sent (*Freiarbeitslager*); camps for prisoners of war (*Kriegsgefangenenlager*); labor camps (*Arbeitslager*), where those deported following a roundup are interned along with hostages, the families of political prisoners, partisans, and foreign deserters; and finally, there are the concentration camps (*Konzentrations-lager*), which hold the victims of the racial purges—namely, Jews—as well as political suspects, saboteurs, illegal prostitutes, pimps and lesbians, common criminals, thieves, murderers, fences, rapists, and the list goes on, "which is not to mention the so-called final solution camps, you get me? Annihilation."

"Yes," I say, nodding.

"They seized me at the factory," he says. "I'm a worker. When they bomb us, I think I'm hearing the racket at my old foundry. In Lille I worked in the blast furnaces. And you?"

"Roundup."

He leans over to my ear: "Where did you escape from?"

I tilt my head: "Back there," I whisper.

"A concentration camp?" He's astounded. "How come they didn't put you in a labor camp?" But then he laughs: "Yeah, of course, what can you expect, what's one slut more or less." He gives me a look. "It happens."

He has sat up and is resting his head against a wooden post of our bunk. He has a wholesome, open face and willful hazel eyes; speaking slowly, looking adamantly straight ahead, he curses the Nazis, his obscene, brutal words standing in singular contrast to the thoughtful, quiet expression on his face.

Moving closer to me, he lies down again, on his side, he too stinking of sweat.

"Tonight they were bombing as though they were being paid on commission!" he says. "Weren't you afraid?"

"Sure."

"Come on, let's make love," he sighs resignedly.

I shake my head no.

"Ah." He relaxes. He looks at me almost affectionately and, stretching out comfortably beside me, confesses that he's sick and tired of this life where fucking is all there is, and that this is the first time since he came to Germany that he's been able to spend fifteen minutes with a woman without having to get right down to business. He explains that women are leeches and never leave a man in peace. All of them, you know? He confides that he likes me well enough and would willingly have satisfied me, but that he'd rather talk—he's troubled, he has a secret, he turns over practically on top of me and pinches my cheek: "I'm going to escape today," he whispers. "What do you think, will I make it?"

"In daylight?"

"In daylight. It may seem strange, but there's less surveillance than at night."

"How?"

"I got hold of a free worker's documents—he died in a bombing. The factory where he worked was destroyed as well. With those papers in hand, I'll go to the Labor Bureau. After a couple of months of exemplary *boulot*, I'll request a leave. And once I get to Lille, I'll go into hiding. That's it." Bending toward the light a moment, he pulls out his ID papers, winks at me: "I'm no fool, huh?"

His imminent freedom suddenly merges with his persona, and, listening to him, I take a sudden liking to him, as if he could free me as well. I get up from the bed to go and lie down someplace else: "Be careful, Jean."

"Did I bore you?" he asks, surprised. (*"Ch't'ai emmerdée?"*)

"No. But you should sleep—if not, when the time comes, you'll be too tense. You only have a few hours."

"Hey, you're right, but you know"—he pulls my arm—"the thought of a little fuck with you is almost tempting, what do you say?" He looks at me frankly.

I laugh wholeheartedly. "Good luck."

Enough, I don't want to hear or see anything or anyone, I want to go to sleep. I wander through the soggy, foul-smelling air in search of an empty pallet. Let's hope Jean de Lille makes it.

But the newcomer with the bangs gestures to me from behind the stove.

"You're from over there, right?" she asks me in French.

"Yes."

"Are there dogs here?"

"So far I haven't seen any."

"Do many die here?"

"I don't think so."

"These people." She looks around. "Can they be trusted?"

"Yes. None of the others know who we are, and between ourselves we have no choice but to help one another. But tell me, did anything happen after I . . ."

"When?"

"Seven weeks ago."

"Pick a number!" She shrugs.

"The Italian girl, from Block Four, at the barrack."

"Oh!" she interrupts. "Maybe . . ." And she clams up.

"Well?" I press her.

"I don't know the details. I was in for . . ." She dismisses her explanation with a wave and goes on: "In short, as you see, being a common criminal, I didn't hang around with the other types. But you know how it is, don't you? All of us with no soup in the evening and . . ." She falls silent again, then shudders: "The other day they caught two outside here and shot them in the courtyard. A girl was screaming and they stifled her with chloroform."

"Who?"

"I don't know, a Jewish girl, they say. I can't take it anymore."

"Don't stay here, right in the middle of the room—go to a corner."

"I'm cold," she says, but she gets up and moves away.

Jeanine calls me:

"She's French, but I don't like her, her neck and ears aren't right. However, if the others want to let her join us anyway, let them. As far as I'm concerned, I'm not proposing anything. Let's go to sleep, it must be almost six, and at seven we have to disappear, because there's roll call in the barracks."

We hear the door slam.

"It must be Polò coming back! But I won't let him see me, that'll teach him not to go roaming," Jeanine says. Then: "Nah! It's the coal man."

A shambling, worn-out man with a skimpy necktie comes in.

La Scopina appears, short of breath, flushed, and disheveled.

"Don't be so upset, my dear," the coal man says. "You were upset by the bombing, weren't you?"

"Yes."

He strokes her hair. The Moroccan's face pops out, observing the couple with a knowing smile.

"I've been looking for you in all the barracks," the coal man says gently.

He sits down on an empty pallet near Jeanine's and mine; La Scopina lies down and rests her head on her friend's lap as he encircles her face with his arm.

"Look how beautiful she is!" the man says, stroking her face with a hand grimy with coal. I sit up and in the dim light of the wooden four-poster look at the woman's slack face.

"She looks like an ad for Cadum baby talc."

Jeanine splutters derisively, and La Scopina straightens up, furious: "Shut up and mind your own business."

"Which is?" Jeanine leaps up, glaring at her defiantly.

"I won't say."

"No, go ahead, say it, that way I'll talk too."

"You know very well why you're left in peace here."

"Why squabble?" the coal man intercedes gently.

"She's a snotty brat!" La Scopina shrugs and lies down again with her head on her friend's lap. Jeanine snorts angrily, but doesn't respond.

I get up, smiling at Cadum baby talc to please the coal man.

The door flies open, letting an opaque dawn filter through, and Paolo walks in whistling.

The Gascon student wakes up with a start, looks at me: "It's awful," he says, "you can't get a single moment's sleep. Look at the Russians, though, they don't hear or see anything, it's like they aren't even here. Western civilization on the other hand frays the nerves and makes us touchy." He goes on—and on, and on—to explain the damaging effects on the nervous system of a coddled lifestyle dependent for generations on creature comforts.

Jeanine is on the alert.

"Where have you been, with all the bombs?"

"You know where," Paolo replies.

"*Busgiardò* [liar]!" she spits at him in her accented Italian. And turns over, facedown, as a sign of protest.

"Good, you're doing me a favor," Paolo retorts, "because I'm dead on my feet."

An irritated shrug from Jeanine, who then falls asleep.

The Gascon has gotten as far as Tsar Peter the Great.

La Scopina wants the coal man to open up his pants.

I move, squeezing among the people crammed together. On the floor in a corner the newcomer with the bangs is making love with François, accompanied by lots of scratching, biting, and shrill giggling.

I head toward the center of the barrack, under the lamp.

"*Signorina*," the natty Italian with the dark slicked-back hair calls me, "can't you find a quiet place?"

I flop down next to him with a sigh: "That's right, I can't. At this rate I won't make it to the end of the war. At our camp it was different: we were all women and at night the silent stillness drove me crazy."

"Are we already having regrets?" He tells me that he is engaged to a German girl, that they love each other very much, that he can't live away from her, that he is anti-Nazi.

I get up again without even saying a word, and I run into Paolo, standing near the window. He grabs my arm: "Carla," he says, panting, "it's starting."

"What?"

His features are changing. From her bed Jeanine cries out and rushes to him.

"Polò, Polò," she calls hoarsely, slapping him.

Paolo goes limp; we hold him up by the armpits.

"Give us some space!" Jeanine yells.

He's drooling, his eyes are staring fixedly, and his legs dangle as if disjointed. As we try to drag him onto a pallet, he slips out of our arms and falls backward onto the floor, striking his head on the boards, and starts kicking and writhing. His eyes become bloodshot, he grinds his teeth with a harsh scraping sound, foamy spittle runs down his face.

Jeanine sits on his chest, heedless of the blows and kicks. "It's delirium tremens," she tells me. "Hold his head. Someone get me some water." Paolo goes on rolling his eyes and grating his teeth. Jeanine moistens the hem of her dress and bathes his forehead. With deft hands she tries to clamp shut his jaw.

"He always winds up biting his tongue. I can sense when it's about to happen to him. He can't stay cooped up indoors, he knows it. It's suffocating in here, he shouldn't tire himself, he shouldn't get drenched, but does he listen, no, now there he is like a cockroach on its back! Drink this, drink!" Meanwhile, she bathes his forehead and closes his eyes, leans down quickly to kiss his brow. "Stay still, rhino. I go with him on purpose, what do you think. I can see it coming soon, the day when he'll be *loufoque* [crazy]. Lie still, I tell you!"

Squirming even harder, Paolo hurls her onto the ground, against the corner of a bed.

"I told him down, I said!" she yells, still on the floor. "Otherwise he'll hurt himself, he'll crack his head!" She leaps up and tries to jump on top of him as he kicks to break free. A few men restrain her while others try to immobilize Paolo, who, released from Jeanine's weight, has started whimpering like an animal.

"Drink!" Jeanine shouts at him, staring at him like a madwoman. "Drink as much as you can, you damn fool, you good-for-nothing you. Gag him, tie him up, I tell you—he's even more worked up than usual today!"

Finally, they manage to tie him up and move him onto a pallet.

Jeanine gets up quickly. "The other night," she tells me, "it happened to him in the toilet, I'd gone there with him because I saw it coming, he started beating me up, I stayed with him until I realized he was about to strangle me, and then I ran for it. But once I was outside, I knew I couldn't leave him there like that, so I stayed outside the door to listen. It went on for so long. I was a block of ice. He was ranting like a mad dog. When I didn't hear anything more, I went back in, I sat on the floor next to him and rested his head in my lap until he came to. Meanwhile, men were coming and going to piss. But you know what? I've got half a mind to dump him." The electric light goes off and we are left suspended in the bleak, milky light of early morning that filters through the two windows. In the gloom it seems like the rain is coming down even harder, directly over us.

"Now the party's over," Jeanine sighs. "Soon the fumigation games will begin. They start at eight. We have to get out of here. Put on one of the Russians' skirts, your overalls stink of Germany a kilometer away. Now how on earth am I supposed to move this pachyderm?" She points to Paolo. "It's a shame, but with the risk of a German raid, you have to be always on the alert, sleep with one eye open. Can you see why I sometimes feel tired? I can't leave him snoring like that. They'll end up taking him for a four-engine bomber and sound the alarm." She laughs to herself.

"Polò, wake up, Polò. Damn this war. Polò."

As if electrified, the fugitives climb through the windows, jump out, and disappear in the rain.

"Beat it," the coal man fusses, "here they are for roll call."

I run to the toilet.

La Scopina appears ahead of me: "Make yourself scarce, there's a guard in front of the toilet."

I head for the garbage dump. In the drab grayness I make out the concentration camp's barbed wire fence. It's plunged in a silence that to me seems menacing and deadly. The rain drenches me to the bone. The sound of footsteps. I drop to the ground. I wish I never had to move again, that I could just lie there on that garbage, become one with that ever-present garbage.

The rumble of trucks, shouts, the shrill sound of military whistles.

I dream that Jeanine and I go to steal a sheep on some dangerous rocks. We find a lamb and break its legs, but it's a small child instead. We don't know where to hide him and we bury him at night. Then we go to an illusive village, which we can't get into, but we creep along it furtively. Finally, we come to a small cottage. The door is wide open and the light inside is on. A beautiful girl with long dark hair tied at the back of her neck comes toward us in her nightgown.

"Don't kill her," I whisper to Jeanine.

"Why would I kill her?" she replies.

Standing on either side of the girl, we push her out of the house and warn her that thieves are coming to steal her treasure.

"Don't go back inside," Jeanine says, giving me a meaningful look, "I'll go in and hide it. You, stay out here with Carlà, don't let them see you, otherwise they'll kill you."

The beautiful girl follows me along the road and I make her lie down in a ditch at the foot of the wall.

"Here they are," I say, and cover her face with a sheet. I wave to Jeanine, who is watching me. Jeanine slams doors and overturns pieces of furniture; then she comes over on tiptoe, behind the girl who is stretched out, and with a hatchet splits her skull. I hear voices and I sit on the victim's head while Jeanine sits on her belly. When silence returns, I remove the sheet; in front of me lies a cheerful little old lady, with two pointy teeth protruding from her lower lip; she looks at me astonished, bleeding from the eyes.

I lift her up, shove her in a sack, squeezing her in, and load her on my back. Jeanine is carrying the treasure. When we get to the dangerous rocks, we throw the woman and the treasure in a ravine and go to the police station to turn ourselves in.

"What are you doing here?" someone says, shaking me. I can't move my limbs, which feel enormous and floppy, like sponges swollen with water.

I turn my head: a German guard is leaning over me. I'm gripped by a terror that dulls my wits.

"I'm innocent!" I cry. "I'm innocent!"

The soldier narrows his blue eyes.

"Get up or you'll catch pneumonia."

"I fell."

The guard slips a flask off his belt and pours a spurt of cognac in my mouth.

"Go back to your barrack, it's time for disinfection."

The sound of the word *disinfection* brings me back to reality, yet given my lethargy, I feel like I'm still dreaming. Still, I have a flash of cunning:

"I have to go to the toilet," I say.

"Go ahead, don't take long."

The guard helps me stand and props me up. Suddenly remembering that he's a Nazi, I gather my strength and rush past him, kicking and splashing through the water. He catches up with me, grabs my arm, opens the door to the toilet, and shoves me inside.

A pale light filters down from a skylight as the rain beats insistently, its incessant, tedious pounding a complement to the squalor. La Pidocchiosa, the one with the lice, is sitting on one of the toilet bowls.

"You're sleepy, huh? It's comfortable in here. I come here to take a rest too. I don't like this life, my fine girl, that's why I don't get ahead. I work just enough to be able to procure the bare minimum needed to eat and smoke, I don't think that's a lot, but I don't enjoy it at all. The trouble is that this temperament of mine holds me back. Jeanine, for instance, is successful: sixteen years old, and she does it for personal pleasure, doesn't haggle about price! Me, though . . . nobody wants me."

The door flies open, and the guard appears again: "Beat it, you!" he tells La Pidocchiosa. "Go on, scram!" He turns to me: "Get going, you too, and cover yourself." He watches me until I go into my barrack. I lie next to a Russian woman with a scabby newborn suckling at her white, firm breast and I fall asleep again.

Harsh, irritated voices as hands rip off my clothes. I sit up on the bed.

Several guards are marching back and forth in the barrack impatiently inciting us. The Nazi, yanking on my collar to wake me, tore my overalls with just one tug; they fall apart as I try to slip them off, stripping for disinfection. François and the French girl with the bangs are also caught in the net. A guard drags over a sack in which each of us must put our clothes. Other guards, in front of the pallets, make everyone strip naked, men and women, one by one. I hide my overalls under the mattress, and no one notices. The Russians are pale and silent. A stocky, pasty-white woman, stark naked, presses her son to her breast, refusing to undress him.

The guards look at her, fed up.

By now all of us are exposed, standing between the wooden frames of the bunks. This is the third time I've been caught in a disinfection. The Russians are sure that they're about to be led to die at the slaughterhouse.

The men weigh their chances with crafty composure, and the women, hugging their cowering, terrified children, refuse to come out of their corners.

The Nazi guards pull out revolvers and herd the groups to the door.

The defenseless masses huddle like sheep as the rain gropes at them frenziedly. The sack full of clothes is thrown into a vehicle stopped in front of the barrack.

I am between François, shamefaced, on one side and the French girl with the bangs, uncaring, on the other.

We are lined up by the Nazis, who are bundled up in raincoats, the rain beating hard on the smooth visors of their military caps.

The SS jump into the truck, which starts moving, and we're ordered to march behind in a column.

The vehicle accelerates quickly and we start running to keep up with it. Prodded by a motorcycle that follows behind us, honking its horn, we bump into one another, as the sharp stones of the gravel jab the soles of our bare feet. The rain pelts down on us, drenching us.

"Even the rain here is a Nazi!" mutters the girl with the bangs, who is running beside me.

With a sudden screeching of brakes, the truck stops in front of another barrack. Surging forward as they run, those in the front rows slam their faces against the rear door. Some are bleeding from the nose. The guards jump down easily in their leather boots. Other naked figures come out of the barrack, shivering with cold when the rain hits them.

All eyes are so filled with hatred, bloodshot from the fury of humiliation and the craving for revenge, that if the Nazis only realized it, they wouldn't go around with such cool, detached insensitivity, but would be a little more anxious about their own well-being. But, then again, they *do* know: our rage excites them, and our hatred slides off their impassivity like rain off their top-quality, well-made raincoats.

The naked newcomers line up with us. The guards jump back in the truck, which sets out again. We resume running like a pack of dogs, trembling from the cold and from rage, freezing outside and burning inside. The guards seated in the truck follow us with their eyes, checking out our bodies, and, short of gesturing, exchange comments and appraisals of us. We cross the camp's lengthy yard, skirting the other barracks, crying in pain from the sharp gravel, shivering from the chill rain, jumping and splashing one another with filthy water, holding each other up, chasing the truck that accelerates, then slows down, urged on by the shrill honking of the motorcycle following us.

We stop again, and our ranks grow to about a hundred.

Those already disinfected look out from the barracks, watching us with dazed sadness or making barbed remarks as they give us the once-over, depending on their mood. By the time we stop in front of a concrete hangar where the truck unloads the sacks of clothes, we are all covered in mud from the water kicked up by our running. Some of the foreigners strike indecent poses in front of the SS to provoke them, but they don't pay any attention to us. I am preoccupied by the thought that I have nothing to put on after this is over, that I won't be able to come out after the disinfection, that I'll be the only one naked, and this prospect is so upsetting that the shame of my current nudity, imposed by the Nazis, seems bearable by comparison

As we wait in front of the concrete hangar, the rain lets up and abruptly stops.

The dripping bodies seem to suddenly come to life. The women start raising a fuss: their shouts are no longer the earlier brief, anguished cries, and the naked men guffaw.

The guards seem almost jovial as they herd us along, slapping at us like you do with cows at a fair; we start running again, jumbled together, without the truck to lead us. The soft forms of the women flop and plop; a weeping girl stumbles at every step because she's busy trying to cover herself with her hands; a disheveled woman with a suckling baby in her arms falls.

The ones in front go the wrong way, do an about-face, now they're coming toward us; we're a mass of flesh and hair, surrounded by shouts and orders as we're shoved about.

Nude children cling to the hands and thighs of the women and cry instinctively, looking around wide-eyed without understanding, squeezed and helpless in the frenzied atmosphere.

Finally, sweaty and feverish, we arrive at a large concrete building.

In groups of thirty, we are placed in a dark room about a dozen meters wide where, from showers placed in the ceiling, a hot liquid with a sulphurous smell is squirted on us, which burns the skin like acid.

Everyone tries to move away, jumping in the dark, shrieking, to shield themselves from that rain of disinfectant that stings and forms rivulets at our feet.

We then go to another big room where there are large sinks all around with small containers of liquid soap and rough cloth towels. The women press to one side, some try to cover up, others, a smaller group, are inclined to display themselves. The men, most of whom are aroused, wash up, spraying water on the women and laughing as they approach them.

The girl with the bangs dries herself off with provocative squirming while yelling, "Pigs, you never miss a chance!"

"We're not stupid!" a man says, stepping forward. Even naked you can tell he's a newcomer.

Awkwardly François tries to rub himself against the girl.

"Stop it," she says, whipping him with her towel. "I don't like that!" She's washing herself with one leg raised and propped on a sink. "You're a child—you remind me of my adolescent years. I can teach you a lot of things, you know. Just remember that I like dark corners and timid men who need to talk a lot. Also champagne, cigarettes."

François, with his paltry, emaciated chest, looks at her and listens, entranced, his eyes already a bit feverish.

She smiles down on him like a goddess; her body is thin, slightly sagging, marked by bruises and traces of scabies.

The children's wailing becomes uncertain and irritable, more lost than ever. Their mothers kiss them feverishly as they wash them.

Someone taps me on the shoulder.

"What a pleasant surprise!" It's the Gascon student. "So I'm not the only one of our group who ended up here."

My initial irritation is followed by the hope that he can help me.

"I have no clothes," I tell him right away, "how will I get out of here?"

The Gascon shakes his head: "I understand noblesse oblige, but this time it will really be necessary to steal. Don't worry, I'll take care of it." He turns, pointing out some foreigners who are grabbing the naked women from behind and humping them quickly while peering around with frightened eyes.

"How easily they've managed to transform men into beasts!" he says, the corners of his mouth turned down.

Three guards burst into the washroom and with contemptuous indignation urge us foreigners to hurry up. At their appearance a chill spreads through the crowd and we file out silently, heading to the body-hair disinfection room. We are let into the room in groups of twelve: a guard at the door counts us off, men and women together, without distinction.

The door closes behind us. Men in white coats give each of us a tube of ointment to smear on our groins and armpits: it's to kill crab lice.

As soon as the ointment is applied, another group of twelve is let into the room, while the first group proceeds to the head-hair room. Those who have scalp lice have their heads shaved by nurses with rubber gloves.

I do not have head lice (I got rid of them at Thomasbräu with kerosene), and I move on with the small group of people who still have their hair.

Next we go on to the skin-diseases room. Each of these rooms is really a very small cubicle, well-lit with powerful bulbs. In each room there are three doctors and some nurses. In the body-hair room I was asked generalities, which I of course answered falsely, and I was given a folder, which I must hand over to the various specialists in turn; in it are recorded the results of their examinations, which are quite scrupulously performed. The doctors are almost all young, aloof, disoriented, and tired. After the skin-diseases room we move on to the genital-examination room; only here are the women examined separately from the men. Then in the lungs room we are given chest X-rays. In the next room an elderly doctor listens to our hearts through a stethoscope; he appears rather nervous, as if he doesn't quite sympathize with his assignment and is about to give it all up and flee. However, he too examines us meticulously and dictates his diagnoses to the nurse. When it's my turn he studies me: "Your heart is fine," he says to me softly, then dictates loudly: cardiac murmur, et cetera. The nose and throat are next. Finally, a tetanus shot in the chest. Many collapse, especially men.

The mothers are grudgingly glad about these medical exams for their children.

We come out into a large room behind the hangar where we left our clothing. The clothes, still scorching hot from the disinfection they underwent, are piled on long tables numbered with the corresponding barrack number—that is, the number of the sack from which the garments were taken.

The foreigners crowd around to retrieve their personal belongings from the piles. I look around for the Gascon. Squabbles arise, with remarks about one another's anatomical configuration. I find the Gascon student, who's already clothed, and he hands me a dress:

"Hurry up, let's get out of here. I took it from the volunteers' table."

"What?" I ask, surprised. "Are the volunteers also disinfected this way?"

"Of course! This is an edifying rite, part of the body cult practiced in the Nazi temple of the Sports Palace: a real man is healthy, nudity is healthy. My dear, they don't do anything without a noble motive! They have to reform mankind, right? And they're full of just pretexts to excuse their brutality. On the other hand, I see that you too have kept your hair," he laughs. "Class is immediately recognizable!"

My warm new garment makes me shiver with pleasure. We go outside where we are again lined up. The Gascon student yanks my arm, however, and drags me behind a barrack:

"Photographs and fingerprints," he whispers. "We have to avoid it at all costs. Let's go join those people over there."

Hundreds of people, dressed every which way, standing three by three with aluminum bowls in their hands, are waiting in line in front of a long kitchen barrack. It's time to distribute rations.

Those who have received their food go back to eat it in their own barrack.

"Will they give us food?" I ask, ravenous.

The Gascon chuckles, walking briskly: "No, we're just passing by to mix in with the ones disinfected earlier. Photographs mean death. Records with photos are sent around to police departments to search for suspected foreigners hiding in the great Reich. If nothing shows up against the subject, they give him an *Ausweis* (ID card). Otherwise, he gets punished according to German war regulations, which state, for some reason, that we're all to be considered German soldiers, therefore deserters. You gave a false name, right?"

"Of course."

While the Gascon talks about the consequences of absurdity typical of totalitarian states, we reach our barrack.

We find a few escapees at the window: "And today we ate as well!" Jean de Lille exclaims.

"Yeah, that too!" The Gascon student nods.

"One less thing to think about, right?" murmurs the French girl with the bangs, who got away before us.

"Here's our little saint!" Jeanine's lively voice rings through the air: "Where the hell have you been?"

"At disinfection."

She laughs heartily: "Imagine how much good it does, with these filthy straw mattresses!" She slaps her forehead. "Why on earth do those guys do it. You, of course, don't have any sense: Polò and I ended up in the toilets, you should stick with me, how many times must I tell you? There are the toilets!!!! By the way, Benito had something to tell you, so much the worse for you."

"Couldn't he tell it to me now?"

"You really don't deserve it; but let's go, come on." She laughs. She jumps out the window. She's wearing a blouse of immaculate white cotton that highlights her immature breasts, a short dark skirt, white socks, and shoes with laces. She has a red sweater tied around her waist.

"You got spruced up?" I laugh, seeing her.

"You too, apparently! Come on." She takes my hand and leads me away firmly, even more chirpy in the snow that has begun to drift down lightly and is settling gently on us and on the things around us. "Well," she laughs. "It's the actor I told you about, sweetie," she whispers in my ear, "he did me up good as new, but mum's the word, otherwise they'll talk about me." She raises her voice: "What do you expect! La Scopina is envious, that's why she says I'm syphilitic and that the Germans sent me here. But everybody knows I ran away! I didn't come from the hospital like her!" She wipes her eyes with the back of her hand and sniffs loudly: "I'm sixteen, you know!" She's crying.

We've reached the garbage dump, where we find Benito, who gives me a huge chunk of bread with two cucumbers. Jeanine lets off steam and sighs. Finally, she takes a pair of cotton stockings out from under her blouse.

"My gift to you," she says, "put them on right away, last night I noticed your legs were purple under your overalls." She laughs again, her eyes shining and mischievous, a dimple in her cheek.

I turn aside to put them on, I don't have any garters; Benito pulls some twine out of his pocket. I slip the stockings on and tie them up, they stay up just fine with two strings attached to a string tied around my waist.

Jeanine claps her hands delightedly.

"Now let's go." She hugs me, glances over at Benito, who devours her with his eyes, like a dog, and overcome by a sudden impulse she says, "Go on alone, I'll join you later." Then she adds, "Only a minute, you know, he's so kind, the poor guy, and so lonely, and he's not so unattractive after all."

I go back to the barrack breathing in the insubstantiality of things in the rising mist. I approach the fence to peer at the concentration camp in the distance. The barracks there emerge indistinctly, desolate and kindly. Who knows what my companions are doing?

Their faces come back to me, frightened, brash, and anguished, reduced to a swarm of horrible, wonderful insects.

"This is the day I've been waiting for," Jean de Lille says, excited and pale. "It's time: the Germans are busy photographing the people with nothing on and feeding the ones wearing clothes."

The Russians haven't returned yet; we're alone in the barrack: Jean de Lille and I, Paolo and Jeanine, Benito and La Pidocchiosa, La Scopina and the coal man, the girl with the bangs and François, the Gascon student, Jeanine's French prisoner, the elegant Italian, and the Moroccan.

"It's time," Jean de Lille repeats.

"I'll go over there," the coal man tells him, "get a move on." He winks and goes out.

"Right," Jean de Lille agrees.

Jeanine rushes toward him: "I'm coming with you!"

Paolo pulls her back: "You're staying here and that's that."

"I'm coming with you," Jeanine repeats, shaken by hysterical sobs.

"The war will end soon," the worker from Lille reassures her, stroking her head.

The Gascon student whispers in my ear, "If you like, if you want, I'll leave everything and we can go too."

"They tricked me, those swine tricked me," Jeanine wails, crushed.

"I'm hungry," the girl with the bangs says.

"Calm down, Jeanine."

"Take me with you!" Jeanine shrieks, clinging to the worker.

"That's enough!" Paolo slaps her, and La Scopina clamps the girl's mouth shut.

The worker from Lille is in a panic: "Do you want to attract their attention? You're doing it on purpose!"

"You calm down too!" Paolo snaps at him.

Jeanine raises her tearstained face.

"Your time will come too," Jean de Lille tells her.

He shakes hands with everyone: "Good luck."

"Good luck."

"Cheer up, don't look that way," Paolo says, "you look like a fugitive! Come on, let's do the ritual farewell."

And in a whispered breath: "Here's to freedom, hip hip . . ."

"Hooray," the others respond in muted tones, their expressions supportive and determined.

"Goodbye."

The door opens a crack; the worker from Lille slips through the opening. None of us speaks.

Suddenly the girl with the bangs begins to tremble; she grabs François and drags him into a corner, down on the floor. In our protracted silence her senseless words seem exaggerated:

"Know what I like? A man who takes you right there, on the floor, in the dark, with at most the glow of a candle stuck in the neck of a bottle you've already emptied, the melted wax sliding down the glass. You know, keeping him guessing up until the last, so he doesn't know what you want, if you're willing to give in to him, if it's the right moment, tease him then discourage him when he least expects it, then tease him again until he can't control himself any longer and wants you at all costs, and meanwhile you yourself don't know what you'll do, whether you'll run off or lose yourself with him."

François, overcome, murmurs incomprehensibly.

A siren's wail rips through the air. It's the siren at the concentration camp, reporting an escape. The girl with the bangs cries out, clings to François.

We all leap to our feet and listen intently from behind the windows.

The girl with the bangs rushes out from the corner, screaming, "My friend, they caught him, I feel it, I feel it!"

"Who?"

"He was supposed to escape from there today."

"Why didn't you say so?"

The coal man comes running in, out of breath: "They're coming with the dogs. Beat it, there are a lot of them."

Jeanine takes my hand. We creep along the barracks to the garbage dump.

The police dogs, unleashed in the countryside, are barking—gunshots, shouts echo through the air, motorcycle engines streak across the plain.

"Poor Jean de Lille!" Jeanine murmurs.

"I'm scared, Jeanine, don't leave me."

"Just think," Jeanine whispers, squeezing my hand. "Yesterday I didn't even know you yet."

"Yeah," I say, "only one day has passed."

Rome, 1954

PART 2

BENEATH THE RUBBLE

AS LONG AS THE HEAD LIVES

I

The bombing went on for three hours, from noon until three o'clock. That day I was sure I would die. I was trembling the whole time, huddled in a corner of the basement, holding my breath as the whistling sped toward me, until the bomb burst in my eardrums and I started trembling again: "I can't take it anymore."

When it was over, I remained flattened against the wall, cringing, refusing to listen to those who were trying to pull me away, assuring me that the Flying Fortresses were gone. Finally, I let them lead me out into the open air. Rubble, dust, flames, everywhere. A bomb had even fallen on the hotel, though luckily it hadn't crashed through to the cellar: it had stopped at the second floor. My legs wouldn't hold me up; my whole body was shaking.

A young Polish man who was always helping me, a deported worker, twenty years old like me, took me to a room on the first floor, where I collapsed on the bed.

He returned shortly afterward and made me drink cognac, telling me that Mainz had been destroyed, which meant that the Americans, who for two weeks had remained at a standstill twenty kilometers from the Rhine, would enter the city at any moment. So for us the war was over.

It was February 27, 1945.

I sat up.

"Johann, let's go celebrate!"

"No one will try to kill us anymore!"

We drank, and I decided to tidy myself up while he went looking for our friends.

I ran downstairs in a flash, to get my little suitcase in the basement, and I felt an energy, a joy, an urge to act. I raced back up. I washed myself thoroughly and put on clean clothes.

Then I looked at myself standing in the wardrobe mirror: You're really safe and sound, life is yours.

"Never mind celebrating!" The Pole rushed in, out of breath. "Our friends ended up buried, we have to hurry."

I followed him reluctantly. I was worried about getting my pants dirty.

It was already evening.

The street was full of people, voices shouting, fires flaring up everywhere. That sight always gave me a barbarous joy, a need to rush, to take risks.

"Behind the door on the right, in the square over there."

We walked briskly, holding hands, and were about to enter when a deafening roar made us jump back as the door buckled in flames. "Luzi! Johann!" our companions waiting farther on called to us. We'd been misinformed: when the shelter collapsed, they'd already been on their way out.

"It's not my day," I said to Johann. "Twice now I've felt it." Returning with our friends, all of them excited, asking and answering questions, I thought: what a scare!

The house adjacent to the hotel had collapsed. In front of it a German girl begged passersby to help her rescue her parents.

"Come on," I said. But there were only three of us, Johann, a Belgian, and myself—four counting the German girl. The others had disappeared.

I was used to it: grabbing passersby by the arm as they were taking off, I appealed to them.

We recruited seven men. The eighth, a German soldier, resisted: "Please, I'm just back from the front today. I have three days' leave. Let me see my children."

There were eleven of us altogether, two of us women.

We moved stones and debris from one side of the collapsed house.

We dragged a huge beam out of a heap of ruins and hoisted it on our backs.

We climbed a ladder to a section of the first floor that was still intact, with only one wall standing behind it. We found a wooden plank, which we used to make a bridge between the first floor and an opening in the side of the hotel. In that part of the hotel water flowed from a broken pipe.

It was six o'clock in the evening. We divided the tasks among us: from above, six of us were to ram the beam as forcefully as we could against the side of the collapsed house that we had cleared, which adjoined the shelter, to break through to those who were buried; the other five had to carry containers of water to throw on the fires burning around us to prevent the flames from entering first, once the wall was breached.

We had to alternate every quarter of an hour, except for the German girl who had asked us for help to save her parents.

I took turns with Johann.

The first round it was his turn to ram the beam along with the others, the second time my turn. The third time, when he was up, he slipped on the plank and dislocated his ankle. I'd been waiting for that moment to go and get water.

"You did that on purpose," I told him. "And that makes three." I caught hold of the beam again.

Jamming down with my entire body for maximum thrust, three people in front of me and two behind, I worked with such a will that I forgot my fear.

When we heard the concrete give way, the men carrying water jumped onto our plank to lend a helping hand with the final shove of the beam, but a cry rose from a group of spectators who had gathered in the street:

"The wall is collapsing."

It wasn't that of the adjacent house that we were trying to breach, however; it was the piece of wall left standing on the floor we were on.

We dropped the beam.

It happened in an instant: I just had time to glance at the wall behind me, turn my back to it, and cover my face with my arms. What a stupid way to go! I thought. That was all.

II

Later I only remember being trapped in the middle of a blaze and having the distinct impression of being in hell. I was suspended by my feet, upside down, my head and arms unbearably heavy, while my legs and the rest of my body drifted in the air, unwilling to come down. I saw myself surrounded by the hotel owner and my companions, and the thought that I would have to spend eternity with them was absolutely crushing.

When I came to somewhat, I was in a compartment that bounced in the dark, my whole body in atrocious pain, and Johann's cracked voice was saying, "Easy, easy, oh God, oh dear God."

Following that I remember some white rooms in a livid light, with rows of beds from which came groans and appeals, and, though I recognized purgatory, I too wanted to sink onto one of those white beds for a moment. Instead I spent an infinite time in darkness, from which I tried vainly to escape.

The following day I regained consciousness for a few hours.

They told me that the wall had fallen down on us, smashing through our floor and the ground floor below us, and plunging us into a basement.

Those saved were: a German soldier, who dropped to the floor at the base of the wall, realizing in a flash that it would fall slantwise from above; the Belgian majordomo, who had the presence of mind to jump down to the street, so that he got away with a fractured femur; and Johann, sitting astride the crack in the hotel's wall with his dislocated ankle.

A brick, which broke off the top of the wall, had shot out with such force that its arc sent it flying straight into the right temple of the German soldier who, standing on the sidewalk across the street, had asked them to let him see his children again: he'd slumped to the ground, killed instantly.

Johann had immediately hopped onto the edge of the caved-in floor, on one foot only, and, amid the flames, lowered himself into the crater opened up by the wall's collapse. Scrabbling through the rubble and discovering the other bodies, he climbed over them until he found me, picked me up, and carried me over his shoulder, steadying me with one hand while trying to find a handhold to pull himself up with the other. And it seems that while he was lifting me up, still on one foot, to get me out, I called him "Drecksack"* and struggled to free myself.

He clambered up the burning stones and debris, but he couldn't manage it and kept sliding back down into the inextinguishable phosphorescent flames that had been unleashed by the wall's collapse.

A German lieutenant who lived in the hotel had come running from the adjacent office when he heard the wall crash down, not to mention the shouting. When he learned that I had been buried and that to save me Johann had also been swallowed up, he moved a ladder over to the aperture, looked down, and called out.

Johann lifted me up, straightening his arms, and the German grabbed me and laid me on the rubble. Without my weight, Johann managed to wriggle out.

He tore off my burning clothes, then tore off his. Together he and the lieutenant carried me down the ladder. Here it seems that I began to cry out nonstop: "Die Füsse runter!"†

They carried me to the hotel lobby, where everyone surrounded me. I kept screaming, "Die Füsse runter!"

Then the German lieutenant and Johann stood me up between them, supporting me by the arms and by the waist. It appeared that I had come to and was looking around, but I soon fainted.

They settled me on a sofa, slapped me, splashed me with vinegar. I cried, then I started murmuring, delirious, "Legs down, I beg you, legs down."

Lieutenant Gauli went to get a car: "I'll take her to the hospital, as a German I can get her admitted right away. If they give me a hard time, they'll be sorry."

---

*"Dirty bastard."
†"Feet down!"

I was known in the neighborhood for always being the first to volunteer in the *Löscharbeiten*, the recovery operations for those who got buried.

He returned soon afterward at the wheel of a car. Johann sat in back with me in his arms.

At the hospital, packed with wounded, the lieutenant insisted they put me in a bed, transferring to the floor a German in less serious condition than me.

There I started ordering them to call God for me right away, then I asked for a mirror, and, when I saw my cracked forehead, my torn cheek and lip, smeared with blood, I said, "It's over," and fainted again.

But Johann stayed by my side all night because, shrieking like a wild beast, I kept trying to jump out of bed with such force and cunning that he had to fight with me to get me to lie back down again.

I had a compressed spinal cord, phosphorus burns all over my body (fourteen of them), a fractured skull, a dislocated right shoulder, broken ribs both front and back, on my left side, and fractured pelvis bones. But I wasn't aware of any of it.

Only the following day did Johann, with his foot in a plaster cast and his burns bandaged up, go with the German lieutenant and a few other men to pull the others out of the basement. Three were dead and four were dying, all of whom died while being transported, except for the German girl, who was a university physics student. A bucket had overturned onto her head, cracking her skull, and had remained jammed on her neck for twenty-four hours. They had to saw it off. But she had such vitality that she survived fourteen days more, battling death, lucid and strong-willed to the end.

As for the people we had wanted to free from the ruins, using pickaxes and wooden supports they had dug themselves a small underground tunnel from the wall opposite ours, and had made it out to the open on their own.

III

I will have to continue the story by combining what I remember with what was reported to me.

The following day I found myself in a small quiet room. Looking around,

I saw two occupied beds behind me, and another one beside me. Their occupants had their faces covered by sheets.

Convinced that I couldn't last long, after I had horrified the patients in the ward with my screams, the doctors had stuffed me with morphine and had me transferred to room 18 on the ground floor, which served as the surgical wing's morgue since the real one had been destroyed.

The dead usually remained there one night and were stored in the bathroom the next day to make room for others, until the funeral van came to pick them up.

In the first month there was such a crush of corpses that I often saw one or two of them on a stretcher right beside the bed.

They also moved comatose patients to room 18 for the benefit of the healthier patients in the wards, since the frequent deaths caused such depression or hysteria among the latter that it affected their physical condition and made it impossible for their will to live to further assist the care they received. Of course I didn't know these things. It seems that during the first days, as soon as my morphine wore off, I would scream mindlessly, making myself heard throughout the entire building, until, after being injected with new, increasingly large doses of the narcotic, I gradually settled into a deathlike stupor. Every morning they cleaned and medicated my extensive burns with cod liver oil salve, but I wasn't conscious of any of this.

I'm told that I refused to be turned over, constantly resorting to the weapon of bestial screaming, and that they had to sedate me numerous times to tend to my back, to reposition my dislocated shoulder, and to stitch up my head wound.

I remember awakening once and involuntarily touching a body with my left hand: a hip, a belly, a thigh—in a word, flesh—that was in my bed, under my blankets; it wasn't my flesh, and it was cold. Intrigued, I stroked and fingered the body, my hand moving upward, until I lifted the covers to peer underneath and saw with horror that the strange body belonged to me, it was mine, marmoreal and numb. I understood in a flash that I had died. *But what about the pain?* It must have been what it felt like to decompose, and, indeed, this body gave off a stench of rotten fish.

So then, consciousness survives bodily death. I remember those moments perfectly, because that was when I felt the most inconceivable terror of my life.

Had the doctors and nuns noticed that I was dead? That was the first thing to determine, if I wanted to avoid being carried away like the others and stuck in the ground, with dirt in my eyes, nostrils, and mouth.

I could see. Which meant they hadn't lowered my eyelids, and that was a good sign.

Shortly afterward, two doctors came in with a nun; I widened my eyes and stared at them. I recalled certain corpses in the Lager whose open eyes seemed to be looking around and winking under their eyelashes at those moving about them.

The doctors approached me and one said, "Never seen such endurance. But she must have suffered a brain injury, there's something abnormal about her gaze."

I listened.

Another nun had entered. "When I'm on night duty, she scares me. I feel those eyes on me constantly."

As long as they don't check my heart, I thought, in the paroxysmal joy of having gotten away with it.

"I wonder if she was baptized!" the first nun sighed. "Perhaps her soul is waiting for the sacraments so it can depart in peace. How could I not have thought of it? I'll have them give her Extreme Unction."

I thought of trying to utter a few words. My lips moved: "*Ich muss nicht sterben*"* came out in a croak.

They looked at me, disconcerted. So then, with concentration and perseverance, I could perhaps bring my body back to life bit by bit. In my exhilaration I gurgled my delight.

"Let's go," said a doctor, twisting his mouth. "What a pity, so young."

As I said, I don't remember any of this.

It seems the priest approached me several times in the following days but as soon as I saw him, I screamed as though possessed; so he backed away, uncertain as to whether I might have grave mortal sins on my soul. They

*"I mustn't die."

called me *das schwarze Teufelchen*, the little black devil. I have no recollection of it.

I do remember that once, seeing the priest arrive, I said to God, "What more do you want from me? After all you've done to me."

I let the priest think that I wanted to confess, that he should wait a moment. He must have notified the nuns, who came running excitedly, giving thanks to heaven; they arranged a small altar, then withdrew.

Speaking slowly and savoring my words, I pretended that I was Dutch, and recited imaginary lapses and sins. Then, satisfied with my vengeance, I recited the Act of Contrition.

Johann came to see me at all hours, and I'm told I always whispered that he should go rob someone because I needed a great deal of money.

For fifteen days I didn't put anything in my mouth, I rejected every drop of tea; they said I was very skinny, my dark eyes haunted.

Then I started drinking milk diluted with warm water that Johann fed me in a baby bottle. I sucked greedily, feeling the liquid flow down my esophagus, constantly convinced that I was nursing my body back to life millimeter by millimeter through sheer willpower.

After twenty days, I had even regained my right arm and chest.

I felt clever because, while the other dying patients flailed and threw off their blankets, catching pneumonia that hastened their deaths, I stayed covered up to my chin, shouting for the nurses to tuck me back up as soon as I felt the slightest draft. In fact, it was March, the cold was back, room 18 had no windowpanes and no door, so we were in the middle of a constant stream of air.

I began to be aware of my condition. I saw that they washed and medicated me every day, and that the fish smell wasn't coming from my cadaver, but from the salve they smeared on my burns.

I noticed that as soon as I felt a headache coming on, when I felt that I'd been squeezed dry inside, drained of blood and saliva, as harrowing sounds began to come out of my mouth, they always injected me with something that gradually, if only partially, restored my equilibrium. I asked about it: morphine. I no longer dozed, but listened intently to what was happening to my neighbors.

Usually, when a patient was brought to my room, he regained consciousness and thrashed about, imploring them to take him back to the ward. Room 18 had a fatal reputation in the hospital, and everyone feared it as though it were the very antechamber of death. Exhausted by terror, these patients merely hastened their own end.

But the nun who was head of the ward, Schwester Vincentia, soon found a way to calm them down.

"Who said you're going to die!" Then "Luzi! Luzi!" she would call me. And I would respond.

"Don't you see that Luzi is alive, hale and hearty? And do you know how long she's been here? For a good three weeks."

This immediately cheered them up. And such was the power of faith that sometimes, after they dozed off, they would wake up again and anxiously call my name:

"Luzi!"

"Ja. Wie geht's?"

We even chatted. I kept talking as they entered their death throes. The first few times I fell silent as soon as I recognized death's breath, but I sensed that this frightened them; so I got into the habit of continuing to say whatever came into my mind. That soon we would feel better, that if I died first I would protect them from up there and they should do the same for me, that I was Italian and didn't hate anyone, and things like that.

By now my only reason for living was to distract the dying, and this unusual activity so absorbed me that my energy soon increased.

I awaited the new arrivals eagerly. I counted them.

There were nineteen people, men, women, and children, whom I accompanied to their ends, by myself, eye-to-eye with them.

At first a nurse or a nun would remain to watch over them until the final moment; then they noticed that my company relaxed those in extremis, while their presence at the bedside only made the patients nervous.

"Luzi," Sister Vincentia would say to me softly, "this one has a mangled belly, I leave her to you."

Or: "With this one it will soon be over—then, at least, he won't suffer anymore."

I so identified with the dying that when I ran out of words, I would sing softly to accompany their death rattles. Sometimes tears even flowed when I sang:

> Tu scendi dalle stelle, o re del cielo,
> e vieni in una grotta al freddo e al gelo.

I stopped when I heard their labored breathing break off and felt the silence of death pass into my soul.

Schwester Vincentia had begun to love me. She often came close to study me; she brushed the hair off my face, gave me a quick kiss on the forehead, and withdrew, shaking her head.

For I don't know how long, we were bombed several times a day.

After transporting the injured to the shelter, where most remained until the danger was over, Schwester Vincentia came back up, stationed herself by my bed, praying, and did not leave me as long as the bombs continued. She intoned the Ave Maria and I answered. In the unexpected intervals amid the thunderous roaring and rumbling, we caught ourselves chanting at the top of our lungs, like lunatics:

> Ave Maria, gratia plena
> Sancta Maria, Mater Dei

We immediately lowered our voices, deafened, but were left with an irreverent hilarity. Once, shrapnel killed a dying woman and a bullet struck a dead man in the skull.

There were solo airplanes, called Japos, which sometimes targeted our wing, no one knew why.

One day, when I was chatting with my dying ones, Sister wanted to transfer me to the hospital wing, but I gave up my place, the only vacancy down there, to a little ten-year-old girl in my room whose legs had been amputated.

"You know, that girl will be gone tonight," Sister said to me, "but you can stay on awhile longer."

Schwester Vincentia was a Sister of Charity, thin, olive-skinned, maybe fifty years old; a no nonsense, even-tempered woman, she worked day and night, lifting the wounded when the orderlies protested.

One morning she fell: her hernia ruptured.

She was admitted and placed in the little room next to mine. They operated immediately. She communicated with me by tapping on the wall with a cane.

Afterward, even with her hernial truss, she would lift and turn the wounded who at night pleaded to be shifted a little to ease their pain.

"Listen," she said to me one evening. "You don't want to die."

"No."

"I'm saying this because you're brave. Now you would die a good death. A patient of mine who, like you, would not die, and was less injured than you, returned to my ward ten years later, telling me: 'If only I had died back then! Afterward all I did was suffer. I can't take any more.' And she finally surrendered to God the soul that she had insisted on keeping from Him for so long."

"Is that so? But I'm not that woman, and in ten years I will return from Italy just to tell you that I was right to live. All I have to do is heal, no matter how long it takes, and you'll see!"

"Will you really come back?"

"Sure."

"Do you mean it?"

"Of course."

"We'll see."

One day, the second day-shift nun, Schwester Johanna, florid, white and rosy, stood on a ladder and removed the portrait of Hitler, which she hurled to the ground and trampled frenziedly; then, clutching the crucifix at her breast and kissing it passionately, she hung it in place of the portrait.

I hope my reader won't lose patience with me if I go on referring to "one day," "one night," "one time," but I have absolutely no idea of the temporal sequence in which events occurred during this period.

One night, a beautiful woman who appeared healthy and strong died without ever regaining consciousness. She had slept for three days.

The night-shift nun, Schwester Petra, told me that she had been raped by Negroes. She asked me if I hadn't heard the angry clamor rising from the city as soon as darkness fell. And, raising her pale eyes to the crucifix:

"Lord, you are about to die on the cross for them, and men have forgotten you."

I asked what date it was. Eight days before Easter. The news upset me. I too had forgotten Christ. I had no quarrel with Him, or with God, because He had suffered, and now more than ever I could understand what that meant. I thought I heard drunken voices and coarse laughter in the hospital garden. Easter was approaching and no one paid any attention. His solitude, the gratuitousness of His sacrifice, wrung my heart.

"Since You are going to die," I told Him, "I'll keep You company as well."

Schwester Petra appeared, syringe in hand.

"What is it?"

"Your morphine."

"I don't want it."

"You can't go without it."

When I insisted, she told me that I hadn't seen my back; it was a hollow cavity with tips of broken ribs sticking out, the thorax exposed, the lungs.

The more she talked the more worked up I got: "Do You hear her?" I said to the crucifix. "Are You listening?"

"I'm warning you, though," the nun said, giving in, "don't you torment my patients with your usual screams, attracting the Negroes to us. One sound out of you and I'll put you to sleep."

The first night wasn't only a series of excruciating, stabbing pains, unbroken agony without a moment's respite; not just torture for my entire body, which, going without food, had quickly become addicted to the morphine; it was also a time of constant vigilance during which I had to work to keep from screaming. By dawn my jaws were so tightly clenched that I couldn't relax them; I was drenched in sweat, my heart pounding crazily. I lost consciousness and woke up with an oxygen tube in my mouth. The ward doctor was nearby:

"You can't go off it so abruptly. We have to reduce the dosage a little at a time."

I wouldn't listen to reason.

"It's not up for discussion, in any case," he said, shrugging, "seeing that you won't make it."

I had a new obsession: it was now a matter of getting the better of the morphine.

I didn't shut my eyes for six days and six nights.

Schwester Petra, who was very pretty, spent every free minute of her night rounds keeping me company. She wove wreaths of tiny flowers around my head, promised me she would never leave my grave without flowers, that she would always pray for me.

On the night of Good Friday she recited the entire scene of Christ's Passion by candlelight, changing her voice and gestures depending on whether she was representing Pontius Pilate, Peter, or Judas.

She later told me that my face wore a look of such suffering that she no longer knew what she could do to alleviate it a little.

The night of the Resurrection, Christ came into my room, which was at least twice as big as usual, with my bed in the middle.

He was tall, clean-shaven, grave, and wore a green tunic.

He closed the door behind Him and came to sit on the edge of my bed.

He looked at me without speaking. Then He squeezed my feet with His hand and shook His head no.

I woke up as I was about to tell Him something.

Schwester Petra told me that I had slept one whole hour. She knelt beside my bed and together we said the rosary, which I listened to, rapt, because I didn't know all of it.

IV

The deaths became less frequent.

On the fortieth day I emptied my bowels for the first time. The fever that had been devouring me from the beginning suddenly lowered. I stopped sucking the watered-down milk—the only food that I could keep in until then!—and began ingesting broths and stewed fruit.

I was detoxified from the morphine

The doctors agreed that I might even live. They gave the order for me to be placed back among the patients expected to survive. But I had become attached to those who were dying and didn't want to leave them. Who would comfort them when they entered that room if the one who had not died was no longer there?

A twenty-two-year-old German girl was brought in following an operation on her stomach, where she'd been stabbed. She had a friend, a handsome young Greek man, who was distraught over her. The girl, whose name was Cunegonda, was so thirsty that she managed to convince her friend to bring her some beer. When she emptied the bottle in one gulp, she quickly worsened, the wound became purulent, she turned yellow, and her family was summoned. She confessed to me that she had cheated on her boyfriend, away at war, by taking up with the Greek, and that God was punishing her; but when she got well, she said, she would atone for it all her life. She was suffering morally more than physically, and she died.

Later on, the Greek boldly came back to see me. He had enlisted in the U.S. Army, was armed to the teeth, spoke loudly, and exuded excessive cheerfulness.

I deluged my neighbors with advice.

For ten days I struggled with the death of a nineteen-year-old brunette, she too German, beautiful, and reticent, who had no resources but obediently did what I suggested. One day, however, she eluded my surveillance and, perspiring, tossed off her blankets on a windy night in April despite all my recommendations. She had no family. Pneumonia claimed her. At that time there was no penicillin in Europe. She called to me to the last.

That death deeply saddened me.

The next day they brought me a long-limbed, delicate woman. She was a doctor in a morphine-induced coma. Every fifteen minutes she implored,

"Morphin! Morphiin!" with avid gasps. She died invoking her god morphine with a cry.

The warbling of the earliest birds could be heard among the trees. I begged the nuns to take me outside and they placed wheels on my bed. Breathing fresh air after two months, I dozed off, feeling comfortable for the first time in my battered body's skin.

I began to make plans.

I got to know some Italian patients with whom I started negotiating to buy a bicycle. I was determined to return to Italy by bike as soon as I was able to walk, to make up for my lengthy immobility with a nice athletic trip. My inactivity was beginning to wear on me.

"How much longer will it take me?" I asked the doctor.

"Nine weeks," he said, and walked away abruptly.

I began to count the days as if there were an exact date.

A few more people died beside me and, to distract them, two Italians with a guitar also came by.

Once, when an extremely uneasy old granny was approaching the end, all three of us started our concert, and she gave herself up to the sound of the music. But family members arrived unexpectedly, crying sacrilege and shame and waking the old woman from her merciful stupor; taken by surprirse, now realizing she was dying, she wept and resisted as no young person ever did, with a kind of greediness that was more irritating than moving.

Johann had arrived, meanwhile, and an inconsolable granddaughter, the most indignant of all, leaving once death had come, climbed on his bicycle and disappeared, pedaling fast. For that matter he too had stolen the bike.

Johann brought me everything I could ask for: clothes, undergarments, table linen, wine, canned fruit, and so on, all stolen stuff of course. He also brought things for the sisters and nurses. I especially recall certain pink mortadellas, a quantity of them.

Sometimes I caught him having a lengthy tête-à-tête with Schwester Vincentia in the corridor.

Whereas during the first few months I never thought about him, I now began waiting for him to arrive. I got impatient if he was late, and, for whatever reason, I pretended not to like the kisses, often mixed with tears, with which he covered my face.

The better I felt, the more I spoke about my imminent recovery, meticulously counting the days and hours of the nine weeks that had passed, and Johann would get gloomy. Sometimes he left without a word. He would show up drunk at night, get down on his knees, and, covering my hand with kisses, ask me to forgive him. He had become petulant. He had it in for the French and the Americans. He always showed up with shadows under his eyes, a shifty air. He stank of wine. He made vague, sinister threats.

I didn't understand. Sometimes I had the orderlies kick him out; other times I was sorry he had ended up like that just when things were looking up.

In early May, there was an inspection by the American health officials. I was in the garden, under an oak tree, one bed among a row of others. I soon noticed that the other patients, the Germans, were frightened. Without anyone asking them anything, they swore again and again that they had never been Nazis. Cowardice has always disgusted me.

When the inspectors stopped in front of me and learned that I was Italian, the most authoritative one said, as though it were routine, "Not a Fascist."

"On the contrary, a Fascist," I replied.

They called an interpreter, and the interrogation began.

It came out that I had been a Fascist, enrolled in the GUF (*Gruppi universitari fascisti*, university fascist groups), a zealot, and that while in Germany I had been a confirmed anti-Nazi; with regard to Fascist ideology in particular, I couldn't formulate an opinion—apart from my views concerning the alliance with Hitler—since Italian affairs had for too long been outside of my immediate interests.

At the conclusion of my interview they expressed their esteem for my sincerity and dignity. The officer had them bring me a big military pack. And from that day on they took me under their wing, one of them coming to visit me occasionally with gifts. We made ourselves understood with gestures and some German.

On another day, the ward physician, whom the patients greeted obsequiously when he passed by the beds in the garden, was arrested for having been a member of the Nazi Party, even though he hadn't taken part in any political activity. As he walked between two policemen, everyone averted their eyes. But I called out to him:

"See you soon, Doctor Niessen!"

His eyes repaid me, and I saw him move on with a more confident pace.

He was released the following day.

He introduced me to his wife and children; the children grew fond of me and often came to play with me, bringing me flowers and cakes.

Representatives of the French Red Cross also showed up, looking for their fellow countrymen. Schwester Vincentia led them to me. When they heard me talk about Reims and Paris and so on with a French accent, and learned that I was born in France and had spent my childhood there, they took a great liking to me and, every so often, they too brought me tobacco and chocolate.

The last ones to turn up were the Italians, very ceremonious, they discussed my condition with Sister, sniffed disdainfully, then told me that I would soon be back in my homeland, and that meanwhile I should have my documents and medical records prepared. They took their leave with a great many words.

Day after day I pressed the head nurse and doctor to give me my papers. The wounds from the phosphorus burns had healed, leaving a smooth, shiny new skin; my back had also scarred over. The nine weeks were almost up. They responded vaguely. I cried. Finally, I was given my documents in a large sealed red envelope.

As soon as I was left alone in the room, I idly opened the envelope.

I read that I was paralyzed from the waist down due to injuries to the seventh and eighth dorsal vertebrae, accompanied by fecal and urinary incontinence and lack of sensation. I could be discharged from the surgical ward because there was nothing more that could be done for me there. They advised electric shocks, massage, and passive exercise, with reservations about the possibility of ambulation with a corset and leg braces due to the brittle condition of the bones, contused and fractured throughout. Included were X-rays of the spine, chest, and pelvis, in various positions.

Maybe my reader realized all this from the beginning.

But I had not.

It was the end of May, and in three months I had never for a moment doubted that I would recover. The only alternatives had been to die or live.

I now understood a host of intimations, of attempts on the part of every-one to lead me toward this realization, to slip me details about my true situation; for example, I had a catheter permanently inserted in my blad-der and a glass receptacle between my legs; some mornings I found myself covered in feces. How could I not have seen it? The more hints I recalled, the more I sank into a dull incredulity. Me! Me stuck in a wheelchair for life, sitting in shit and urine.

I couldn't believe it.

But malicious reason kept telling me that it was true: you're paralyzed. No!

I grabbed a bottle of cognac from the bedside table and gulped it down in one swig. I raved and vomited all day. Johann kissed me and beat his head against the wall. He gave in to my insistence and brought me more cognac. Again I drank it down in swift gulps and threw up all night. A third bottle the following morning. I vomited and had diarrhea all day.

Johann did not leave my side for a moment. Schwester Vincentia fought with him; I had never seen her so incensed.

"If you don't feel you can do it," he kept telling me, "we'll die together."

The second night we each drank another bottle. Schwester Vincentia had him taken into custody. Then she got angry at everybody and finally she mocked and insulted me:

"Is this what you call being strong? I'm disgusted with you. Where's that resilience? Shameless!" And on and on.

It felt like everyone around me was crying for me.

"I'm not paralyzed. *Ich bin nicht gelähmt*, I'm not paralyzed."

But as much as I hoped to drink myself to death, just the thought of co-gnac now made my bowels churn. The disturbance that such drinking causes is truly the most repellent thing imaginable. After twenty-four hours of writhing and retching, constantly nauseated by the taste of excrement in my mouth, I ended up falling into a heavy slumber.

I was sick for days. I couldn't eat or drink, speak, or think. At times the reminder stabbed through me like a knife: You're paralyzed. But it didn't stick.

At daybreak one morning I awoke, fresh and clear, to the singing of birds in the trees. I listened admiringly to their limpid, irrepressible, vibrant trills. That's why I hadn't died. This was where He wanted me. Okay then: I would accept the challenge.

V

That same morning I called for Schwester Vincentia; we hadn't spoken to each other since the evening she reproached me. I asked her if I could still stay in her ward, or if I was now compulsorily discharged. She replied that no one had sent me away: I was the one who wanted to leave. We both had tears in our eyes, but we spoke in polite tones and avoided looking at each other. I said I wanted to buy a wheelchair.

She nodded thoughtfully: "How much do you have?"

"The money set aside for the bicycle." My voice cracked.

She grabbed a glass from the bedside table and cleared it away. "I don't like having a mess around. How many times must I tell you?"

But she soon returned, with an odd, stern expression on her face, and started tugging the white bedspread from all sides, unfolding and refolding the towels hanging on the headboard.

I told her that I intended to get used to sitting and moving about in a wheelchair. I had to get some books to study, to improve my languages, get reacquainted with philosophy. Finally, I said:

"I'm not going back to Italy: I'm dead."

She spoke to me about my parents, about my mother's sorrow.

"They haven't heard from me for ten months now."

One day I watched the Corpus Domini procession from the corner of the hospital's drive. The gravel was strewn with flowers. Sweet little children and clerics with candles marched along singing. When the baldachin passed by, the faithful around me knelt.

Suffice it to say that You killed Your son, I told Him.

Johann greeted the news that I would stay in Mainz with extraordinary relief. I learned that he had decided to follow me, that he would have had to cross the border illegally; he was worried about his chances of finding work in Italy. I noticed that he had grown a mustache and sideburns, perhaps to look more like a southerner. He was always fond of Italians, feeling glad when someone mistook him for one of them. I noticed that he talked loudly, gestured a lot, walked with a swagger, gave provocative looks. He was no longer shy and retiring. He wasn't gloomy and brusque anymore either, like when I used to talk about my recovery. Moreover, I saw him less often: he didn't come every day and usually stayed only a few minutes. At times I thought I recognized his step and a warmth would spread through me. I pinched my leg until it left a mark: It's all just suggestion, I told myself, *you can't feel anything.*

I had the Americans give me a pass with which I could borrow the books I wanted from the university.

I would wake up at dawn and study Russian for three hours—I already knew a little.

Then I bathed and exercised in the water under the guidance of the masseuse; sitting in the tub, I stretched out my arms and touched my toes with my fingertips; hands on my hips, I rotated my torso; on my knees I pulled myself up to sit on my calves, then I lowered myself again.

After lunch I read the philosophy books I borrowed or that Johann stole for me from the university: Spinoza's *Ethics*, Kant's three *Critiques*. In them I found the rationality that eluded me in life. Around five o'clock, I got dressed and sat in the wheelchair to enjoy some fresh air in the garden.

I had made friends with a Russian girl with a mutilated arm, who was soon repatriated. Saying goodbye, she had given me the threadbare stuffed dog that she always pressed to her chest with her one little hand.

"His name is Tobik," she said, handing him to me gently.

I lived with that dog and never went anywhere without him. I told stories featuring Tobik to the convalescent children who came running over to me as soon as they saw me come out of the ward—some hopping on one foot, some hobbling, some with plaster casts; and as I spoke I would straighten a limp ear, make him bark, lift his paw. Each time they would ask me, "What did Tobik do today?" They begged me to let them touch him and were overjoyed when I allowed one of them to hold him for a moment;

it was a prize I awarded to those who had not been naughty about eating or taking their medicine, subject to a note from their head nurse declaring: *Today so-and-so was a good boy or girl*, along with the details.

Even the adults who were getting a breath of air approached and listened to the stories I made up, which I embellished more and more as my audience grew.

A German soldier in a wheelchair, with a gangrenous leg, was set to have it amputated the following day: surrounded by the circle of children, he asked me earnestly to lend him Tobik for the occasion.

Afterward he sent him back with a little leather collar he'd made himself.

Since Tobik was too floppy and stalks of straw stuck out of him from all sides, the ward doctor decided to operate on him as well. In front of my kids silently gathered in the operating room, with bated breath, he put on his white mask and rubber gloves while Schwester Vincentia handed him the instruments, shaking her head from time to time; the doctor cut open the dog's back, stuffed him with straw, stitched him back up, and solemnly gave him back to me. The doctor was about thirty years old, with dark hair receding at the temples and dark eyes; in the evening he would come to my room and chat.

Because my wheelchair stowed in the hallway was in the way, it was decided that we would leave it under the portico in the evening. But the day after this decision, we found the tires flat, the brake unscrewed: it had been my little friends, simply eager to snoop around something that belonged to me.

In a small room in the isolation unit there was a ten-year-old girl, her entire body burned as a result of having touched a high-voltage wire. She had heard about me and had sent her mother to call for me. She studied me with her big eyes and finally asked me to give her Tobik. I didn't give him to her. Later I felt sorry, but on the other hand, if I had given him to her, it would all be over. I myself had become attached to that dog and I couldn't sleep if I didn't have him next to me, with his snout tucked under my arm. "We have only each other," I told him.

I went to see the little burned girl right away and, not realizing the cruelty of the ploy, I suggested she tell my little friends that she had been reduced to that condition by playing around with my wheelchair:

"We'll say that there's a particular spot, you don't know where it is, through which a strong electrical current passes, and which is therefore dangerous to touch. I'm the only one who can. Do you understand? Can you remember it? They'll come and question you, you know."

That same afternoon I told the children about the terrible accident that had happened to a friend of mine who had climbed onto my runabout when I wasn't there.

They looked at each other as if to say: This is too much!

"You don't believe me? Go and see her. I'll wait for you here." And I told them where to find her.

They came back still looking incredulous, but—all in all—alarmed. From that day on I was able to safely leave the wheelchair under the portico. The sisters told me later that in the morning the kids came to check it out from a safe distance, daring one another; one reached a finger to a spoke of the wheel or to a screw, and quickly drew back, saying he'd felt the shock.

They constantly went to see the girl devastated by burns, and she no longer hid her disfigured little face, she was no longer lonely like before; she was excited and eager to recount ever new variations of her amazing adventure with my wheelchair, stories that she believed more than the others, and was religiously listened to as a heroine. I went to see her too and we talked seriously together about how strange many things in life were. Her mother laughed and cried.

By then the little girl's flesh was crawling with worms and she died.

After I'd been sitting up and doing exercises for fifteen days, I realized that I was humpbacked. Someone in the garden always managed to brush against my hump. Maybe I had strained myself: my back wouldn't support me, and I sat slumped over. Besides that, my belly was always swollen, and often my legs and feet as well, which were bluish due to poor circulation. I didn't feel embarrassed. I looked at my body as if it were that of an unfortunate relation of mine. The only thing you're good for is to annoy me, I told it, giving it a few maternal pats. I baptized my legs: Lazarus, the left one, and Cunegonda, the right.

"Cunegonda is twisted," I would say, and the nun straightened my right leg. Lazarus was the husband and Cunegonda the wife. He was firmer, straight, a real man, whereas she always buckled and seemed to have a simpering disposition.

Schwester Petra, the night-duty nun, had fallen ill due to severe exhaustion and had been replaced by a young Red Cross nurse, sweet and kind, Schwester Luise, the war widow of an engineer.

One evening she brought to my room a little picture of the Madonna, which she had stitched for me during her breaks from work.

On the morning of my twentieth birthday, I awoke to find my room full of flowers, small gifts, cards, which Schwester Luise had arranged on tiptoe. The patients had shared the date in secret to surprise me. I spent the day receiving visitors, bouquets of lily of the valley, clusters of currants, and other offerings. I had a lump in my throat over the generosity of the human heart.

Johann was the only one who did not show his face. He showed up around two in the morning, very agitated, unsteady on his legs: he asked me to marry him. He couldn't live without me. "I need your help, you don't know what a state I'm in." That said, he seemed to calm down and slipped a metal wedding band on my right ring finger.

Schwester Luise had a hard time persuading him to leave, he had to go or she'd lose her post; it wasn't like before, there were visiting hours now.

In the confident frame of mind I was in, I suggested that the sister accompany me to the city the next day, to where Johann lived, in a former army barracks, to surprise him. So around 5:00 a.m. we started getting me ready, and, as soon as she had finished her shift, we went out.

The crisp morning breeze filled my lungs. Schwester Luise pushed me, striding quickly down the sidewalk, and I felt like a baby being taken for a walk by her mother.

In a few months the Germans, like ants, had restored their city; all around were houses with uneven wooden planks for walls, aluminum sheets for roofs, paper covering the windows, geranium plants and flowering violets on the windowsills. The streets were clean, the rubble heaped in orderly piles.

When we reached the immense courtyard of the former barracks, I asked for Johann. Disheveled women and hard-faced men in sleeveless undershirts gathered around me. They spread the word. I saw a girl with a scrubbed, gentle face run up, a small sprightly brunette, German, who seemed to be expecting me yet looked upset:

"You're looking for Johann, right? Come, come with me," she said. And to the curious onlookers, with an air of setting things straight, "It's his sister! His sister from the hospital." And she led us through the yard, her hand on the arm of the wheelchair, her head high. "How young you are!" she exclaimed, no longer able to hold back. "I imagined you old, mean." She explained that she had so often pleaded with Johann to introduce her to me, but he cut her short, saying that I didn't want to meet her. And one night when she had followed him to the hospital, he had beaten her on the spot, so hard that she had not dared try again. They had gotten together in March, three months ago. Her family wouldn't have anything to do with her anymore, especially her father, who had fallen ill (as if to say: not only his relations are opposed, but mine as well). She was a shop assistant.

Schwester Luise said that it was getting late and we had to return immediately, she was responsible for me.

"Wait just one minute, I'll call him. Otherwise he'll beat me." And the girl showed us the bruises she had on her arms and legs.

But Schwester Luise said no and we started back. The girl walked partway with us: she was trying to gauge the impression she had made on me, whether I would allow my brother to marry her, when we would leave for Warsaw, what Johann's and my parents were like. Plainly I had been a nightmare for her and she couldn't get over her disbelief:

"So nett!"* she kept saying.

At a crossroads we hugged, calling each other sisters, and tears slipped out as I pressed my cheek to hers too vehemently.

Without a word, Schwester Luise and I made our way back to the hospital.

With Schwester Vincentia and Schwester Johanna hovering worriedly, Sister Luise put me back to bed.

"Bastard. Polack," she said.

"He has a German girlfriend," I announced. "She would be my sister-in-law, because I'm supposedly his sister."

---

*"So nice!"

"All sluts nowadays," Schwester Johanna said, blushing.

As soon as I was left alone, I threw off the sheet, feeling like I was suffocating. The first thing I did was take the metal band off my finger and fling it out the open window.

I couldn't think straight. Finally, my mind formulated the words *he'll pay for it*, and I felt relieved. Clinging to this new purpose, I had to determine a course of action to take. But as soon as I got distracted, I remembered instances of his ill-concealed impatience to leave, the inept excuses he came up with: one time he said he had to remain hidden because they were searching for foreigners to be repatriated; another time that he was working to set aside some money. Not to mention his fruitless plans. In short, he said a lot of things. His new way of swaggering; the way he apologized too much.

He'd never even asked me if I loved him.

And me, placid, blind, deaf.

Only because I was paralyzed. Wincing, I recalled that I had twice voided my bowels in his arms as he was about to put me in the wheelchair.

Back in March when he'd met her, I'd still been dying. All he had to do was disappear then: I wouldn't even have noticed.

He felt obligated to love me. *Me.*

The more crushed I felt inside, the more worked up I got in the intoxication of battle. My mind enjoyed wallowing in humiliation, while outwardly I wept with strange noises in my nose. I was at just such a combative moment when I recalled the face, the energetic body of his healthy girlfriend, and me in comparison. For the first time I experienced such profound shame over my condition that I lost my senses and fell asleep.

I was awakened by a familiar voice. It was him, arguing heatedly with Schwester Vincentia; he threw open the door and rushed into my room, followed by the nun, who said bitterly, "You can never know a person well enough."

"I have to talk to you!" he said to me arrogantly.

Sister motioned to me from behind him, to see if she should leave. I nodded and with my eyes indicated the bell. She went out, closing the door behind her.

Alcohol must have given him courage.

Practically shouting, he accused me of never having loved him, of having always treated him like a slave, of not having the feelings of a woman.

I immediately assumed a contrite look (my heart pounding over the triumph that I allowed myself).

"You're right," I replied softly, shamefaced. "I don't love you. You've always been so good, so generous with me that I never had the heart to tell you."

When he grasped the meaning of my words, he laughed scornfully until he turned pale and told me that he should have known that I was false, treacherous, a true Italian, he explained.

"You're right," I said again, with an indifference that made me feel proud.

He threw back at me the fact that I had let him kiss me.

"I was so sick then! What did I know . . ."

I should have stopped myself at that point, but I couldn't resist the misguided temptation to add, with a hint of derision, "But now I see things clearly. Now I'm recovered, even if I'm paralyzed."

Hearing that word, he couldn't take any more; his fighting spirit vanished, and he begged me to marry him because I was the only one he loved. If he had never known me, he might have been happy with the other girl, but as it was, he was always thinking of me; he spent his time drinking and making love, just so I wouldn't always be on his mind, and he'd turned into a brute and it wasn't a life worth living.

When he said "making love," my heart shrank. "I'm dead," I told him, and rang the bell.

"Don't send me away!" Footsteps were approaching. "She knows I love you, I confessed everything, she understood, she's a good person, we broke up."

I smiled scornfully.

"You've always hated me," he said, talking fast. "You despise me."

"See how intelligent you are? So spare me your pity." I was about to burst into tears.

"That's not true!" he protested. "How could you think that. You don't understand." The orderlies, at a sign from the nun, stood alongside him. He glanced at them distractedly.

Then he turned impetuously to Sister: "Which one of us is more pitiful," he asked, "Luzi or me?"

When he was gone, I finally let myself go, sobbing under the covers. Was living really worth it in the end?

VI

I woke up suddenly, with a thud, as if I had fallen, and found my hands gripping the sides of the mattress, my heart pounding, in the dark, alone, with no one who could understand my struggle, who could help me. Sister Vincentia herself had advised me to die.

I relaxed my grip; I had to breathe deeply. I closed my eyes and waited. Nothing had happened.

Johann had never existed. *Before*, in fact, he hadn't interested me.

No.

Johann existed and, just as I had grown attached to him after he saved my life, I would now, as naturally, forget him. That's all. I had not been defeated. "You won't bring me down," I whispered to God, but it wasn't an accusation; I felt He was on my side. Moreover, even the worst father is relieved when a child can manage on his own and doesn't always go running to him. I could just imagine all the prayers, lamentations, and complaints that men addressed to Him: "I'll bet You must be tired of it too," I said with a sigh, and went on to reflect on life.

It was beginning to be clear: it seemed to me that I was preparing for something far-off and difficult for which I would perhaps struggle all my life, though in the end I could not fail. I was calm and confident and I grew drowsy.

Around nine o'clock I was awakened by a caress from Johann, who stood there studying me. I smiled at him and winked against my will.

"Out!" The voice of Sister Johanna rang loudly as she descended on the room. "Visiting hours are the same for everyone, Thursdays and Sundays from three to five!" Her face flushed, she swept out the door with a great rustling of her skirts.

Soon afterward Sister Vincentia appeared and with a gesture encouraged him to leave. They stopped to talk in the hallway. I couldn't make out what he was saying; then she replied calmly and distinctly:

"Everything is fine, but leave her alone, she hasn't asked you for anything. Luzi doesn't need anyone."

I underwent treatments and did my exercises and spent every free moment studying.

By now people were no longer dying and in any case the real morgue had been rebuilt. Brought to my room were annoying middle-aged women who'd just had stones or ovaries removed, who rang the bell for no reason and complained endlessly.

"Luzi!" Sister Vincentia approached me. "How come you don't call? Can you be the only one who never needs anything?" And every so often, during the hot hours, she came in with a cool drink, an apricot juice, and massaged my behind. "There, now you're nice and cool," she said, lifting my foot to look at it.

In the afternoon I received several visits: from Germans recovering in the hospital, and from American and French soldiers with whom I had become friends and who had the right to come in at all hours.

If Johann appeared, "Go away," they whispered to him, "the doctor doesn't want visitors, you're not a soldier, you have to keep to the normal visiting hours." And in front of him, I became more expansive toward the soldiers; a sudden familiar mood came over me. Sometimes I even went out with them. "Bye-bye!" I said, apologizing to Johann, who would arrive all worked up. "I have a prior commitment, I can't cancel."

As the soldiers pushed my wheelchair through the streets of Mainz, people would look at our little parade and I smiled, thinking about the impression all those healthy young conquerors surrounding my vanquished body must have made. I gazed at the trees, at the faces of passersby, as though watching a pageant.

Often Johann followed us on his bicycle, skinnier than during the time of the Germans, unshaven, his eyes flashing. The French guys warned me when he showed up. And together we laughed at him.

I got along better with the French than with the Americans because it was easier to talk and because our way of seeing things was similar.

With one or the other group, I usually went to the park. They even sat me on a grassy flower bed, under an oak tree. We played games. I had started the fad of playing *cocuzzaro* among the Americans. They had to pronounce the ritual phrase in Italian. Seeing those hulking young men, both whites and blacks, seated in a circle on the lawn, their faces diligent and focused—watching them jump up when their number was called and stumble over the words *"Perché quattro cocuzze"* (Why four pumpkins?), I couldn't keep from laughing, and they laughed with me. Toward evening we ended up making such a racket that knots of curious onlookers stopped to look at us, laughing in reaction.

The Americans particularly liked to shower me with gifts of food, and at every outing, a new one appeared asking permission to come too.

One afternoon toward sunset when I was in the shady park with my two best French friends, one of them was raising the wheelchair's footrests to allow Cunegonda, swollen and sweaty, to stretch out, when Johann rushed at him. The other young man jumped on Johann from behind, Johann pulled a knife, they twisted his arm, and Allied soldiers came running to help, dragging Johann away.

Some time later, Johann jumped through the window into my room one night—luckily I was alone—with such an expression that I was truly frightened. Still, I made sure to act as though I were worried about him, as though I were concerned that the night watchmen might arrest him, whereas I had actually asked the watchmen to do just that, because I'd been expecting a break-in like this from Johann sooner or later. I played my part so well that not even five minutes had gone by—he was planning on kidnapping me, freeing me, was talking about the doctors and orderlies as if they were my jailers—before he let me convince him to leave so as not to get me in trouble.

The easier it was for me to handle him and make him change his mind, the less he counted in my heart. Very soon I reached the point where seeing him that way—filthy, shabby, eyes always on the alert—compared to the trim Germans in their Sunday best, and even more so with the Americans and the French, so upstanding in their immaculate khaki uniforms, made me ashamed of him.

By now even the gifts he brought me looked like they were stolen and were no longer permitted, including cans of vegetables marinated in oil and vinegar, in keeping with the German practice of preserving anything

edible: chickens, rabbits, eggs. He would pull them out of his shirt with a furtive gesture, too imprudently, so I insisted he hide the stuff as quickly as
possible in the bedside table or in the suitcase under the bed. Seeing him
coming and worrying about making a bad impression became one and the
same to me. At first thinking about his German girlfriend rekindled my
malice; now, though I rarely thought of her, it only made me shrug.

"This is not the way to drive him off." Sister Vincentia voiced her
disapproval. "It's not charitable."

"And I don't want his charity either!"

"Don't you ever ask yourself what you gave him?"

"I didn't mistake him for someone he isn't. Let him learn to know someone the next time before he comes forward."

"It's you who provoke him," she replied.

"He should regret me as long as he lives."

I remember that at that time I was constantly agitated and emotional. I
would wake up at night repeating lists of foreign words, constructing sentences, thinking; the chirping of birds before dawn, the rustling of the trees
in the evening, the impassioned shrieks of the maimed and crippled children
playing with boisterous fervor in the garden, everything gripped my heart,
moistened my eyes, gave me a warmth, a "yes" inside.

There were also the Germans and their problems. They were hungry
and I had provisions, from the soldiers' gifts and Johann's, that I willingly
handed out to them: Sister Vincentia took care of the distribution. But
above all the Germans had favors to request of the occupation authorities—
special permits, certificates, various licenses—and since I was visited by the
Americans, the Germans came to respectfully ask me to intercede for them.
They entrusted lengthy petitions to me, they left gooseberries and asparagus
on my nightstand, though their eyes were famished. I would attach a note
and pass the papers on to the Americans. Often the supplicants received a
note summoning them to Command and obtained what they wanted and
would have obtained just the same without me. But they preferred going
through my channels and considered me an important person.

Some gave me letters to be forwarded to America. Civilian mail wasn't functioning yet. Word spread and, curiously enough, they schemed more to give me their letters than they would have done for useful concessions. They were seized by a fervent epistolary mania. The American soldiers, who mailed these letters with their own sender's address on the back, asked me to please go easy on them because they were forbidden to include non-military correspondence in their mail and they didn't want any trouble with the military censor. But the Germans were unreasonable on that point, doubling the gooseberries and asparagus: putting the sheet of paper and envelope in my hand.

I decided to go through the letters on my own, eliminating those that were too obsequious or incoherent. In the evening after dinner, I went to the treatment room, wheeled in with my bed and all, and, along with another victim from February 27, a witty forty-year-old German woman, began the secret reading. Schwester Luise brought us raspberries sprinkled with sugar and helped us in between her rounds.

The letters to be discarded were torn up and thrown in the toilet; I pulled the chain, and the following morning I told the interested parties that I had mailed them by sea. The sensible ones, instead, I gave to the soldiers, telling the letter writers that they had gone by air.

I remember a German who wrote to a distant relative of his wife, whom he had not heard from in twenty years, as it turned out. He proposed setting up a toilet paper factory in the Rhineland, explaining that toilet paper was a much sought-after commodity in Germany, which had been suffering for years because Hitler, swine that he was, had sabotaged its production. The man asked the relative for an exorbitant amount of dollars for the initial setup costs—but by return mail, before anyone else stole the idea.

After laboriously deciphering it, Fräulein Schwarzmann exclaimed: "What a bright idea! Meanwhile, not to waste time, I'll use this one to wipe myself."

One morning in late July a man with a folder came to see me. He was from the hospital administration: he wanted to know when I would vacate my place.

"I don't know."

What? What was the Italian Red Cross doing instead of assisting their wounded?

"I put off my departure."

He didn't understand.

"Many foreigners remain in Germany."

Perhaps these foreigners were self-supporting: "But who pays for you here?" So I had to leave, there was no need to be alarmed, they would officially see to having me repatriated.

To buy time I made up a story that my parents had moved to France and were expecting me there, and that I was just then waiting for an important reply.

I got a two-week extension, but I had to sign a document to the effect that if I had not left by the end of the fourteen days, the administration would decide my case with no restrictions whatsoever.

Two days later I received a communication from the French Ministry of Health, at the hospital's request, according to which, having been born in France, I could move there once I presented: (a) my birth certificate; (b) my parents' French residency certificate; and (c) a document from them summoning me, certified by the consul general, in which they guaranteed to provide for me economically.

Having turned twenty-one, and due to the privilege that being born in France conferred on me, I could opt for French citizenship after at least a six-month residency on French soil, and from that time on I would be able to benefit from France's rights for war invalids.

My case was not a simple one because obviously in my condition I wouldn't contribute any revenue to the French coffers, but the health office stationed in Mainz had nonetheless recommended me highly thanks to the good contacts that I had there.

I had to confess to my friends that my parents were living in Italy and that I had fooled the administration because I did not want to go home.

They didn't give up, but with no relatives in France, there was only so much they could do for me.

The Italians in gray-green, with the health department armbands, showed up one morning, called to my bed by the administration, despite the extension. They were the same ones as before, based in Wiesbaden; they had that difficult way typical of Italian males with women they consider homely or undesirable, whereas they make everything easy for attractive girls. I got rid of them quickly, declaring that I was Italo-French from Paris and stressing the French r, which inspired them to utter a few gallant phrases to me.

The very thought of Italy depressed me.

I went from the one extreme of yearning for my country to the other extreme of a terror that was practically aversion, with no middle ground.

I dreamed of my mother often, and in the morning I felt a need to lean on her and sleep some more. I thought back to my friends there, admirers; I would recall an episode and laugh, all by myself, moved, but when I thought of seeing them again, of being with them again, a chill came over me. If I imagined scenes of meeting them, I actually froze. No place in Italy where I had been appealed to me. I was especially wary of any relatives. "You wanted to see for yourself. Look what came of it. If you'd only listened to us. Naturally it had to happen, you had to have it your way." And at my slightest initiative, a chorus of protests: "Isn't what happened to you enough?" And a whole wall of prohibitions, for my own good.

And my parents, surrounded by these comments, torn between the pride of not showing how deeply my adversity struck them and their apprehension over what new misfortunes might await me. Unable as I was to act on my own, my father would have inevitably ended up laying down the law: "That's not appropriate; this is unsuitable," according to his uncompromising criterion of what is good and what is bad for a female child.

I thought about Mama's ingenuous ideas of what is noble and what is not worthy of a "proper" person's interest; I thought about everything that I had seen, observed, learned. *She* was the inexperienced child. But how to make her see that? She would always feel the need to guide me, fortified by my misfortune: "What did we gain, chasing after ideals? What good was it, I ask you? There was no one under that wall, and you went rushing in."

I did not agree.

The wisdom of adults—"When I was your age I too wanted to do this and that, at your age you always think that . . . then you calm down and realize instead that . . ."—had poisoned my adolescence. I was not like them, I would not settle, surrender, be directed. Don't lose heart, in the long run the truth triumphs, I kept telling myself. If it seemed that evil was successful, it was because of the positive values that made it effective, its joie de vivre, its knowledge of the world, its unconventionality and daring; if it seemed that good was oppressed, it was because of its inertia, its sentimentality, its ignorance of reality; if it didn't protest this or that outrage, opening its eyes too late, this only meant that it lacked the requisite energy to act, and so it wasn't genuine goodness after all, but mere passivity.

My brain worked nonstop during the night as I awaited dawn, as if only then could I lower my guard and rest.

At times I remembered with a jolt that I was paralyzed, as if it were something new, and that fact reconciled me with everyone and everything, with my youth, with my memories of my parents. A lump in my throat, tears streaming down: "Mama, Papa, goodbye."

I knew, from the time I accepted His challenge, that I would go to Russia, "where they repudiate You," but my two French friends were against it and wanted to try someplace else first.

They accompanied me to the American Command center, at the town hall of the lower city, where I was received by various officers, one after another. Each of them listened to me affably, questioned me over again, and let me speak at length, after which they declared that it wasn't possible for them to send me to America. I could, however, return to Italy, relying on the charitable operations of the Vatican, which would put me in contact with a benefactor willing to assume my travel and living expenses and ongoing care costs: such philanthropists abounded in the United States, and it wasn't out of the question that one might be found for me. I explained that I knew several languages and was able to work and pay for myself. If I had been in good health, of course, they themselves would have hired me, gladly, but as it was, they told me that I was very smart to know so many languages (which I had listed for them), that I should continue to study, and they wished me all the best.

My French friends then accompanied me to the International Assistance Bureau for concentration camp survivors, which was located behind the eighteenth-century palace of the Carnival prince, on the Rhine. The great river was cool and refreshing to behold in the suffocating heat of that continental August. Unfortunately, the International Bureau dealt exclusively with persecuted Jews. There was, however, another German institution on the other side of the city, near the public park, that might be appropriate in my case. There they handled only former German political prisoners. Nevertheless, they did not let us leave until they had demonstrated, especially to my French friends, that the current German administration offered victims—more specifically those of Nazi tyranny, which had oppressed everyone without distinction—compensation for damages, albeit overdue, in the form of an apartment, a car, a refrigerator, a generous pension, and various privileges, including a weekly distribution of food and medicine parcels normally unobtainable.

The Frenchmen, disappointed because this was our last attempt, and Russia was the last resort for me, insisted that the German bureau give me a parcel for my trouble, but those gentlemen were sorry, no, at which the French criticized them loudly as the most hypocritical people and wheeled me away. That day on the way back they gave anyone who turned around to look at us a withering look, treating them like brutal Nazis. I, on the other hand, was cheerful. I had set out curious about the outcome, as in a game of chance, and with each slap in the face, seeing those expressions of sympathy, my heart flickered, ready for battle: "And I'm supposed to capitulate because of *them*?"

The Frenchmen, who'd wanted to see me settled, had to give it up because they were leaving that same evening: one transferred to Berlin, the other, with TB, to a sanatorium in the Alps. They were twenty-three and twenty-two years old.

We spent the whole afternoon together. The one who was going to Berlin was sad and looked anxiously back and forth between his companion and me. We two instead joked around. There was talk of love. I said that I was one of the Lord's chosen ones because He granted all my prayers, maybe even a little too literally. I had wanted to sacrifice and He instantly buried me under a wall; I had argued that, for a woman, love, as currently conceived, meant subjection to a man and He promptly had put me in a position of not being able to love . . .

"*Dieu nazi!*"

At that time, in the German regional capitals, each of the four victorious powers still had a military post, and the smaller countries an agency, to reclaim those who had been deported.

The Soviet Command was located in a green house not far from the barracks where Johann lived.

On the tenth morning following the hospital's ultimatum, I went there with Schwester Luise.

I asked for the comrade commander. A man in his fifties, stocky, with a deep voice, wearing a bottle green uniform and high boots, came out of the house to the garden. He sat down on a bench, to which he pushed my wheelchair, and prepared to listen to me.

I knew Italian, French, and German well; I understood, wrote, and read Russian and Polish; I remembered Latin and ancient Greek fairly well; a little Romanian; I was studying English; I presumed that the Russians might be interested in a polyglot with a humanities background and that, by its very ideological tenets, communist society would recognize the sacrosanct right of every human being to work.

As I racked my brain to dredge up the clever little phrases, repeated so often during my sleepless nights, that were to lead to my explicit request to go to Russia, and which now escaped me, the captain stood up, went to grab the broom out of a soldier's hands, and started sweeping vigorously, calling the man a slowpoke.

Then he came back to sit beside me, puffing, and gave me a concerned look. I had to laugh at the thought of my little contrived speech, and I told him straight out that I wanted to go and settle in Russia because I was paralyzed, I didn't want to be pitied and kept in Italy as a survivor of myself when, if anything, I was stronger now than before because I knew things that others couldn't even imagine, and I was capable not only of providing for myself, but also of being useful to others, and I was not afraid of life.

"You're not really a 'run-to-mama,'" he said, using the name the Russians called Italian soldiers during the war.

"We run back to mamà, true, but only after putting up a good fight," I retorted, feeling stung for my compatriots.

He laughed heartily: "*Khorosho*, very good!" and he had them bring me a bag with a huge slab of red, fresh beef that I had not seen for years, a lump of butter, a sack of sugar, a loaf of bread, and some cucumbers.

But then he stood in front of me and looked as if he were getting ready to leave.

"Well?" I asked. "Will you let me enter Russia?"

"Are you serious?"

"Yes, I am."

"How can you even think of it?"

"I'll get Russian citizenship."

"In that condition?" He pointed to my legs.

"Bravo!" I retorted. "Congratulations."

We stared, gauging each other. He sat down again. He slapped his hands on his thighs and said:

"Just my luck that this one had to show up here!"

"Yes." By now I was sure that he wouldn't send me away with a conventional excuse.

A small group of soldiers had gathered around us. They eyed the young, attractive Luise and, perhaps to appear important, brought the absorbed commander cigarette paper and matches, told him the time, all with great familiarity, until he lost his patience and, with an unwarranted burst of anger, threatened to have them all shot on the spot. They vanished. Still frowning, he slumped back on the bench.

"You know," he said finally, "one's own land"—he paused on the word *zemlya*—"is always one's own land."

I wrinkled my nose: "Come on!"

He frowned again.

"You were a partisan?"

"No."

He hesitated, studying me: "Fascist?"

I didn't answer.

He rested his elbows on his knees, his broad ruddy face in his hands. "Go on. Speak," he said softly, brisk and somehow trustworthy.

I was eighteen when the Badoglio government, following the armistice of September 8, 1943, upset the front against the Allies during the war, and the German roundups began; people were terrified, confused, left to their own devices, hiding, feeling as though their earlier ideals were crimes, and any promises just words in the wind. So I wanted to put myself to the test, to see if I too would retreat at the first difficulty. I was troubled, as I am now, searching for the best decision. Thinking and rejecting, thinking and rejecting, I realized that the only way to learn the truth for myself about Fascists and anti-Fascists—many said that they could no longer figure it out—was to ascertain it firsthand. Understanding this, I had to go to the places about which the most outrageous stories were told: the Nazi concentration camps. That's why I ran away from home on February 8, 1944, and went to Germany as a simple volunteer worker, with pictures of Mussolini and Hitler in my backpack, sure about what I was doing. But after spending a few months in a labor camp near Frankfurt am Main, my comrades organized a strike at the factory, the IG Farben, where I worked in the Ch 89, the chemical division. As a result I was jailed, then later transferred and detained in Dachau. In order to survive, I escaped from there in October, and for a couple of months I remained hidden in Munich. Then I left, following the death of the friends who were helping me: a pregnant Polish woman named Dunja who died in childbirth, and a Frenchman killed by the police. I headed back to my first Lager, traveling partway by train without a ticket, crouched in the toilets of the cars, partway on foot, spending the night in bomb shelters, in abandoned cattle cars, in foreigners' barracks, I also worked as a *garzona* (waitress) for a few days for some farmers in the vicinity of Donauwörth; in mid-February I arrived in Mainz. I also met up with an old comrade from IG Farben, Johann, one of the ones with whom we had organized the strike in the factories. He had fled in time and so had avoided arrest. He was working as a kitchen boy in a hotel in Mainz, under a false name. He managed to get me hired as well. I had been working for a week; by then I was safe, I was a waitress at the Königshotel, where . . . —I choked up—and here I am.

The captain couldn't get over his surprise: "A strike! Escaped! But didn't the Germans catch you again?"

"Communications had been disrupted for some time."

He shrugged. He started pacing up and down. He came back to where I was waiting. He bent down to my ear and whispered, "Don't mention volunteering. You were a Fascist, but with the genuine spirit of a comrade.

In Russia, you'll see, you will be treated humanely and well." But he went on: "I still can't put you on the list. *Nie magu*," he spelled out. Only then did I have doubts about being rejected. I couldn't breathe because of the heat, and, feeling overcome with no further recourse, I let myself go and wept silently, with my eyes alone. He clenched my wrist: "*Podozhdi, devchonka.*"* He disappeared into the house and came back with two glasses of vodka.

"If only you were married to a Russian," he sighed.

"Over there, though, is it certain that I could get divorced?"

"Of course!" Then, thinking about it: "Why, is there a man?"

I laughed nervously. Johann was born in Russia, he spoke Russian as well as I did French; he had no papers, but he could pass himself off as Russian. Still, I didn't say that to the captain. Instead I asked, "How much time is needed for a wedding? I only have four days, after that they'll throw me out of the hospital."

"Bring the man here, with your documents. I'll see to the rest."

As Luise wheeled me away, I turned to look at the captain, who was watching me with something of a stunned expression. My head was spinning strangely, maybe because of the vodka. I was overjoyed. There were no obstacles too great for me, Lord.

On the way back, I wanted to stop by the barracks. Luise objected. So I begged her to leave me at the gate, let Johann know I was there, and go away. He would see to getting me back later. She was extremely troubled to do it, but I insisted and she did what I asked.

Johann appeared very annoyed to see me. It was noon. Apparently I was in the way and he didn't know what to do with me. A far cry from the imploring, suffering air when he came to visit me or stalked me during my outings with the soldiers. He became more and more irritated each moment that passed. Finally, he wheeled me into the barracks courtyard, picked me up in front of a staircase, and carried me up hurriedly, as if afraid of being seen; he set me down on a cot that stood alone against a wall in an empty room: "Be right back," he said, and rushed off.

An hour went by, two, three. I had not unplugged and emptied the catheter from early that morning and I was worried that I had wet myself. I felt

*"Wait here, dear."

down there to check; luckily I was still dry. More time passed. I tried calling out. No one heard me. I called louder. The sound of footsteps stopped behind the door. I called out again. The door opened partway. A woman's head appeared in the opening; she closed the door again, came back with another woman. One at a time, with curious glances, several people came in.

They all talked at once: it was the fault of that floozy who looked down on them when she was worse than anyone, shameless, stealing the man of a poor unfortunate like me, *poverina, so lieb*, I would have moved a stone; and he let himself be led around by the nose by her, he couldn't get over her, jealous since her boyfriend had returned from prison, he'd become so emaciated he looked like a corpse, at twenty years old, and her, one day she'd say yes to him and the next she'd stroll by him with that chump of an ex-convict without even saying a word.

The sun was setting.

I asked to be taken back to the hospital. It seemed like a huge task, opinions and counter-opinions, orders and counter-orders; four of them lifted me. God willing, I found myself back in the wheelchair in the courtyard. Not so much as a trace of him. We set off in a group of half a dozen or so, prostitutes and burly men, all outraged, watching over me like a baby chick.

The nuns welcomed me back, raising their eyes to the heavens. They quickly sent away my companions, who were still talking about the episode with two nosy women in the ward.

That night I came down with a high fever. I'd returned with the wheelchair soaked and the catheter expelled from my bladder. My buttocks were swollen, hard and hot as coals to the touch. I was delirious. God had done this so that I wouldn't become proud; by now I knew Him, I didn't get mad at Him anymore.

Schwester Luise, angry, watched over me all night, and the next day the other sisters were also surly and cold with me. Johann didn't come all morning. I managed to persuade the masseuse, who had a car, to go and look for him and bring him to me. In the afternoon one buttock split open and emitted copious putrid matter with an unbearable stench, yet the fever remained high at forty degrees. Johann finally showed up in the evening; the masseuse had not been able to track him down earlier.

I asked him if he still wanted to marry me. He made me repeat the question. He threw himself at me, covering my face with kisses, as when I was first injured, and asked me how come. I struggled to find an answer. Finally, we would leave, we would start from scratch, he apologized to a patient in a nearby bed who had come in that day, to an orderly, he kissed Sister Vincentia's hands as she muttered *"Armer Kerl!"*★ and looked at me resignedly. Then he hugged Schwester so hard that her bonnet went askew and she tottered.

We were all touched; I stroked his head. But, alone, I composed myself: despite the fever I had noticed his excessive enthusiasm, the shifty glances. I mustn't care, what mattered was that I achieve my objective, whatever the cost. "But," I said to Him up there, "make him pay dearly."

It was easy enough to obtain papers in those days. All you had to do was request them from a special office based on a simple declaration countersigned by four witnesses. You could readily give false information. That was what we did: Johann declared a Russian surname, and proclaimed himself Russian; I gave the name under which I had been working at the hotel and with which I'd been admitted to the hospital.

The following day, the thirteenth, we went to the Russian Command with two German couples as witnesses. Although the fever had subsided to thirty-eight degrees after my other buttock had split as well, my head was pounding and I felt myself swaying in my chair like an inanimate object.

The commander looked Johann up and down and called two soldiers, who stood at either side of him.

"Are you Russian? From where? Why didn't you report to your command before now?"

Johann, who in Russian was now Janka, explained that he had waited for me to be in a condition to face a long journey.

"This marriage then turns out to be convenient for you as well, otherwise I would have written you up." And in a harsh voice: "Were you SS?"

"No."

"Examine him."

The soldiers took Janka by the arms and led him away. The SS men had a tattoo like two lightning bolts in the armpit or on the shoulder or elsewhere.

★"Poor boy!"

Standing at attention, the soldiers declared that there were no markings; the commander wanted to check for himself. Then he had me brought into the house.

We handed over the German documents that the commander tossed on the table as if to say, I'm going to let it go, signed a register, and a military clerk issued us a certificate. The comrade commander seemed to relax, and slapped his fist on Janka's back:

"You're lucky that I'm already married," he shouted jovially in his deep voice, a quip that made the soldiers who were present laugh uproariously.

Then he completely ignored my spouse and, waving his arms to drive the soldiers out like chickens, asked me if this marriage was serious.

"No, pro forma, that way it will be even easier to get divorced." The commander thought as much: I wasn't meant to be tied down.

Wheeling me down the corridor, he informed me that the first convoy was leaving in a week and that meanwhile he would vouch for me with the hospital administration. If he could, he would personally accompany me to the first link-up point of the journey, Homburg in the Saar, because I was a courageous, honest, and, yes, beautiful girl.

Janka wanted to take me to the former barracks; I really had no desire to go there, but I felt drained, after the stress we'd been under, and conciliatory. They'd been expecting us, because we were immediately surrounded by men, women, and children who popped out of doorways on the four sides of the courtyard. Janka's eyes kept looking around for someone. In front of the flight of steps he wanted to pick me up to carry me upstairs, amid the applause and coughing of the onlookers, but remembering my last visit and thinking about the foul smell that the bedsores on my behind would have emanated when he lifted me up, I told him I didn't feel well and wanted to go back to the hospital.

As we argued, someone called him aside, greatly agitated. He came back to me ashen, beside himself: "She cut her wrists." And maybe because I remained unfazed, he repeated bitterly, "She cut her wrists." He stopped a twelve-year-old boy who came by: "Stay with her, take her wherever she wants," and he rushed off.

The boy planted his eyes on me, sullen. I promised him chocolate to console him, but nothing coaxed him out of his sulk.

When, along the way, I suggested that we bet on who would touch my hump as they passed by, his face brightened, and he had a good time maneuvering the wheelchair to make it easier for people to brush me hurriedly. I counted to myself: in odd numbers, they would bring me luck, even numbers bad luck. I tallied seven.

Back in bed, relaxed, in a daze, I thought of the great pains that I had gone to, running around, planning, doing everything I could to get to Russia, when it might turn out that I'd arrive just in time to die there.

Janka reappeared on the eve of the departure to pack my bags. After he did that, he knelt beside my bed and buried his face in my arm:

"You're strong, you'll help me," he murmured.

"From the Saar you can easily return, move someplace else with her where nobody knows you, Worms or better yet Mannheim, take back your true identity, marry her for real, and declare yourself to the Polish delegation in that city. She'll be happy to follow you. All I needed was to be allowed to join the convoy. Once I'm on the way your presence is no longer required."

He stood up again. "You're kind to everyone, except me."

The next day at ten o'clock the Soviet commander's car arrived. It was August 20 or thereabouts.

"Time to go," I murmured, saying goodbye to Sister Vincentia. "I'll see you again in ten years."

"God willing."

But when the moment came to get into the car, I hid my face in her apron and wept inconsolably, clutching the armrest of the wheelchair.

"*Versuch' zu beten*,"* she said to me, handing me the crucifix to kiss. Then, after a pause, she added: "Perhaps someday you will be able to find what your bizarre mind is seeking. Now lift your head, sit up straight, we two can't let ourselves go to pieces."

---

*"Try to pray."

The trip was pleasant. I sat in the captain's car, beside him in the back seat, surrounded by cushions. The chauffeur drove.

We followed a caravan of vehicles, one of which also carried Johann; the last truck was a prison van transporting Russians who, during German captivity, had enlisted in the SS. The Soviet Commands would search all over for them and, once they tracked them down, they'd arrest them and send them to the USSR, where they would be tried for treason by a military court.

The landscape was welcoming as we sped along toward the south. When we skirted a vineyard and I mentioned Italy, the captain looked at me, had the car stopped, and got out. He stepped cautiously into the vineyard and returned with two stalks, from which hung a few golden grapes.

"They're not yet ripe!" he apologized.

The men in the vehicles sang with commanding solidarity:

Esli zavtra vojna, esli vrag napadet,
Bud segodnia k pokhodu gotov!*

At the border between Rhineland and the Saar we were stopped first by the Americans and then by the French, where the occupation zones changed hands.

Toward dusk we entered the transit camp, in the vicinity of Homburg.

The captain kissed me on the cheeks three times, as is the Russian custom, and I clung to his neck.

I was put into an ambulance and we left.

The hospital was nearby, on a hill, a big complex with numerous pavilions, one of them for Russians.

VII

The Russians assigned me a nice room on the second floor with two windows, streaming with light, which Johann pompously adorned with double curtains of velvet and tulle, adding vases, books ranging from university

---

*"If tomorrow war, if tomorrow battle, / be ready to fight today."

physics texts to treatises on palmistry, and a large damask duvet that I kept and still use; the foyer was also at my disposal.

At first they gave me two Russian women, one for the day shift and one for the night, who took care of the cleaning, because the actual medical care was entrusted to a German nun and a nurse. Soon they replaced the Russian women with a young Polish girl of sixteen, an orphan, thrown into the camps, whose name was Barbara; blonde, with cheerful bright eyes, she was brisk and always ready to have fun. Barbara moved in to share the room with me, and Johann went into the foyer, where a bed was set up for him.

Johann had entered into the role of husband; he welcomed the Russians from the pavilion who came to visit me, and in the evening he appeared with friends from the transit camp.

He tried to get close to me but I pushed him away, overcome with fury.

I had actually expected his attempts to approach me, curious about how he would manage it and how I would feel, but when the time came, my awareness of my condition was stronger than my curiosity. By day I thought he did it *out of duty* and that he was secretly quite relieved by my rejections; that he persisted out of male obstinacy. I remained aloof. Nevertheless, I had them empty the urinary catheter more often, I combed my hair, I acquired some cologne, and even tried furtively moving my legs.

At night I asked myself: What if no other man would later feel any desire to come near me? If this were my last chance? He loved me from before and therefore may still feel a certain attraction. But another man?

And should I take advantage of a feeling kept alive by memory? Calling back the past?

Then too—a tiny glimmer of hope—who's to say that one day I might not find true love?

I had always had an invidious respect for this mystery. Even if I missed my last chance, rejecting it was worth it rather than taint my pure, passionate, mystifying notion of love. What could be worse than a fumbling, eager contact with Johann, what with the catheter that could be dislodged, the odor of urine, the sores, my deadened flesh, and me, maybe not even wearing the appropriate expression? A pitiful affair, no, better to save face with a detached air of having other things on my mind.

At this point my sense of irony took over and I began laughing under the covers at the thought of how worried he must be about contriving to be intimate with me.

I had a fever. When I washed myself and touched the wounds of the ischia, my fingers could feel two slimy grooves between hard ridges, right and left, which exuded a smelly serum, and I thought about Johann.

Before long he began to lose his patience; in private he gave me intentional looks, with that cold, masculine premeditation that arouses embarrassment and that humiliated me; abruptly he began scowling at the people who came to see me. Thinking that his change of demeanor was to prepare the ground for his departure for Mainz, already decided from the very beginning, I acted kind and sincere, out of spite, while watching him struggle between a sense of guilt and the desire to provoke an argument that would justify his flight.

One evening when he had gathered some friends in my room, a handsome, funny Soviet man named Piotr suggested that Johann give me to him; he was syphilitic and a marriage abstainer, he grinned, it was just what he needed. As if on cue, they all laughed and laughed.

Johann left the room, and when the door opened I saw him sitting in the foyer, by himself, his expression strained and vindictive. The Russian spotted him too and in a thunderous voice boomed, "Italian lady, marry me. What do you want with that phantom?"

The next morning Johann entered without knocking, his accordion over his shoulder.

"You're making a fool out of me. I'm leaving," he announced.

"It took you this long to get up the courage to tell me?"

He stared at me with hatred, and was about to reply, but turned sharply and walked out, slamming the door. It was August 30; he had lasted ten days.

One morning they found my bed wet, the catheter clogged, and there was no way to replace it, since the area was so swollen. I was leaking urine drop by drop, unable to retain any of it, and within days a single wound formed.

The pavilion doctor, a yellow-toned Caucasian, shy and taciturn, had them summon German specialists. I wasn't in pain but I was delirious due to my temperature, which had settled at forty degrees. No more urine was coming out. The skin of my lower abdomen was taut with a protruding lump.

Impossible to insert a catheter. After thirty-six hours I was urgently transported to the operating room, at night. I saw the flesh on my pubis split, making a rasping sound under the scalpel like fingernails on a blackboard; a jet of urine gushed out into the surgeon's face, but he remained serious as I burst out laughing before his glaring assistants, and a big rubber tube was inserted into my belly from which the pee would come out from then on.

After the suprapubic cystotomy I thought that if my body was of no help to me, at least it didn't hurt me. I could consider myself fortunate to be unfeeling. The poor thing was ailing and I was living peacefully, noticing its afflictions only because of the soporific effects of the fever.

Whether because my condition made me the center of attention, or because I felt free of Johann, I had a lightness about me, a vivacity; I kept everybody cheerful and they smiled fondly at me. Already by the beginning of September the visits had become nonstop: Russians from the pavilion, those from the camp, foreigners from the other wings.

I don't know how it popped into my head, but I had a nice multilingual sign made up, which I had hung outside the door. It read:

GOOD MOOD ROOM

with rates for visits below. A single session cost one cigarette or one chocolate per minute; there were also group rates. People paid upon entering.

Maybe it was the foreigners' clothing that had prodded me: they'd come out of the camps as beggars, and when looting the German warehouses and wardrobes they had not only grabbed what they could, but had taken a fancy to certain items of apparel. As a result you saw thickset farm girls wearing elbow-length gloves, simple peasants sporting flowered hats that didn't suit them, sensible men with wide-brimmed, floppy hats set roguishly on their heads, and young men in smart German military jackets and black ceremonial trousers wearing sandals and red cotton bandanas around their necks.

Barbara acted as my secretary. When someone knocked, she would ask his name and particulars. She then closed the door again and described him to me. We waited awhile to make ourselves seem important and already we started giggling. Then we let the person in. Seeing him come forward with a little bundle in his hand as he cast furtive glances at the curtains and books, we laughed like a couple of lunatics. The visitor glowered, and of course the more offended he was, the harder we laughed. We invited him to sit down and grandly offered him a drop of wine and a tissue-thin slice of black bread with a hint of jam on a tray complete with doilies. Our laughter was contagious because the person ended up joining us, and then I would ask him to help us draw his friends into the joke. The first customers became allies. The jolly Russian, Piotr, became fond of us and was soon the animating spark of our shared evenings: he publicized our services at the transit camp, and because he enjoyed a certain prestige, he always brought us new visitors.

"That Janka is as much a Soviet as I am Canadian," he told me with a wink.

Within a few days we gained quite a reputation. And if for once I couldn't come up with something to say and remained silent, the visitor laughed just the same, as if it were a new clever ploy. They showed up already having a good time.

I said a bunch of silly things. For example, I had a piece of a flaking, broken mirror, and Barbara would ask me why I didn't throw it away. For heaven's sake, it came from the ruins of Pompeii! And I would describe the find so dramatically and convincingly that a couple of impromptu antiquity lovers came to ask permission to examine it.

Every so often we singled someone out. I confided to an arrogant little Czechoslovakian lieutenant that my father was a municipal street cleaner and my mother a washerwoman, and that in Italy all the daughters of street cleaners know Latin and speak at least two modern languages.

Even an Italian priest, dressed in civilian clothes because of the Russians, came to see me, with the intention of hearing my confession and saving my soul. I embarked on a very learned philosophical discourse according to which God was perfect, owing to the detachment that left Him objective; that is, owing to His insensitivity.

"I wonder," I concluded thoughtfully, "if we won't one day find out that God is paralytic."

Usually, however, my only thought was to cheer people up. When former deportees came, looking defensive like everyone who's been buffeted by fate, a weight was lifted from my heart each time their expressions were slowly transformed, first with a charged, forced gaiety, then becoming naturally joyful, their faces untroubled.

Among the many who appeared were the regulars; to proceed in an orderly way, I wrote up a list where I numbered them in priority order. Barbara announced them to me by number. Some paid extra to get a better number on the list. Sometimes the Caucasian doctor showed up; urging us to sing, he sat apart, melancholic, to listen.

At first when someone asked me about my husband, I was left speechless; I forgot my new surname, and got our names wrong, his and mine. All in all, in front of third parties, my marital status seemed like just another game.

Often people wanted to see me to tell me their troubles and ask my advice; I told them what I would do in their place. Later, at night, turning over their difficulties in my mind, I was struck by such doubts that my heart raced. But, faced with their worried expressions, I answered confidently, undaunted. To lighten their spirits, I read palms. The way the lines on the palm were drawn seemed to me a geological history as precise as the formation of the earth's rivers, mountains, and valleys. I remember a clearly scored, very sound life line that inexplicably stopped, cut short, on the hand of a young Russian man with docile, startled eyes. I later learned that he had been in the SS. The soldiers with the red star and the comrades treated him like all the others, except that when they saw his vacant stare, they nudged him compassionately as if to say: Don't think about it. He had turned himself in voluntarily to the local Soviet Command after months of hesitation and hiding.

Barbara and I had gotten into the habit of consulting the tarot cards, which we obeyed religiously. Once they decreed that we stay in bed until two in the afternoon, and when anyone knocked, we yelled out, laughing: "We can't, the cards won't let us!" Another time they made us start our toilette at five in the morning.

That late September the weather was bad, we had no heating, and a windowpane was broken. In the morning the room was plunged in fog.

One evening there was a pelting rainstorm that, with its flashes of lightning and bursts of thunder, felt like a bombing. Can we go to sleep? we asked the cards. No. Is anyone coming? Yes.

At ten a fearful little knock. We sat up, yawning and numb with cold, and Barbara ran to open the door: it was Adamo, the pavilion's innocent. We hadn't even put him on the list, nor had we ever received him in a private session. We offered him a chair, we stuffed him; I read his palm where the lines seemed to have been wiped away, I played a little tune on the harmonica for him and he grinned, flushed and befuddled with pleasure. At eleven we consulted the cards: they answered yes. We said goodbye in a hurry; Barbara walked him to the door and turned the key in the lock. From under the bed she pulled out the box in which we kept our haul, which we gazed at endlessly and divided up each night.

Piotr traded the stuff that our customers brought us for clothing and money. Barbara favored silk stockings, transparent lingerie, and handbags of all shapes and sizes; I was given to long oversize shirts, woolen shawls, rabbit fur wraps, a Persian muff, as if I were going to the Pole. I still have a blue pleated dress with lace from that period. I had rings, necklaces, watches, and four thousand marks corresponding to forty thousand Italian liras at the time, a negligible sum in Germany, where a kilo of black bread gummy as glue cost sixty marks under the counter, but considerable in Italy and, I hoped, in Russia. Our good mood business was booming, all in all.

The nurse, who sized up all foreigners as potential boyfriends (though, fearing they would make fun of her, she bombarded them with questions and went from one letdown to another), gave me, in accordance with the custom followed by German girls of the time, a sampler with words she'd embroidered herself: *Humor ist wenn man trotzdem lacht.**

My fever fluctuated because, although the abscess at the entrance to the urethra had burst, a third wound had opened at the sacrum: I couldn't manage to get my body back on its feet.

On the last day of September a tragedy occurred.

In our pavilion, on the ground floor, there was a thirty-five-year-old German communist who was applying for Soviet citizenship on the grounds of the three years he'd endured in a concentration camp because of his

---

*"A sense of humor is being able to laugh in spite of everything."

views. His big brown eyes twinkled in his puffy face. He lived with an eighteen-year-old German girl, excited to be the free-thinking girlfriend of a political martyr. He taught them all, his voice now weakened, citing himself as an example and recalling the tortures he'd suffered. He made me feel depressed and I was ashamed to find him so annoying. For his part, he was rightly disappointed by my frivolity, given that I was a fellow internee—we would speak about Dachau together.

The girl's father, an invalid in a wheelchair, was also hospitalized with us, through the intercession of the former detainee. The elderly soldier could not forgive the young "idealist" for taking away his only child without marrying her; for him it was a dishonor, and he constantly accused his wife of not raising their daughter properly, of having ruined her. She, in return, asked him why he accepted the benefits that he received from his daughter's boyfriend if he hated him so much.

"Where else can I go?" the man shouted in exasperation. "With no house or job, you want me to kill myself?" She, for spite, turned to the young man, calling him "our benefactor" in front of her husband.

The two men were completely incompatible.

"What does he want from me if they persecuted him?" the old man whispered to me. "What can I do about it?" Deep down he thought the younger man was exaggerating, that he was a clever poseur.

For his part the young man expounded on free love, offering him abstract arguments, and told me he regretted the poor invalid's reactionary narrow-mindedness.

One evening, mother and daughter, who were also living at the Russian pavilion, returned home after a ride in the former internee's car, and had to break down the bedroom door, where they found the old man on the floor, dead.

He had slipped a noose around his neck, tied the other end of the rope to the handle of the locked door, and jumped off the side of the bed opposite the door, strangling himself.

We learned that the convoy would head out again on October 3. But the Caucasian doctor told me that the German urologist had vetoed my departure. Having already pictured the journey in my mind, I rebelled, ordering him to transport me together with the group of wounded men because I was a Soviet citizen and I would not submit to a German; what's more, I would file a complaint with the Russian Command in Mainz. In his unassuming, mournful way he spread his arms: he didn't feel confident taking me with him, I wasn't well, I could die, I had septicemia, I might as well know it.

The lengthy convoy, which had swelled in Homburg, set out toward Leipzig, which was the second link-up point. The transit camp emptied out and only Barbara and I remained in our pavilion, since she had refused to move on without me.

Piotr, who had repeatedly urged me to leave Janka for him, insisting "I'm getting better!," did not say goodbye.

The German doctors took over the ward. The whole atmosphere changed: silence, schedules, a medicinal smell. Barbara took down the GOOD MOOD sign, but Sister didn't like that and had it hung back up in its place.

As if they'd been waiting just for this, the Germans subjected me to medical examinations, X-rays, tests, hypodermoclysis, intramuscular and intravenous injections, enteroclysis, blood transfusions, and the scrutiny of a dozen physicians under the command of a Dr. Ort, a reflective man who was lean and wiry, his white hair closely shaved at the back of his neck.

I assigned the chief ward medic, Dr. Hasslocker, the first and last number on my now totally decimated priority list. I had been told by Sister that he was a staunch misogynist, due to having been deceived. I told him that he could trust me because, as a result of the malevolence of war, I was a kind of half woman, half fish, a modern-day siren who couldn't betray anyone—only cheer up passing sailors.

In the short breaks between one treatment and another, the nun would introduce me to a German man or woman in the room, urging me to cheer them up. People came to the good mood room from the adjacent wards. They were terrified of the Russians, who were stealing what little they had left after the bombing and looting; they started at every sound and leaped to their feet, wary. If they were needy but dignified, I gave them something to eat, because we were provided with abundant rations and now I even received packets from the French Red Cross stationed at the hospital; but if they vented their feelings uncivilly, I let them leave empty-handed.

At times I thought I had an advantage over those who were sound: precisely because I didn't really have a body, I was free from countless small anxieties and material insatiability.

As soon as the Russians left, a group from the French Health Bureau made an inspection tour. Speaking my mother tongue, I seemed to recover a little gaiety. Some of the men came to see me every day: they were very young, all volunteers, fervently anti-Nazi. They passionately discussed the Nuremberg trials that were beginning then, and they were irritated by the sight of the Germans, who, when they appeared, retreated, their expressions drawn.

The Frenchmen had it in for everybody, even the Allies, especially the Americans, the newcomers, but they also distrusted the Russians. As far as these young men were concerned, no nation had sufficient political conscience. I admired their zealous fervor; I thought about human suffering and I justified my reluctance to delve into political issues with the excuse that I was ill and had no stomach for hate.

In the evening, a German doctor, Ellen Marder, a thirty-year-old writer's war widow with three young dependent children, came to knit in my room. She was very tall, with piercing blue eyes and a heartfelt laugh. She said I had the unexpected in my temperament, like her fallen husband. She gave me one of his novels: it was the story of a young man who ends up dying. Its sense of loneliness and emptiness makes it one of the most desolate, disquieting works that I have ever read. It seemed that he had been very witty in life and sociable, hungry to live. He had left for the front with wholehearted enthusiasm. Of course, I thought, with that desperate restlessness in his heart, the war was the ultimate opportunity for him.

Neither the doctor nor the French volunteers admitted that I was paralyzed.

After ten days of treatments, examinations, lavages, and restorative therapies, Dr. Ort, articulating the words clearly, said he could attempt surgery. The two affected vertebrae, by slipping and overlapping, had formed the hump with which I was afflicted; certainly it would have been better had I been operated on and put in traction six months earlier, at the time of the trauma. Now the osseous callus was such that he could not guarantee he'd be able to decompress the medulla. In any case, he wouldn't touch me without my explicit written request.

"Could I die?"

"Possibly."

"Could I be healed?"

"Perhaps."

I won't describe the excitement that came over me. And here I thought I had accepted the paralysis, that I had discerned its positive aspects. I saw the hand of God in my non-departure. This is why I had been left here . . . to be healed. All night I thought about Italy with rapture, desire, a sense of belonging. The earlier reservations had only been a defense. In my imagination I was already standing, I was running, my face in the wind, my hair blown back, my chest constricted by the air rushing by. Divine Providence. Sobbing with gratitude, I hugged and kissed the pillow as if it were God. How could I have lived without walking? How could I have tolerated such an abomination? It had all been a nightmare.

But the dawn, the usual gradual clarifying light of dawn, brought me back to reality. I could die. No, because by now I was somewhat of an expert on nature's discriminations and I knew it was not my time. And what if I did die? What did I think lay before me? Though I had attained a certain knowledge and understanding of life, overcome a few trials, there was nothing left for me to do in this world. If that were so, however, I would die even without the surgery.

I had risked death for others. Couldn't I risk it for myself? I talked about being strong and at the first real test I was pulling back.

That morning I signed the request for a laminectomy.

The surgery was scheduled for October 20. It was the sixteenth.

Unexpectedly Johann showed up. He'd gained some weight, looked neat and tidy, and brought gifts that included a Telefunken radio.

He'd learned of my decision and was against it.

The doctors declared that they could not act without his consent.

I hurled the blankets to the floor. "What do you want from me? Look at me! Don't you see the condition I'm in?"

The rubber tube protruded from my sunken lower belly, between the angular projections of my hips.

Johann turned pale.

"And you'd like to be cut up again by these people, for their experiments? Former Nazis?"

"I want to live. I'm sick of having this corpse for a body."

"Stop it! You're more alive than I am."

There was no way to get him to give the green light, his "no" became more and more authoritarian, not subject to appeal; he moved around the room with that vain air he'd had earlier at Mainz when he'd been having the affair with that German girlfriend of his and I hadn't suspected a thing.

I was seized by a trembling fit of impotent rage. True, my cunning in having used him was coming back at me, but I had never gone so far as to interfere in his personal affairs. How dare he? If it weren't for the bladder complications that occurred after he'd gone, by this time I would be in Russia, alone. Nor in a month and a half had he bothered to ask whether I was alive or dead, though he had left me racked with fever from the septicemia that was already spreading through me, and he knew it, the Russian doctor had spoken to him. What gave him the right now to dictate the law to me, like a master? By what justification?

I summoned the French volunteers, who came immediately. I'm one of them, I thought.

After listening to me briefly, they urged me to move quickly before Janka appealed to the Russian manager of the Homburg camp for permission to take me away. Four young men came to my aid, hovering in front of the pavilion and making an occasional sortie to check around and reassure me, with protection straight out of a romance novel. A German doctor was able to divert Johann, with the pretext of taking him to see Dr. Ort, and the nurse led Barbara away with her.

It was the morning before the date set for the operation. One of the Frenchmen stood guard down the hall, another in front of my door, while two others quickly dismantled the tents in my room, emptied the closet, and gathered up my bags, then put me on a stretcher. When everything was ready, the Frenchmen on guard loaded the stuff on a little truck, and the other two lifted me on the stretcher and carried me down the stairs to the outside, running along paved drives, gravel paths, and flower beds to the far side of the hospital, where the French pavilion was located. Every so often, when they thought they were being followed and speeded up, I pitched and swayed as I lay on my back on my stretcher, looking up at the pale gray sky.

"It's like the rape of the Sabine woman," we said, feeling as though we were playing some sort of prank.

They took me to a ground-floor room, spacious as a salon, and quickly settled me as they argued heatedly on a plan of action for my protection. And to outdo the Russians, they placed green plants on the windowsill and a warm brazier next to my bed. I was content. They stood guard outside my door in pairs, taking turns every hour, while a young girl named Madeleine, black hair and blue eyes, stayed with me, ingenuously enamored of her mission.

In the afternoon I heard Johann's angry voice and the undeterrable voices of my bodyguards. He went away and the French guys, describing the exchange to me, beamed about the victory they had achieved. But when they saw him return, armed, wearing a Soviet army uniform, they hastily recommended a change in tactics: they could not forbid him to enter.

He came in. We were alone.

"I am a Russian soldier," he pronounced.

"And I'll have the French take me to Mainz, and I'll report you to the Russian captain as a Polish spy."

"And I, as my last wish, will ask to be shot before your eyes."

After that we started laughing. And as if there had never been the slightest disagreement between us, we planned what we should say to the Russians if they looked for me: given the delicacy of the operation, I'd preferred to have it done with people from the land where I'd been born, and with whom, especially after the anesthesia, I could more easily make myself understood.

He, however, insisted on the condition that he be able to be with me, otherwise as a Russian soldier he knew what he had to do.

"Your blackmail works as long as I want to go to Russia."

"You don't want to anymore?"

"I'm not sure." I was thinking of the outcome of the operation. "But someday I'll go there, even if it means waiting twenty years. They were the most supportive people in the camps and they've been good to me."

I stayed up all night. If I had to die, I wouldn't waste a single minute of life. The French played the accordion and Johann performed Cossack dances squatting on his calves.

Only Barbara, who had later tracked me down, wept, sniffling in bewilderment.

"Why did you leave me? I stayed behind for you." Then she'd get distracted, watching the group, but would suddenly remember herself and, screwing up her little face, cry, "Now what am I going to do all alone?"

VIII

Dr. Ort, when he cracked the bony callus of my hump, did not find the medulla sawn in two, as might be expected after months of friction against the vertebral points, but in the shape of an S compressed between the two segments of the spinal column that had slipped and overlapped each other; it was only *partially* crushed. He extracted the wedged plates and, after four hours of surgery, had to stop at straightening my back, leaving the injured vertebrae side by side rather than pulling the two sections of the spine together to make them meet, because my heart couldn't take any more. He fashioned a bed of plaster in which I was laid.

The first thing I remember thinking is that another wall had collapsed on me, and no one was helping to free me.

I felt pain for I don't know how long, an overwhelming, dark pain disproportionate to the huge, heavy body sunk in the bed like lead.

Between the comings and goings of the Frenchmen, swift as wolves, Johann leaped up every time I moaned, handing me this or that, anxious to guess what I might need, but I never wanted anything and I took it out on him.

Dr. Marder later told me how, at the time of the operation, she had indicated the bed with me already under the anesthesia and sighed, "It would be better if she never woke up again."

At which Johann blurted out, "No!," his eyes filling with tears. "No, Luzi, no." The foreign words escaped him. "Here"—he had finally tapped his forehead with his fingers—"here . . . *solang der Kopf lebt.*"*

They'd found him outside the operating room after waiting four hours with bated breath, his eyes asking: Is she alive? Then he collapsed; they had to keep him going with injections.

One morning, touching myself, I found that I was skinny and small, not voluminous as I felt. I had a belly, two legs, two feet. Inside there were thousands of pins that were triggered whenever someone brushed by my bed. Sometimes a leg would leap into the air, tugging on the medulla like a cord; when I placed the palm of my hand on it, it released. I even had a nail stuck in my belly. I went to pull it out, but I squeezed a rubber tube: I remembered the suprapubic catheter and left it alone.

As soon as I dozed off, I woke up worried that my body was no longer there. Yes, it was there. At times I gave in to the joy of pain: an injection was a stab; other people's touch a jolt on bare nerves; I moved the catheter up and down to exacerbate the burning in my flesh.

I discovered early on that I could move my pelvis a little: I wriggled my rear end uncomfortably for hours in the plaster bed, enjoying the sting of the pins gone haywire. There was no chance I would ask for sedatives to ease my suffering! Which earned me a reputation for exceptional resistance to pain.

In short, the relationship between my paralyzed body and the rest of the world was not yet that of precise discrimination by touch, but a subjective one of pleasure and pain.

But it was nice to clench my teeth and tighten my fists, so tense that I shook, spasmodically, mentally willing my legs to move: they remained inert. I dreamed that I was running. I would wake up panting and each time I had the sensation of having arrived a fraction of a tenth of a second too late, just long enough for my legs to stiffen back up. I thought I could feel them becoming immovable.

The director of the French Health Bureau, Madame Martineau, her gaze responsible and concerned, came each day to inquire about my progress and to give me instructions:

*"As long as the head lives."

"The destruction is accomplished in an instant, but to restore what was done takes time and patience. *Ne soyez pas pressée, ma petite Lucette*, don't be in a hurry."

In part to distract myself from the pain, I took to reading and listening to the radio again. I heard the vibrant voice of the news commentator give long accounts of the Nuremberg trials, which my friends talked about with horror, and I with endless anguish.

Some Germans sought me out, but the French didn't take kindly to this.

The nun from the Russian pavilion came to see me and with a conspiratorial air asked me to put in a good word, if possible, so that at least two Germans in serious condition—"simple soldiers called to arms, who did their duty and nothing more"—might be admitted to the hospital; they had arrived in a freight car full of wounded Germans expelled from the Strasbourg university hospital; she wouldn't even ask for the others, but those two! She was asking in the name of Christ, it was an act of charity. "They'll die soon," she added as a final endorsement.

The French, courteous but brusque, arrived to let me know that I had no business dealing with such matters: many foreigners were still breathing their last on straw pallets.

Besides, they took care of patients on their own, and they did their utmost to exclude the Germans from assistance, even clerical support, which the atheist Russians had granted them:

"We are prepared, we don't need them." And to the doctors on their rounds, they politely said, "Thank you, *merci beaucoup*." Then, when they were alone: "When will the French doctors get here? And our priests? Headquarters in Paris doesn't realize the importance, the political urgency for us . . ."

The hospital was in fact filling up with sick and injured foreigners of every nationality, some skeletal, weighing about thirty kilos, disoriented, waiting. I met several Italians who, having heard about me, introduced themselves warmly.

"We're Italian!" they repeated, shaking my arm vigorously, gripping my hand.

A gaunt, elderly Venetian, with a severe duodenal ulcer: "When I had a good stomach," he mumbled, toothless, "I never had anything to eat. Now that there's enough to feed an army, I can't even tolerate baby food."

Nonetheless, he was serene. I chatted happily with him and he told me about himself: the story of an emigrant, with two world wars behind him, a prolific wife, children scattered around the world to find work, German captivity.

Barbara had been picked up suddenly by the Polish Command in Saarbrücken.

The German communist had gone elsewhere because his girlfriend and her mother had been put out of the hospital. Moreover, behind the formal deference for his past, he himself felt the silent accusation of being German:

"We are now the detested race," he sighed, saying goodbye to me.

During that month I spent time with a Ukrainian student whose name was Dunja Babiak, a pale, undernourished, eager girl, with renal tuberculosis, with whom I exchanged grammar lessons, she Russian, I French. Applying ourselves to our studies gave us a sense of purpose in those uncertain circumstances.

With the Italians I relaxed: they cooked spaghetti with tomato sauce; from their walks in the fields they brought back hedgehogs, snails, and chicory, which we made into tasty dinners.

Johann had left, I don't remember when, nor does it matter any longer. As much as he hit it off with the Italians, that's how much he disliked the French, whom he considered corrupt, arrogant, and politically at fault, along with the British, for having deceived Poland with their guarantees at the time of Gdansk, leaving the country prey to Germany and ultimately trapped between the Nazis and the Bolsheviks. Even while we were staying in the Russian pavilion, he would sometimes mutter under his breath, "I am a true Pole: all I do is change masters."

Piotr would deride Poland, a nation of dandies, in front of Johann, and he could not react. But I hadn't been aware of Johann's torment.

"I gave up my country for you," he muttered bitterly, and, though he'd always boasted to the Germans about being Polish, showing off the *P* in his buttonhole like a decoration, I didn't believe the strength of his feelings and in my heart accused him of merely employing rhetoric meant to disguise his intention to return to his girlfriend.

"Your master is still the same," I replied. "Still German, only the gender has changed from masculine to feminine."

His time was divided between Mainz and Homburg as though between two families. He spent a few hours with me, arriving on a motorcycle, mostly to make sure I wasn't doing anything rash. Practically speaking he lived with the other one, Grete, and in a couple of weeks he'd flourished again and regained his strength: he appeared clean shaven, dressed with care, wore clean underwear and an air of well-being for which I did not forgive him.

I could very well confess to not being his wife, a sham, unconsummated marriage, and regain my freedom, but I was not reckless to the point of closing my eyes to the risks of such a revelation. The mood was uncertain. The Nuremberg trials, in addition to prompting a resurgence of rancor against the Germans, had also triggered a state of political surveillance among us foreigners, a kind of reassessment of our positions, and had repressed national spirits. Each group observed that its people would never have committed the atrocious crimes of Nazism. We Italians, suspect due to the Rome-Berlin axis, asserted that we were good, humane, incapable, even in a climate of dictatorship, of falling into the fanatic zealotry of the Nordics, thanks to a Latin critical sense, to the restraint of a skepticism attributable to millennia of civilization and historical experience.

My need to go to Russia had dissolved by itself, almost without my being aware of it. When I looked at my future in the Soviet Union, I had a new feeling of cowardice, as if, given the paralysis, my independence had a limit that was called Italy.

Johann informed me that as soon as I was able to withstand the strain of the journey, we would leave. We would stop in Warsaw, where, introducing me to his parents and consulting them, he would decide what to do. Freshly shaven, he spoke soberly, looking around slowly, like a husband; and I watched him, wondering who he was; I didn't know this man, we had nothing in common he and I, and the idea of living beside him seemed inconceivable to me.

In order to silence me, he occasionally alluded to the fact that he was a Russian soldier and sometimes appeared in uniform, though he only stayed a few minutes, as if uneasy. His going back and forth, acting on his own with no rules or regulations, did not convince me.

Olga, buxom, dark haired, and vivacious, was a local fifteen-year-old girl who had taken a liking to me as a model to imitate. She judged Johann to be a shady opportunist and made it her duty to follow him with an intent hatred; for this reason she quietly left for Mainz, on whatever form of transport was available—rather rash, considering the times—and looked for him, relying on information she'd wheedled out of me. She found him in a room at the former barracks, sitting on a bed in which his Grete was lying, wearing a U.S. Army uniform. At a loss for words, Olga blurted out that I had sent her there from Homburg to ask him for an alarm clock! She returned that same evening, pale but proud, to report the outcome of her investigations.

So he was not a Russian soldier; who knows what scam was behind his changing uniforms. He must certainly have to avoid attracting the authorities' attention to himself: he no longer intimidated me. I started smoking again. I put on lipstick.

After about ten days during which I didn't see him, he showed up in my room one afternoon when I was talking with two Frenchmen and the Italian with the ulcer. Noticing my displeasure, he announced that I was painted like a French whore and that I was ruining myself by hanging around with those people. When I shrugged, he slapped me, actually just barely a tap, but my French champions intervened and the Italian as well. Johann then ordered me to say that he hadn't hurt me, that he was my husband, and that the others should back off, but I remained silent. They came to blows and he punched the Italian squarely in the stomach, knocking him to the floor. At a whistle from the first two Frenchmen, their comrades rushed into the room and immobilized Johann while one went to get the handcuffs. He appeared dismayed and so meek that his keepers relaxed their hold, but then he unexpectedly wrenched free and climbed out the open window.

They searched the hospital grounds to no avail.

The Frenchmen transferred me up to the second floor for fear that he might return through the window and beat me at a moment when they weren't there.

That night, in bed, alone in the second-floor room, I heard a thud; a figure dangled in the shadows outside the window, occasionally bumping against the wall, like a hanged man, then stepped onto the windowsill. I heard the screech of diamond on glass, the clink of glass shattering on the floor, felt a cold draft, then the handle turned and Johann leaped into the room. He turned the flashlight on and then off, and sat down on the edge of the bed. "Get it through your head that I will get to you no matter where. I'm not the same as I was before. Your viciousness has made me a man." In the darkness, in the silence, I could hear him breathing hard. "Now listen to me: either you take it upon yourself to ask to return to the Russian pavilion, by tomorrow, in which case I'll wait for you as long as you like, I'll be here for you—"

"In Mainz," I interrupted.

"In Mainz or wherever I choose, no one can forbid me to get elsewhere what I can't get from you."

"Or?"

"Or the following day I'll take care of things myself and we'll leave for Russia at once. Answer me."

I replied that I was paralyzed, I couldn't see my way clearly, I needed time for so many things, I couldn't think about him.

"You bring up the paralysis when it suits you."

"I learned that from you."

He left through the window, leaping onto the same tree on which he'd been perched earlier, watching as the French searched the grounds before moving me to the very room facing it. Then he slid down.

The following morning, blindfolded, I underwent a neurological examination with pinpricks, pinches, hammer taps, hot and cold stimuli applied to my body and my legs, articulations of the lower limbs. It turned out that while I had no epidermal sensitivity, the deep sensitivity of movement, temperature, and touch had returned, attenuated as if through a cloth and altered. I again felt bowel and bladder stimuli but I was not yet in control of those organs. My intestines were not working properly. A doctor suggested applying an artificial emission duct for stool, a tube made of special material with a tap at the end to open and close at will; it would eliminate the filth and reduce the risk of infection due to there being excrement in my wounds.

Johann's words about the experiments of former Nazis came to mind;

having had a laminectomy just a month ago—I told the doctor—I had no intention of undergoing further surgery for the time being.

"We'll talk about it again," the doctor said, smiling imperturbably and confidently.

The following morning, three Russian soldiers came marching into my room: two of them, one being Johann, carried a stretcher; the third one, in a helmet, indicated me.

I rang the bell as the agreed-upon alarm signal. The blue eyes of René Payoux, the "old man" (twenty-three years old), stared through the upper pane of the door. Shortly afterward a platoon of Frenchmen arrived, followed by René.

They asked the Russians to please wait.

I whispered to René to ask Johann for his documents.

Shooting me a sarcastic look, Johann handed the Frenchman his papers and waited, legs spread, hands on hips. I insisted on checking for myself: the document seemed in order, complete with stamps and signatures.

Dr. Marder was summoned.

When she saw Johann, she laughed, relieved: he knew very well that I couldn't be taken away like that!

"Do you know what Luzi did to me? She incited them to throw me in jail, and it's not the first time."

Frau Marder didn't want to know about it; what was between us was none of her business. She judged people on their own merits: "I know each of you individually. You, Janka, are a fine young man who does not want Luzi to die," she said, reminding him of the day of the surgery.

"Luzi must understand that I'm serious," he said, already upset.

"From this moment on Luzi will understand that, don't worry, I myself guarantee it."

I asked Johann to forgive me; I promised to change my ways with him, to be decent. I wept, partly because of what I was saying, partly due to the fright I had had.

He had to leave that night for Mainz, where, after Olga's "incursion," he had enlisted in the Soviet army as a volunteer reservist. When I decided to leave, he would be demobilized, provided he perform military service in Russia in the city where I would be hospitalized. I asked about the captain; he'd been gone for some time, they said he'd been called back to Russia.

The two Russians who had come with Johann, however, would not bend; they had received orders to take me away.

The French demanded a written mandate.

The soldier with the helmet, who was a sergeant, presented it.

The French declared that they had to submit it to their superiors, who were now absent, and that they were not authorized to hand anyone over.

Since I was married to a Soviet soldier, the French really had nothing whatsoever to do with me.

Nevertheless, I was in territory under French jurisdiction from the moment I entered that room, which the Russians had invaded illegally.

The French had initiated these illegal actions the day they'd taken me away from the Russian pavilion.

No, because they had carried me away with my full consent.

But I was a Soviet citizen.

But I had purposely taken refuge with the French to apply for a divorce, which would release me from Russian citizenship.

Johann pricked up his ears: "Good to know."

Both sides threatened to protest to higher authorities.

The Russian with the helmet put a stop to it, saying that they would return the following day with instructions so clear that no one would dare prevent them from carrying out their orders. He turned to me with contempt:

"And you too, comrade, will have to answer for your conduct. One who has the honor of being Soviet defends it."

They went out with their sturdy, martial gait. I called out to Janka, who followed them without looking back.

That same afternoon a supervisor from the French Health Bureau arrived: he had received a protest from the Russian Command at the transit camp in Homburg.

The Frenchmen were harshly reprimanded for having arbitrarily abducted me, instead of having me obtain the transfer through regular legal procedures.

In the evening an officer from the French police came to tell me that the diplomatic incident was assuming such proportions that, because the French were in the wrong, they were obliged to hand me back to the Russians with their deep regret.

Finally, at ten in the evening, Jean, one of my friends, informed me that the next convoy to Russia would leave within forty-eight hours; he had just learned, unofficially, that I was on the list and that Janka was assigned to guard me and some Russian SS prisoners, on pain of death.

At midnight, Frau Marder, bundled up in scarf and overcoat, having been informed of everything, came to offer me a solution: before dawn a freight train with two cars of wounded German soldiers would pass through the Homburg station headed toward Bavaria. I could leave with them; the German Red Cross nurse who had assisted me at the Russian pavilion was willing to accompany me. If I wanted to go, I had to prepare quickly, covertly, because the French, having committed to the Russians, were obliged to hinder my escape. She handed me my medical records, but they were labeled with my Russian surname. I told her the story about the false names. It was now two in the morning, and she hurried off as the nurse stealthily entered to pack the suitcases. At three Frau Marder reappeared with a duplicate of the documents labeled with my real name, which I hadn't used in fifteen months. She also left me the other copies, so that I would have duplicate documents available. "Just in case," she said.

At five in the morning a German ambulance came to pick me up, along with the nurse and the luggage.

The French soldier on the night shift, Jean, also got in; he stopped by the stockroom, from which he took five cartons of provisions supplied by the Red Cross and gave them to me. The ambulance set off again.

At the station I was carried onto a cattle car and settled on the straw in my plaster bed, surrounded by wounded Germans, by the stench. It was still night when the train left, with a screech of clanking iron. I had not said goodbye to my friends, not even Frau Marder, no one, and they had all aided and supported me with no questions asked, without a word of thanks.

IX

The first morning in the cattle car, in the hovering stench of rotting flesh, ointments, and urine-soaked straw, interrupted by waves of cold seeping through gaps in the floorboards, in the dim light, among the skeletal features of the wounded on their backs and the listless faces of those seated against the walls, swaying as the train rattled along, in that lifeless silence broken only by moans and cries for help, I thought I might die.

Each lurch of the train reverberated in a stabbing pain in my back and legs, and I clutched Tobik tighter to my chest.

This was my second time traveling in a cattle car. Back then I was hale and hearty, the thought of pain did not defeat me, and my companions, though emaciated and enterocolitic, had an intense resilience about them as a result of the unjust offense, an aggressive look, a scornful twist to their lips. Now I was broken, no longer rebellious but anxious and fretful, and my new companions were destroyed inside. I will always be with those who are suffering, I thought.

Someone begged for a cigarette, and I remembered Jean's cartons. I asked a little man in a shirt, who was leaping about spryly among the bodies, to divide the contents among the soldiers. The distribution sparked a brief animation that quickly faded.

A handsome young man, his head wrapped in bloodstained bandages, who lay beside me on the straw, turned his feverish eyes to me and stretched his mouth in a grimace: finally I realized that he was smiling at me.

At a rural station two German girls in a uniform I'd never seen before stormed into the car. Supporting the wounded men's heads, the girls helped them drink, their faces so intent that it seemed not a drop of the watery broth would be lost.

A French soldier looked in and the nurse, wedged among the bodies, shouted at him: "*Italienerin! Italienerin!*"

I spoke in French and got a food parcel.

I wanted to share it, but someone called out, "It's a long trip, you'll get hungry, keep it for yourself."

The others agreed. The train creaked along on the rails. With a small voice that rang out crystal clear in the din, I ordered the nurse to throw the parcel out the door, into the fields. They protested.

From then on, at every godforsaken station, I had them carry me out of the car on a stretcher and take me to the first-aid office, where I demanded food and medicine by presenting my Italian papers (the Russian ones were hidden at the bottom of the trunk).

By the second day of the trip we had come to know one another, as well as the wounded in the other car, to whom we sent part of our haul.

To have some fun, I began speaking in the Rhine dialect, acting the part of a peasant girl from "*Menz am Rhoin*," Mainz on the Rhine. The bloodied young man next to me was my boyfriend; the nurse, my rival, had shot him out of jealousy; there was a mayor, a parish priest, and other characters as the wounded men gradually joined in the performance, each of them passionately playing his role.

The situations became so convoluted and comical that we had to lower the curtain to catch our breath.

In the evening we sang in unison for a long time:

> *Wo die Nordseewellen rauschen an den Strand,*
> *wo die gelben Blumen blühn im grünen Land*
> *und die Möwen schreien grell im Sturmgebraus,*
> *da ist meine Heimat, da bin ich zu Hans.**

When we paused and particularly when the train stopped, we heard, like a response, from the adjacent car:

> *Im grünen Wald, dort, wo die Drossel singt,*
> *und im Gebüsch das muntre Rehlein springt,*

---

*"Where the waves of the North Sea crash against the shore, / where yellow flowers bloom in the lush green countryside / and seagulls screech raucously in the storm, / there is my native land, there I feel at home."

wo Tann' und Fichten stehn am Waldessaum,
*verlebt'ich meiner Jugend schönsten Traum.**

Absorbed in intoning the spacious words of sea and forest, we forgot the cramped car, the jolts, the festering wounds, the hunger, the shivering.

The third morning a wounded man went into a coma and died. In the afternoon, another one had a seizure.

At the first stop I had them call an ambulance, saying I didn't feel well. I got in with the German in crisis. At the hospital in town they assigned me a bed that I gave to him. The doctor objected, it could not be done.

Why not? What could happen?

He could lose his job.

"That's why you crushed a defenseless people," I said, "so as not to lose your job."

Because the order, which he made me put in writing, was from a foreigner who seemed so confident, the doctor accepted my protégé.

At each village, with the same ploy, we found hospital care for the wounded men who, unable to bear the hardships of the trip, became delirious or unconscious.

With the gold that I possessed, and a few bills from the German soldiers, we bought cognac.

On the fourth night my boyfriend reached for my hand, squeezed it, and blinked repeatedly; his big gray eyes told me that he was dying. The nurse alluded to a concussion. I stroked his hand all night, I kissed him, whispering that I loved him, that he should sleep, I would watch over him; whenever I fell silent he pressed my fingers until I started whispering to him again; by dawn his hand was sweaty, getting colder and colder, his features assuming a certain purity, like that of a child. He was seventeen years old.

The door was partly open; in the distance, in the hovering mist, the gleam of a lake in the dawn light could be seen. It was the *Selbstmörderin-nensee*, called the lake of suicides because of the vast number of women

---

*"In the green forest where the nightingale sings / and from the brush a sprightly doe leaps, / where pines and spruce stand at the forest's edge / I spent the sweet dream of my youth."

who had jumped to their deaths during the first months following the end of the war.

At noon we pulled into the Munich station, where the train ended its run. It was raining under the dark dome of the sky. It was November 23, 1945.

I was loaded into an ambulance, by myself, without having had time to thank the German Red Cross nurse who had cared for me during the entire trip.

I hadn't seen Munich in nearly a year: I watched the city pass by through the window of the ambulance: rubble, chunks of wall, interiors of houses split open like stage sets, neighborhood after neighborhood deserted, even more dismal beneath the heavy, steady downpour that washed the stones.

X

It was night and I was still alone in the emergency room of a large modern hospital on the outskirts of the city, in the dark, not having eaten since morning, with an aching, full bladder, bowels on the verge of voiding, exhausted from five agonizing days on the freight train, from being moved painfully on stretchers and ambulances, from the strain of talking and contrived cheerfulness. With no word of my luggage. And Tobik looking at me with the shiny button of the one eye he had left.

Finally, someone came in, turned on the switch that lit up the white room, and busied himself at a small table where he started opening and closing drawers, leafing through charts. He wore a hospital coat and had a bushy gray mustache.

I called to him and he rudely told me to wait, not bothering to look at me.

I kept an eye on him and when he seemed to look up, I smiled slightly, but he didn't see me. He went out.

I vented my feelings with Tobik; we were really unlucky, the two of us, but he shouldn't worry about it. I sensed a presence behind me and twisted my head around: the man who was here before was back in the room without my having noticed. Standing at the head of the wheeled gurney on which I was lying, he was studying me. He smiled, suddenly interested in me, and, pointing to the stuffed dog, asked how he was. Encouraged, I explained that the poor little dog was hungry, cold, and sleepy: he had traveled in a cattle car and was paralyzed as a result of a bombing.

"Poor thing!" He nodded and, pushing my gurney, said, "Let's go."

Corridors, elevators, courtyards, padded doors that sprang closed on me; my head was spinning, in a daze. I opened my eyes and saw that a chubby nun was now pushing me. Men in white with a knowing air surrounded me, glancing hastily at my papers. A small female figure in a striped robe slipped in front of me and stole the shoes that were lying beside my feet, on the blanket, because in the past month I had become obsessed with shoes and I always kept a pair on hand. In the distance, someone was screaming.

I was taken into a small, narrow room, crammed full of strange beds with high sideboards on either side, replete with fastenings; they laid me on one of them.

The fat nun, muttering that I was disgusting, grimy, filthy—wasn't it time she introduced herself?—set about washing me along with an orderly. They lathered me up, turned me over, and brusquely applied medication to my wounds, not very gently. I cried out, asking them not to be so rough, but they harshly ordered me to be quiet and went on in even more of a rush, cracking my plaster brace.

Someone tossed a metal bowl on my nightstand.

Half-asleep, I thought I glimpsed sly, cunning, imbecilic faces moving around me under the greenish glow of the night-light.

I was dozing when a young nurse with a gracious tone, the first civil voice in that place, bent over me:

"Is this cute little dog yours?"

"Yes."

"What's his name?"

"Tobik."

"Is he paralyzed?"

"Yes," I sighed, and added: "Most of all he's sad, terribly sad." My eyes wept, watching the gentle face of Schwester Gisela.

"You're not crazy," she whispered in my ear. "Ring this if they bother you," she said, putting the call button in my hand.

During the night the person in the next bed moaned voluptuously at first, then began growling, seemingly fighting hand to hand with someone. The high sideboards that separated us prevented me from seeing. All of a sudden someone bent over me, brushing my face with an asthmatic breath. I rang. The nurse came running and turned on the overhead light. My neighbor straightened up: it was a beautiful girl, her eyes bloodshot, foaming at the mouth, her wrists bloody; a firm, rosy breast peeked through her torn gown.

"*Lieber Gott!* You got untied again! How did you do it? No, I won't tie you, no, but you have to be good, come on now."

The girl calmed down. Whispering in my ear, the nurse warned me to be careful, she was dangerous, the only one in here who was, they were to transfer her any day, she was syphilitic, an Italian from Milan.

When the nurse went out, I heard whispering in the back of the room with giggling, sighing, little cries.

My neighbor had set her sights on me:

"*Wer sein du?*" Who are you, she asked in German, in a guttural voice.

I replied in Italian. She didn't understand. She spoke only a mutilated German with all verbs in the infinitive. But the Italian sounds must have pleased her; she remained kneeling on her bed until the early hours, gazing at me and listening to me.

I spent the following days trying to convince the doctors that I was not insane. They listened to me smoothly, complacently, they petted my stuffed dog, pursed their lips, pinched my chin, tugging it this way and that, then quickly went away.

During a medical examination, irritated, I pulled a doctor's chin myself, asking, in his own absent tone, how was he, hmm? poor thing.

I planted my eyes on those of the fat nun and the disagreeable orderly, and gave them instructions in a calm, arrogant voice, staring at them the entire time they stayed around me; they became more gentle, their expressions softened.

But I got along better with the crazies. They loved me with a primitive love, awestruck, jealous of one another. I had to take care not to give the impression that I had favorites, when in fact I favored my impetuous neighbor, who punched everybody and dominated them with her unbridled vitality. Yet all I had to do was call her in Italian and she settled down docilely. They had a need for human kindness, for consideration, for affection, that gripped my heart. There were a few who were treacherous, with a bestial gleam in their shifting eyes. All nine of the women were cunning, scornful, lewd, and very belligerent. They didn't understand my words, but they sensed the spirit behind them. I had to stay alert, like an animal trainer with his tigers. They demanded justice from me and resorted to my judgment for every little tiff; they did nothing but squabble heatedly.

I remember a Romanian Jew, a loner who didn't bother with the others, who would constantly talk to herself about the Nazis and the gas chambers. As soon as the doctors entered followed by the aides wielding syringes, her whole body began to tremble and she would back away and hide under her bed, giving out earsplitting screams. A nurse had to inject her with something to knock her right out; they would then drag her out, inert, throw her on the bed, and put a straitjacket on her. This scene was repeated twice a day. The doctors watched the operation with a shrug, ill at ease but indifferent.

One morning I couldn't resist and told them that they should be ashamed, that the crazy women were better than they were. Demented as they were, at least they weren't killing me. In fact, they protected me.

The syphilitic girl put her hand over my mouth, terrified. I pushed her hand away. "Let me talk, honey, I know what I'm saying."

Whereas the high and mighty doctors, in their lucidity, have no conscience, they think they're superior owing to that glimmer of reason that they can't even use with humility; a fine feat on their part, terrorizing a frightened woman.

My eight loonies had formed a close circle around my bed and were silent, lying in wait.

Let the doctors try to deny that since I'd been in the ward the madwomen were calmer; the nun herself had acknowledged it, and it had only been six days so far.

A short time after the doctors left us, there was a knock at the door and Johann appeared, emaciated and dusty. He came around and hugged me:

"Look where you are! What they've done to you!"

I kissed him back, my savior. "You found me! How are you?" I said, touching his face; it was really him.

On the morning of November 20 he had returned to Homburg, to the French pavilion, to take me away and had learned of my escape. He had abandoned his Soviet uniform and left to follow me. He'd looked everywhere: when he heard about me by chance from the station master, he'd been able to narrow his search. He'd been in Munich for three days, visiting all the hospitals, this was the last one, he'd been going from ward to ward, presenting his Soviet military papers, and here I was.

I hugged him to me, closing my eyes.

When we'd calmed down, we considered the future. The afternoon was advancing and, increasingly distraught and resolute, I realized that I was seeing him for the last time; the more he talked, the more difficulties and complications crowded into my mind: the impossibility of it. I would never marry. But I didn't dare tell him so. Enthusiastically he described our life together in Italy. He darkened only when he mentioned that he would be forced to remain Russian until the day he died, bound by false names. That observation gave me my chance: he absolutely had to return to Mainz, making sure he didn't get arrested by the Russians for desertion, and obtain his Polish identity certificate at the German registry office; he could use the landlord at the hotel where we'd worked together as a witness—a man whose warty nose quivered like a rabbit's and who, for money or for fear, would get him any document he wanted. We would travel to Italy as Russian spouses, so that he could cross the border, but once there, we would be married with our real names.

He was reluctant, however, and we argued about it all night. Finally, he estimated that he could make it there and back in two days. He wanted me to caress him at least, but I begged him not to insist.

"Afterward, though, we'll work out a way to make love. Promise me?" he said.

"I promise."

"Another separation for forty-eight hours, but it's the last."

"Yes, the last one."

"Why do you say it that way? Are you falling for me? Does it bother you that much that I'm going away?"

"Yes."

"You're sorry that I'm leaving," he repeated contentedly. "Now do you believe that we're good together?"

"Yes."

I looked at him, and at the crazy women wandering around on tiptoe waiting for a sign from me; every now and then I called one of them over and kissed her. Johann's face tightened.

Finally, he left.

Shortly afterward two men came to lead my neighbor away. The girl sensed something; she grabbed the bedside table and hurled it at a nurse, kicking. She jumped on me: "Mama!" she shouted, sobbing, clutching me: "Ma-maaa!" And she bit me.

I kissed her like a daughter. As they brutally tore her away from me, I screamed worse than her and thought I would faint.

But I had no time to faint. Johann would be back in two days; I had to get away before then, flee again.

I was summoned to an interview at the ward doctor's office.

A doctor and a lady from the bureau were there. We talked a long time. They were outraged over the error; traumatic paraplegia; the misunderstanding of the stuffed dog was clarified.

Without explaining anything, I told him that for personal reasons it was essential that I leave within twenty-four hours. The woman seemed to hear me with emotion. The next day she informed me that a "white" train of Italian prisoners coming from Russia, stopping in Munich, would be departing for Italy that very night. She had booked a place for me.

That night an ambulance brought me, with what little baggage I recovered, to the hospital train. I was settled in a bed in the infirmary car. I was the only woman among the travelers and male Red Cross staff. Throughout the trip, war veterans from Russia came by to greet me. They elected me their mascot.

The following morning, on December 4, 1945, we crossed the Brenner Pass. The veterans in my car had hung Tobik from the ceiling as a lucky charm, and stuck a lit cigarette in his mouth.

Rome, 1961

PART 3

FIRST ARRIVAL IN THE THIRD REICH

IN THE CH 89

Gradually I had developed a curious image of myself. I thought I'd been a slender girl, with delicate wrists and ankles, who had gone through hell without changing her appearance. But I also saw myself as having a button nose in a rather round face, my features somewhat jovial despite the thin lips and sunken eyes.

If I recalled scenes of anger or terror, I pictured myself as a small, restrained figure amid a mob of frenzied people.

Perhaps I carried this easygoing girl in my mind so that she might transform, seamlessly, into the "half woman, half mermaid" creature I now believed I had to turn into.

But the face that appears in the photograph of a factory badge and on the last fake ID card that was issued to me in Mainz, before the wall collapsed on my back, is a different one: a sturdy face, heavier, not given to dreams. In that smooth face of an eighteen-year-old, with her childish cheeks and wiry hair, there is a willfulness discernible in the downward turn of the tight lips, in the dark eyes staring starkly at the lens.

Looking at those photos, I reviewed in my mind the circumstances in which the student from a good family had become that disillusioned, stubborn girl during the first months of living in a Lager, as a worker at IG Farben.

I

The first few days, Lucia felt relieved: life in a camp was less harsh than what it was rumored to be. True, the nine-by-five-meter barrack housed twenty-two women, but it was used only for sleeping, from eight in the evening until four in the morning. The rest of the time was spent in the factory, in the canteens, in the street. If her barrack mates had been a little more well-bred, they could have adapted even in such a cramped space.

The two-story bunks, paired side by side lengthwise like double beds, faced each other in two rows, with the heads against the walls and the feet toward the center of the room. Six bunks were lined up two by two along one entire wall and five on the opposite wall, at the end of which was the door. Stacked against the wall, between the heads of the beds, were metal lockers in which each internee placed her stuff, padlocking it protectively. The space between each pair of bunks was one meter wide. Quarrels broke out continuously between the women on the mattresses below and those on the upper pallets, to appropriate the space from which to get to the lockers. The women below argued that those above could open their top lockers while lying on their beds, without blocking the aisle. The women above argued that the aisle belonged to everyone and that they intended to come and go from the lockers to the stove without having to climb up and down each time. Squabbles also arose over the stove in the middle of the room, in the roughly nine-meter-long aisle between the two rows of bunks. Someone had a roasting potato stolen, another a strip of paper she'd left to dry for rolling a cigarette, another a mess-tin of water being heated; no one wanted to move away from the stove lest some roommate carry off her property.

Other scenes took place over the small sink behind the door. It was impossible to go to sleep before ten o'clock at night as long as the bright overhead light was shining on the eyelids of the women in the upper bunks, not to mention—at varying times—the intrusion of a night guard pointing his flashlight in your face, the barking of the two German shepherds who roamed around on the gravel between the barracks all night, and the frequent air raids.

At four in the morning people would get up more tired than when they went to bed.

Lucia couldn't manage to get to sleep, especially thinking about the long predawn walk to the factory, five kilometers from the camp.

Since the second day she'd developed two open sores on the big toe of her left foot and one behind the heel of her right foot, caused by chafing from the wooden-soled felt boots whose scratchy seams protruded on the inside, rubbing the flesh raw at every step. The chamois leather shoes with the cork lifts, with which she'd left home, had become riddled with holes while traveling; they'd fallen apart completely in Villach, on the Yugoslav border, the day she'd spent nine hours standing in the snow, along with hundreds of volunteers and those seized in roundups, waiting outside the station for a train that would enable them to continue on.

Her companions wrapped their feet in sheets of newspaper, but they wouldn't give her a piece even when she asked them nicely.

"I got them for a fuck," a French girl told her, waving two newspapers under her nose. "You'll just have to earn them yourself, my dear miss, using this," and she'd patted her on the behind, substituting the gesture for the word.

"Watch what you say," another French girl said, nudging the first. "She's one of them."

"I don't think so," a girl named Martine had intervened. "If she'd come here to spy on us, she wouldn't have revealed herself the first day. Instead of introducing herself as a Fascist volunteer, she would have posed as one of those from the Italian Resistance caught in a roundup and we would have swallowed it."

"Still, she's one of them," the girl with the newspapers insisted. "At the factory they assigned her to monitor the machines, like a German."

"Because of class solidarity," Martine said. "She's hardly a worker like us. She's studying at the university and they take that into account."

"She's got you spellbound too, apparently."

"So tell me something." Another girl stepped in, hand on hip. "Since you're always getting on our nerves with your anti-Nazism and your stories about class, I can give it to you straight, right? Seeing as you trust the college girl"—she smiled tightly—"how do you explain the fact that someone who speaks several languages like her doesn't work in a nice warm office, or sleep on a real mattress in a sturdy house, and instead comes here to get mired down in a barrack with us, huh? You don't see anything fishy about that? Trust me, sweetheart!" she ended shortly, laughing in her face: "I'm on my guard."

Martine flushed. In her mid-twenties, she was petite, with a lean body, brown hair cut short, a thin, pointy nose, and lively, penetrating eyes; her thin moist lips traced a red gash in her pale face. With a shrug, she climbed up to her pallet and from up there said, "Fine, let's do a test."

The five Italian women in the barrack were more apprehensive. They whispered among themselves, but as soon as Lucia was watching, they fell silent with shifty smiles meant to be ingratiating. They allowed her to get past. They tried to assume a courteous tone when she spoke to them but they never spoke to her first. Two of them, from Bergamo, in their thirties (one of them pregnant), were always together and fought over the same guy: a puny, prim man in his forties who was the only one of the internees to have an umbrella, which he never seemed to part with, not even in the coed lavatory before dawn.

Another inseparable pair was a worker from Sondrio and an apprentice hairdresser from Rome, both sixteen, who shared every crumb and whispered late into the night on their adjacent mattresses, with muffled giggling. The last of the Italians was a gaunt, taciturn young woman, about twenty-five, who slept on the upper level of a corner bunk, facing the door. Raised in an orphanage, she'd been adopted at eight years of age by an old man who'd satisfied his desires with her. When he died, the old man had left all his property to his grandchildren and not even a handkerchief to the little girl. She'd worked as a domestic here and there until she left for Germany as a volunteer; there she'd found a position in the Lager by taking up with a Croatian sous-chef for whom she worked as a dishwasher. She was the only one who had margarine, salami, jam, which she sold at a high price, sometimes for goods but preferably for money, which she counted scrupulously, thoughtfully, as if she regretted not having asked for more. She would re-treat up above, on her pallet, hiding her earnings on her person as she pulled out the key to her locker, which she kept around her neck. She refused to open the locker unless all the room occupants withdrew behind the stove, on the other side of the barrack. She would shut the door as soon as one of them took a step forward and stare at the intruder with feverish eyes. With incredibly swift gestures, she would unwrap, cut, and wrap the agreed-upon goods, close the padlock, slip the key around her neck, and suddenly relax, sliding down to the floor, where she handed the buyer a little bundle, her big gray eyes both modest and kindly in her pinched face.

At times Lucia was struck by the "pettiness" of her companions, by their "attachment to the little things," by their "small-mindedness." It's more than miserliness, she thought, it's meanness. And, almost not admitting it to herself, she thought that her parents weren't all wrong when they said, "Stay where you belong, forget those pipe dreams. You can't get too familiar with people of the working classes. They don't understand, they don't appreciate things. The only thing you can do is try to educate them a little. Otherwise they'll turn against you, that's what you'll get."

"They're people like us," she'd told her father. "Of course," he'd said, smiling, "poor souls, it's not their fault if they lack refinement. It's like being humpbacked! Do you want to become a humpback too?" "Why is it necessary to become a worker," her mother had insisted, "when you can be much more useful in a ministry office? You're capable of performing tasks that are beyond the reach of those who are ignorant. Believe me, everyone must keep to his place."

It was true that the women in the barracks had no dignity: when faced with the *Lagerführer* and the guards, they assumed a servile expression. And they let themselves be treated like animals. For example, men and women were forced to undress together in common washrooms.

Lucia went to the office of the *Lagerführer*, a tall, robust man in his fifties who always went around in a ski sweater and boots; he carried a whip that he switched through the air as he walked, always followed by two German shepherds.

She requested that he grant the women washbowls, one for each of them, so that they could wash freely in the barrack, away from men's eyes.

"I would even give you two if you'd like," the *Lagerführer* replied, amused, "because you're a well-bred girl and have a sense of decency. But those women? Dregs, understand? Scum!"

Lucia stubbornly dug in her heels and was given washbasins, if not for all the women in the camp, at least for herself and those in her dormitory. With her arms full of twenty-two enameled basins, she entered her barracks.

"You see?" she cried, victorious. "If you address the situation, you get somewhere," she told her stunned roommates: "I explained to the *Lagerführer* that the internees are not animals."

Both the French and the Italian women were thrilled by that turn of affairs and the following day, when the wakeup call sounded, they set about washing up in the barracks.

"Good for the college girl!" they laughed. "She did well." "*They*'re the pigs." "No dashing out in the cold, just hop out of bed and there you are, a nice wash-up in a warm room." "A real godsend." "Filthy swine!"

The twenty-two basins took forever to fill from the trickle of water that dribbled from the single tap in the tiny sink behind the door, from which you could barely drink; and twenty-two women could hardly find room to wash up in the narrow aisles between the two-story bunks that crowded the room. Only about a dozen of them had managed to wash when the muster call rang out from the camp's loudspeaker, signaling that it was time to assemble in columns for departure to the factory. The notorious basins ended up in a pile outside, behind the barracks, where they remained to peel and rust.

Lucia then realized that at four in the morning, wakeup time, everyone entered the common lavatory with a sullen look and heavy-lidded eyes, their faces dour. They soaped up and rinsed quickly, paying no attention to their neighbor, man or woman. And later, the next month, she thought that even if someone were to make a racy comment or a double entendre, what was so awful about that? It put people in a good mood, it raised their spirits.

But in truth she found it especially revolting to wash with those people who thought nothing of blowing raspberries or clearing their throats to spit in the sinks. It hadn't been decency that motivated her as much as revulsion for such coarseness. She wouldn't admit it to herself, but her companions had noticed her disdain. And once the story about the basins spread through the camp, the French and Italian men started calling her "Miss Turned-up Nose!" "Who do you think is looking at you!" "Who wants to see you anyway!" "You'd like that, wouldn't you?"

Offended, Lucia stood on line in the camp canteen at seven in the evening, in the press of sweaty bodies reeking of machine grease and boiled vegetables; she felt her stomach turn. Afraid of vomiting in public, filled with bitterness and contempt, she went outside, forgetting about the camp's two German shepherds, known for sinking their teeth into anyone who went around alone or stepped beyond the boundaries.

She was running toward the barrack when, about thirty meters in front of her, she saw a dark form emerge from the night and leap toward her in the snow. She was so angry that she stopped abruptly and snarled at the dog in German: "Go on, come a little closer. Try it."

The animal came to a halt a couple of meters away from Lucia, who could hear him panting. "Lay one paw on me and I'll strangle you," she said, her hands like claws in front of the shepherd, who, grinding his teeth, shrank into the shadows, ready to rush forward at the girl's slightest movement.

"Cowards, all of you," Lucia muttered as she went past, never taking her eyes off of him. "Swine."

The dog padded slightly behind her, with silent steps. They kept an eye on each other. Lucia walked slowly, constantly glancing back at him: fur bristling, teeth and pupils glinting, ears flattened back, he kept growling and wagging his tail. Still watching him out of the corner of her eye, she slowly entered the barrack and, once inside, glued her face to the window. The dog immediately rose up and showed his fangs, wrinkling his nose in anger. Seized with fury, she shot out the door. "Beat it," she ordered the animal, again in German. "Shame on you, you're just like them. Taking it out on a helpless girl. I could use a whip, *raus*, get out of here." And she added more softly: "Go bite your masters." With tears in her eyes, no longer looking at the dog, she went back into the barrack, starving, and realized that she had pissed her pants.

II

Indeed, the protagonist of this story had been assigned light work on the fourth, topmost floor of the Ch 89. All she had to do was monitor various kinds of thermometers placed in a machine with cylinders, pistons, and looping tubes, and record the temperatures every hour on a nearby blackboard. If the mercury rose past a certain red line, she had to lower a switch applied to the thermometer, which turned on a light in a panel exposed in a long glass-enclosed booth suspended over the equipment as if on stilts in which the foreman sat. The latter would then join the girl and turn some cranks, explaining their function.

The ground floor of the factory held huge, greasy black machines, whereas on the upper floors—galleries accessed via small iron staircases— the machinery grew smaller, more complex, and cleaner as you gradually made your way to the top.

From the fourth floor, leaning against the railing, Lucia often looked out onto the dissonant, diverse screeching of the assorted gears and equipment, watching the workers on the ground floor. They labored under faint electrical lighting in a building whose windows were permanently darkened, and Lucia had to get used to the dim light to make out what the men below were doing. At times, when her eyes tired from the effort, she would lose herself in contemplation of the metal beams that supported the black sloping glass roof. Every so often a glass pane glittered among the window coverings, stirred by a silent breeze amid the din of the engines.

When she got too bored between one temperature check and another, the girl pretended to go to the toilet and would sneak out of the shop and wander aimlessly among the factory shops. She watched the French prisoners who worked at the lathe in a hall smeared with pitch, adjacent to the Ch 89, where she was employed. She lingered to watch Soviet prisoners carrying huge sacks on their backs, Russian women rolling heavy bins to the tracks of the internal railway. One afternoon she ventured a bit farther and had to ask a guard on a bike how to find her way back to her shop. When she returned to her post, there was no German there to question her. Moreover, Lucia noticed that the Germans greeted her politely, but

seemed to avoid her. The foreigners instead looked her up and down scornfully, even though she greeted them with a smile whenever she stopped to watch them work. The French prisoners spread the word when they saw her coming: *"Les collabos se baladent,"** someone snickered. The Italians from the next barrack became especially animated: "Enameled washbowls!" one sang out, as a peddler would, or "washbasinnns!" another called. The only ones who didn't deign to look at her, as if she were transparent, were the Russians and the Poles, those wearing a triangle that read OSTEN or P in the buttonhole of their coveralls.

The first days of her stay at the Lager, Lucia was nauseated by the way the workers ate, noisily slurping up the soup from the spoon, spilling it on themselves, licking the mess-tin, jokingly pretending to belch as if they were full, telling vulgar jokes. "Ill-mannered" people, as her paternal uncle used to say; he was chief engineer at the land reclamation works in the Pontine marshes and, to hear him tell it, had taught hundreds of unskilled laborers and peasants to "behave properly at the table."

Hundreds of workers took turns at the IG Farben canteens, which during the midday break had three staggered, one-hour shifts from eleven to two, but friends would agree to eat together at the same shift and couples met up on the same bench.

The canteens fell into two distinct groups. The buttonhole triangles, the Russians and the Poles, to whom the Slovenians had been added, ate in the canteens of the Slavs, behind the factories along the canal. Perpendicular to the canal, along the internal railway, were the canteens for "Westerners": Italians, French, Belgians, and Croatians. At the time everyone thought in terms of nationality and internees tended to congregate with their fellow countrymen, but everyone ended up going back to the canteen he'd happened to go to the first time, together with those from his work shift. Little by little the nationalities mingled, though the division between peoples of the East and West was a given.

Even in the uninterrupted flow of men and women who lined up at the counters, bumping and colliding with one another in the narrow aisles between the tables before reaching the desired spot, the diners always

---

*"The collaborators are taking a stroll."

noticed when a newcomer appeared. Knowing glances as, one by one, heads turned toward the intruder.

Lucia had not gone unnoticed. "Spy," someone would hiss, blocking her way, or "*provò*" (for provocateur), but in general they merely kept their distance, leaving a certain vacuum around her. Only Martine sat beside her, pretending not to hear the stentorian voice of Etienne calling across the canteen, "Martine!" Etienne, a war prisoner, was her boyfriend; a stocky young man with an alert face, like her he was from the outskirts of Paris. To follow him, Martine had come to work as a volunteer in Germany.

After a couple of futile calls, Etienne decided to come to their table. Lucia tried to talk with him, but the young man gulped down his soup without saying a word, raising his lively brown eyes to Martine every now and then with a look that was both questioning and challenging.

Word had just spread about the "washbowl crusade" when a smelly, hairy old French vagrant—crawling with lice, with snot in his nose—sat down beside Lucia in the factory canteen. Martine was not there.

Lucia changed her seat and the vagrant, dispiritedly shuffling his feet, followed her, sitting close beside her again. The nearby tables fell silent as heads turned to watch.

The next day, at the same French-Italian canteen, sitting down at a table with a full bowl, Lucia saw that the lice-ridden man wasn't following her. She suppressed a sigh of relief and reached into her jacket pocket to get her spoon. But it wasn't there. She rummaged through the other pockets of her jacket and thick twilled trousers, growing more and more anxious, until, looking at the table to see if she hadn't already put the spoon there, she sensed an unusual silence. All eyes were on her. Bastards, she thought, they stole it from me. As courteously as possible, she asked a man if she could borrow his spoon. He shook his head no and kept looking at her. The same refusal from a woman, then from another. An Italian man came forward to offer his spoon and was shoved back. A wall of men in coveralls blocked him from view. The tramp, who was sitting at a table across the way, got up with a toothless smile. After hawking and spitting on the floor, he mumbled, "Want mine?" and held the spoon out to her. "Thank you," Lucia said, smiling at him, and, grabbing the spoon that she could see was filthy, dipped it into the soup. She tried not to touch the spoon with her lips, while at the same time nonchalantly bringing it to her mouth and swallowing.

When she finished eating, she rubbed the spoon with sand under the tap at the back of the canteen; it was so encrusted with dried particles that no matter how hard she scoured it they wouldn't come off. She nearly vomited the soup that surged up in her mouth, swallowing it all over again. She made her way back to her table and returned the spoon to the tramp with a beaming smile: "If you lose it someday," she told him, "I'll give you mine." And in a sudden fit of hatred she turned to the others: "Shit-faced bastards!" she shouted.

"Same to you, Fascist," Etienne muttered under his breath.

"Hey now!" Alain scolded her; a French prisoner of war, around forty years old, he normally never spoke. "You shouldn't swear, missy. What would your mother say?"

The others snickered. They had formed a circle around her. Lucia began elbowing and shoving her way through and Alain grabbed her arm. "Or," he said with a straight face, "are you by chance becoming a human being?"

But Lucia tore away from his grasp and, with tears of hatred in her eyes, said scornfully as she went past him: "If I don't submit to the dogs, I won't give in to you either."

That evening she ran into Martine in the barrack: "You ducked out today. You all hate me, you want to crush me. You're the *collabòs*."

"It's gnawing at you, huh?" Martine replied grudgingly, red in the face. "You want the privileges of being a Fascist student without the drawbacks. Fancy that, look how crafty this mama's darling is!"

"What privileges? Don't I live like the rest of you? Don't I work in the factory like you? Don't I eat the same slop?"

"What! You liked it so much! The first two nights, you even got a second helping. You savored it as if it were caviar."

"I was starving, don't you understand? Three days of traveling, numb with cold, with nothing to eat."

"Go on. You said yourself the food here seemed more than adequate, I heard you myself, you know, with my own ears."

"That's right, I thought it would be worse, so? At home we got by solely with the ration card because my mother was against the black market. She made me focaccias with bran and I devoured them, okay?"

"Stingy too, your dear mama."

"No, my mother did it out of patriotic love."

"Then you're also a fool," Martine said curtly.

"Don't try to sidestep the issue again," Lucia parried. "Do you know that my father is undersecretary of state for the Republic of Salò? If I wanted privileges I wouldn't be here now."

"Good to know. So why did you come?"

"To find out the truth."

"And did you find it?"

"I'm doing that, and at my own risk, without taking advantage of my status."

"That's what you say. If you must know, your foreman at the Ch 89 is up to his ears in demands the Germans make on your behalf. But he has orders from above to 'let you adapt,' to cut you some slack. If anyone else took the little strolls you take through IG Farben, he wouldn't get away with it like you do. And your ridiculous little washbasins, if one of us had asked for them, do you think she would have gotten them? A slap in the face, that's what she'd have gotten. So shut your mouth and go peddle your philanthropic bullshit to someone else. Why do you try to excuse yourself? You are who you are."

"I'm not a *collabò*."

"Then why do you keep pictures of Hitler and Mussolini at the bottom of your duffel bag?"

"So you went through my locker. And I'm supposed to be the spy, right? Thieves and spies, that's what you all are."

"Report me to the *Lagerführer*."

"I'll do that."

Martine climbed up to her pallet, pulling the covers over her face.

Lucia tossed and turned all night. She had completely forgotten those pictures in her bag (how could she have?). She couldn't sleep, in part because of hunger. Almost all her roommates had secret supplies they managed to get somewhere, but she ate only the food that was doled out at the canteens. And at first she had even relished it. After only two weeks, the more she wolfed down, the hungrier she remained, despite even finishing the chickpea purées and the turnip and potato soups that Martine left in her plate. It occurred to her that during the argument with Martine the other French women had not intervened with their usual sarcastic remarks. They'd listened in silence.

III

The following morning she felt sick at heart. I'm eighteen years old, she thought, and the only ones who understand me are German shepherd dogs who obey Nazis.

She was walking to the factory in a column and realized that only in the shop did she have any peace. As she approached the IG Farben plant, she noticed that the burnished bricks gave her a sense of familiarity, and she stepped up her pace toward the plumes of smoke billowing from the smoke-stacks. Inside Höchst, the column slowed up as it moved along the buildings; the smell of minerals filled the air as engines purred. Groups peeled off to report at their specific gate.

In front of an open area, between massive apartment houses from the early twentieth century, Lucia passed through an imposing, iron-plated double door, followed by the eyes of two guards in glass watchtowers, and punched the factory card, heading for the shop.

That morning she didn't leave her workplace for a minute.

But at noon, as she was walking to the usual canteen, the idea of being back among those harsh faces made her hesitate. She decided to go and eat at the canteen with the people from Bergamo, an entire community of laborers and unskilled workers who never split up. She was already on her way there when she convinced herself that she would be subjected to the same rejection all over again by the new group. Suddenly she decided to join the Russians. She would show the Italians and the French that she was more democratic than them. They snub the Russians, she thought, they think they're more evolved than the Russians. I'll show them.

She didn't know that any association between the two groups of people—those from the East, including the Slovenians, and those from the West—was severely prohibited by the authorities. She set out behind the factories and entered one of the canteens for Russians and Poles, finding herself among hundreds of bundled-up bodies, loud male voices, women's shrill cries, and hands offering bowls.

She made her way to a table and, from the first spoonful, noticed a rotten taste in her mouth: there was no comparison with the soup they gave to Westerners. It was all mashed turnips without a hint of potato. And the dark bread was so gummy it stuck to the fingers.

She left the soup there and headed for the factory administrative center to complain. She demanded to see the director himself. The clerks were taken aback by her assurance. After being shown to a waiting room, she was taken to a large, bright, comfortably plain office. She walked toward the gentleman sitting behind the glass desk; dressed in light colors, he was thin with closely cropped red hair and sunken eyes behind thick-lensed glasses. Enunciating the words clearly, she told him that the food given to the Russians was inedible. Director Lopp just looked at her.

"I understand," the girl continued. "You can't believe it. Come see for yourself," she insisted.

Herr Lopp's expression was more and more puzzled. When he rose to his feet, he seemed thinner and younger than when he was sitting down.

"You speak German properly," he said. "Where are you from?"

Lucia explained: "I studied it in school, and as a child I used to spend vacations in the Tyrol and in the Black Forest."

"What did you study?"

"Humanities and philosophy at the University of Padua. My family moved north following Mussolini's government."

"How old are you?"

"Eighteen and a half."

"So young and in college?"

"I skipped two grades, in elementary school and high school."

"Good for you." Then with a brief bow: "And now you may go."

"Oh no." Lucia stood her ground. "I came about the Russians' food. The soup is a disgrace, it contradicts the Nazi-Fascist promises of civility."

"How long have you been in Germany?"

"It will be two weeks tomorrow."

"*Achso*," he replied, "I see." He sat down again behind his desk: "I will take care of it," he said, and waved his hand for her to leave.

"Director," Lucia said excitedly, "as you know, only the equality of peoples can construct a thousand-year peace."

Herr Lopp pressed a button on his desk and, when a clerk appeared at the door, pointed his chin at the girl. The man, his posture stiff, touched her arm, ushering her out. They passed modest offices, one after another, with long tables and built-in bookcases of unfinished maple. The clerk led her to the service exit, a spiral staircase at the back of the building.

As payback, the day after her complaint to the management, Lucia again showed up at the canteen for Russians and Poles.

Men and women sat at the tables with the rancid turnips, their unwashed bodies and clothing crowded together; letting her eyes slide over the long rows, she spotted a pair of deportees' jackets folded up on a bench in a corner.

She tore the cloth triangle that said OSTEN off of one of them—the label the Russians had to wear in their lapel—and later pinned it to the jacket of her coveralls.

On the fourth day she ate with the Russians and Poles—where she met Johann—Lucia was picked up and taken to the director's office. Herr Lopp shot up. Motioning to the guard to leave, he approached the girl and told her that she was in danger of going to Dachau if she didn't settle down.

Lucia replied that threats were not necessary, what was needed was justice for all foreign workers hosted by the Third Reich. She walked out on her own initiative, satisfied that she had beaten him to it. She ran to the canteen, but was immediately stopped and brought back to her shop, without eating. The foreman informed her that she'd been transferred to the ground floor outside the factory; there she was to load and unload blocks of sulfuric acid frozen at seventy-eight degrees below zero, together with the Russian prisoners and the Warsaw insurgents.

He added, "Since you love them so much, go work with them."

Not a week passed before Lucia's hands were cracked and covered with lacerations that stung day and night; she also had lesions on her chest from carrying the big blocks of sulfuric ice that seeped through her clothing and rubberized canvas gloves. Her feet were scraped raw, inside the wooden-soled felt boots, and oozed a foul-smelling fluid. The chafing at each step made the pain unbearable.

It was cold and wet, early March '44. Russian soldiers, Polish partisans, and Lucia loaded and unloaded in the rain.

In a silence empty of thought, Lucia felt at peace when passing a block from hand to hand; it seemed like a gesture of solidarity. She was finally accepted. Though every so often a Russian prisoner motioned for her to take that OSTEN off her jacket.

The blocks were stacked on a truck or sometimes on a wagon drawn by two prisoners, as though they were horses.

Afterward the workers had to go and unload them from the trucks in the little station fronting the canal, and carry them in their arms to some factory that always seemed to be on the opposite side.

Lucia sometimes had to walk more than a kilometer with sulfuric ice against her breasts before reaching the intended shop. Accompanied by the clanking of the machinery, she ran among the IG Farben plants, blackened buildings that seemed to turn their backs to the deserted streets.

From time to time a group of ragged people appeared and disappeared, sucked into a dark doorway.

Some days, when the siren for meal time had sounded and Lucia rushed off to eat, away from the area where the canteens for the French and Italian workers were, where she had eaten at the beginning, she felt like heading over that way and would slow up. But she kept going, ordering herself not to turn around. Let the soldiers on guard duty see that she didn't give a fig about not being able to enter. Actually, she had tried, but the Nazi officer had denied her access, threatening to transfer her from her Lager to that of the *Osten*.

Out of sight, Lucia stopped to stare at the murky, oily water of the canal that slowly swept IG Farben's discharges to the river. Viscous clots floated on the surface. She told herself that perhaps she should break all ties with the "Westerners" and move to the *Osten*, even though their camp was so jam-packed that they slept thirty or forty to a dorm. The Italians and the French would realize that they had wronged her with their pranks.

But the *Osten's* camp was even farther away, and three more kilometers worried her when the five kilometers that separated her camp from the factory already seemed endless.

Sometimes the French prisoners called to her when she passed by their factory, empty-handed, on the way back from transporting some sulfuric ice. But Lucia turned her head.

At the end of her shift she felt almost sorry to leave IG Farben. As they formed into columns outside the plants, she sniffed the pungent odors of the damp night; all she could hear was a muffled hum after the deafening rumble of the machinery that lingered in her ears.

Six weeks had passed since her departure for Germany when she finally received two letters from her mother at the same time. In the evening, after returning to the camp, they were handed to her by the *Lagerführer* during roll call.

The *Freiarbeiter** were allowed to write a note to their families every fifteen days, on an aerogram obtained at a window at the camp canteen, and then mailed, open, in the mailbox provided. The delivery was recorded, and if the note happened to get lost, that mail opportunity was missed.

As soon as she'd arrived at Höchst, Lucia had written to her parents telling them not to worry about her, the food was sufficient and the barrack well heated. She had then bought, in exchange for her scarf, two aerograms from the pregnant Bergamo woman; in those notes she had alluded that she was learning a lot from the experience, said that her shoes had fallen apart, and asked them to please send her the pair of mountain boots that she'd left at home. In another aerogram that she was later allowed, she begged them to hurry up and send her shoes and boots and *stuff to eat*, adding that it was impossible to understand things from a distance.

Glancing at the postmark for the date it had been sent, Lucia opened the first letter from her mother. In her slanted, effusive handwriting, her mother replied that she was glad to hear from her. She had never doubted that what was said about the Nazi concentration camps was slander, "so it seemed pointless for you to endanger yourself this way to verify truths that were not in question." She had spent "atrocious days" since her daughter

*Volunteer workers.

had run away from home without saying goodbye, leaving only a farewell note on the empty bed, until she'd received the first sign of life from her. "Now that I know where you are," she wrote, "I'm a bit calmer." Worried most of all about the bombings but also about the cold, she added, "My dear daughter, bundle up when you go out." And "I urge you, Lucia," she concluded, "uphold your dignity."

The letter was signed "your mother, anxious about you."

Only late that night did Lucia decide to open the second letter from her mother.

The writing was more imperative (the bars crossing the *t*'s, the accent marks, small clues). "My dear daughter," it began, "you are not being well treated. Why don't you come home? Meanwhile, you have only to go to the Italian consulate in Frankfurt and talk to the consul himself about getting you a more suitable job. The consul will understand." The letter ended with: "Let's at least hope that this experience has served to make you see that everyone must keep to his own kind. In the words of Manzoni, 'experience human affairs sufficiently enough so as not to attach too much importance to them.' See you soon, your mother who is waiting for you."

(Later her mother resigned herself to her daughter's "stubbornness" and sent her one package after another, after the events of this story had already taken place.)

Lucia tucked the two letters in her duffel bag. She tore up the third aerogram she was allowed, which she had picked up the night before. At dawn she got dressed without washing and, arriving earlier than the other internees, waited for them in the open space to form a column to walk to the factory.

By now she kept to herself in the barrack. She no longer spoke to her roommates. In the canteen she quickly gulped down her portion, and even finished her neighbor's soup, paying no attention to whether the individual was filthy or clean. She herself had become slovenly by now and she didn't wash anymore. When she unwrapped her feet before going to bed (a Russian had given her woolen bandages), she welcomed the stink as retaliation. A woman might give her a piece of bread and Lucia would snatch it without saying thank you. Jacqueline, the French girl who had refused her a sheet of newspaper, was the most generous with her.

Lucia began to distinguish the sixteen French women in her dormitory, only four of whom she saw regularly, since the others had different work shifts (they were in the barrack when she was not there). Above all, she was careful not to meet Martine's eye, even accidentally, though she felt her presence. Some nights she would leave the barrack, pressing her hands on her chest to ease the sting of the acid on her flesh; followed by the German shepherds, she would stop near the barbed wire fence and think about taking her life.

On nights when there were bombings, when the blasts exploded deafeningly in their heads, the internees never able to judge their distance in the darkness, she lay on her pallet, or wandered among the barracks. She'd gradually come to hate the Lager's air-raid shelter. To Lucia this subterranean concrete tunnel of about a hundred meters, which could hold only a thousand or so of the three or four thousand internees, standing or sitting on the ground, seemed like a long snaking intestine that made the ground bulge slightly as it wound between the rows of barracks; walking over it, the gravel crunched with a screech that made you clench your teeth at every step, while the empty cavity reverberated.

When everyone pushed and shoved "to stuff themselves into that bowel," crowding in from both ends since there was no access in the middle, Lucia told herself that she wasn't afraid of death, but she didn't want the bombs to fall on the exits and bury her in that tunnel-coffin, asphyxiated with the others before the rescuers could clear the obstructed openings. Let them all die, it was immaterial to her.

One night she huddled on the ground outside her dormitory, letting the March rain soak her. Wrapped in a blanket, her arms around her legs that were tightly drawn against her chest, she listened to her heart hammering. She leaned her back against the rough planks of the back wall of her barrack, which she thought would shatter at each explosion. In the pitch-darkness of the camp, she watched the blazes that burst out on the horizon despite the rain falling from the sky; though subsiding, the booms continued to echo in the distance for quite some time. Until finally she heard the all-clear, and the excited voices of her companions returning from the shelter.

When the wakeup call sounded, she could feel she had a high fever. She couldn't stop coughing. She would not come down from her bunk: "I'm reporting sick," she told the guard.

"If you take the OSTEN off your collar, okay, you can go to the infirmary. Otherwise *raus*, get to work." Lucia dragged herself up and went to the factory.

After eating, during the lunch break, Lucia joined the *Osten* and P. When it wasn't raining, they lay on the bank of the canal behind the factories, under the pale rays that broke through the milky sky, snuggling close to one another to keep warm.

Lucia stretched out beside Grùscenka. They had met at the Ch 89, where the Russian girl tended to the underground toilets, a strategic place, she explained, that allowed her to study the workers' moods.

Grùscenka was slim and, though tattered and filthy, had an elegant bearing. Lucia had noticed that even the Germans were charmed by her oval face with its high, slightly curving forehead, arched eyebrows, aloof blue eyes and slender nose; a face so perfect as to appear cold, almost abstract.

Twenty-four years old, she had studied at the Naval Academy in Moscow to become a captain in the merchant marine. They had arrested her near the front. She was fortunate that they had only deported her, she said unemotionally.

The two girls whispered intensely in German, a language that the Russian knew better than Italian.

They got into the habit of lying side by side, amid the whiff of decay that rose from the canal and mingled with the animal reek of their coveralls. Beneath the fog, in a language foreign to them both, they dreamed of stealing shoes and clothing. It was a quiet, slow dream that soothingly shaped their words, in which the only problem was not getting caught. Grùscenka, in a crystalline voice, suggested they get hired as maids in private homes, so they would have all the time they needed to choose the stuff to carry off at the right time. Lucia, constantly gripped by hunger, proposed they set their sights on money, provisions, and food stamps instead.

Huddled together beside the two girls, taking it easy, were two Polish civilian deportees, Johann and Stanislaw. Every so often they yawned a few words, especially when Johann, pricking up his ears at the women's whisperings, mumbled a rejection or encouragement to a proposal by the Russian or Italian girl. Stanislaw, who didn't understand German, added his own mutterings just the same, as soon as Johann told him what stage the girls' planning had reached regarding the possibility of getting work in the private home of a German family.

IV

Throughout the shift, Grùscenka and Lucia plotted together happily. Lucia went down to the toilets of the Ch 89 whenever she could escape the foreman's eye, and listened intently to her friend's proposals. The wife of one of the camp's wardens, through her husband, had sent for someone to wash clothes at her home. Both the *Lagerführer* and the wardens lived with their families in a cluster of stone houses at the edge of the camp, by the road. One of those buildings also housed the administrative offices, and a small platoon of camp guards was stationed in another.

In the evening, returning from the factory, the warden accompanied Lucia to his home. To make a good impression on the warden's wife, as agreed with Grùscenka, Lucia had cleaned up thoroughly, taking a shower in the locker room after work. Though she had then showed up looking quite presentable, she was led directly into the laundry room, where she scrubbed clothes from 7:00 p.m. to 11:00 p.m. The German woman, standing with her, occasionally recounted the linens, constantly fearing that some item might have disappeared. A woman with a meek, frightened expression, not only did she marshal her eldest son by her side, but, rather than leave the foreigner alone for a moment, she repeatedly called her younger daughters to bring her more bleach, another bit of soap, or a forgotten pillowcase, then waved her hands to send them away immediately. The two little girls pointed at the foreigner, their eyes taking in the patches, the frayed hem.

Lucia had wanted to wear the last personal clothes she had left, a dark green woolen dress and a gray coat with Persian lamb trim that she kept in her locker. But when the time came to put on the dress, she realized that it didn't fit: she had gained so much weight in just over two months that the seams in the armpits and on one side had ripped. She'd had to show up in the thick twilled jacket and pants the camp supplied to the internees, which for that matter went better with the wooden-soled boots (she had removed the OSTEN from her lapel).

The girl had a mental image of herself that she had carried with her from Italy and did not see how she had become: bloated in her coveralls, her face heavy, her eyes wary behind her courteous manner. She offered herself as a laundress to all the camp wardens but no other private home accepted her services. Instead, she sold them her gold Omega wristwatch for eight two-kilo loaves of bread, the coat for five loaves, and the dress for two.

After she sold her watch and ate two loaves in a row one night, wrapped up in her blanket or hiding in the toilet to avoid being seen, it occurred to her that she was behaving exactly like her roommates, whose ability to eat on the sly, ignoring the famished eyes of their companions, she continued to despise. In the few days in which she went through the supplies, she spent her time feverishly calculating how many grams per person it would take if she shared her loaves with the ten Russian prisoners and the four Warsaw partisans she worked with at the Ch 89, not counting Grùscenka, Johann, and Stanislaw, in addition to the twenty-one occupants of the barrack, not to mention the Italian prisoners of the Ph 32 opposite her shop, twenty or so dejected men, called *"badogliani"* by the Germans and "Fascist sheep" by the French prisoners, to whom she could not deny at least a loaf. The Italian prisoners of September 8, 1943, were the only ones, together with Soviet prisoners of war, who did not enjoy the assistance of the International Red Cross, from which the French and the Anglo-Americans received food parcels. She certainly could not deny them a piece of bread.

In the evening, lying on her side on her bunk, which fortunately was the last of those against the wall opposite the door, she turned her back to the woman in the next bed and, still under the blanket, meticulously cut the slices to be distributed, splitting them ad infinitum so as not to exclude anyone, until the overhead light was turned off. Upon awakening, she stuffed the slices under her jacket and took them to the factory. Once there, suddenly ashamed of her frugality, she doubled the rations, promising those who were left without that she would give them their portion of bread the next day. She was so absorbed by the effort of dividing, multiplying, and distributing grams, every so often remembering someone whom she had neglected, that she furtively gobbled up pieces stolen from her mental calculations and, after ingesting half a loaf, would be devastated at having to start the computations all over again to equitably reduce the others' rations. Fearful of gorging too much by herself if she made her cache of bread last too long, she sped up the distribution, and it was a relief to her when, after six days, the eight loaves were finally consumed. It was Hitler's birthday, April 20, 1944, and the loudspeakers at the factory and at the camp transmitted martial anthems and festive chorales alternating with brief messages exalting the Führer.

As they lay on the canal bank during the midday break, Grùscenka observed that the Nazis seemed like a metaphysical entity, omnipresent and invisible. She'd gotten a glimpse of them when they arrested and deported her, but afterward she'd no longer been able to spot one, except for the *Lager-führer*, who for that matter acted through the guards and wardens, rarely appearing in the flesh. In the factory, moreover, the foreman didn't look like a Nazi and the few German technicians seemed mainly concerned with holding off the foreigners' repressed violence: "Put yourself in their place. We are at least eighty percent of the workforce, from ten to fifteen thousand."

Johann whispered that the German guard at a warehouse of pure alcohol had taken him aside that morning, telling him, "I want to celebrate the Führer's birthday with you: I'll let you take a few bottles of alcohol and I'll look the other way. But I warn you, if you get caught, I'll come down on you even harder than the others."

The last quarter hour of the break was spent planning the thefts. By now they were on their feet and, stepping over the nearby bodies, went off behind a shed.

Grùscenka suggested that the French prisoners also be involved in the caper, since they could sell off the alcohol as a product of the parcels they received from the Red Cross: "They can keep the price up. But if we *Osten* and *P* resell the alcohol," she said as if it were the name of a company, "people are going to think we stole it!" The last words were spoken with mock consternation. Then her expression hardened: "Anyone is apt to report or blackmail us. So see to it that the French have a joint interest in this, Lùszia, otherwise all we can do with this alcohol is get drunk."

"Hey!" Johann laughed, winking. "Is it so awful to have ninety-proof fire buzzing in your veins?"

Stanislaw, tall and lanky, went on talking in Polish, his eyes lively in a fuzzy face; he kept slipping his closed fist here and there under his jacket and in his pants, as if he had bottles hidden in there. Johann translated: "Anyone leaving at night with a bulge somewhere ends up getting noticed"; he added that Stanislaw insisted they organize a chain so it wouldn't always be the same internees who carried the stolen goods out of the factory.

The young men hastened to make arrangements for the following day. Like the Westerners, civilian internees from the East were lined up in columns on the road, outside the factory; workers from the various shops were able to walk to the gates in scattered groups, and could therefore mingle with the French prisoners without attracting attention. (The Russian and Polish war prisoners were the only ones made to form a column as soon as they left their shops.)

"Tell the French to agree to meet us a couple of times between one factory and another, where the streets we walk every day come together inside the IG," Grùscenka said, "so we can negotiate the percentage they demand for reselling the alcohol for us and, if we agree, pass them the loot."

"Much safer under cover," Johann said. "It's easy to switch locker rooms, no one notices. Tell them this: each of us will let the other know which locker room he goes to in the evening to wash off, then instead of going to his own, he mistakenly goes to the one used by the comrade who has to carry out the stuff and delivers it to him."

That night in the barrack, Lucia called Martine aside. They had not spoken for eight weeks, since the argument following the prank with the tramp's spoon. The French girl invited Lucia up to her pallet; close to the door, hers was the only bunk that wasn't paired with another. Squeezing in to make room for her guest, Martine quietly confided that for some time now, in partnership with Etienne and Alain, she'd been stealing sugar and soap in the factory: "Once," she recalled proudly, "I carried off half a kilo of sugar in one fell swoop."

Lucia explained the locker rooms plan: "It's a chance to become friendly with all nationalities, we can even eradicate the gap between East and West. I could be useful to you, you know?" And counting on her fingers: "I sleep in the Westerners' barrack, I work with the *Osten* and I know the languages."

Martine unexpectedly stiffened. Eyes bright, her thin lips redder than usual, she assured her in a dismissive tone that she would speak to the

French internees the next day about taking in Grùscenka and Lucia, Johann and Stanislaw as a group.

On leaving the factory, Grùscenka showed a bag full of harmless rags and bundles, which she let the guards inspect thoroughly. Alain appeared up ahead speaking falteringly with the warden. Martine slipped the stolen goods into Grùscenka's bag and began yelling at her accomplice, who was detaining the warden while others froze to death waiting. She pushed him aside, offering her body for inspection, arms outstretched. Grùscenka sighed with the resigned expression expected of an *Osten* and humbly went out.

Or else Lucia would sneak a bottle of alcohol under the jacket of her coveralls, holding it in place with her arms crossed over her chest and hands under her armpits, as if she were cold; head held high, she passed through the booths where the guards patted down the workers as they went out, pleading, "Quick, my column is leaving." A warden quickly felt the pockets of her jacket and trousers, and the girl walked off.

But they had to come up with new methods all the time. One warden, in fact, demanded that Lucia spread her arms. The girl slipped one hand only out from under her armpit and with an accusing look held it out to him, livid and bruised. "Go on, go on!" the warden barked, annoyed, and Lucia slipped quickly through the gate.

"Heaven protects us," she whispered to Martine as they walked together in the column to the Lager. "Just today a hammer shot out of someone's hand and bruised my fingers. Otherwise, what would I have shown the warden? Look here, the wounds I had for weeks have disappeared. Hands and feet, the hide of an elephant, not even the smallest crack."

The two girls were now getting along well and often talked together in the evening, in the barrack.

The night of the Führer's birthday, careful not to let anyone see her, Lucia had torn up the photographs of Hitler and Mussolini that she'd kept in her duffel bag and thrown the pieces into the stove. Afterward she continued to check that the padlock of her locker was secure, so as not to let her roommates win.

"You still don't condemn Fascism," Martine said point-blank as she undressed on top of her pallet. "You find extenuating circumstances for it as opposed to Nazism."

"I'll have to think about that," Lucia said, taken by surprise. "I need to come up with a criterion by which to judge it that doesn't fall short the first time it's tested. Here I've been able to see things from the other side, but there? I know nothing about it."

"Never mind her," the girl who scraped by through prostitution cut in. "Don't you understand that she grew up in polite society?"

But Martine wanted to know what the Italian girl had ever found good about Fascism.

As she listed the merits of her country, its dedication to the cause, its fortitude and courage in difficult times, Lucia felt a sense of vagueness that humiliated her and for which she held Martine responsible.

"Why do you call her the Italian?" Jacqueline asked. "You can see she's still here with us, she's more French than you and me put together."

"No," Martine retorted, "it's one of two things: either she's more aware of the class difference when she's with her fellow countrymen and feels she's above them, or she's ashamed of being a Fascist."

"But I lived in France, where I was born, for fourteen years, and later spent only four years in Italy, so what are you talking about? I don't feel I'm above them. I'm less familiar with the Italian mentality, that's all."

One night when it was drizzling, Lucia had seen Martine confront her boyfriend on the way out of the factory: "It's a mistake to want to pull the rug out from under her all at once."

Putting his arm around her shoulders, Etienne had walked along slowly with Martine in the rain. And by his gestures, it was clear he was explaining his reasons.

Martine's behavior was erratic. At times she would tell Lucia, "Don't let them intimidate you," and at other times she would mutter, "Go ahead and keep your Fascism. The worse for you when you're ready to spit it out and no one will want to hear it."

"Up till now I've spat out judgments on things I didn't know anything about," Lucia retorted. "So I will only judge what I know, doing my best with the values I have—that is, the ones I'm discovering."

"And what are those values?"

"Solidarity, for example, which is different from Fascist unanimity."

"We'll see."

The French prisoners working on the lathe adjacent to the Ch 89 had become friendly toward Lucia, who again would stop and talk with them after a sulfuric ice delivery.

"Take that OSTEN out of your lapel," Alain, the elderly prisoner, told her. "It's what the Nazis ordered."

The man curled up his lips: "You draw too much attention to yourself, you don't fit in with us."

"So who ever wanted to?" Lucia leaped up, stung.

"Exactly. Someone who wants to stand out doesn't interest us," Alain repeated offhandedly.

Chauvinists, Lucia thought—they don't hang around with Russians. They deign to talk to me only because French is my mother tongue.

But just the same she had a feeling they were studying her as if they wanted something from her.

And toward the end of April she began to connect certain details. With exactly the same casual tone Grùscenka used, Martine pointed out that the Germans at IG Farben were a negligible minority compared to the foreigners.

Moreover, Martine often asked about her childhood and adolescence spent in France: What had she observed in people's behavior, strangers to her, that was lacking in Italy? In turn she told her that she had worked at Renault, on the assembly line, since she was sixteen, but had not had time to experience the strikes and sit-ins in the factories because war had broken out with the immediate occupation of the invaders.

Lucia then recalled the processions of Parisian protesters who paraded through Rue Monge, where she lived. She remembered the echo of the rallies that followed her on the way to school—emphatic, incomprehensible words reaching her ears.

So, unexpectedly, as they walked in a column to the factory one morning, Lucia had an extraordinary idea: "Martine," she whispered in her ear, "why don't we organize a strike?"

"Have you lost your mind?" her friend laughed at her. "And while we're on the subject, what's come over you recently that's made you go around saying you were deported to Germany? I've already heard it from three people. A volunteer is what you are, stay that way."

Lucia had never intended this white lie of hers to reach Martine's ear and, caught in the act, replied in a choked voice, "I should have expected it: you're all afraid. You bark constantly but you never bite."

V

For more than a year (Lucia would never have imagined this), a number of French internees had been planning a strike at IG Farben.

Alain was a French partisan who had gotten himself deported to Germany along with other *maquisards* like him, to organize an uprising of foreign workers; there were said to be about fifteen million men and women transported to the Third Reich, including six or seven million employed in industry.

Fifty-two guerrilla fighters, who together made up an entire command, had let themselves be rounded up by the occupying forces as military prisoners or ordinary civilians, making sure they were arrested at various times and places so as to be put on board trains headed to different cities. They were all highly skilled workers, certain of being hired at major industrial complexes. For reasons of control and logistical organization, foreign labor was concentrated in large factories that turned out parts, but absent in plants which produced finished military products. The task of the French militants was to ensure that an uprising of foreigners employed in the factories coincided with the Allied landing in Normandy, in order to weaken the Nazis on the home front and accelerate their surrender.

The Frenchmen communicated with one another in code, persuading some compassionate, innocent German to transcribe the messages in his own hand and mail the letters in his name.

The most sensitive information from their base of operations was reported to them verbally by people like Martine, whose volunteer status allowed her to choose her destination venue. Assisted by Etienne, Alain had informed and involved about a dozen French workers. Martine maintained contact with the others, since she had more freedom of movement as a volunteer.

The French militants had drawn a topographic map of the Lagers that spread over the plain on the west side of Frankfurt-Höchst, the side overlooking the Rhine.

There were four camps for prisoners of war, one beside the other, each with its own kitchen and its own *Lagerführer*, though jointly sharing some services such as disinfestation and access to the air-raid shelter, laid out in the usual arrangement of East and West: the two camps for the "Bolsheviks" and Polish inmates farther away from IG Farben, those of the French and Italian internees closer. And at the end of the row, isolated from everyone, the small camp of the Warsaw insurgents.

Across the road lay the barracks of volunteers and civilian workers who'd been rounded up, divided into two clusters of unequal density, with seven to eight thousand people in the camp of the "Slavs" and about half that number in that of the "Westerners."

Drawing the human map of IG Farben had been more complex, not so much due to the irregular distribution of the buildings as to the mixture of peoples. The factories did not adhere to the sharp distinction between groups from the East and those from the West, on which the separation of the Lagers and the factory canteens was based. Workers with or without the triangle, military prisoners or civilian workers, were employed in the same factory though distinguished by levels. The upper floor was given over to machinery, alongside the workshops, for distilling or monitoring: skilled, light jobs assigned to the Germans, of course. Moving down, the levels expanded, going from the French and Belgians to the Italians, Greeks, and Croatians (situated at the same level), down to the base of Slovenians, Poles, and especially Russians, who were given the toughest tasks.

This pyramid arrangement in the factories, however, only seemingly facilitated the planning. No foreigner could go up to the gallery or to the workshops of the Germans except briefly, to transport material, with the exception of "one of them," namely Lucia; not so much because the girl was a Fascist—the few French Pétainists and pro-Nazi Romanians of the Iron Cross remained on the lower floors—as because of her higher social status, which she never missed an opportunity to make known.

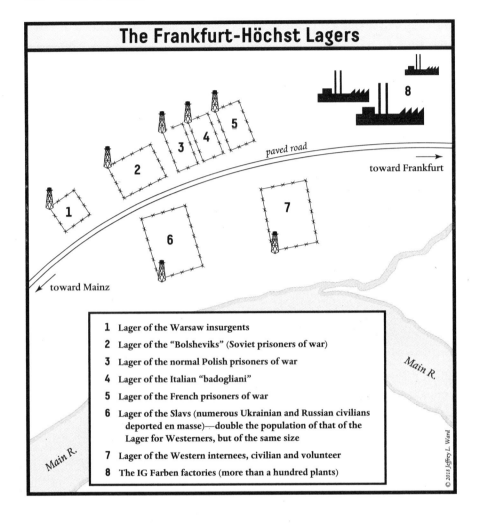

The Frankfurt-Höchst Lagers

paved road

→ toward Frankfurt

← toward Mainz

Main R.

Main R.

1 Lager of the **Warsaw insurgents**

2 Lager of the **"Bolsheviks"** (Soviet prisoners of war)

3 Lager of the **normal Polish prisoners of war**

4 Lager of the **Italian "badogliani"**

5 Lager of the **French prisoners of war**

6 Lager of the **Slavs** (numerous Ukrainian and Russian civilians deported en masse)—double the population of that of the Lager for Westerners, but of the same size

7 Lager of the **Western internees**, civilian and volunteer

8 The **IG Farben factories** (more than a hundred plants)

© 2018 Jeffrey L. Ward

As a result, being able to count the Germans had required time and complex calculations on the part of the organizers. Those assigned to count the Germans' faces when passing hurriedly in or out of work were always likely to describe them in such a way that others wouldn't recognize someone who'd already been counted: "The one I mean is a different one," the next counter would answer. He was taller, or shorter. They lost time sketching a picture, okay, it was someone else. But the resulting number would mean too many Germans and they had to start over. Then they all turned out to be the same man and the number became too few.

Besides counting the Germans, for the purpose of effectively planning

the strike, establishing the distribution and number of the various nationalities of the foreigners in the individual workshops had also required
patient, painstaking work.

It should be noted that there were no concentration camps (reserved for
Jews, political prisoners, homosexuals, and common criminals) connected to
IG Farben, only labor and detention camps. So there were no exterminations
that could upset the calculation of the masses in the fenced-in camps. After
taking into account fluctuations due to the arrival of new convoys, exchanges
with other factories, sudden relocations of entire communities due to
demands for reinforcements elsewhere, a satisfactory estimate could be de-
duced, namely, that the foreign labor force accounted for between fourteen
and sixteen thousand workers, a good quarter of which were women.

If the distinction between military prisoners and civilians was evident
at first glance, in part because the former wore the military uniform with
a big KG printed on the back, among the civilians, on the other hand, it was
hard to distinguish the volunteers from those rounded up and deported en
masse. The former, in fact, as soon as they looked around, tended to deny
their volunteer status in order to blend in with the other internees.

At first the French militants had considered it essential to distinguish
the two categories, regarding the volunteers as less trustworthy. But after
wasting several months on that virtually useless exercise, they had gradually come to realize that, with the exception of some lumpenproletarians
who had lived in the most abject poverty in their countries of origin, most
of the volunteers harbored an even greater hatred toward the masters than
the deportees. And when they heard someone laughing his head off about
the alluring promises Nazi propaganda made to entice suckers, they realized that one of the suckers was the person speaking and that he wouldn't
back down when the moment came to strike.

Time available to the organizers was getting tight since, in November
'43, Martine had brought word that preparations for the foreigners' rebellion in Germany had to be in place by May '44, ready for it to begin at the
first signal.

The planners were still gauging the actual makeup of Germans in
the factory. Though they had managed to estimate their number, they now
also had to distinguish between German citizens of the first degree and

German citizens of the second degree, a difference that a foreigner could not read on their faces.

German second-degree citizens, that is, *Volksdeutschen*, were less numerous. They came from countries variously appropriated in the Third Reich, such as the areas surrounding Gdansk, Alsace and Lorraine, several Czechoslovakian territories, and Dutch and Flemish regions. Enlisted in the *Arbeitsdienst* (the Labor Service), they were transported to Germany. They constituted a large part of the skilled workers, truck drivers, and transport workers in general, served as accountants in the offices and in the camps, and were the head cooks in the factory canteens.

The pure Germans, on the other hand, namely, the *Reichsdeutschen*, were more numerous. These citizens of the first degree constituted the entire management staff down to the lowest chemistry professor; the clerical staff, comprised almost exclusively of women; the platoon of soldiers who escorted the detainees and foreign deportees; the nucleus of soldiers from FLAK (anti-aircraft forces) assigned to IG Farben, as well as custodial personnel.

The strike's organizers paid particular attention to the *Reichsdeutschen* working in the factories, the foremen, the *Vorarbeitern* and technicians who with few exceptions were men unfit to fight, elderly, or exempt from national service. All those able to fight were at the front. In addition there were the chemical assistants (*Laborantinnen*) trained to prevent foreigners from gaining access to the laboratories, to avoid acts of sabotage that would have caused incalculable damage, given that the products were flammable.

On the other hand, the foreign workers feared a fire as much as the Germans did. That was the reason why everyone was especially fearful of the factory being bombed: what with chemical powders, acids, huge tanks of fuel, the plants would go up in a chain explosion that would spread into a single conflagration. Everyone was relieved to have escaped such a danger till then. All the same, the growing anxiety of the lab staff could be seen in the white skull and crossbones that appeared more and more frequently on the doors.

Ultimately, adding up the *Reichs-* and the *Volksdeutschen*, it turned out that about eighty-one to eighty-three percent of the workforce was made up of foreigners.

Once these preliminary studies were complete, the French militants made contact with elements of other nationalities. At times the difficulties seemed insurmountable. There were patently delicate situations: most Poles did not forgive the Russians for having sided with the Nazis at the beginning of the conflict, for having invaded them and for continuing to occupy them even after they had become allies again. Only the one hundred thirty-eight men of the Warsaw Uprising supported the strike as a bloc, even before the organizer finished revealing the plan. They were all emaciated, their eyes reticent. They were forbidden to exchange a word with anyone, and everyone, both their countrymen and other foreigners, fell silent as they passed, torn between respect and apprehension.

The Nazis had fostered the irredentism of the Ukrainians, promising them independence from the USSR; they had fueled the separatism of several Lithuanian villages in northern Poland, and backed the preeminence of the Croatians in Yugoslavia at the expense of Serbs and Slovenians. And it wasn't easy to convince such heterogeneous communities, divided by conflicting passions, to set aside their internal hatreds and give precedence to the fight against those who had in some way unified them by deporting them from their fatherland.

Finally, there was the French's contempt for the Italians, whom they accused of stabbing them in the back on the eve of the occupation, to steal Nice and Savoy from France.

Nevertheless, given the greater concerns, a number of prisoners and deportees of every nationality joined the French militants, with whom they gradually spun a web of provocations and clandestine connections. Since the base of local operations was in the lathe workshop attached to the Ch 89, the decision was made to proceed with the plan of persuading the workers in a spiral fashion, starting with the more distant plants and circling round and round to the closest buildings. The organizers wanted to avoid having too great a proximity prompt the workers informed of the plan to constantly ask for news and information, displaying an excitement that would eventually arouse suspicion. As a result, the job of persuading the

Ch 89 was saved for last. Not for a moment did the strike organizers forget that the most insignificant whisper could derail an undertaking of such scale.

Things had seemed to be going well when, at the beginning of February '44, in the Western civilians' camp, that girl who proclaimed herself Italian had appeared, seemingly reckless, too rash to be credible. Martine's line of reasoning, namely, that if Lucia were a spy she would have pretended to be an anti-Fascist partisan, only partially convinced the French militants. It could in fact be an astute tactic of reverse psychology on the part of the masterminds whose instrument the student was, to make her seem like a naive innocent who goes over to the opposite side when shown the facts. After all, Martine herself had fallen for it. And if Lucia wasn't a spy, that didn't make her any less dangerous, given the unpredictability of her behavior.

So they considered various tactics. At first they tried to repulse the girl so that her reactions might in any case provide some clue. But every act on her part lent itself to a double interpretation: it could be a pretense to win over the detainees and be asked to forge links with the Russians, for instance, to then reveal the ploy at the right time; or it could be a sincere display. In fact, since the girl had been born and raised in France, Lucia's Fascism might well be more superstructural than she herself suspected. It was therefore possible that the clash with reality might strip her of an adolescent infatuation for the regime's mythology. Martine, who leaned toward this hypothesis, namely, that Lucia was acting in good faith, sounded her out to that effect. Etienne, on the other hand, judging her to be an insidious, bourgeois schemer, held to his opinion. Alain vacillated, leaning slightly toward Martine's theory. The other militants felt that no opportunity should be dismissed out of hand. If their wariness was excessive, they would effectively lose a valuable mediator: given her knowledge of languages, once the girl was persuaded to take advantage of her earlier reputation as a Fascist and make the most of the indulgence the Nazis still accorded her, she could step up the final contacts and contribute to the success of the endeavor.

To that end, it was essential that she not alienate herself from the Nazis completely but give them at least a sign of having second thoughts. Hence Alain's instruction that she remove the triangle from her jacket.

When Lucia ultimately had the idea about a strike, the French decided to continue trusting her to a degree. They agreed to make her responsible

for the entire initiative. That way she would be so involved with the internees that she would no longer be able to betray anyone.

"If one of us had acted as erratically as you have," Alain said, coming
up alongside Lucia as they left the factory, "they would have thrown him
into Dachau without thinking twice. They certainly wouldn't have been
satisfied with transferring him to another work area. You could afford to
have those fits of anger, my so-called heroine. And whom did they benefit?
Neither you nor anyone else."

"I don't take instruction from those who don't bite."

"Now you're even speaking in metaphors?"

"How cultured you are!" Lucia scoffed.

"Does it surprise you that a worker is educated and knows the word
metaphor? What an embodiment of class consciousness you are! You feel a
distance between us and you!"

"I feel it because it's there," Lucia replied distractedly. She wanted to
savor the prisoner's humiliation: she too was learning to offend him pleas-
antly, wearing the same preoccupied expression he wore.

"You're wrong, my poor girl," Alain sympathized. "Open your eyes,
finally: here there is no distance between you and us. We have exactly the
same social status, all barrack dwellers. Before there was a class difference
and maybe there will be one afterward as well   imagine someone like you
not going back and retreating to her social rank. But here, in Frankfurt-
Höchst, in the IG Farben camps, whether you like it or not, we're equals.
In fact, you're lower down because you're uneasy and we're not. The reasons
why you came don't mean a thing given the fact that, in this situation,
you're in up to your neck."

Once again she resented that man: "And you, why do you always insult
me? What do you know about how much it cost me to do what I did, even
if to you my actions seem like impulsive fits?"

"Because in your place I would have acted very differently!" Alain exclaimed, suddenly cheerful. He slowed down, since by now they were
nearing the gate. "If I could pass myself off as a Pétainist, as a *collabò*, I'd be
in the saddle by this time. I would kick up such a racket, my dear, that I'd
make their hair stand on end."

"But when I suggest organizing a strike, you're not in favor."

"You, a strike? With that OSTEN in your buttonhole? Go on! Who do you think you're kidding?"

"Didn't I steal with you in the factory, with the OSTEN in plain sight on my jacket?"

"Then you don't know what you're talking about! You mean to compare a little theft to an uprising? Well then . . ." And the man walked away.

VI

Lucia decided to fight alone. She would take advantage of her comings and goings from one workshop to another at the factory to air the idea of a strike.

She now volunteered to carry bags of coal on her back, rolls of plastic on her shoulders; once she'd had them load and tie on her back a machine weighing nearly a hundred kilos, which she had carried up a flight of stairs. She had become incredibly strong. In one of the *Sicherheitsdienst** examinations to check her personal characteristics, she read on the scale's indicator that in three months she had gained more than twelve kilos over her normal weight: she weighed sixty-four kilos and was one meter sixty-five centimeters tall.

She couldn't, however, let them discover her. The French were right, it was unwise to draw attention to herself. And how to go about approaching a stranger to suggest he go on strike? Internees were always proposing some act of bravado.

She decided to use the technique of grousing. And with every foreigner she ran into, she griped: "What do they think we are, slaves? Why don't we go on strike?" She'd learned to say words like that not only in Russian and Polish, but also in Greek and Slovenian. She met few workers, however, because most of them performed their jobs inside the machine shops. And when she incited them by urging "What do you say, huh?" those few simply returned her greeting. At most they responded with a hand gesture, as if to say: "It's just talk!" Or else they winked and snickered, "Sure, why not?" It seemed like a prank with no consequences.

Even the Russians, with whom she slogged away in the Ch 89, merely

*Security service.

smiled broadly at her. One merrily clapped her vigorously on the back, making her stagger.

At the camp, Lucia considered it pointless to divulge her suggestion. In the evening, at the canteens, the internees only wanted to gulp down their soup and they reacted by swearing if anyone disturbed their apathy. In the lavatories at dawn it was even worse: they washed up in a daze, like automatons. As they walked in a column, back and forth from work, parading through the barracks, men in front and women behind, she could only speak with her dorm mates. But the people you live with, she thought, are always the last ones you should inform.

At the factory, however, they were all alert and ready to revolt. There was more drive, the nationalities were mixed. The ideal thing would be to get to the military prisoners. Hadn't Grùscenka said one day that she envied the KGs? "*By convention*, even in the eyes of the Germans, they have a right to passive resistance. They can take more chances than civilian deportees, even the Soviets, see, because of the respect the Nazis have for *military* virtues. Only the Warsaw insurgents are at serious risk." Grùscenka was right: the KGs were more united than the civilians, they could be influenced.

At a moment when the supervisor was distracted, Lucia snuck into the shop opposite hers. She had decided to change her tactic, that is, to assume a different tone depending on the circumstances. She thought it best to adopt a firm, thoughtful manner with her compatriots: "We can't go on like this, we must rise up," she began, but she had to raise her voice to be heard above the clamor in the shop. "We have an exceptional weapon: we can strike."

The five Italian prisoners in the Ph 32, whose curiosity had been piqued when they saw her come in, exchanged weary glances. "We don't have enough trouble, all we need is to satisfy an urge just for the hell of it!" someone shouted at her in the din and asked: "Can you imagine what they'd do to us?"

Lucia had another go at it the following morning, again eluding the foreman's attention. But the Italian prisoners continued working around the furnace, amid the sparks of red-hot metal plates that they slowly fed into the presses, surrounded by the sizzle of tiny filings shooting out from all sides.

"We are no longer puppets," Lucia shouted, hands cupped around her mouth. "From now on we will act on our own."

"You think you're on the balcony of Piazza Venezia?"

The girl would quickly crouch behind a press, going round and round the machinery depending on the movements of the *Vorarbeiter*, who, perhaps drawn by the voices, strode in to inspect the Italians.

She met them again later, on the way back from the canteen after the lunch break: "Hey, *Osten* from Rome," a *badogliano* called to her, "what do the others say?"

"What do you expect them to say?" his neighbor interjected. "Everybody knows already: it will come to nothing."

"Sure!" a third man said, smiling to himself. "Just let them try it and within fifteen minutes we'll see: if they don't slaughter us all in a single burst of machine-gun fire, we might at least get some small satisfaction!"

Within a few days Lucia had gotten used to standing up to the wary ones. At a glance she would decide whether to bring up the subject with a confidential or challenging tone, though an assured, even somewhat casual pitch almost always caught on better.

The Slovenians, who'd fought in Yugoslavia against the pro-German Croatians and were persecuted by the Nazis, started giving her imperceptible smiles of consent with complicit looks. They worked near the small station of the internal railway.

Using gestures, a Greek made her understand that, if everyone refused to work, he was in. But if only a few of them striked and the majority continued to work, then no, count him out.

An Italian civilian internee, who worked on the first level of the Ch 89, took an interest in the issue. To Lucia it was almost as if the man, an immigrant from Puglia, all nerves and facial expressions, were lying in wait for her so he could express his point of view: he objected, he suggested strategies, he predicted counter-moves by the Nazis, he would seem to support the idea of a strike, then suddenly shrug, "Impossible, it can't be done."

The more sensible the girl found the Apulian's observations to be, the more torn she was between the need to get his promise of support and the desire to slip away whenever she saw him silently approaching out of the corner of her eye. A whistle from the overseer usually resolved her dilemma.

One afternoon when Lucia was pulling a cart and passed in front of Alain and Etienne's doorway, they motioned for her to stop. Three or four Frenchmen busied themselves around a machine that they had carried outside; unscrewing a cogwheel and hammering bolts, they asked how things were going.

"In spite of the lily-livered cowards, beautifully," the girl said.

"Did any sucker take the bait?" Etienne said with a faint smile.

Lucia exaggerated the show of consent from the Russians, Slovenians, and Greeks, not mentioning the skepticism of the Italians.

"Interesting!" one of the Frenchmen muttered occasionally, pretending to concentrate on his work.

"Don't you want to participate?" the girl asked.

"Us?" they said, laughing their heads off.

The following day Lucia again saw them in the open area near their doorway, still crouching, busy fumbling around a piece of machinery. As if to catch her breath, the girl let the sack she was carrying on her back slide to the ground and stopped. She explained that there was a good chance of success. The French, looking distracted, let her talk, occasionally tossing out a question, a little "technical detail" (they said) about her plans:

"And where are you going to stop working? In front of the machinery?" "All of you jammed in the toilets?" "Who's going to give the signal?" "Are you going to use a flute or a trumpet?"

Lucia noticed that they kept exchanging glances behind her back and winking at each other; then their faces would suddenly harden and they replied in monosyllables.

"You know what I say?" she snapped angrily. "I'd like to wipe my ass with you." She tried to reload the sack on her back, and Alain and Etienne hastened to help her. "How vulgar the little schoolgirl has become!" Alain sighed as he adjusted the load, pushing it higher up her back. "What do you think, pal? You can't bring her to the debutante's ball!"

Lucia couldn't forgive the tone in which they had asked those questions. She couldn't find the right words to crush them. She rejected *worms, animals*: too weak. Finally: "Pack of riffraff," she said indifferently.

Her relations with Martine had also worsened, since the French girl teased her about the Italians, suggesting that with them it would be a fiasco, especially the war prisoners, too defeated, too distrustful. "Don't you see how they are? They walk with their heads bowed, and if you talk to them, they look at you as if you were trying to make fools of them."

"Well, aren't they right? Given the insults that you and the Nazis reward them with, do you expect them to start dancing?"

"You pass yourself off as French by birth and then, if someone touches your Italians, you'd think he'd stepped on your tail."

"It's a legacy handed down from you people, my dear girl. At school, in France, the words *macaroni* and *mandolinist* were repeated to me so often during recess that I became proud of them."

When Alain came up to her as she left the shop, she put him off, saying sweetly: "I don't have time for those born to be slaves." It was a phrase she had prepared at night.

Luckily there were Grùscenka, Johann, and Stanislaw, who mobilized their friends in organizing the strike. From the depths of the foreigners' toilets, Grùscenka circulated suggestions of individuals in the Ch 89 who were most prone to being tapped for the initiative. With her lazy manner, she roused more people than Lucia with her head-on approach (it was Grùscenka who finally obtained the Apulian immigrant's support).

Stanislaw spread the word to the most trusted Poles in his Lager while Johann, who knew Russian well, plotted with the Ukrainians; they welcomed him affably enough, offering him a cucumber, but then demurred. Ukrainians were the most skillful at rooting out cabbage and cucumbers from the fields, on the way to and from the factory. Feigning urgent bodily needs, they were permitted to hurry off from the column to relieve themselves behind a bush. Nonetheless, they were reluctant to strike.

For three weeks now Lucia had been living solely for the strike (it was nearly the end of May). She felt like she was moving in a vacuum, with nothing to show for it. She had pleaded her cause with two, maybe three hundred internees, but there were several thousand foreigners. At this rate it would take an infinite period of time to approach them all, and by the time the last one agreed, the first one would already have forgotten about it. Furthermore, after the first few days of euphoria, she was beginning to feel scared. The overseers in the various workshops had given her a good talking-to and chased her away when they spotted her around. As soon as she got within earshot, they demanded to know where she was wheeling that bin or pushing that cart and, irritated, pointed out that she was going in the wrong direction.

The girl had hoped that her willing readiness would persuade the French to take part in planning the endeavor. She had never really doubted their fighting skills, and it seemed to her that without their contribution, the results were much more uncertain, despite her reliance on the *Osten* and Poles.

Grùscenka had focused her attention on putting together the general aspects of the plan and was mainly occupied with organizing and administering its implementation. She repeatedly conferred with the military prisoners, both the Russians and those from the Warsaw Uprising, who worked in the Ch 89. The latter, in turn, arranged things with their fellow militants in the Lager, some of whom maintained contacts with the French activists.

The support of the Russian civilian deportees was not a concern. For the *Osten* the call to stop work was merely a continuation of the course of action already adopted at home: though few had taken part in guerrilla actions, all of them had engaged in passive resistance against the invading armies.

On the other hand, it wasn't easy to unite workers from East and West, to vary the arguments and convince workers of such different backgrounds to strike together, without setting their sights on such ambitious aims as a general insurrection. It was obvious that, in the state of permanent abasement in which the internees lived, the idea of plunging back into an active war, weapons in hand, could only terrify them.

The Soviet prisoners, who were ordinary soldiers, respected Grùscenka, recognizing in her the qualities of an officer. Nevertheless, since at IG Farben the girl was only a civilian deportee, the soldiers, trained in military intelligence, didn't let her in on the plot with the French prisoners. They did, however, pose the most intricate practical problems to her and saw to it that her orders were carried out.

"The situation is clear," Grùscenka explained to Lucia. "We can only establish one thing: how to stop work. Other than that, we have to act based on the way the Germans react. But we have the first move, that's something."

Occasionally Grùscenka relied on Lucia to approach a "hard-ass" pointed out by her companions: "You have a way with words—let's see what happens."

Other times she cautioned her: "Careful, Lùszia, the determination to stop work must reach a fever pitch at just the right time, which must be synchronized throughout the shops. So cool down your incitement in this area." She gave the same warnings to Johann and Stanislaw, both nineteen and, like Lucia, unprepared to consider the organic unity of the overall plan to be primary. "Measure out the propaganda," warned Grùscenka, who seemed to be back at the Moscow Naval Academy, calm and authoritative, her manner laid-back. "We don't give a good goddamn about those dim-wits fed by the Red Cross," she added, referring to the French military prisoners with a callous smile on her composed, pretty face.

But Lucia had taken in the objections raised by the "hard-asses." She ag-onized over the Germans' resources, their methods of repression. She spent her time in bed lying awake, brooding over the complications. And if she dozed off, she experienced scenes of terror like those the Warsaw insurrectionists had described to Johann. One night she dreamed not only about the French abstaining, but also about the mass defection of the *Osten*. Only Grùscenka, on the main deck of a ship, was left standing, a slender figure in the rags that clothed her. When a towering breaker was about to crash over her, Lucia woke up screaming.

She was afraid to fall asleep again, and, feeling her limbs grow heavy, she shook herself, pulled on her coveralls, slipped into the wooden-soled boots, and left the barrack. The air outside was so dry that the Lager's two German shepherds heard her footsteps from far off. Lucia heard them come trotting over on the gravel. They must have recognized her scent from a distance, because they slowed up. One jogged off while the other waited. As she approached, Lucia heard him panting, his breathing agi-tated. He looked like the one she'd confronted on one of her first evenings there. She thought she saw him foaming at the mouth, his big tongue loll-ing out, his breathing harsh and shallow; the animal seemed to be reading the fear in her mind.

Now the dog was sniffing her. The girl was about to hide her hand in her pants pocket but thought: Oh God no, he'll think it's a threat. She kept her fingers still, pressed against the outside of her pocket, where she remembered she'd stashed half a sausage: He can smell it, he thinks I stole it, which means I can't be one of his masters. But I'll show him I'm not loaded with sausages!

And impulsively she tossed him the precious piece bought with the proceeds of a theft, watching the animal sink his teeth into it on the fly with a snap of his jaws.

That was the dog under whose nose a guard had placed a stolen garment. And after feverishly poking at the cloth with his snout, the shepherd had started leisurely wandering around the Lager, sniffing the ground or breathing the air until he'd set off at breakneck speed. A man, herded into the yard with a group of internees, had started whimpering, turning himself in before being knocked to the ground.

Half a sausage is still better than a plate of lentils, Lucia thought, disheartened by her schoolgirl humor as she cast wary glances at the animal, who'd started wagging his tail beside her.

In the morning she fell asleep standing up, like a horse, at the factory's little station where four of them were waiting for a freight car of methane to unload.

At the end of the shift Alain stopped her. "Excuse me"—Lucia tried to dodge him—"but I don't have time to argue."

"We're willing to go along," Alain said.

Lucia shrugged and headed toward the gate; the man walked beside her and kept talking to her, though she didn't answer him and wasn't really paying attention to what he said.

"Are you listening to me?" he said, taking her hand.

"Excuse me?" She felt bewildered.

"I said you did a good job, both you and Grùscenka in the Ch 89 and Johann and Stanislaw in the Na 14."

"We weren't alone."

"I know."

On the way back, Lucia joined the column of Italian girls from her barrack, who made room for her without all the fuss of the past.

She mentioned the strike.

"You can count on us," the pregnant Bergamo woman replied. "They'll have to drag me on the ground to force me to work."

"Me," the other girl from Bergamo chimed in, "not even if they pull me by the hair. I'm not moving."

Carla, the tall, strapping, sixteen-year-old worker, a brunette with rosy cheeks and big teeth, who had formed an attachment with a *badogliano* war prisoner, stepped between Lucia and one of the Bergamo women: "My boyfriend and I also did our part," she said with a gentle voice, turning her velvety eyes on Lucia, "and without all the ballyhoo."

"What fun!" Pina, the apprentice hairdresser from Rome laughed. "Much better than playing hooky!" Often alone since her inseparable friend had found a "fiancé," she'd started acting even more infantile.

"I can't stand that simpering girl," the gaunt, taciturn woman from the orphanage grumbled, irritably moving to the outer end of the row.

"Did you hear that?" whined Pina, the petite Roman. "She's the la-di-da one, you'll see if she strikes! Bloodsucking bastard is all you are."

"In fact," the woman in question replied with dignity, "I'm not joining in. But I'm not a traitor, nor a scab. When the time comes. I'll say I'm sick."

That same evening Martine called Lucia up to her pallet: the strike was scheduled for the following day. All the foreign workers would be informed during the trek from the various camps to IG Farben. At the same time they would learn the details of the operation, which Martine meticulously disclosed to Lucia in advance, revealing behind-the-scenes activity that the Italian girl was not aware of.

Their heads side by side under the blanket, Martine whispered in Lucia's ear for an hour. As she murmured, "With the advance of the Anglo-Americans tomorrow, all the foreign workers in Germany . . ." she fell asleep without finishing the sentence.

VII

The internees left the Lagers at dawn, in column formation as usual, walking briskly. The announcement of the strike circulated from row to row: as soon as they reached the factory, the workers were to start heading toward their workshops, those who had a short way to go walking very slowly, the others a little less slowly; but nobody was to hurry because everyone had to be at their locker rooms the moment the six o'clock siren wailed. When it sounded, all the foreigners in each of the factory's plants were to simultaneously proceed to the lavatory, where they usually went only in the evening to wash off the machine oil. Once inside, they initially had to pretend to wash their hands or pee in the urinals, so as to keep the Germans confused for a few seconds more. They were then to remain in the lavatories, not moving from there, until further notice. They should keep in mind that as long as they were scattered throughout IG Farben, the foreigners could control the situation; but if they let the Germans round them up, they were done for. The workers would be informed of the progress of the strike as it went along. But they should beware: the Germans would certainly spread false rumors. No one should pay any attention to hearsay. The watchword was: wait for instructions.

Punching their cards one by one at the various entrances to IG Farben, the foreigners peeled off single file toward the workshops, slipping out to the lavatories when the work siren sounded.

Carla, who in her excitement had stumbled, falling facedown to the ground, had not had time to reach the factory where she worked and had crept into one of the lavatories of the Ch 89 with Lucia.

After they'd spent a few minutes crowded into the same room, with a row of sinks on one side and urinals on the other, the guards appeared: "Back to work, let's go!" they ordered.

The foreigners, about thirty of them, looked at them placidly and went on scrubbing their hands under the faucets or pretending to pee against the wall tiles in front of them. The two guards advanced toward the internees to force them to move from there, first pushing them and then also kicking them. But in a sepulchral silence the detainees thronged so closely around them that the two guards, immobilized by the pressure of bodies whose every muscle they could feel tensed, feared for their lives. The Apulian worker, nose to nose with the German soldiers, gauged them with his eyes and said through half-closed lips, "We could gag and disarm these two, if we were sure that all the lavatories were holding their hostages." Lucia translated quickly into French. "But if we're the only ones," the Apulian continued, "they can blackmail us: either release the two soldiers or we'll toss ten hand grenades into ten lavatories. Some choice!" He concluded: "We have to let them go." And with his shoulder he shoved a way through. Outside, the shrill sound of brass whistles mounted, strident and imperious. Reluctantly, the foreigners made way, the press of their bodies driving back the guards, who, disregarding decorum, slunk out once they reached the door. "Aah!" Everyone breathed a sigh of satisfaction. "We may not have acted too diplomatically," said a Frenchman who had worked at Höchst for four years, "but they had it coming."

"What a kick, guys!" exclaimed an Italian, stretching with pleasure.

Little by little, however, their courage shrank. Everyone shushed his neighbor then, listening silently; some nodded approval. not a sound of machinery could be heard. For seconds the stillness was broken by the sudden roar of an engine speeding beyond the walls that men and women, white-faced, huddled against.

"My stomach hurts," someone said.

Perhaps a quarter of an hour passed and still nothing happened.

"They'll force us out with gas," a man's voice rose to say, "and once we're out, they'll exterminate us," he whimpered.

"Shut up, you goddamned jinx!" a woman silenced him.

But, overcome by terror, the man who had spoken broke away from the wall and went to the door, where he was swallowed up in the dawn. Across the deserted street, the leaden buildings emerged lifeless, or so it seemed. Maybe a minute later, the worker reappeared, dazed: "It's working!" he told them. After turning the corner, he had run into the foreman and the small group of *Vorarbeitern* from his iron metallurgy shop. Standing idly at the door, they'd looked at him as though seeing a ghost. And he'd made an about-face and run back to the lavatory. "The strike is working . . ." he repeated incredulously, his voice faint.

"They disarmed us psychologically, hammering into our brains a fearsome image of their cruelty," the French veteran of IG Farben, who had also been a fighter in the Resistance, began. "This image we have of the Nazis, you have to get it through your heads that they were the ones who fixed it in our brains. That way, fearing their reactions, we'd never dare make a move. Just remember that they're men just like us, with weaknesses and fears, and so—"

"You sure love to preach all the time!" said a woman who had grown impatient.

"It's true, he's right," said the man who had left and then taken heart after seeing the "paralysis" of the workshops around them. "The fact is that the strike is working."

As they argued, the warning siren sounded.

They looked at one another: "At this hour?" It was about 6:40 a.m.

"What's going on?" the Frenchman interned at Höchst since '40 worried. "There's never been an alarm at this time, not once in four years."

Pairs of footsteps on the pavement were approaching.

"To the air-raid shelter!" ordered the same two guards from before, rifles in hand, but in a normal tone of command. "All of you to the bunker, quick! An unprecedented formation of Flying Fortresses has been reported!"

With meaningful glances, the foreigners remained motionless, as if bolted to the ground between the sinks and the footrests of the urinals.

They struggled to hold on to a feeling of strength as the guards remained in the doorway. Despite the Germans' outraged expressions, they hadn't beaten the workers with their rifle butts; finally they went away.

The French militant used his sleeve to wipe the sweat running down his face. He grabbed his neighbor by the back of the neck:

"It's clear," he breathed, "we're not alone. All the factories, get it?" Then the *Vollallarm** slashed the air with its piercing undulating sirens that gave you shivers just hearing them.

Shouting could be heard outside, human voices moaning and sobbing, a running clatter. The alarm's wailing never ceased.

The seasoned Frenchman looked out: "Bastards!" he shouted to be heard over the shriek of the sirens. "Go back to the lavatories!"

"We'll all be roasted alive here!" a voice shrieked.

"Come back!" the Frenchman shouted at the top of his lungs. "Victory is in hand!"

Someone in the lavatory moved swiftly to the door. The Frenchman blocked his way. "I have to shit, I can't help it," the man said, shaking, as he jerked free and went out.

The two guards reappeared together with a German civilian. It was the foreman of the Ch 89 himself. The thought that he had not rushed to the armored shelter *"nur für Deutschen,"* only for Germans, calmed the strikers down for a few moments. They also noticed that, incredibly, behind the guards' backs, the foreman was giving them signs of complicity: his eyes

*The red alert.

indicating the sinks and the walls, he signaled by winking. The foreigners looked at one another uncertainly. Then the foreman stepped in front of the two guards and spoke harshly to the strikers crammed into the lavatory: "To the bunker, you good-for-nothing trash, *Dreckleuten*," he ordered. Meanwhile, he slipped his thumb in his vest pocket and pointed to his chest with his index finger, then, making fists, crossed his wrists over his belly, in a gesture indicating handcuffs.

Everyone immediately averted their eyes, assuming glowering expressions toward the foreman to spare him the guards' suspicions. "Thank you for your kindness," Carla whispered in Italian, her eyes sparkling.

"Get it?" They nudged one another when they were alone again. "They wanted to trap us in the shelter!"

"Very clever, the foreman! Who would have thought?"

Some had sat down on the floor, others on the sinks, calculating aloud how many hours they would need to hold out. They did not intend to return to the Lagers that night, planning to stay put and simply occupy the factories and the canteens with all the food supplies. They had almost forgotten the bombing danger when the *Vorentwahnung*★ rang out.

"I'm going to my boyfriend," Carla announced. "I'll continue the strike with him." And she ran out. The others heard her scream and for a moment saw her pass in front of the open door, kicking and writhing, two guards dragging her by the arms. The shrieks of women and a scuffling of bodies amid the barking of male voices could also be heard in the distance. And again the *Vollallarm* rose with its urgent undulations, its wailing twisting everyone's bowels.

"Planes!" a woman screamed.

Petrified, the foreigners in the lavatory listened to the drone of the powerful engines, which seemed to rise from every corner of the earth, the pregnant, muffled buzz they knew all too well, which came just before the sighting of bombers in the sky.

"I'm going to the shelter," a man decided firmly, when it seemed that the aircraft's roars were increasing. "God help anyone who stops me," he said, turning a murderous look on the others. Four people followed him.

★The all-clear signal.

Everyone expected the bombs to crash down on the factories at any moment. Each of them estimated the flammable substances being processed in his own workshop, determined to disobey orders at the first explosion, in his mind already running toward the gates, amid collapsing walls and flames, stoked by acids, leaping up to lick at the fuel tanks.

Lucia buried her head in her arms as the rumble of the planes grew in intensity.

"Someday they're going to destroy the IG for sure," the Apulian muttered bitterly, sitting cross-legged on the floor and rocking.

"But did it have to be today when we're striking?" the seasoned Frenchman shot back, having understood the Italian words. "Just today?"

"We would have been better off taking hostages," the Apulian whined over and over.

A breathless worker appeared in the doorway, clinging to the doorposts: "It's a trick," he said in Italian. Short of breath, he could barely get the words out. "Those aren't bombers." With an effort he straightened up: "Spread the word," and he disappeared.

Meanwhile, the roar of the planes came closer, making everyone's hair stand on end. The vibration was stronger than before.

"Bastards," muttered the French militant. "We thought of everything, prison, the firing squad, being gassed en masse in Buchenwald, but not this elementary trick of letting the strike collapse with a false alarm, with a fake air raid." He sat slumped on the floor. "Could they have simultaneously exterminated the foreign workers in all the German factories who revolted on the same day? And what about military production? What would have happened to military production? Who would have manufactured their weapons for them? Their only option was to cause the strike to fail. As simple as that! How did we not think of it, I mean . . ." He stared ahead, dazed. "It was the first move we should have expected . . ."

"We underestimated them," a young Belgian woman admitted, she too stunned.

"They're not bombers," the other French and Italians crouched against the walls kept saying, terrified by the uncertainty that they might be, when the blasts rang out.

A woman rushed out the door, hands in her tangled hair, with a bestial wail that was chilling.

Lucia had hunkered under a sink, fear giving her gooseflesh.

"They're not bombers, right?" a man croaked, leaping furiously to his feet. "The strike isn't a suicide mission," he spat at his companions, and with a sweeping gesture of his hand said. "Everybody to the Na 14's armored shelter, let's go!" He ducked out the door, doubled over to protect himself from shrapnel.

"Don't fall for it!" implored the French soldier and the Belgian girl, forming a wall against those who wanted to leave. "Let's think calmly," Lucia spoke out, joining them. "It's the tension of the strike that's playing nasty tricks on us." The Apulian who'd remained seated on the floor stretched out his legs, tripping a man and a woman, who tumbled to the ground.

In the uproar that followed, someone from outside thumped the backs of those barring the door, who quickly turned around. Everyone suddenly fell silent as the man, wearing an *Arbeitsdienst* (Labor Service) armband, stepped into the lavatory. "Don't be afraid!" he fired out in German. "It's the FLAK." He smiled, pressing a hand to his chest, his face flushed, and with a brief wave of benediction, vanished.

"It's not bombers, just antiaircraft guns shooting into the air," Lucia translated.

"It's a trap to make us burn alive."

"No," the veteran Frenchman thundered. "That man was telling the truth. He's a Protestant pastor who sympathizes with us, I know him."

They kept silent, worn out. In fact, the blasts were followed by a mixture of rat-tat-tats and unusual thuds, intense rounds from machine-gun belts; not the piercing hiss of bombs falling but a more muted pressure of air, typical of gunfire. They listened intently, but even the repeated reverberations were too closely spaced. But outside, the hustle and bustle and scurrying footsteps continued. The young Belgian woman left the lavatory to try to detain the foreigners who were running to the shelters. The Apulian, the French Resistance militant, Lucia, and a few others followed her.

"They're firing into the air," one of them shouted.

"A fake bombing," another yelled loudly. People stopped, peered around, squinted up at the sky.

"Don't let them trap you—it's psychological warfare."

Then the blasts of real bombs were heard, with the relentless hiss, the booms, the hollow thuds.

The confusion in people's minds was immeasurable. (Only later did they find out that the bombs had been dropped intentionally in the open country-side, on a restricted area pitted with craters from repeated carpet-bombing.)

A few hundred foreigners remained in scanty groups in the lavatories. Lucia ran into Martine and Etienne, who took her with them.

Alain was leaning against the wall, eyes closed.

"Here's your enemy," Martine joked.

Alain made an effort to smile at her: "We're fucked," he said, but he couldn't keep his tone light. "At forty years old, it's tougher."

By now convinced that hundreds, thousands of tons of explosives would be dropped by the American flying fortresses hurtling through the sky, they shuddered as a matter of course, apathetically.

But little by little the explosions diminished, the blasts lost their momentum until at 11:00 a.m. the all-clear signal (the *Vorentwahnung*) rang out again. Immediately a crackling sound, inexplicable at first, spread through the air. Then an amplified voice swept through the loudspeakers in all the workshops. Though clouded by the radio transmission, Lucia recognized the voice as belonging to Director Lopp.

He spoke gently but firmly. He said the war was intensifying and all the workers in the German factories were increasingly subjected to the threat of air strikes, regardless of nationalities and ranks, united in the same risk of death.

Sober, persuasive voices repeated the director's words in different languages, in Dutch, French, Italian, Croatian, Russian, Polish, Greek, and Slovenian.

Lucia noted that the Russian translation had not been relegated to last, probably because of the numerical strength of the *Osten*.

It was essential that they remain united, Director Lopp went on, in order not to give in to the enemy forces, namely, to rich nations that hurled their weapons of death on women and children, on German citizens and foreign workers alike, on enemies and allies, in their attempt to wipe out civilization.

After the round of translations, Director Lopp, revealing a chink of conscious generosity, announced that despite the extreme rationing of the German people, an extraordinary measure had been taken.

The versions that followed without pause heightened the expectation.

"Today," the director's voice rose, "in all the canteens, for all foreign workers employed at IG Farben, there will be pea soup and a boiled egg apiece. I repeat, in all canteens at the midday meal, making no discrimination between nationalities and ranks, everyone—volunteers, deportees, prisoners of war from every country—will be entitled to pea soup and a boiled egg."

As the loudspeakers continued to broadcast the communication in the internees' languages, the streets of IG Farben filled with workers as swarms of people streamed toward the canteens.

A hundred fanatics tried in vain to oppose the tide: "This is when we must not give in." But the famished workers were pleased with themselves, crying, "We won! They were afraid of us and they're giving us an egg."

"No!" the activists barked. "Only if we refuse their alms will they really be scared." They had joined solidly together, arm in arm in several rows, at the junction where the streets for the East and West canteens branched off: Stanislaw, Grùscenka, the Apulian, Lucia, Johann, Martine, Etienne, Jacqueline, a Russian prisoner, Carla, her *badogliano* boyfriend, a Greek man, Alain, and many others. "Now the strike will really begin," they chanted.

The German guards watched without intervening. Sure enough, the tide that pressed toward the canteens prevailed. The hordes streamed toward the smell of food, mouths watering.

Lucia, disconsolate, savored the pea soup in small spoonfuls, while Martine meticulously peeled her egg with silent tears on her haggard cheeks. Over the canteen's loudspeaker, a male voice quietly repeated in French and Italian:

"The air attack was repelled. The danger has ceased. You can safely go back to work. And if the flying fortresses that could hamper supplies don't return, tomorrow there will be a new distribution. Tomorrow, a herring apiece."

Rome, 1975

PART 4

THE DEVIATION

I

There is a fact that I evaded. By so often saying that I had been deported to Dachau, I ended up believing it. But it's not true. My companions were transferred to that Lager. Not me. I was repatriated.

Four days after the strike, on June 6, 1944, a Tuesday, I was stopped as I punched my card at the entrance to IG Farben and loaded into a police van, where I found Martine and Grùscenka. We just had time to exchange looks that said no, deny everything and that's it. At the jail, the officer who transcribed our details patted us down and emptied our pockets—Martine had a penknife and Grùscenka a piece of string—informing us that we'd been accused of theft at the factory. At that, we looked at one another, reassured, since we hadn't stolen anything for some weeks. But climbing the stairs, Martine muttered:

"We're fucked."

I was in front of her, and when I turned around quickly, she pushed me to keep going. Only at the fourth landing did she explain what she meant.

"When do they ever tell you why they arrested you? And just now, a simple theft? We won't get out alive."

On the sixth floor, one of the two jailers who were escorting us led us down a windowless corridor, with bolted iron doors on either side.

He began turning one key after another in the three locks of the first door—the turns of the key were endless, screeching by fits and starts as the gears caught.

Martine came alongside me, touching my arm, and, looking at that iron door, her lips barely moving, said:

"Save yourself at least. Play your Fascist cards."

I stared at her so deeply hurt that she shook her head almost imperceptibly: "You'll never understand a thing," she whispered.

The iron door opened, grinding on its hinges. A muted whiff of metal and urine spilled out; I gripped Martine's fingers. Grùscenka, her arm grabbed by a jailer, was dragged past us, white-faced, a faint smile of goodbye in her eyes. She didn't turn. More clanking from inside, out of sight.

"Grùscenka," I called, "Grùscenka." She didn't answer.

Martine was swallowed up at the next door. Then it was my turn. The ward I entered contained nine cages, four on the wall where the door opened, and five in front of the unbroken wall, at the top of which a long, narrow window allowed daylight to shine down on the metal outlines of the cells.

I was locked up in a cell against the wall, facing the door, which held a pregnant woman with a high protruding belly.

I won't describe those ten or so days. I had to settle for the floor because the woman kicked me as soon as I tried to sit down on the plank. Brown-haired, with undefined features, she avoided me with disgust. I was sorry I hadn't changed my clothes. Just the night before, three parcels had arrived from Italy at the same time (from my mother) and I was so agitated that I had put off dividing up my goodies until the next day. There were socks, underwear, three dresses, two sweaters, a pair of shoes, and the boots I'd asked for, boxes of canned and powdered milk, jars of jam, biscuits. If only I had gorged all night. I kept seeing in my mind the articles of clothing I could have worn. My mistake had been to want to disinfest myself first (1 was infested with crabs as well as head and body lice). Meanwhile, my cellmate spat up a mouthful of yellowish fluid whenever she accidentally crushed a bedbug with her hand. She'd told me her story in a nutshell when they'd first locked me up with her.

"What did you do?" she asked me indifferently.

"I'm accused of theft at the factory, but I didn't steal."

"*I* did, more than a hundred parcels."

She was German, and had managed a post office (I think in Okriftel) with her husband. Both of them had stolen parcels meant for German soldiers at the front; the more lavish ones were for the Russian front, coffee, chocolate, cold cuts, everything you could wish for, wonderful months, years. Investigation time had come. Tried by martial law, her husband had been shot immediately; she would be executed right after she gave birth.

"The war might end in the meantime," I replied, not understanding how I felt. My words must have upset her. She didn't speak to me again, didn't hear me if I said anything to her. I myself was happier with that silent hostility. At night, wrapped in my blanket on the floor, I heard her muttering off and on, huddled up on the plank with her face to the wall, "*Dreckausländer*"* and other hateful words.

I spent my days with my face against the grille, talking to the people in the cells around me. The iron partitions that separated us made the prisoners invisible to me. Thieves, prostitutes, a murderer, all foreigners speaking loudly in unconstrained pandemonium, intent on planning a collective fart each time the jailers entered. They would announce to one another that they were about to fart and were urged to hold it in, soup time was coming.

"*Y a les chleux,*" here come the Krauts, I warned them as soon as a jailer's eye appeared in the peephole of the door opposite my cell.

And when the two jailers entered with the "swill," the concert of blasts and splutters started up with such a stench that we didn't breathe, letting it fill the guards' noses.

My cellmate, the only German in that place, was overcome by nausea,

*Filthy foreigners.

bent over her belly. When she very slowly recovered, she would feel her abdomen, listening with her hands, a secret smile in her eyes.

One night I woke up and saw her standing on the plank. In the shadows she was fumbling with the grating that served as the cell's ceiling. I realized that she was tying something to it (her stockings, I thought right away, since every evening she caressed and kissed them after taking them off). When she then slipped her head into the noose, I leaped up and grabbed her legs. Her hands clutched the grating above her and she tried to kick. Standing, I held tight to her knees, my cheek against her belly. I felt the fetus stirring gently through the cloth and taut flesh.

"Don't touch me," she croaked, gagging with disgust, spitting up a watery, acidic vomit that ran down my hair and forehead toward my mouth; it seemed like liters and liters.

All at once it occurred to me that I could shout. "Help," I yelled, *"au secours!"* more and more frantically.

The adjacent cells awakened slowly. The woman above me was pleading with me: "Thank you, you saved me, now please be quiet." Her sweet voice was striking. "It was a moment of confusion, but be quiet now, stop screaming." Shocked by such a capacity for gentleness, I stopped shouting and heard her say: "Help me put my feet back on the plank, be quiet, okay . . . that's it."

"First take your head out of the noose," I told her softly, feeling vulnerable.

"Ja, natürlich, but if you don't loosen your grip I can't, you're holding me so high that my head is squashed, the grating is cutting into me, please," she implored, still sounding grateful to me. "You have to prop me up by the feet. Go on, sit on the plank, I'll support myself with my hands and put my feet on your shoulders."

"I don't trust you."

"Grip my ankles."

The other cells strained to hear. "Lucia," they called with unusual wariness, "what's going on?" I heard their alert breathing around our forms clinging in the shadows. My companion kept whispering to herself, "Thank you, thank you, what was I about to do to you, my son," her body increasingly limp against me.

Then, bracing my forehead against her legs, which I continued to grip with my left arm, I liberated my right arm to grab one of her ankles. But her knee shoved me sharply under the chin and made me waver; immediately another thrust caught me right in the face. I instinctively put my free hand up to my bleeding nose and a kick in the throat from her released foot almost made me fall backward onto the plank. I nearly hung her myself, pulling her with me as I fell. But by some reflex I managed not to lose my balance, my arm wrapped around her right thigh like a claw, so that even bending that knee she couldn't strangle herself. As I focused on not loosening that hold and on trying to stop her other leg that was kicking out wildly, another blow caught me on my once-again exposed nose. I could no longer tell what was hitting me. I remember that when the foot I couldn't grab lost its shoe, inside I reveled in the scuffle, in the need to grapple for the sake of grappling, to ease my cramped hands. But that instant cost me the sole of her foot pressed against my face, toes in my eyes, clinging like a suction cup, as though we were one flesh. In a flash I thought of biting her and twisted my mouth. What if I licked the foot? Tickling it with my tongue would make her loosen her hold. To do that I had to slacken my other arm, and a hail of kicks, knee thrusts, and curses rained down on me; however, I had managed to grab the ankle of the foot that was in my face and to bend her calf under her thigh, keeping her sitting in air, like a Buddha.

"Filthy bedbug!" she hissed, her voice piercing. "What business is it of yours? Who are you? What do you want? How dare you, *how dare you*? What do you want from me, it's *my* life," she screeched, panting, "filthy bitch . . . *my* life! *How dare you!*" And thrashing about, she made the grating snap. The sharp wrenching sound softened into the plop of her dangling body and me knocked to the floor. Only then did I hear the deafening racket of mess-tins and rhythmically pounding feet from my neighboring cellmates, who were hoarsely shouting for the jailers.

The interrogation, that same day, was strangely undemanding. I was led to what turned out to be the courthouse, to a room I couldn't see, where men in plainclothes sat behind a table. My battered face was meticulously described in the minutes: swellings and bruises on my forehead were enumerated, scratches on my cheeks, neck, and hands were measured with a centimeter-rule (I couldn't explain the scratches), a cracked incisor tooth was listed, nasal bleeding noted. Not only did they exonerate me of any responsibility for the suicide of the "pregnant prisoner," but they also commended me for trying to save the unborn child for the Third Reich, snatching him away from the demented perpetrator of infanticide. As a result I was granted probation. I was allowed to go back to the Lager. I would be summoned for information related to my arrest and that of the other foreigners. My conduct in jail was a sure indicator of having reformed. Nazi justice did not doubt my will to cooperate.

My barrack was still empty. My companions would soon return, however. Hunger dehumanized me. I ran to my locker. The padlock was forced, the shelves empty except for the floppy duffel bag with my mother's letters in a pocket, next to the packets of rat poison that Grùscenka had given me: she'd taken them from her supply of disinfectants for the toilets when I told her I saw two sewer rats pawing through the bins behind the barrack. In a fragment of mirror I saw hateful eyes watching me and turned around slowly, terrified. There was no one. I buried those eyes back in the mirror.

I tried to force my roommates' padlocks. Unsuccessfully. I peeked through the slits in the locker doors to see if I could make out my stuff and sniffed the scents. Pausing awhile with one eye glued to a vent in Jacqueline's locker door (my palm over the other eye), I glimpsed a pale blue color. Aha, it was the little cotton dress, shirred at the waist, the jauntiest one, that my mother had sent me. Nasty bitches. Silent tears flowed as outrage clouded my thoughts. I sat down to wait for my roommates, legs apart, hands in my pockets, leaning against the bunk in front of the door, the one whose upper pallet had been Martine's.

They arrived singly or in pairs, glanced briefly at me, and walked past, keeping to one side (hurriedly, however). I began with Jacqueline, the only one who had looked at me with an "Ooh" of surprise that seemed affectionate, almost happy.

"I want my stuff back," I managed to get out. "I want my food back."

"Oh yeah?" The other women who had dodged me turned around slowly and approached me. I glared at them.

"Thieves," I hissed.

"You sold out the others," one of them said, shrugging. "That's how come you're here." She turned her back to me.

"Yeah," another one came forward, "the Nazis were right. 'The student talked,' they said. Just look at her, that hateful face. And we didn't want to believe it!"

"No!" I couldn't speak. I rushed at them, punching and jabbing.

"You spilled your guts, you slut, you sold out." They were all talking at once.

I went for the lockers. Tip them over, I thought. They realized it. Each one ran to protect her locker door, ready to defend it with her life.

"Filthy bitches, you wanted me dead," my brain was screaming, but no words came out. Dully I kept repeating: "I want my things back. I want my food back."

"And what about Martine? And Carla? How come you're here alone?" The voices came thick and fast as they grouped in front of the lockers. "They weren't traitors, they stood up to the beatings, the torture."

"No," I started moaning again, "no, no." The pain was impossible to control. I had to do something, do what? and who would be first? "That's right," I started yelling. "I sold you out but good! You'll all end up in jail," I laughed.

In the brawl that followed, amid the fray of bodies and voices—"Bitches," "traitor," "you'll give it all back, every last crumb," "Nazi swine"—the stove rolled to the floor, belching puffs of black smoke that filled the room. We didn't even notice that the door had been thrown open. It was the crack of the *Lagerführer*'s whip, thrashing us, that called us back to the situation. Slowly we straightened up; as I crawled out from under the others, I saw a strand of my hair in someone's hand.

"They stole my stuff," I said, breathing hard in the absolute silence. Only then did I realize that I too clutched a hank of black curly hair between my fingers. I stared at my speechless companions one by one and victory died in my soul.

"What did they steal from you?" the *Lagerführer* asked me with patent understanding.

"She's the thief," the women blurted out, huddling together. "She stole alcohol at the factory."

"My stuff," I repeated.

"She left the machinery unattended."

"My things, my food."

"Sabotage," they threw out chaotically, "she's guilty of sabotage . . ." A trembling voice rose: "She wanted us to strike."

All eyes turned to look coldly at the older woman who'd uttered the unspeakable and in a faint voice stammered, "She wanted to provoke us, to put us to the test, but we didn't . . ."

"What did they steal from you?" the *Lagerführer* repeated kindly. The kindness only cruelty can give you, I thought.

"A box of powdered milk," I said blankly.

"Is that all??" the *Lagerführer* asked with amiable irony.

"Yes," I said firmly.

"Are you sure?"

"Yes."

"Really?"

I nodded.

"Fine. I'll have the lockers searched. Take out your things, everything will be checked against the contents of the packages that you signed for when you picked them up. And if they stole anything else from you, don't worry, you'll get justice. They won't lay a finger on you."

Turning to my roommates, he said, "A report will be prepared. You will sign your accusations."

"What accusations?" The women crowded around. They knew nothing. Rumors, hearsay, nothing.

Jacqueline spoke up. "Her father came looking for her, he's a government official, you can't charge her."

"We'll see about that." The *Lagerführer* strode out, leaving two armed guards outside the barrack. The dogs were whining.

"My father came for me?" I whispered to Jacqueline.

"Like hell. Who'd be looking for you?"

Bruised, scratched, bleeding from the nose and mouth, we assembled my stuff on my pallet while four of the women on sentry duty at the window covered our movements from the guards. Several things that had been eaten or traded during my absence were missing. Each woman took out one of her garments, a lump of sugar, a pinch of tobacco, until we thought we had put together a plausible equivalent of the three parcels. There remained the disparity I'd complained of, the box of powdered milk: it was gone. We agreed to blame the pregnant Bergamo woman for the theft, since she'd been repatriated for the birth and couldn't be prosecuted. We took heart at the thought that whatever charge might be made against me I had only to assign the blame to her. Having cooled off, in part due to exhaustion, we sat down to await the inspection. The minutes ticked by.

"I'm hungry," I said.

"So eat. With all the food you have! Look, it's all yours, what more do you want?" a voice said from her pallet.

"You want us to stop breathing?" another voice piped up.

"Us *too*?" a third voice chimed in (could it have been Jacqueline?).

I huddled at the head of my bunk, in front of the stuff, not tasting so much as a crumb of bread. So it was just an apparent truce. They believed the Nazis. I would never convince them. I would never convince anyone. My parents? I laughed to myself. The hours passed in silence.

Occasionally a woman got up to sneak a bite from her locker. Hiding it from me as she glanced at me out of the corner of her eye (I could tell). After all, I had reported them. No, I couldn't convince anyone. Essentially I couldn't even convince myself. Too much effort.

Half-asleep, sitting on my pallet with my knees pressed against my chest and my sore cheek resting on them as I kept an eye on the bread and sugar beside me, I remembered the packets of rat poison. Relief knocked the breath out of me. How could I not have thought of it before?

I took my time thinking about it. Still, I had to make up my mind if I didn't want to be rescued when my roommates awoke. It must have been at least 11:00 p.m., maybe even midnight. Let's see. I returned to the Lager around five. The women showed up about six-thirty or seven, stopping by the barrack before going to the camp canteen (they even missed supper to-night, or rather the watery soup). Not more than an hour must have passed before the *Lagerführer* showed up. I wondered if the guards were still out-side. I thought of going out to pee. No, don't change the subject. I was say-ing: Had it all been over by nine o'clock? Each woman in her bunk? More likely by ten. Don't get bogged down in details. Take things in order. Surely it was later than I thought, could it be 1:00 a.m.? Soon, no hurry. What did I have to lose by dying? They say that, but it's routine. I'd learned Latin (I laughed). And tomorrow?

At the thought of tomorrow and the days to come, I made up my mind. Everything that would follow rose up against me, crushing me all at once: What would I do with what I'd experienced here? Suddenly I saw the mahogany furniture, the fine china, the English silverware in my family's home, and I laughed with delight. A satisfaction filled me as I pictured them and erased them, presto, gone, all gone. Feverishly I took off my shoes and slid to the floor, unsteady because of my numb, tingling legs; slipping a hand into the pocket of the duffel bag, I felt around for the packets beside my mother's letters. I pulled them out, heaving a thankful sigh, and counted them; whatever lives dies—there were sixteen of them. I felt light.

I took my aluminum cup and, on tiptoe, went to the sink to fill it. The trickle of water on the metal was a refreshing sound to my ears. I poured eight packets into the first cupful of water, stirred it with my finger, and, closing my nostrils, drank it down in one gulp. Hurriedly, I emptied the other packets into a second cup of water and, holding my nose again, tried to swallow without breathing but I couldn't do it. I counted thirteen sips. Half a cup of clear water on top of it, to make sure everything went down. I felt a great peace. Maybe I should walk back and forth like Socrates. It took so little. I paused in front of my bunk. No, I would die on Martine's pallet. Martine wouldn't have believed what the Nazis said about me. I climbed up slowly so as not to wake the woman below. I lay supine, molding myself to Martine's straw mattress. I was done. Martine would have believed me, Alain too, and Etienne and Grùscenka as well, already so distant. They would have believed me. I could let myself go. Finally. I slipped into a drowsy trance.

All on their own, the strands of hair on my head stood up one by one;

my skin became drenched in a cold sweat; shivers came and went in waves from head to toe; my teeth chattered in my skull; a tube-like thing inside my stomach, maybe the esophagus, writhed; and I broke out in goose bumps. I felt like I was about to burst. But it didn't last long. Horror swept over me. In every pore, a horror of death, my eyes bulging out of their sockets as a sense of irreparability plunged me into that overall horror with the full weight of the miserable thing that was me.

What's really stayed with me, intact and vivid, from that night, whenever I think about it (which is as seldom as possible), is the utter sense of wretchedness that I felt at a certain moment of my poisoning (the rest is entirely reconstructed). That *I* would deny the universe my life seemed so miserable—I have no other word for it—that it overwhelmed the horror, drowning out the evidence. Yet even amid my body's turmoil, the determination not to ask for help prevailed, with a murky (and futile) awareness that the refusal to demean myself in front of the women was in fact the very lowest depth of my wretchedness.

I wanted to get up but I couldn't. I wanted to turn over on my side but I couldn't. Two fingers, the whole hand in my throat, supine, goggle-eyed, I realized that even if I wanted to—and by then I wanted to—I couldn't scream; not a sound came out of me. My flesh twitched, nerve fibers and organs convulsed. Streams of vomit flooded my face

I woke up in a neat white and blue hospital room, with tulle curtains, varnished beds, a drip in my arm. It was blood. I had transfusions totaling four liters, which had been donated to me by the anemic, famished internees in the Lagers. I'm even taking your blood, I sometimes thought in serenely bitter, quiet desperation during the weeks of convalescence that followed; even your blood, as I read the *Confessions* of Saint Augustine, which the pastor of the Italian consulate had brought me as a gift.

The morning I'd ingested the rat poison they found me drowning in vomit and blood, my jaw dislocated. What had saved me was the excessive dose I'd swallowed down in one gulp. The violence of the poison's effect had activated the body's defenses and made rejection possible. Had I taken only half the amount, I would not have survived. Only the kidneys had been damaged, permanently; some renal vascular duct was fragile and at the slightest strain oozed blood.

The consul himself came to see me. Director Lopp had notified him.

"Why didn't you turn to me? You will be officially repatriated," he informed me.

The consul was a hale and hearty, benevolent man with graying hair, who above all did not want to hear any details. He'd sent word of my circumstances to the Italian Foreign Ministry. He was anxious to convince me that he hadn't known and that, as soon as he'd been informed, he'd moved heaven and earth to afford me the assistance that was due me, owing to my status. He indicated the curtains, and in a lowered voice confided:

"A hospital for Germans only, *nur für Deutschen*," and with a sly wink: "*Reichsdeutschen*," he explained, raising an index finger. He was on edge because he didn't know whether the girl who'd attempted suicide was my father's daughter or the one imprisoned by the Nazis, the girl beaten by the internees or the one with the OSTEN in her buttonhole.

He proffered a question but immediately took it back: "Don't think about it anymore. It was a terrible nightmare. It's over."

He sat stiffly upright at my bedside, with a monocle that I could not stop staring at, leaning forward only to emphasize the difficulties he'd had to overcome to have me admitted "here," he said with a sweeping wave of his hand, turning his gaze of approval on the walls. I observed the capillary veins on his moist, ruddy face, on the pale forehead and receding chin. I was aware of how drained I was compared to him. I felt only a faint, brief flicker of sympathy when, with a certain consternation in his eyes, he considered my father's self-discipline: "A true Spartan," he said, in fact, a man "who despite the ability to pull so many strings, didn't ask me to do a thing for you, Signorina Lucia."

"He doesn't give a damn," I replied sweetly. The consul took his leave.

II

I boarded the train without being allowed to go back to the camp. They brought my stuff to me at the hospital. I had been there six weeks. The doctors had visited to philosophize with me. The nuns approved of Saint Augustine on the nightstand. A clerk from the consulate was present to witness the tally of my clothes, ready to file a complaint if I was missing anything. I hated that pale blue cotton dress, those sweaters and suede shoes, the stockings and panties, I wanted to destroy them. I was about to ask the clerk to send the entire suitcase (a gift from the consul himself) filled with my stuff to the women in the barrack, but I sensed that he would have kept it for himself. I summoned the pastor but at the last minute I didn't trust him. I insisted that he be the only one to accompany me to the station. He had a sidecar. Once I got him complaining about the Nazis, he opened up. So I told him to pass by my old Lager. When he refused, I threatened to report him, and he drove me there. I slipped under the barbed wire fence, shoving the German shepherd away with a kick. I left the suitcase under Jacqueline's bed with a note. I kept the boots I had on, and I was wearing a pair of trousers I'd gotten back from the clerk and a sweater around my waist; in the duffel bag on my back were a loaf of bread and Saint Augustine.

The boredom wore on. I smoked throughout the trip, lighting one cigarette from the butt of another. I handed my documents to the inspectors, ignored the seatmates who asked me about opening or closing the window. After twenty hours or so I was in Verona: a sunny morning, stalls with peaches outside the station, at a few liras per kilo. A forgotten hustle and bustle, and Italian words everywhere, surprising me at every step. I didn't know where to go.

All I remember of that morning is wandering around the city, staring at the people. They all looked like faces that hadn't seen war. Buy a peach, I told myself, eyeing the velvety piles at the fruit stands. I approached a woman who was feeling them, but my smile faded when I saw her unwelcoming expression. Surrounded by talk and gestures that didn't concern me, clearly in the customers' way, with the shopkeeper standing there, I reached out my hand, quickly pocketed a stolen peach, and made off, obsessed. I turned the corner and bit into the flesh, the fruit hidden in my hands, sucking the juice slowly before continuing to walk. But by the third time I did it (a plum this time) I felt isolated by my stealing—it was out of step with the passersby.

In a trattoria I ate three plates of roasted polenta topped with tomato sauce and two slices of chestnut cake. I was eating my food placidly when two soldiers at a nearby table ordered *pastasciutta*. I didn't see them hand over any food stamp vouchers and called the host:

"A *pastasciutta* for me too."

"I already told you, you don't have a voucher."

"You gave it to the soldiers."

"Of course."

"Without a voucher? I'm going to report you."

"What do you mean, without a voucher! They gave me vouchers all right!"

"I'm going to report you just the same," I said, making a move to get up.

The man changed his tune, he was sweating.

He quickly served me a plate of spaghetti *aglio e olio* (with garlic and oil), a glass of wine, a small piece of pecorino cheese, and a large hunk of bread as well. I savored every mouthful, chewing slowly.

"Did you have enough?" the host finally asked; he was around forty and had a wary look. I nodded my head and started laughing. Suddenly he winked at me: "What was there to report? I gave you this food because I wanted to, my dear girl, I took it out of my family's mouth, I took it from our rations."

"How much is it?" My good mood was already gone.

"You decide, young lady, ask your conscience, such things are priceless these days."

"How much is it?" I repeated, hardening my voice. "I want the bill, written and signed."

I paid a few liras. Outside in the street I laughed to myself over the host who couldn't figure me out. I went to sit in the sun on a park bench. I awoke as the sun was going down, peaceful, satisfied.

I counted the money remaining from what the consul had issued me (one hundred Italian liras) along with two cartons of cigarettes. I had eighty-two liras left. Five for water on the train and thirteen for the meal, it added up. I stretched. I had to find a place to sleep, but first a toilet. I was in a little park in the middle of a piazza; I just had to ask. But the faces that passed were all absorbed in their own little world, as if that were all there was, and I put it off until the next person came by. Why spoil my freedom?

I roused myself: I'd find my own way. I knew I looked decent again; after the suicide attempt I was back to my old weight of fifty-two kilos, deloused, clean. I returned to the station, where some soldiers came up to me:

"Want to spend the night with me?" one asked. They looked like inexperienced, violent boys, *repubblichini* with a fez worn backward or over the eyes. I recall two insistent ones with whom I ended up in a bar: one was tall, brown-haired, with a kind of dapper cheeriness, the other shorter than me, dark, with a mocking air.

"Are you Fascists?" I asked in a low voice.

"You can say it out loud," the short one laughed with his affected swagger. "They saw things get ugly, so they all turned tail. When the ship is sinking, the rats are the first to flee, but I'm holding firm. Those fucking whores go with the Germans, would you believe? But not with us, no, they turn up their noses," he said, wrinkling his nose to imitate the girls who rejected him.

"And you?" The tall soldier leaned down to me.

"I've come from the Lagers and the German prisons."

"Oh."

"How is it over there?" the dark one asked, lowering his voice.

"It's like they say here," I replied.

"Oh."

"How did you get out?" the tall one whispered. I was standing between them, at the counter of the bar, a cup of chicory with saccharin in my hand, and I looked at them in the mirror opposite us.

"I tried to kill myself and they sent me back to Italy."

"You're going home? Lucky you."

"Watch out for the partisans, they don't answer to anyone," the dark one said.

"Are your parents expecting you?"

The thought of my parents, up till then avoided, oppressed me. Unexpected tears welled up in my eyes.

"I don't know where to go anymore," I uttered, exhausted.

"Come on, let's get out of here."

The three of us walked the streets until late at night. I told them what I'd been through, about my situation, my fear of going back to my parents, of standing up to their opinions. I described in detail my father's thought-less way of saying hurtful things, my mother's way of looking down on the lower classes.

The tall soldier tried to reassure me at all costs; they would welcome me back, he said. "They will forgive you" were the words he used, inter-rupting my constant outpourings and justifications with suggestions such as: "Why don't we go have a good meal? It'll be easier to talk, things seem less bleak on a full belly."

The short soldier instead shook his head: "They won't understand a fucking thing." Nevertheless, he agreed that going to eat was a great idea.

Stuffed as I was, I said I wasn't hungry and they sighed; to them I must have seemed like a spiritual creature.

At the restaurant, however, I devoured everything they ordered for me, maybe twice what they ate.

"Damn, you eat like a horse," the short one chuckled, pouring me some wine.

The other one pressed his leg against mine under the table, about to sug-gest a good night's sleep. I focused on the dark soldier, who struck me as more sincere.

"I don't want to have sex with you," I slurred, tongue-tied from the wine. "Not with him, though he's trying to feel me up under the table without you knowing, nor with you, even if you're more frank. So tell me how much I owe you and no hard feelings." This time I cried on purpose, to move them so they wouldn't make me pay my share.

"No, no!"

"Don't be silly. We're not skirt-chasers, you know. A Fascist is a man of honor," the dark one exaggerated, he too slightly tipsy. "We can see you don't feel like it, you know, given the bad situation you're in!"

"I did it to cheer you up," the tall, brown-haired one said, taking offense, "given how tired I am! What can I say, you were so down."

"Whatever," the dark one reproached him, "you were taking advantage of her, I wasn't." And to me he said, "I'm not tired and I'd make you reach the stars. But I'm a man of honor and, if you don't want to, friends like before." He winked at me: "Think about it a bit . . ."

"Right." I said I had to go to the toilet. I left by a back door without saying goodbye to them. I was proud of the trick I'd played on them. Maybe they would have paid the bill at a hotel, but this way there were fewer complications. I could always go and sleep in the waiting room at the station. Meanwhile, what was stopping me from taking a walk? I checked the money in my pants pocket. I'd managed to do okay, at this rate I had enough to live on for a few more days before having to go home, to Como, to the villa the Mussolini government requisitioned for my family. The party's over, home at sunset, my mother's eyes aimed at the grandfather clock in the hallway if I was late coming back, worse, my father's orderly glued to me, tacitly decrying all I'd put them through, maybe sending the chauffeur to pick me up if I lingered someplace too long, or not being able to go out anymore except accompanied by my mother, to those unbearable ladies' teas like in Rome. Back then I'd amused myself by cultivating a retinue of mothers-in-law: to evade boredom, I practiced ingratiating myself with mothers who had sons, for any future prospect. But now that pastime seemed insipid. The very idea of receptions and concerts, with my mother in a veil or wide-brimmed summer hat to shade her lovely face, me with dainty lace gloves smiling staidly and demurely, gleaming officers clicking their heels here and there with a haughty expression, the gracious atmosphere—it was all so predictable that I had to remind myself of the suicide attempt so as not to run and hide somewhere.

I got lost in the darkened streets and was stopped by a patrol of *repubblichini*.

"Documents!" they demanded. "Don't you know there's a curfew?"

Surrounded by an escort of soldiers, a dozen or so holding machine guns, the rhythm of hobnail boots on the pavement and a scent of oleander in the still darkness of the long avenue, the disorientation that had confounded my pleasure at being free since I'd stepped off the train vanished. I was myself again; with every measured step I came to life, marching to the factory in a column with my fellow internees.

I realized that I hadn't thought about them throughout the entire day, not once from the moment I arrived in Verona, as if they had never existed, and I had a strange sense of fear at seeing how easy it had been for me to pass over those recent months, too rooted in the present moment, as if there were nothing more. All of us wrapped up in paltry ambitions. I would not return home. I would go to work in a factory in Milan, better yet in Turin, farther away from my parents. I had to be very careful, however, forget about stupid petty thefts and anything that could attract the authorities' attention, keep in mind the curfew, go unnoticed. If the consul had revealed that I'd been repatriated, my father would surely look for me. He would lose face if I didn't go back home.

We came to a building that turned out to have been a school. In a classroom with desks stacked along one wall, an officer behind a teacher's desk interrogated me. When had I arrived? Why hadn't I immediately taken the connection to Como, which my ticket showed was my destination? Whom had I had contact with in Verona? What was I doing well after midnight in the center of the city? Who was I looking for? Questions peppered with insults and threats. I got distracted comparing the Italians' interrogation methods with those of the Germans, the latter contained, the Italians brutal. It was as if I had committed a personal affront against that officer, whom the soldiers addressed as marshal. Strike a human chord, I thought. "Marshal, I have nothing against you," I said. "Look at my papers, here, you see? It's the Frankfurt prison stamp: *Gefängnis*, do you understand the word? I was in prison. And look here, there is also a certificate from the hospital. They freed me because I was innocent, but I was ill. And being back in Italy, with people talking excitedly, peaches liberally sold in the streets . . ."

"The sun," he empathized.

"Yes, the sun, everything, after nearly six months of detention between the Lager and all the rest, I wasn't about to rush, I felt like taking a stroll."

"I understand, but try telling those higher up. Who's going to tell them? Are you going to tell them?"

"If no one says anything, I'll keep quiet," I promised. "Let me sleep somewhere, tomorrow morning I'll leave for Como and that's the end of it."

Another dozen or so soldiers were lying sprawled on the ground, some snoring, some awake and following the scene.

"And who's to say you're not one of *those*? I don't want a brothel in here. Inspections come thick and fast, my dear girl. If you'd been a partisan, you would have been fair game, we could have fucked you all we wanted. There would have been some merit in disrespecting you. Hitler himself might have arrived and found us with our dicks up: an act of war," he declared, drawing a line in the air with his thumb and forefinger joined together. "We would have been in proper order, see? But *they* released you, complete with documents and stamps, *their* documents, know what I mean? Who can trust you? It could well be a trap, my beauty, and I'm not falling for it."

"But where should I go now?"

"You're asking me?"

They brought a bench into the middle of the room.

"Lie down here. And if you make a move to 'service' any of them, I'll take you to the Gestapo."

I fell asleep at once. They shook me a long time before I woke up: "Get up, dummy, and get out of here. If we catch you around again, I warn you, you're in for it," the marshal said. And, irritated at having protected me, he shoved me out with a kick in the butt by way of goodbye as I was leaving.

I headed for the station, following their directions. It was dawn, the air fresh, and I filled my lungs. I thought about what to do, walking briskly to get away from that area. I would turn off at the right moment.

But reluctantly I slowed up. I was afraid again. Who knows what bad blood existed between local contingents and occupational forces, between Fascist and Nazi authorities. The radio at the Lager canteen had called Mussolini's new regime a "phantom government." True, the stray troops, like the two soldiers from whom I had sponged supper, spoke of allegiance to the staunch ally stabbed in the back, but at the top? In fact, my father had always been vexed when my mother and I exalted the moral virtues of the German people. Yet his mother, my paternal grandmother, was of pure German blood, a descendant of Bavarian families transplanted in Italy at the time of the Napoleons, some of them related to a school of artists founded by Klaus associated with Canova. The first to stray was precisely my grandmother Bettina, who married an Apulian from an aristocratic family, namely my father's father. But what did my grandparents have to do with anything now? I was losing my train of thought. Oh yes, my father. In Germany there were foreign ministries involved, here it was different, he couldn't very well do as he did when I was in the Lager, when to punish me for my rash action he hadn't lifted a finger for me, though in his position he could have come a hundred times to see for himself how I was living. Here if I ran into one of his colleagues, how would it look for him to be ignoring me?

My suicide attempt had satisfied his pride (of course the Frankfurt consul had reported it to him, to crow about the assistance he'd given me), and now an act of clemency toward his daughter the black sheep was essential. The more I thought about it, the more confident I was that it was now a matter of honor for him to find me. And how could I be sure that the marshal wasn't sending word of my imminent arrival to the soldiers in Como? With a cool head, my story about wandering aimlessly around because I was happy to be back could have looked different to him, all the more so if he was afraid the Nazis might have freed me to use me for their own ends. He'd clearly said as much. So he'd acted like he was being hospitable and released me in deference to their documents, while still doing his duty to keep an eye on me; Machiavellian as he was about the question of fucking, he wouldn't have taken any risks in this case.

I was quite certain that he was telegraphing not only Como but also the train station in Verona, as well as the bus terminal for coaches to Lombardy, and all checkpoints. This was not the time to head west. I was better off going east, farther into Veneto. It was futile to hope to pass unnoticed. In the hallway of the former school where I'd spent the night, I had seen wanted photos of fugitives with rewards on their heads, people from Piedmont, from Friuli, those nearly hypnotic faces on ID cards, the inexpressive stare waiting for the click. I pictured my face alongside them with an even higher reward—appropriate to my father's prestige—for anyone furnishing information about me; after all, I thought in my malevolent mood at the time, he would still find a way to not pay (I needed to hate him, to buck myself up). Besides, it was a difficult time, no one trusted anyone else, who would go out of his way to hide me? I had no connections, how would I? How could I establish contacts, at the drop of a hat, the daughter of Fascists, my mother secretary to the Fascist Party since the days of France, with two gold medals from the Grand Council for her assistance to emigrants (she worked night and day to establish nurseries, send children to summer camps, organize theatrical performances, arrange for Fascist Befanas, distribute weekly food parcels). The daughter of notorious Fascists, more than ever in view, repatriated from the Nazi camps. Martine had correctly expressed what everyone would think: that I had saved myself by playing my Fascist cards. What's worse, those cards had played themselves. There had been no consul to release Grùscenka or Martine. In the words of the marshal, they would have been fair game. The little schoolgirl could afford the luxury of playing Joan of Arc because when all was said and done *she wasn't taking any risks*. Being who I was, whatever I did was indulged.

I was crushed by a sorrow and shame that paralyzed my resolve. I had to shed my social class. Changing my name in Italy would be of little use unless I were able to pass through the front. But I despised the Americans and the king. And then what? I would find safety, nothing more, given that I didn't feel like joining up with the Americans. Assuming getting through the front was feasible. My face lined up with the other wanted persons stared at me from the hallway of the former school I'd just left, as if I had actually seen it there the night before. To begin with, I had to get rid of the documents that I had in my duffel bag. A tremendous decision, and time was against me. It wasn't salvation, but it was one less risk of being found.

Coming down a side street, I saw a bunch of people being herded by several SS soldiers. They were heading in my direction and I stopped at the corner to watch them. Men and women in civilian clothes moved along slowly, their legs jerking when a Nazi boot kicked them in the shins. The SS, their machine guns pointed at the prisoners' backs, kept glancing behind them and looking up at the windows of the houses, meanwhile scanning the human pack from side to side, shoving their gun barrels into stragglers' backs at times.

When they drew near me, an SS (there were six in all) pointed his gun at me, motioning with his head for me to get out of the way. They're afraid, I thought, they're in a hurry; they won't shoot me because they don't want to wake the neighborhood. I stood there, staring at the SS. Another one caught up to him and came running toward me, his footsteps silent, like in an ambush.

"*Pass auf, ich schreie*," watch out or I'll scream, I told him distinctly in German. Maybe he was surprised by the language, because he stopped. "Take one more step toward me and we'll all scream," I said. "Mind you, it's our signal."

In an instant the SS sergeant who was following the captives pronounced *"Alt"* and stepped forward; with his head he motioned two soldiers to go to the rear of the small procession, pointed two others to the sides and a fifth to the head of the group, facing the prisoners, each soldier with his finger on the trigger. When he reached the spot where the SS to whom I had spoken had been standing, he said in a soft voice that did not shatter the early-morning stillness: "Join the column at once or we'll kill you all. On the count of three. *Eins zwo . . .*"

I jumped into the ranks. There was only the clatter of my boots. I absolutely had to get rid of my documents and the repatriation certificate. If they found them I was lost. All I could do was dump the duffel bag. A pang at the thought of the money. No, it was in my pocket, I touched it.

"Hands where I can see them," said the soldier who was gripping me tightly. "Try putting a hand in your pocket again and I'll shoot you."

In fact, I got so distracted thinking about where to hide the money so they wouldn't seize it that I forgot that the problem was the duffel bag. After several deserted streets, doors began opening. The SS pushed harder to make us hurry. I faked a sprained foot and, bending over in simulated pain, let the duffel bag slip to the ground. Promptly prodded by the barrel of a machine gun, I looked back at the bag as if I wanted to recover it, but the soldier shoved it aside with a kick. I glanced quickly at the number of the door where it lay on the ground and, hopping along on one foot, engraved on my mind the outline of the building and the houses that followed, counting the doors until I read the name of the street. For what it's worth, I thought, for what it's worth. I continued memorizing the streets we crossed, sometimes pretending to set down my sprained foot painfully, distressed at not feeling reborn, at not experiencing the importance of what I had done, unable to enjoy my private freedom due to the anxiety of not forgetting the name of the street and the effort of having to hop along on one foot only, alongside those who had been rounded up and who looked at me unkindly; I was oppressed by a sense of exhibitionism stronger than any other motivation.

III

That this is how it happened, I later denied even to myself. I had to turn fifty before acknowledging that I had been repatriated. What I said initially—so often that I came to believe it myself—was that I had been deported to Dachau with my comrades after the strike. I buried the act performed on that distant August 2 in Verona as something to be forgotten. I wanted it to be the Nazis who had captured and imprisoned me, so that gradually my first months as a volunteer were obscured, the period at IG Farben became hazy, and even my time at the K-Lager in Dachau faded into the shadows, lest the situations it held force me to remember all the rest.

The memories shrank. They focus around the escape from Dachau, then reappear at the hotel in Mainz. What remained to me of that entire wartime experience were a few patchy weeks of wandering through the Third Reich, between a solitary escape and the wall falling on my back: a time apart whose memories—not even disclosed in full—skimmed the surface and did not cause any problems. Suffice it to say that I referred to that period as "my German parenthesis," as if it were a concluded preface, a preamble to the wheelchair, without which I was unable to move, the historic background to what was more a technical inconvenience than anything else (so I told myself).

The reader encountered it at the beginning of this book, where I described my escape from the concentration camp and my first weeks of life as a fugitive. The girl in "Thomasbräu" and in "Asylum at Dachau" hardly seems the same as the one from "In the Ch 89" and the fugitive from Verona. Judging by how I saw myself in '53–'54 when I wrote those early pages, I'd been a runaway concerned solely with surviving, with coping, avoiding any attachments so as to have more freedom of movement. Not a trace of the need to "fight together" that had animated me at IG Farben, of the compulsion to find myself back among comrades that in Verona had driven me to join the deported strangers. My going to Germany and my returning there had contracted into a single sensation of escape, and the images I'd retained all centered around this amputated perception.

It took me until 1961, when I wrote "As Long as the Head Lives" (later

I will describe under what circumstances), to dare to acknowledge openly that I had gone to the Lagers voluntarily. After fifteen years of confiding it in secret, whispering it to only a very few individuals, increasingly intimidated by others' reactions to that "rash action" of mine, until its significance had nearly been erased from my mind. And even then, in '61, I mentioned it only in passing, merely as a topic by which I had tried to move the Soviet captain to pity so that he would take me into Russia.

And then it took me another fifteen years to admit that I had returned to the Lagers of my own free will. Why so much resistance? Why in particular was my about-face in Verona the last memory to surface? Even a year ago, when I wrote "In the Ch 89," I was unable to get to the repatriation. I described the strike up to the time it fell apart. I stopped my memory at the part where it failed.

That's what I'm now interested in understanding. What was the origin of that mental block; how had I been able to successfully ignore the tangle of that violent past for so long, believing perhaps that I was putting the lesson to use? Given that I've slipped back into my social class, as Martine and Alain had predicted, how had an experience that so marked me been able to settle at the bottom of my thoughts, almost as if it had never happened? Or maybe it had been at work subconsciously, despite my having wanted to ignore it, seeing as it has at last become clear to me, now that I no longer have reserve worlds in which to invent myself. It all came back to me, even that dawn in Verona, the *repubblichino* marshal's words in my ears, the human herd steered from the end of a side street by the SS, the consul's face superimposed over the softened voice promising "the assistance appropriate to your status" in the neat clinic in Frankfurt. Decades to find myself face-to-face with that leap that I had impulsively and blindly made thirty years ago (and meanwhile my hair has turned gray).

But to be able to reconstruct when this repression lasting thirty years of my life began, I must first fill in the gaps of the repressed experience, to see whether folding a social exigency into an individual vision was entirely my subsequent interpretation, or whether that memory lapse hadn't had its origins in reality, in harsh situations that I didn't dare remember.

―――――

Already on the freight train to Dachau, I knew what it meant to be truly on the other side. Four days crammed in with about fifty deported "Aryans" (Jews were in another car), with only the packed lunch that they had given us in Verona—bread, cheese, and fruit—regretting not having swallowed enough water in the drink they'd allowed us before loading us onto the train. Between endless stops when we flung ourselves against the sealed doors and begged for water, making a deafening racket before falling silent, unmoving, worn out by the waiting, the train would start creaking and jolting on the rails again, and we went back to moving around the car like a caged pack of hounds.

I remember certain sensations. We sat in the straw, between one another's legs to save space. I was crowded between the thighs of my human backrest, in whose company I spent the entire trip. I'd asked another young man who was leaning against me to let me draw my legs up a moment, since they'd fallen asleep on me, and to use my knees as a seat back for a little while. So I was huddled up in a sort of fetal pose, except for my head, which slumped on the shoulder of the man whose chest supported me. His face was leaning on my cheek, and he breathed the sour stench of wet coal into my neck. I in turn took in that rotten egg smell, which rid my nostrils of the persistent reek of diarrhea that polluted the freight car. It must have been night because no light seeped in. The shafts of light that earlier filtered through the chinks in the car had been obliterated. Clasped in that embrace we fought wearily, amid the lurching of the train, the clatter of the moving wheels, the moaning of people racked with thirst. In a parched voice that croaked in his throat, the man spat words of suspicion into my tympanum, and I muttered sarcastic remarks in his ear with some difficulty, because the grating of my tongue scraped my palate; meanwhile, in the dark I tried to read the indistinct gleam that was his eyes, whenever he raised his head to counter me.

My human backrest was one of the deportees from the group in Verona, twenty-five years old.

"I was rounded up by mistake," he'd said, introducing himself to me when we started out.

But in the freight car, in his detailed way of asking questions, I'd recognized that certain probing tone, the look, the words, typical of Martine,

Grùscenka, and Alain. And I surmised that he was not someone rounded up by mistake.

The third night I decided to let off steam: "Stop lying," I told him. "You're a communist partisan, I know it."

I felt him get defensive, physically. And, a little at a time, he came out with words along these lines:

"Not bad, your little performance in Verona, too bad you then gave yourself away, oh yeah, you made the mistake of forgetting that you had twisted your ankle and, as soon as they piled us into the Kommandantur, I saw you walk normally. The Nazis didn't notice, everyone knows they believe in miracles, but I'm more skeptical . . ." And: "Cute, though, that SS sergeant, with the nice silencer he had, he could have bumped you off, right? The hell he could. When you told him watch out or I'll scream, it's our signal, he immediately lowered his gun. See, it just so happens that I know German. But tell me: whose signal?"

"Idiot," I hissed in his neck, my throat dry, "I'm sitting here in your excrement . . ."

"Excuse me, you're the one shitting on me," he corrected.

"If we deportees don't trust one another, it's over," I went on. "*They're* the ones who divide us, that way *even our morale* is in their hands. Isn't bodily shit enough for you? You have to soil my mind too?"

"You want me to confide to you where our partisan bases are in Veneto? Locations, strengths . . . ?"

I don't know how many hours later, our human tangle was on its feet again (we took turns sitting on the floor). Making our way through the car to reach one of the two cans for feces that were at opposite ends, with my friend-enemy leading me by the hand in the continuous bustle of people going up and down nonstop to the cans, amid the groans of dismay and distress (and then also of relief) of those who let go and shit in their pants along the endless route, I suddenly forgave my vilifier. He was right, I was at fault; I demanded that a comrade trust me when I myself hadn't trusted him (I hadn't told him anything about my history).

After waiting for each other at the can, we were able to continue the trip glued to the wall: a coveted spot; those who secured it defended it tooth and nail. My friend-enemy welded himself to it. Standing, his back against the partition, he stuck to it with a kind of blankness, his face touched by a shaft of light coming from a nearby chink.

"Ah," he sighed, "stick close to me." He closed his eyes, his mouth open, his breath increasingly dry and fetid.

Clinging to his neck, against his chest, practically locked together because I had to talk into his ear amid the jolts and groans and din of the moving train, I told him about my life, about volunteering, IG Farben, my parents, repatriation, everything. As I told him, I wept. "You see? They accepted me," I said. (I was alluding to the Soviet and French workers.) But just then I had to dart away to the can.

When I came back to look for him, he was gone. He had even given up the wall spot to get away from me.

For hours I went back and forth in the car from one can to the other, zigzag, scanning the faces in the shafts of sunlight, but he must have been moving too because I didn't find him. For the fourth day in a row they hadn't opened up the car, and thirst intensified my aggression (at least I think so); added to that, the bag of plums we'd each been given when we left had acted as an infernal purgative. As soon as the sliding doors opened in the night, I hurled myself like a wildcat toward the gusts of air that streamed in from outside, smelling of hay. Maybe I shoved my way through a bit heatedly, not to say punching and kicking, because a hand grabbed me, an arm closed around my neck, and *his* face, bathed in a ray of moonlight, gave me a hateful look as he said, "Fascist blood lives up to its name."

Every ounce of energy drained out of me, I looked at him, half-strangled, my head twisted in the vise of his arm: "That's all that . . ." I stammered.

He let me go, saying, "I may be thirsty, but not thirsty enough to drink up your bullshit." He pushed me away with his elbow and slipped in among the deportees.

Not long afterward we reached our destination. He helped the sickest passengers jump down off the train. It was still night, amid deserted tracks in the middle of the countryside. I sat on the edge of the floorboard so I could slide down. He gave me a hand.

"The performance is over," he whispered to me, "you can go home."

Subsequently, I met my friend-enemy only once more, about two months later. I was in line in front of a K-Lager infirmary to pick up an ointment for the scabies that gnawed at me. He was a few meters behind me, on the men's line that stretched alongside ours, the women's queue. His eyes signaled me not to speak. He looked at me as if seeing me lifted a weight off his chest. Still gesturing with his eyes, he suggested changing places, to get closer. Shaved head, dark circles under his eyes, a shadow of himself.

I had so hated him during those two months that I was surprised to be glad to see him. We were now side by side, close but separated by a hundred insuperable centimeters.

"*Ciao*," his lips said.

"*Ciao*."

"We should keep in touch."

"Now?" I had already planned my escape down to the tiniest details, it was a matter of days.

"Why? Did you give in?"

"Me?" I felt a wave of resentment: "Fascist blood?" My anger quickly passed, however. "Listen," I said, barely using my voice, only moving my lips, which he stared at intently, "I'll tell you a secret that I haven't told anyone. I have a plan to escape. Listen to me, come with me."

"And the others? Have you thought about the others?"

I contemplated the wraith of a man who had spoken those words. Sorrow strangled me; how to communicate to him, in the few seconds we had, everything that had built up in me during my time at the K-Lager in Dachau? My line, not as long as his, was moving more quickly. He kept moving a place ahead to stay beside me, running the risk that the deportees might get angry, that the SS might bash his head in with a rifle butt. Finally, I replied:

"The others? I despise victims." I looked at him, torn apart by a kind of savage love for those victims I despised. I stepped back a place, pushing the woman who'd been behind me into my spot. My eyes sought an answer from my friend-enemy as he looked at me from the depths of his gaunt face.

"I searched for you," I told him.

"They tortured me," he said, holding out two fingers without nails, the sensitive flesh exposed to the quick. "And two months in solitary confinement. But I didn't talk."

"Come with me," I told him, moving back another place.

He shook his head no.

"Do you blame me?"

No again, and he couldn't contain a boyish smile.

I was about to step back again, but the Kapo, quicker than I, lashed me with her whip. "You have to come, understand?" I cried loudly now, as an SS dragged me toward the infirmary. I broke free, exclaiming "Heil Hitler," standing at attention in front of the jailer, who, not knowing how to interpret the authoritative tone of my Nazi salute, took his hands off of me.

I just had time to turn around and glimpse the face of my friend-enemy: "You have to live," my lips repeated with a complicit smile. "Let's go," I then ordered the SS, glancing at the Kapo with a sudden feeling of indulgence and turning one last time to my tortured comrade, who silently mouthed "Good luck" (were his eyes laughing at me?).

My Kapo was a middle-aged black triangle, a former druggie; they said she'd even sell her brother for a pinch of snow, and now she had us to trade for a rare Gardenal tablet.

My memories of the K-Lager have not faded. I can summarize them in a few paragraphs.

Dachau took me by surprise. I hadn't imagined it to be the way it was. It was talked about at Höchst, horrible rumors floated around, but they had no substance in our perception. It was like the ogre in fairy tales, at most an oppressive nightmare in which monsters transform into one another and facts have no veracity.

Astonishment was perhaps the strongest feeling I experienced on arriving in Dachau. To the point of sometimes not believing what I was seeing with my own eyes at the very moment I saw it. Perhaps this was one reason why, back in the civilized world, I suppressed for decades those abysmal depths that were roused only in my sleep when a scene from the past gripped my soul like an octopus, raking up ghostly appearances that again seemed unreal.

The shock I felt at the time is still today something that I never forget when talking to someone who has never been in a K-Lager (concentration camp) or T-Lager (death camp).

In the twelve weeks that I remained in Dachau I did not for a moment stop being stunned by the incredible number of privations the human body can endure. I even laughed at the thought of how outraged I'd been over the foreigners' treatment at Höchst, where, by comparison, people lived in comfort and freedom, including the *Osten* and P. Yet here, where we inhaled the intolerable, indignation virtually died in a kind of dazed stupor.

To be truthful, at the beginning I got a little worked up; I was disheartened by human nature, seeing the incredible speed with which a thinking brain (mine first of all) adapts to the most unlivable conditions. Later, however, I realized that it was not surprising if minds in weakened bodies were extinguished as well. The light of reason was focused on its own vital breath. The body's sluggishness made the brain drowsy; it had only enough energy to get by one more month, one more day, one more hour. And in a few weeks I was wholly absorbed by another discovery that then turned all my criteria at the time upside down.

I'm referring to the absolute normality of crime, physical violence, informing on others, and perversion as routine practice in day-to-day dealings, all quickly seeming natural, familiar. I had already felt a strange joy at being alive, there in the freight car; a kind of rapture when, upon arrival at the K-Lager, I'd dropped to the ground in the middle of a bunch of women, on the gravel of a courtyard, where we were then kicked, beaten, spat on, all of us lying there, docilely apathetic, until they shoved us into a barrack where the bliss of being finally able to stretch out on the floor abruptly erased our torments. On the faces of my companions, who lay on the floor with real gasps of pleasure, I had seen the same taste for brutalization that shamed me in my sleep.

At first what humiliated me was the immoderate ability to enjoy the least bit of relief. It wasn't like at Höchst, where I restrained my anger. Here I was so engrossed in what I was doing, meticulously wrapping myself in a blanket, salivating over a mouthful of bread slowly chewed in a corner of the barrack, that basically every other thought remained abstract to me. I ignored the reproachful looks, which didn't even begin to get through to me.

"What? Is this what you came back for? To sleep with lice? To drool over the most rancid swill? What about the struggle? A couple of weeks and the struggle is forgotten?" Silence. I yawned.

"Who would I struggle *with*?" I answered myself.

The first fifteen days had ticked away slowly in one of the isolation barracks, in Quarantine Block, along with dozens of foreigners dehumanized like me and like the SS men who occasionally came to inspect us, Ukrainian and German lumpenproletarians, even Tartars, in whom brutality was so natural as to seem guileless. I had to keep telling myself "they're monsters" so as not to let myself be taken in by their *Selbstverständlichkeit** in enjoying their cruel impulses, like slapping you around, kicking over a full mess-tin, hawking a gob of spit on a blanket—not spitefully, though: just as a matter of course, to pass the time.

Then came the biggest discouragement. The Nazis did not issue me a red triangle—assigned to political detainees—but branded me with a black one, allocated to the "asocials." And they assigned me a bunk in one of the black triangles' barracks. The red triangles' Block was situated on another street inside the K Lager, and I couldn't easily get to it. The men were even farther away, separated from the women. The *Osten* and *P*, like the male and female yellow triangles (the Jews), were virtually inaccessible to us Western and Central Europeans. Impossible to know if Grùscenka was there. The barracks seemed endless to me. Some said there were twenty, some fifty, and some a hundred thousand of us interned in the camp, but I didn't know anyone who had made a map of the K-Lager and its outbuildings, like my comrades at Höchst had done, and to this day I am unable to estimate.

I know that for days I looked for Martine. I didn't find her. I scanned all the faces at the canteen, at roll call, in the lavatories: no one from IG Farben.

Gradually I began to wonder if I had really come here to share the fate of my old comrades, since each day I cared less about not finding them. I reached the point where I dreaded running into one of them.

*Matter-of-factness.

IV

I had to do as Grùscenka had done from her surveillance post in the underground toilets of the Ch 89: look around to form as accurate (and exhaustive) a picture of the situation as possible for myself, and quickly too, before I became so malnourished that I would no longer have the strength to think. The most likely time for observing was during evening roll call in the yard, when the K-Lager internees returned from work, but I mustn't overlook the lavatories at dawn. In addition to Sundays. And at night I could get to know my bunkmates when they returned from their shifts in the factory or in the quarries.

My barrack contained mostly alcoholics of all ages. I counted twenty-two drunks when I arrived. They were all flabby women, their features blurred by alcohol, docile and whiny about the utter tedium. Though genuinely embittered toward the Nazis, they couldn't be trusted: one drop of schnapps involuntarily loosened their tongues.

There were also two nervous petty thieves who were always stealing our rations. When a prostitute reported them to the management, they accused her of having instigated them to revolt, and the woman was exterminated in the infirmary, with an injection, like they usually did with the incurables (in fact, she was suffering from last-stage syphilis). One night, the two petty thieves robbed each other, partly because by now it was difficult for them to steal a single crumb from one of us: we had set up sentry shifts in the barrack, one hour apiece day and night, and if they made the slightest suspicious move, we were on them, beating them up: "Call the Nazis if you can." They stabbed each other, and were immediately immobilized by the German shepherds and shot down by machine-gun fire in the yard.

The most quarrelsome, however, were the professional prostitutes, about ten of them, from every country, most ravaged by venereal diseases. I remember a young Bohemian with clouded vision who felt each object with her fingers and took tiny steps when she walked, and who, for fear of being exterminated, firmly insisted that she could see quite well as the women waved a hand in front of her unblinking face: "Lucky you, with your good eyes!" they laughed, winking at one another.

"That's right," the young woman replied. "I can see."

"So what's this?" They held up a potato. The girl reached out her hands. "No, don't touch. Guess. Go on, guess." Her face would light up when by chance she got it right.

But the "asocial" who made the most lasting impression on me was a Flemish girl who came from a camp of free workers.

One evening she went to sleep in the barrack of a Slav whom she'd recently chosen as a friend. After having sex with her, the guy had gone to the toilet and sent another man back to the bunk. After a certain number of successions the girl had become suspicious, not only of her friend's virility—every half hour he was ready again—but also of certain differences (one time he was fatter, another time thinner), until she noticed the coming and going between the bunk beds and started to resist, futilely, in a silent scuffle. She couldn't say when she'd started to scream, howling so loud that the guards had come running. She filed a complaint against the Slav, but the facts (and male mentality) were against her: Why hadn't she stayed in her barrack? They assigned her to a brothel on the Russian front. But when she raised her fist against the portrait of Hitler, blaming him for all the abuses she'd suffered (her words), they deported her to Dachau. Here she practiced a degrading prostitution, going off to the latrines with SS of the lowest ranks, German or Ukrainian farmhands. She would return to the barrack good-natured in her loose skin of starved fat, her eyes gentle, and she always offered some of us a little piece of her measly earnings, a bit of wurst, a hunk of bread, a packet of jelly.

Three pink triangles lived on a pair of top bunks: Danish (or Norwegian?) lesbians who ignored the entire universe; always intent on washing together and combing one another's hair, spotlessly clean given the environment, refined, gaunt, they showered one another with concern and caresses until late into the night, consumed by a communal ardor that made them seem happy in our eyes, beyond hunger and brutality, wholly immersed in reciprocal tenderness. When approached, they answered politely but in monosyllables, and hastened to retreat to their bunks. Sometimes I saw them spoon-feeding one another in turn, all three from the same mess-tin.

We had only one green triangle in the barrack, that is, a common criminal. She was a French prostitute, an infanticide, her face disfigured by some kind of incident as a result of which she had no chin, almost no nose, and a slit for a mouth; her eyes were constantly wide open because the skin was drawn taut by the scars. It seems she was exceptional at giving blow jobs. I was there when a well-built, good-looking SS sergeant spent his nights at the window of the barrack begging her to come out, giving her as many as three chocolate bars at one time, just to tempt her to join him. Someone had reported him. Rumor had it that it had been Lulù herself. The Nazi sergeant seemed desolate, not so much for being sent to the front with one of those *Strafbataillonen* in which discipline was harsher than in the Foreign Legion, as for no longer being able to see Lulù. Before leaving, he gave her all his pay, even his savings, and countless things to eat. She uttered something in a toothless mumble, through the scar with no lips, as she put away his gifts and, noticing that I was watching her, moved close to my ear: "There are many ways to make them pay, you too should learn them."

I never quarreled with those women, who on Sunday regularly came to blows, except for the three lesbians. Spiteful tricks, mockery, accusations, and scenes always played out on Sundays, when forty-two women got in one another's way in a cramped, overcrowded room (eleven by five meters) with seven three-story double bunks. They ripped one another's coveralls, tore out what little remaining hair each had. On weekdays they were taciturn; at most they talked to themselves, feverish, after evening roll call, when each would lie moaning on her pallet, sighing to herself with her eyes open.

It was awesome to hear them swear their hatred for the Nazis, weary of the guards who had enjoyed making them "sing" for a drop of schnapps or a pinch of tobacco.

Even though I was the only Italian and no one understood my language, I lived in terror of talking in my sleep. That was another reason why I didn't want to think about my old comrades: What if I dreamed I was talking with Martine? I might give myself away in French, let a mention of Frankfurt-Höchst slip out, say my real name.

There wasn't a bunkmate who didn't mumble words in her restless sleep, and I had the feeling I wasn't the only one straining her ears to catch some meaning in those scraps of disconnected phrases. I scrutinized each face when I awoke, looking for a possible Judas smile as evidence that I had revealed something. If I had exposed myself, how long would it then take the camp's management to send my new fingerprints to IG Farben? To have them compared to those that were kept on file there, to see if by chance they were identical . . . ?

As soon as one of us slipped away, we all surrounded her. We made the drunkards breathe in our faces and the first one who smelled vaguely of alcohol had to account for how she'd gotten it, prodded by pinpricks and burns.

I couldn't even rely on the support of other internees. The black triangles were shunned by everyone, especially by the red triangles, who feared they were informing to the SS. The "asocials" were considered much more treacherous than the green triangles, ordinary criminals, who had their own code of silence. There was talk of a well-known anti-Nazi militant, whom the *Lagerführers* had purposely assigned to the "asocials" to undermine his reputation among the deportees from the start. Their plan had succeeded: the man had remained isolated until he slit his wrists.

At one time I'd been saved by virtue of my notoriety as a Fascist volunteer; the Italian consulate knew I existed, there were too many factors that stood in the way of cleanly eliminating me. And above all, let's face it, I had not been considered dangerous.

But now things were different. No one would have claimed the existence of an Elena Pareschi, a recidivist and a clandestine. The false identity that I had given the Nazis was their license to kill me.

So, best not to breathe a word. Only your companion from the freight car knows who you are and even if he despises you, he won't betray you. Continue looking around without attracting attention, but be quick about it, before you're too debilitated to be able to do anything.

Meanwhile, every morning and every evening I washed from head to toe in the lavatory, hastily to avoid the complaints of the women in line at my faucet, yet at the same time I took care to scrub my skin clean with the harsh soap they gave us (I was gripped by the nightmarish fear of being infected by my syphilitic roommates). Then I vigorously rubbed myself with a cloth to make the blood circulate, standing naked among the internees who looked at me as if I were off my rocker.

"You have energy to spare?"

"She must want to get noticed for the officers' brothel."

"Take it easy," I answered.

"Save your strength while you still have it," they advised.

Pay no attention to them, I told myself, keep an eye on them. I practiced giving orders to the German shepherds behind the SS's backs, mute orders with my eyes, with my little finger, with a minimum of gestures. And I forgot about hunger. But watch out, autumn is coming, with the cold you won't make it. Get a move on (though I didn't know what move to make).

As I obsessively kept repeating "none of this is normal," I had the chilling sensation that any time now I would lose all hope of being able to make it: the K-Lager's population only brought the jumble of the outside world to a fever pitch, *it was not another reality but merely an extreme form of the same order that existed outside.* This feeling grew in me during the hours spent lined up at roll call, at the canteen, all the occasions where they crammed us together on our feet. I forgot about my fatigue in the task I'd assigned myself: to study faces, to ask *who are you? where did you come from? what did you do in civilian society?* At night I then concentrated on weighing and assembling all the bits of information the way a miser counts his money.

One constant evolved in my mind: just as in Frankfurt, there were no rich or powerful in Dachau.

But although it was understandable in the camps connected to industrial plants—a factory requires workers, not upper-class gentlemen—in a K-Lager it was suspicious: Could it be that there were no anti-Nazis in European high society? Or weren't they persecuted?

Jews themselves were almost all rounded up in Central European ghettos, a sea of artisans, workers, small merchants, a handful of intellectuals, especially doctors, chemists, and engineers, those who possessed the "mental capital" (as the Nazis called it) that could be useful to the Third Reich. The big financiers, the *truly* wealthy, were sheltered abroad. Economic discrimination was therefore even stronger than racial discrimination—indeed, wasn't economic discrimination actually the basis for racial discrimination? Jewish lives as hostages, as flesh to be bartered . . . In the brief time that I was in the K-Lager I heard whispers, I don't know how often, of Nazi negotiations with the Swiss government for the sale of a supply of Jews. I don't think it was just a delusion on the part of the huddled masses we saw passing behind the yard from our barracks—we *Untermenschen*, that is, we subhumans; though we were still one level higher than *them*, in part because *we belonged to more economically developed countries*—we Western Aryan deportees.

Those most knowledgeable about the subject were the red triangles, because they were the group in which the percentage of *Akademiker* (as those internees with any academic degree were called) was greater than among the other colors. In large part employed in the registration and administrative offices, and in the infirmaries, they kept a concerned eye out for those like them, whom they assigned to the kitchens. Clerks, accountants, nurses, potato peelers (still subordinate to German internees), these *Akademiker* were better off than those who worked in the quarries, in the blast furnaces, or tarring the streets. I viewed them critically for that very reason, because their "mental capital," although unexploited, kept them shielded from much harassment. They could continue to act according to the values they had held in the "civilized" world more easily than the lower grade of inmates could.

I said as much to a nurse I knew, one of the rare internees who had risen to that position (women were usually excluded from such assignments, considered a lower species even among the deportees): "Why do you beleaguer us with your ideals? You can afford the luxury."

I'm unable to think the way I did before I came to know this hell (I thought). And I kept questioning the nurse, a Dutchwoman whom everyone respected for her tireless efforts in the *Krankenrevier*. Forty years old, a hint of self-sacrifice in the pallid face with its depleted features, she didn't avoid me like the other red triangles did, but responded patiently to my questions when we met at dawn in the laundry room. Both doggedly rubbing clothes with a sandy soap in the dim grayness of the unlighted room, at times we laughed together over the idiocy of that determined scrubbing. She told me in German about the type of people she had seen file by the day before. We estimated that even among the red triangles the middle classes were a minority. The ones who systematically fell into the hands of the

Gestapo were the workers, the unskilled laborers. According to her, this was due to the fact that communist workers were much more numerous than intellectuals of the same beliefs. I, however, saw it as proof that economic discrimination prevailed even over that of ideology:

"Excuse me, Ellen, but if the Nazis assail the ignorant more in terms of ideas as well, it means that even in politics their first yardstick is money, because the ignorant, we know, are the poor."

"You can't confuse things that way . . ." the woman replied, slamming a tattered garment against the laundry's corrugated concrete counter: "Ideas still matter, all the more against savages like the Nazis."

"And how they matter!" I argued. "Especially the idea that in this world money matters more than anything."

Each passing day strengthened my conviction. Among the Catholics, the internees were all lower-ranking clergymen. Ellen couldn't bear the thought. One morning she came with news of two deported Polish bishops and a Dutch cardinal.

"That's it?" I laughed.

"An Italian princess too."

"Oh!" I scoffed, adding, "How do you explain the fact that even among Italian military prisoners, among the *badogliani* as they're called, only soldiers are forced to work, while officers may refuse to do so and the higher grades are actually exempted? You don't call *that* class discrimination?"

The next day I pointed out that the common criminals were all very low-class people, brought up in orphanages, in overpopulated urban fringes. (The criminals answered my questions about their childhoods more willingly than the others, warmed by the thought that someone would recognize that they had once been children.)

"You're insulting the poor." The nurse stopped rinsing. "They're more moral than the rich."

"That's what I'm saying! An illiterate thief is less despicable than the rich man who sends him to prison."

"I don't care for your way of thinking. Besides which, at your age it's dangerous. You're too young to judge. You want to overthrow everything. You make me sorry I gave you so much information." And, involuntarily, her eyes slid to my black triangle.

"You too think I'm an *asocial*," I said. "Like the Nazis."

And so I lost Ellen's trust. I continued my probing on my own.

As for the Nazis, even our guards were of the lowest social class. It was almost as though one of them was acknowledging his childhood roots when I asked him: "Where did you live as a child?" and he answered: "In the Black Forest." He was the son of woodcutters who were driven from their land when it was deforested, and who had moved to the city when he was still a boy. This guard was a stocky man, a drunk, inclined to violence.

The officers didn't come around much, but by their strutting ways—my father would have called them "parvenus"—they appeared to be of modest origins. I saw four of them in action during my stay in Dachau, some ordering whipping and solitary confinement for internees who had not responded to roll call, and one who personally shot a runaway, with a slightly annoyed scowl.

Now I wondered: If I accused the Nazis of dehumanizing us foreigners, whom should I blame for the dehumanization of the Nazis? To whom are they *Untermenschen*? They take it out on us because we've been allocated to them as subhumans; better yet, they themselves designated us so. But are they free men? Reduced to the low-level jobs of slave drivers, jailers, exterminators, plunderers, torturers, and therefore ultra-subhumans. Acting on whose behalf? There must still be men somewhere who don't do these things, without necessarily being victims themselves. Or is all of humanity subhuman? Only tyrant-slaves and slave-slaves, the former rounding up and guarding the latter? A universe of victim-slaves and executioner-slaves? Impossible.

Think about it.

The war industries are profiting from all this low-cost labor.

Director Lopp was very refined. He would never have laid a hand on a foreigner on his own. His manner was civilized, humane, forlorn, his voice distressed over the loudspeaker when he talked about the inhumanity of the aerial bombings, of the *"Massenarbeit,"* the massive air strikes against defenseless populations, women and children, the old and the infirm, Germans and foreigners, enemies and allies, without discrimination. Yet he employed thousands of underpaid, undernourished foreign workers in the plants he managed.

When I later worked in the sewers, I once found myself lifting a manhole cover with a Warsaw insurgent. He told me how a German industrialist in that city hid the ghetto's revolutionaries in special shelters, and was paid for his protection in ready labor, day and night, in record numbers. By then I had chosen my path and the Pole's revelations only strengthened my resolve. Having realized that I was dealing with slaves had given me infinite vigor, a kind of liberation from the need to rebut the Nazis head-on, as if they were individuals who controlled their own actions. They were not. They were the executors of those whose consciences had dissolved, starting in the twenties, with the dizzying collapse of the mark that had bankrupted millions of small savers and reduced millions of German workers to poverty.

You just couldn't let the air of authority that the tyrant-slaves put on scare you. It was an empty mask, behind which there was nothing. The point was to nail them to their role of slave.

I had gone through so much terror and so many bouts of colitis to convince myself that they had no power over me unless I myself gave it to them, that I was truly relieved. It never even crossed my mind that my analysis could be subjective. For me its objectivity was indisputable, proven by the very effect it had on my mind: *I no longer felt afraid.*

V

The German shepherds were the first to notice the change in me. They wagged their tails when they saw me, something unprecedented (evidence for me that my analysis was accurate).

I made my first attempt with the human dogs on a September evening. I was crouched at the corner of the window with Lulù and, in the twilight, we watched two soldiers out behind the barrack, who had forced the Flemish girl onto the ground. One of them (the guy from the Black Forest) held her legs apart while the other one, from Hamburg, dangled a rat over her belly, the creature squirming in his hand. They laughed, telling her that they would stick it into her vagina. On her back, her body spread open on the ground, the Flemish girl was kicking. I could see the whites of her dilated eyes as she stopped up her mouth with her fist, certainly fearing that if she screamed they would kill her. Now the woodcutter's son was securing her pants that he'd pulled down around her ankles.

"Lulù," I whispered, shaking. "Why don't you promise to suck them off if they leave her alone? A blow job apiece . . ."

"Are you nuts? They'll get even more excited, worse yet. We have to startle them, that way they'll drop the rat."

"Okay, I'll try," I said, and abruptly opening the window, I sang out, "*Deutschland über alles*," in a shrill voice, eyes fixed on the sky.

Caught by surprise, the soldier really did let the rat slip out of his hand. I went on singing, though I hadn't seen anything of that Germany, "*über alles auf der Welt*." But they were stepping over the Flemish girl, coming toward me. I met their grim scowls, one by one, with an icy look (I myself was shivering) and said slowly, softly, in my most polished German:

"Since when is it forbidden to sing the anthem of the Third Reich?" Then I asked what time it was, sociably, as if I hadn't seen anything, and I closed the window. Lulù immediately gave me an entire chocolate bar and the Flemish girl ran back to the barrack, where she fainted in my arms, making me slip to the floor. I was so happy and all three of us—Lulù, the Flemish girl, and I kept kissing one another in the corner below the window.

I experienced several occasions of contentment during those September days. I had found the tone that disconcerted the low-class SS forces (another proof that my analysis was real). I was very formal in addressing the guards; I approached them indulgently, a distracted firmness in my voice, my body composed, my gaze focused elsewhere. It was a thrill each time. I then confided to Lulù and the Flemish girl, "Remember: treat them like pesky gnats."

Lulù had another admirer: the soldier with the rat.

"I'm his spider," she said, opening her slit of a mouth, "you'll see."

I must confess that I didn't even hate them anymore. Instruments of a power they didn't understand, they deluded themselves into believing that they weren't automatons by committing cruel acts that no regulation required of them. Nail them to their role of slave. Don't forget that every time you despair you're giving them a gift. Just remember that the further into degradation one falls, the more brutality becomes your last glimmer of humanity.

I had already read and reread, starting at age sixteen, *The House of the Dead*. It's just like Dostoyevsky says: in order not to go crazy doing his job, a jailer must really "put himself out," until he gets to the point of flogging the inmates "for the sake of his art," and the skill with which he applies the whip makes him feel like a man.

So you know, let's not make a song and dance about it. Don't get taken in by a sense of firmness, sturdiness. The only difference between them and the tsar's jailers is that these Nazis have put so much of that art into their job that they've joined hands with the society that spawned them. That's all, a quantitative difference.

So don't lose heart and think you no longer have any choice. During these weeks you've become sufficiently familiar with crime, see what you can get out of what you've learned. Being able to keep them at bay isn't enough.

It was the beginning of September and I still hadn't been called to work. This worried me. Had they decided that I was unfit? They could choose not to give me any more subsidized food rations, given the plethora of labor that continued to arrive, one convoy after another. Recent reports spoke of tens of thousands of insurgents from the "Paal republic," robust Poles, not to mention the Warsaw Jews who kept pouring in—the muscles of warriors, it was said, the resistance of steel; there were also rumors about a new contingent of those virile he-men, the Russians, strapping hunks whom not even a nonstop double workday could fell. What was I in comparison? Wouldn't it be more economical to incinerate me? If I'd been in their shoes, I wouldn't have hesitated.

The very idea that I could die made me a nervous wreck. I've never been as terrified of death as in the K-Lager, maybe because hunger and debilitation make you obsess over bodily things; it's like an intoxication, the desire to sleep that I mentioned earlier, to stuff yourself on scraps.

The first imperative, therefore: I had to get them to assign me a job.

It would also afford me the immediate benefit (besides that of not dying) of coming into contact with more people, maybe with outside workers, thereby escaping the segregation of the K-Lager and of my own Block, which my un-employed status consigned me to—I was the only such case in my barrack.

I consulted with Lulù and the Flemish girl, both of whom had also worked in the civilian world—one had operated a milling machine and the other was on an assembly line—and I had them teach me about the equip-ment you need to handle, what you have to do, so I could apply for work without being immediately exposed. Now that I was no longer scared, it seemed foolish to have waited so long for them to call me. One morning I told Black Forest to take me to the *Arbeitsbüro*. "*Schwarzwald*," I said to him with a smile, "March!"

But while I was awaiting my turn, a platoon of sewer workers came in. Their guard was saying that he needed more men. Right away I thought I'd found the ideal occupation, hundreds of manholes in the outside world at my disposal, dozens of clogged toilets in the factories, endless possibili-ties of meeting people with whom to weave a network. Forget about being stuck in a workshop behind a single machine. So I volunteered for the job. In a resigned, impassive tone, I asked the *Obersturmführer* sitting behind the desk, looking through him; he gave me a quick glance and motioned me to join the pipe-uncloggers, instantly turning his bored face to the internee behind me. It was the end of summer. I had to face the approaching cold.

For several days I'd been subjecting the Flemish girl (my age) and Lulù (thirty years old) to a flight of fancy that in the early days, during the idle hours, I had projected in my mind like a film, once I'd convinced myself that the Nazi exterminators were a reality. The idea was to make connec-tions with the new arrivals, who were fresher, not yet weakened. Once we'd formed a plan, a few thousand or so of us internees would take a hundred scattered guards by surprise, and knock them out with shovels, tongs, any tool we could get our hands on. Once the SS were disarmed and their guns were in our hands, we would occupy the munitions depository, while de-portees working in officers' private homes saw to killing their families. Then we would incite all the others to attack the offices, storerooms, and garrisons, with a very simple argument (I had repeated it to myself so many times that I still know it by heart):

"We all know that millions of Jewish and Russian internees, and Westerners as well, have been gassed and machine-gunned while their exterminators have not suffered a single death. So why not revolt en masse, united, tens of thousands of slaves? We certainly can't lose more men than they have already massacred and that they will go on killing until the end of the war. There will be decimation, true, but think how many of our torturers we can assassinate, just the enjoyment of seeing them piss their pants . . ." (The final words were not up to the standards of my models—Thucydides, Julius Caesar, and Plutarch—but seemed necessary.)

I had soon abandoned that pipe dream. The new arrivals at the K-Lager were already crushed, dazed, ready to fall in line to avoid being kicked, or to be able to cradle a bowl of soup. I was aware of the perfect rationality, from the Nazi point of view, of those transports in freight trains or cattle cars, idling and interminable, the victims without food or water, crammed together in the airless darkness. Once they reached the K-Lager, the daily spectacle of the death of the frailest of them would do the rest. In fact, everyone (including me) became inured to his neighbor's agony, his mind focused on his own survival, reduced to being alone in order to stay alive.

But when I started working in the sewers, that old daydream took shape again in a plan that Lulù, the Flemish girl, and I honed at night (whispering in French). I had also built up my strength by learning to rummage through the garbage bins in the streets when they unloaded us at dawn in Munich or in the villages: I always found extraordinary prizes, like cheese, fruit, potato peelings, boiled meat bones with tendons and cartilage, even crusts of bread. The technique I used was simple: I would distractedly sing a Nazi anthem to myself with perfect *Hochdeutsch* pronunciation.

"*Die Fahne hoch, die Reihen festgeschlossen,*" I sang, lifting the lid of a garbage can, "*SA marschiert mit ruhig festem Schritt,*"* I went on as my hands felt around among the scraps, "*Die Knechtschaft dauert noch nur kurzer Zeit.*" This last line I sang with particular conviction: slavery won't last long.

The illiterate soldiers of the SS followed me with uncertain eyes. I gave them a friendly nod every so often, to get them used to me, so they wouldn't be alarmed when I moved on.

---

*"Raise the flag! The ranks tightly closed! / The SA marches with calm, steady step."

I caught mange but I put on some weight again. I shared the yield of my raids with the Polish insurgent and brought whole handfuls of vegetable peelings back to the barrack. "It's full of vitamins," Lulù said happily.

Then an incident occurred that upset my plans.

One evening in the toilet, between the rows of toilet bowls, as I was pulling down the pants of my coverall, about a dozen internees came at me. I wasn't expecting it and found myself on the ground, my lowered pants immobilizing my legs. The women scratched me and beat me black and blue; trying to protect my head with my arms, I couldn't fight back. With each hail of blows they taunted:

"This is for people who sing Nazi anthems."

"This is for the apple of the SS's eye."

"This is for the Dachau bitch."

More than anything, I was paralyzed by the inability to believe what was happening to me. That my devious singing was *our* ultimate weapon against the Nazis seemed categorically evident to me, a method anyone could use. I didn't realize that I had always thought about it alone and that what I assumed was clear was plain only to me. I was so crushed by the injustice I was suffering that I even stopped trying to defend myself.

I must have lost consciousness, due more to moral than to physical pain.

I don't know what time of night I returned to the barrack.

Lulù, sitting on my pallet, occasionally changed the damp cloths on my face. "They did it to me too last winter," she said in a toothless mumble, exhaling cigarette smoke, "because I suck the Nazis, they said. They didn't try it again. The ones I recognized . . ." she explained, pretending to inject something into the vein of her arm. In the dimness I thought I hadn't seen her clearly, that I'd misunderstood what she meant. But the next day, at the first light of dawn, she repeated the gesture, saying, "Anyone who lays a hand on Lulù," as her hand slashed the air.

So she had denounced the women who had attacked her. And, to hear her tell it, they had been "*gespritzt*," so to speak: intravenously eliminated.

I'd been working in the sewers for about three weeks, but that day the Polish insurgent wasn't part of my all-Western squad. It was the first time we were going to spread manure in the fields, and I didn't know whom to ask for advice. After the beating, every move was a stabbing pain; hot tears flew like sparks.

On the way back, trudging along a trail in the woods, I was tempted to hide behind some bushes until our platoon moved on and then make a run for it; after all, the K-Lager was a good distance away, there were no German shepherds for a number of kilometers, I could always find a hayloft in which to wait for the already approaching night. In the dark I could keep going and put hours of walking between me and my pursuers. Why hadn't I thought of it before? Come to think of it, the job I'd chosen didn't present as many opportunities for meeting people as I'd thought it would, but it did offer prospects for escape.

That would teach them to malign me. Hadn't they left me unconscious in the toilet? At the mercy of the dogs . . . Was I supposed to worry about the reprisals they would suffer for my escape? One injustice deserved another. Club-wielding bitches, degenerate lowlifes, Dachau's Fascist squad. I slogged along, dragging my aching body, one eye swollen, my lip split by a canine tooth that had broken. Okay then.

But don't act impulsively, this time you can't make any mistakes. Every move must be calculated, every risk assessed down to the least foreseeable. So I began testing the waters.

I was at that stage of my preparations when I ran into my freight car companion on line in front of the infirmary, as recounted earlier. It was toward the end of October (I can't remember the exact date).

My facial swelling had almost disappeared and my bitterness toward him must have subsided due to the thrashing I'd received in the toilet. Seeing him so wasted away, I don't know what I would have done to again inspire in him the cruelty that he had shown me during the journey, which for months I had held against him in my heart and which now seemed to have deserted him. Just now when he understood me.

As I lowered myself into a dark cesspit, I was sure that he too was going over our meeting, wondering what I meant to communicate to him by the way I handled the jailers, since he no longer trusted me (I had sensed that). Perhaps something could still be done.

If what Lulù had told me about her own retaliation was true, my enemies had attacked me with the certainty that I would then report them. Day after day they must have been surprised when no one summoned them to the camp office.

The nurse from Holland, who had long since stopped talking to me, approached me one morning in the laundry room: "Is it true they beat you up?"

"Who?"

"Some internees, they say."

"Bullshit. No one ever touched me. Why would they beat me?" There you go, I thought, if they sent you on ahead to feel me out, they'll be left empty-handed.

That night, on the way back from the toilet, I skirted the barracks until I slipped into one belonging to the red triangles. I woke up a woman.

"I came to talk."

"Who are you?"

"The apple of the SS's eye, the Dachau bitch."

I realize now that I hadn't chosen the best opening for a peace talk.

"Wait, I'll call the others," the shape whispered to me in the darkness.

I wanted us to return to the toilet, but it was clear that they were afraid of an ambush. We crammed into the tight space behind the door.

There were a half dozen of us, our faces close together, pale spots over bodies crouching in a circle. I kept repeating the same thing in French, German, and Italian: that our jailers were slaves, that we had to bury them using their own practices, wage psychological warfare, and so on.

"Why are we here?" jeered a voice in broken German (which meant she didn't want to reveal her nationality). "If all we wanted was to applaud the Nazis, we could have done it when we were free!"

"I didn't say applaud."

"Singing their anthems is the same thing."

"Would you rather die?" I said.

"Rather than debase myself, sure."

"It would debase me more if I didn't try to find a way out."

"Become a savage like them and you've found your way out," the same voice said.

A form was rising to her feet and another leaned on her to pull herself up.

"Anyone who separates men into savages and non-savages is already a Nazi," I said quickly, before they moved away. "If you can suggest another explanation for what we're experiencing, I'm ready to listen to you. I told you what I think, now it's your turn." I held them back. "We can't let ourselves be completely dominated."

"You're the one who's dominated. Even if they torture me, in here I remain free," she said, and I saw that she was pointing her finger at her chest.

"And they remain masters of the camp."

"But they know I despise them."

"They don't give a damn."

By now we were talking by ourselves, at the same time, the mysterious voice and I; the other figures had melted away, denser shadows in the darkness that enveloped us.

"I'm only suggesting a tactic to confuse them," I persisted. "We have to disorient them, all of us together, so as to attack them when they feel most secure. Deluded into thinking they've morally subdued us, they'll relax their vigilance." I translated my words for the shadowy forms around me (some others had sat up on their pallets).

"You're the one who's deluded," said the only voice that responded.

"And you're all slaves, *schiave, esclaves, Sklaven.*"

"You're wrong." The voice seemed to have joined the figures rustling in their bunks and from a corner spoke distinctly: "You're the slave, that's why you know such a lot about slavery."

I raised my voice; I sensed the forms stumbling about, bumping into one another, as I said, "You don't want to fight, that's the truth, you're too scared, cowards is what you are, attacking a poor scarred cocksucker for political reasons." (Repeated in three languages.) "You can't get more debased than that!" My hands were itching with fury; I was breathing hard. Okay, I told myself, that's enough. I left with a sense of theatricality that shamed me.

Today I couldn't say whether in my distress I wasn't also buoyed up by murmuring *I'll escape, I'll escape,* as I ran along hugging the barracks, breathing in the scent of snow in the air on that late October night.

"Work sets you free," I laughed to myself the next day, reading the slogan on the K-Lager entrance. However, I didn't want to compromise my Jewish or Slavic comrades. I waited to find myself back on the squad made up of Western Aryans only. Meanwhile, I was so hardworking and disciplined that the guards neglected to stick by my side. As a result, it was easy for me to escape. I didn't write about all this in "Thomasbräu," but I will now.

VI

When I wrote those accounts in '53–'54 I remembered myself as being a lot more idealistic than I had been. There was also my memory block, due to incredulity about the past, to the fear that I might seem to be exaggerating, and to still more that I will later try to clarify.

For now I will only say that the facts described in those pages are accurate, but that there are omissions. The most yawning omission stems from not having understood back in the fifties, when I was recalling those events, that the experience in Dachau had plunged me back into the mindset that I'd had in Höchst, before I joined the French partisans and the Soviet prisoners, when for me everything was a question of courage, of individual morality: of responding with the truths of one's own convictions.

In Höchst we all worked together in the same factory; there were objective conditions so that I too could acquire a social conscience.

But in Dachau . . . Even when it did not kill individual people, the concentration camp managed to achieve its real purpose: to destroy the social conscience of the internees. What is most certain is that while in the outside world the Nazis tried to present an impeccable image of themselves, *in the K-camps they did everything they could to be hated*, so as to terrify most unprepared inmates and arouse such moral repugnance in the more combative ones that they were too sickened to fight their tormentors. In a word, the Nazis duped them. In fact, *hatred of the Nazis became an exclusive passion that did not socially unite the inmates*. Already cunningly divided into arbitrary communities of yellow, red, green, pink, and black, the deportees felt threatened not so much as unified members of dominated classes, which they were, but as individuals. And along with his physical existence, each one fought tooth and nail to defend his personal identity. Hence the fever pitch at which we enacted our eccentric behaviors, each individual's uniqueness making effective cohesion among the internees that much more impossible. And there you had it. I experienced it firsthand. Though believing I'd understood it, convinced to the last that I was thinking in collective terms, I was unaware of having *isolated* myself in the strategy that I thought I was formulating for my fellow internees. To the point of *not seeing* that my conduct was creating real problems, especially for those who now found themselves in a K-Lager precisely for having refused to adopt that strategy when in the free world.

Only today am I capable of gauging the solitariness that Dachau imparted to my thinking, driving me into a conceptual impasse (the effects of which lasted well beyond the collapse of Fascism). Further and further back, to a mentality stolen from the adversary: it was only a matter of cunning, of quick reflexes, of skill.

That was one of the reasons why I became really attached to Louis, whose toughness and solitude I admired—I don't know if it comes through in "Thomasbräu." It was he who kept me at a distance, having been made antisocial by a society that had trampled him since he was a child. He wanted me to be unreachable; too absorbed in his break-ins and robberies by then to turn back, only by denying his affections could he put his life on the line with no regrets. And ultimately it was fine with me, because I was afraid of plunging into the desire for self-destruction that had already seized me at Höchst, in Dachau. After all the mental machinations in the K-Lager, I took pleasure in not thinking, in gorging myself thanks to the ration cards, the money, and the provisions that Louis passed on to me. But his death left me drained. This too I did not write. As I slept, someone stole the money that the Sicilian had delivered to me and that I'd sewn into a breast pocket inside a pullover I'd bought at Sendlingertorplatz. Light hands, which had snipped my sweater without waking me.

But the fact remained that in the outside world it was much easier to get by than any of us had ever imagined in the K-Lager. How to let those inside know that? In the continuous flow of convoys that kept arriving . . .

I didn't say that I went back to Dachau to try to communicate with my friend-ex-enemy and give him all the advice for escaping that would have saved him.

I walked all night, a long December night from the time the sun set at five in the afternoon until dawn broke around seven, when I saw a wire mesh fence come into sight. Since I didn't know of the existence of a transit camp in the area, I mistook it for an extension of my deadly Lager. And suddenly I was afraid. I feared the internees' revenge for the reprisals that I had caused them. I dropped to the ground, covering myself with fresh snow to camouflage myself. I shivered thinking about the German shepherds: Would the dogs recognize their atavistic mistress in this creature flattened on the ground, soaked? They would swoop down, leaping at me before I could pull myself up. Anyway, if they were already sniffing the air, they'd also sensed my fear by now.

But how would I locate that gaunt partisan, which barrack was he in, whom could I ask about him, where would I find him? Why did I always put myself in untenable situations, each time because of that damned mania of rushing to somebody's aid, of anxiously putting myself out for someone, to share a discovery, a hope? Lying in the snow, numb with cold, expecting to see the dogs bound out at me—there was an entire pack of them at the K-Lager—I no longer had any desire to save myself.

Until I rubbed my eyes. Was it possible? Men and women in civilian clothes were coming out of the barracks in ones and twos, not hurrying; casually wandering about here and there, they formed little clusters, then separated. Some even leaned against the fence. My heart skipped: Was I seeing things or was it real? Two guys appeared at the gate. This is no time to lose your head, I told myself; wait a moment and watch.

They stood at the entrance, foreigners to all appearances.

I'll try them. I stood up, brushing off the snow with my hands as I continued staring at the two figures. There was no doubt about it, they were flesh and blood.

Racing over, I joined the idling groups and little by little blended in with them, as I read the happy inscription on the gate: DURCHGANGSLAGER (transit camp).

But no escapee could feel safe in such close proximity to his certain death. So I fled again, always moving alone, filling the need for companionship by engaging in solitary dialogues with friends who'd been lost: Martine, Grùscenka, Alain, Johann, Jacqueline, the Flemish girl, Lulù, my human backrest from the freight car without fingernails in Dachau, Dunja, the Sicilian, Jeanine, Benito, Polò, all of them, squabbling back and forth with myself in a foreign voice, in German, in a kind of insane assembly, with Louis's spirit suggesting thefts for me to attempt, places in which to spend the night. Instead of going to Switzerland, which was closer and was a much safer haven, I retraced the route of my repatriation, back toward Frankfurt-Höchst. The patent absurdity is that, even as I returned to the first comrades I'd ever had, I was actually isolating myself mentally, becoming more locked in my solitude each day. Until the paralysis, which stripped me of any illusion that a person can ever really escape.

But the reader knows that story. He has already read the (outwardly) matter-of-fact account of that all-encompassing imprisonment, as I lay in a body that I could no longer feel, that supposedly belonged to me but did not respond to me, did not know me, existed for its own processes that did not concern me, the me within it (where?) unable to destroy it because that damn body was alive, extremely vital, fond of living; stronger than me, it held me prisoner, forced me to go along with its wishes, vomited my inebriations on me, so that I didn't know where to turn, what with my broken ribs, exposed back, burned skin, split forehead, useless organs, so I poured my whole heart into foolish inanities, as compensation, in the need to matter in some way, futilely, superficially, to endure the blow, to loosen the hold of that body that immobilized me and kept me alive. And I clung to finding goodness in the people around me, warming myself with forced sentiment to try to melt the ice that bound me, that *was* me. Because this body oppressed me, I didn't want to be alone with its storms, which raged continuously within the ice. That was partly why it had gotten on so well with the crazy women in the asylum in Munich, in Bavaria; there was a current that ran between bodies that had escaped the minds they housed, organisms that lived for themselves, which even seemed to feed on those mushy brains, flourish against all logic, including my own.

Retaliation is what it was, getting back at that half-wit that was me, reproaching the doctors, boasting about being loved by the crazy women. It was the same in the cattle car with the wounded Germans, the same solidarity of bodies struggling against death had created a visceral understanding, made up of shit and urine and gangrene, which I had entered into with my small, petulant, ubiquitous "I" who'd had herself carried in and out on a stretcher in the stations the train passed through, rooted in paralysis on her bed of plaster, with the suprapubic catheter mentally wielded as a weapon, demanding food, hospitalization, respite for those human bodies abandoned on the straw in the stench, the same colitic, feverish bodies as in Dachau. In the fitful need to not identify with the devastation of her corporeal prop, that small self, with her frenetic attempts to see to things, her determination by then metaphysical to not allow herself to be devoured, extolled herself by handing out little lessons right and left, by distinguishing slaves in her own way, in a bizarre racism that reversed that of the Nazis, equally physiological, in which the physically afflicted were those who had eschewed the rules of the game, answering to no one, deserving of love.

Victories over the body urged it on. Paradoxically, perhaps, but in appearance only. Having shunned traditional relations of power, individuals answering to no one could ultimately understand and help one another and, together, recover from the death forced on them. I was living proof of it. In the cattle car, in the asylum in Munich, and on the "white" train, in less than three weeks, with makeshift treatments, with no hygiene, the sores on my ischia and coccyx were healing. The tissue was growing back by itself, activism on its part as well, a swarming of cells parallel to the bustling of my small self driven to obtain food and medications, to shepherd the whole heap of rotting flesh that lay groaning on the planks, slammed about as the train rolled along the rails. In embracing the crazy women, stroking their faces and uncoordinated limbs, my flesh was healing unbeknownst to me. I realized it in Merano.

In '45 the rules of the game had been crystal clear, as hopeless as my devastation. There was nothing to understand except that the bulk of humanity was at the mercy of factors over which it had no control.

I was so crushed by my destruction that I saw it everywhere. In the rubble. In the foreign workers still amazed at having survived the Lagers and the bombings alive, dubious about looting food and clothing so long denied to them, millions of beggars throughout all of Europe who had learned to accept one another, only to return home marked by the subjugation they'd endured, scattered as before, on hand for the next war that would again mobilize them, shunting them back, on opposing sides, to mutilate and mangle one another, until the next truce, when they would be obliged to thank the winners.

I saw my inability to govern my own body extend into the starving, bewildered German population, which after seeing its cities razed to the ground, its men killed in the war, its youth shattered, found itself saddled with the guilt of the regime that had suborned, enticed, and deluded it. I couldn't stand the fact that, just at a time when these people could reflect on the mechanisms that had influenced them—might understand that they had let themselves be led by hopes of collective advancement, in a unanimity that did not face facts and therefore did not consider *at whose expense*— that just at that time these German masses were prevented from dispelling the fog but were sent back, hammered, frightened, and demoralized, and made to keep exonerating themselves, to justify themselves, to go begging. Those who submitted once again as they had submitted to Hitler were absolved. Accordingly, bow your head, always.

So I reasoned then. And, constrained by the irrelevance of my paralyzed body, I recognized my limitation in the very air I breathed, measuring the vanity of the rancor that had driven me to join the deportees in Verona, and to escape from Dachau in order to convince my fellow internees that one did not have to bow one's head. And for what? To end up in a wheelchair.

I was beaten. Here the most unseen enemy awaited me. *There was no collective salvation.* The final struggle was an individual one, with death. And it was a struggle so hideous, irrational, and unequal that the rest was nothing by comparison.

If I looked at someone and thought about the fact that he would die, it took great effort to apply reason. Faced with the disproportion between men's blindness and their extinction, I was amazed that they continued to keep going, to trudge along, to convince themselves of something. I admired them for that. How could I confound them with the final truth (the one I carried in my body)? All I could do was distract them, cheer them up, give them confidence, restore a slim measure of continuity: not to cringe,

at least, not to devote what little time there is to fear, to anxiety, to the minute cowardices that crumble the insignificant nothings that we are.

I certainly had not been able, at age fourteen, to prevent the outbreak
of war in '39, nor was I now able to arrange it so that it had never happened:
you couldn't be any more insignificant than that. I'd been a drop in the
ocean of tens of millions of people moved about from one front to another,
from one Lager to another. I had taken part in it with such a mass of humanity that it couldn't be considered a personal matter. How to determine
why one individual had cracked and his neighbor had remained undam-
aged? A calculus of probability that not even the most powerful electronic
brain could solve.

What I actually needed, no matter where I'd been on the day and time
of the accident in Mainz on February 27, 1945, was for things not to have
gone any differently. Not because it was destined, mind you: I just happened
to be there. A sequence of events in which I had gotten caught, but it could
have happened to someone else. Twists of fate humanly impossible to control. When I recalled the wall's collapse, I never failed to say that at that
moment I should have been filling water buckets at the adjacent hotel; I
should not have been on that slab under the wall ramming the beam against
the nearby shelter. But Johann, who should have relieved me, had sprained
his ankle. And I had stayed at the beam with our companions, to balance it
out and ram it more forcefully into the gap that widened under the thrusts;
after each shove I looked to see if the opening was wide enough, furious at
the Pole, the buried victims, the damned concrete, jamming down with my
body's full weight to break through . . . I never forgot the German soldier
killed on the spot by a brick across the street, where he'd thought he'd
be safe.

The very idea that I could have escaped the fate that fell to me drove
me crazy. It knocked me senseless, weighed down by the same impotence
that had crushed me on the night I attempted suicide, when I wanted to go
back to life and couldn't. I couldn't bear to think about it for more than a
fraction of a second. For years it would flash across my mind whenever I
unexpectedly caught a glimpse of myself in a mirror or in a windowpane,
sitting in a wheelchair or else standing, leaning on a walker with my legs
supported by braces around my knees. Suddenly my condition plunged me

into my body. Steady (I told myself), as I very slowly pulled myself out of that slump. Paralysis is a practical complication to be resolved on each occasion, nothing more (the important thing was not to let it mark you).

From what I've recounted so far, it's clear that the deviation in my mind had already begun when I was still experiencing the events that I later repressed.

That gesture in Verona, which was the most social act of my entire life, had become in my hands a moral act (of which I was ashamed) as soon as I had done it, from the moment my partner-in-diarrhea in the freight car had directed it against me. The need for social justice, which had seized me in Verona, was instantly reduced to an incommunicable episode, a private secret in my personal story. I was so voluntaristic, my feelings about the social chasms was so recent and generic, so black and white (rich/poor, educated/uneducated, slave drivers/slaves), that I was certainly incapable at the time of continuing to follow, solely on my own, the path embarked upon in Frankfurt-Höchst, shown to me by the comrades who had organized the strike at IG Farben. The rapid succession of unforeseen turns of events prevented me from dealing with the difficulties that lay before me. And the daily necessity of surviving made the shifts of my mind imperceptible to me, though today it makes me shudder to think that, after throwing away my documents in Verona so that no one in my social class could save me, I ended up as the girl in "As Long as the Head Lives," in the hospital in Mainz, that Luzi in a wheelchair who gets to the point of boasting about having been a Fascist, as the last act of liberty left to her after all she's been through.

At the time it's still understandable, given my upbringing, my inexperience, all the mixing and clashing of feelings . . .

But afterward?

Rome, April 1977

VII

Reader, I'm back. It's been six months since I left you at the preceding page. I spent that time trying to answer the question "But afterward?" on which I had (once again) gotten stuck.

It was a grueling task, which nearly brought me to the edge of insanity, reviving the relationships, endeavors, and struggles of thirty-one years of life, looking for that memory gap that was everywhere and nowhere. It became a kind of hallucination in which I continually disassembled and reassembled recollections, rooting through passions that awakened under my mind's touch, confounding my purpose, so that I no longer knew what I was looking for.

In fact, things I did not believe emerged, errors, swerves, obstinacies, completely forgotten facts, those too repressed, which I now saw as the most pivotal. But as soon as I examined them, they no longer responded to my question. It was never the event I was looking at but one close to it, the one just before or just after it, that would have clarified the underlying reason for my repression. That event too, however, studied more closely, took a new turn. Not only did I not uncover the *need* for such a long silence concerning the episode in Verona, but I also wondered why I had reacted that way and not differently, so that each recollection became a new problem.

Yet I had to admit that the huge gap in my memory had determined the course of my existence. On the other hand, common sense made me ask: Did a person necessarily have to repress two long-ago periods of voluntary service in the Lagers in order to get married, give birth to a son, obtain a college degree, teach, and publish several books?

So I changed my technique. Follow the facts, I said to myself, and we'll see what emerges.

But even here I found myself in trouble.

The facts were voluminous and presented such an eventful picture of my life that what remained was a dissatisfaction, almost too much of everything, both joys and sorrows, the ruminations, the activities, the resolutions. It seemed as though I was always just about to hit on the right path, a succession of turning points. I had to come to terms with that as well. And I willingly set about examining the facts one by one to see where the road had forked, where the choices had lain, and whether I had taken that path or not. And so the summation of my life stretched out for hundreds of pages.

I had to acknowledge that I was dealing with an immense story that I did not know what to do with: it went beyond the account of the distortion of my German memories from which I'd begun, but had not broken free of them. As a result, it was neither the clarification it was intended to be nor a narrative that stood on its own. It had the same flaw that I had noted in my life. This in itself demoralized me.

But that wasn't the worst part.

All those forgotten events had brought me face-to-face with a series of subterfuges enacted by my memory. Curiously, it was almost always the unpleasant scenes, behavior that was at the very least embarrassing, that I had stored in a place of oblivion. For example, I would remember an argument. Unintentionally, I got into the part, I became heated: the quarrel had arisen from the fact that the other individual had touched a raw nerve, some feeling that I now understood had its roots in the repressed experience of the Lagers. I had no sooner reassured myself when presto! some overlooked detail popped up (a gesture, a look) to show me that it hadn't been like that at all.

I was dejected. I knew it was the wrong way to reflect on one's life and I reproached myself: It doesn't hold up, does it? You retained a quite different picture, didn't you?

My new objective became the unmasking of my mental tricks. By now I mistrusted them to the point that I saw them everywhere. If a positive memory appeared, I felt ashamed and rejected it, viewing it as a trap meant to serve the ideal image that I had sifted from my reality.

Whether because of the intensity with which I went about it or for some other reason (that too yet to be understood), my memories were of no help to me. They joined forces to coalesce against me as a team and would not let me pass. It was like a traffic jam. No sooner had one collided with another when a third one sprang up, and so it went; new ones kept coming so that their respective positions were constantly changing. And then they got angry with me. Each one insisted it was a true memory, not that domineering one that wanted to outshine it with a push from my imagination. From time to time each of them was so convincing that I made changes to its neighbor, which, however, took offense, until I was no longer able to distinguish between what was real and what was fictitious in what floated up from the past.

"Enough," the literary compartment of my brain told me, "don't you see that you've digressed? Can't you understand that your assumption was wrong, that you can't attribute to one single repression a sequence of griefs and joys, of ties and attitudes that, for better or worse, had an internal necessity of their own, their own motivations? Haven't you realized that you can't relate your every action to that mental block regarding your Germany? Yet you continue to compare your actual life with what it would have been *if you hadn't forgotten*. No wonder you feel like a worm and can no longer distinguish between what happened and *what might have* happened. This path won't get you anywhere. If you continue on this way, you won't be able to make head or tail out of this or any other story."

"To hell with literature!" I said. "I want to know who I am, who it is I've been carrying inside me for half a century, don't you see?"

So while the literary compartment of my brain continued to dissuade me, the ego from its little corner wanted clarification and, sometimes in the dead of night, I would slip out of bed to rush to the file cabinet in my wheelchair and check my old diaries and agendas, piles of faded letters, to see if invention (in its sense of rediscovery) had restored the incident to me, or if I had imagined it. Depending on the response and my frame of mind, I would resume frantically delving into the past or I would lie down, inert. But vigilance would not keep still on command; from the mind's magic treasure chest I continued receiving information about my past that overturned yet again memories that had already been verified. Even when I put down my pen, the task continued to rise in my brain as if fermented by a frightening yeast. Memories erupted on their own by now as if a dike had burst, worming their way in even in my sleep. In my dreams I rewrote scenes already written while awake, and the next day I tried to capture on paper the fleeting trace of those nocturnal variations.

After four months of such total concentration, I no longer dared stir up my memory. For entire days I remained in bed, in the dark, while outside it was sunny mid-August (remember, reader? I had left you in April), lying supine like a corpse, for fear that the slightest sign of life would bring back the full weight of the past that hung over me, unstable.

In one of those moments, drained and dead tired, the enormous effort of my life suddenly hit me. It's curious how the body has no memory.

In rummaging through my papers, I had found an infinite number of medical reports, X-rays, analyses, hospital records, which showed that I had undergone fifteen or more surgeries, had about a dozen plaster casts put on my pelvis, that I'd lived for years with a fever, apparently while continuing to work to earn a living, to study, to take care of the house, to love. Whole periods when I didn't stay in bed but went out, even traveled. One summer at the beach, I swam every day, with a toxic myocarditis that cut off my breath each time a wave slapped my face (the heartbeats gone haywire). Bizarrely, in chasing the past, I had skipped over all that, I hadn't given it any importance, an insignificant aspect. I had reconstructed my feelings, my human relationships, my actions, glossing over the trying physical conditions in which they had all taken place. The infinite application to reactivate my muscles and restore my functions. Hours and hours contracting and releasing the bladder to urinate on command. And what about the training sessions to facilitate sexual intercourse? (I had not forgotten my embarrassment at Johann's approaches.) Hours of exercise, supine on the bed, pulling up my legs as though they were lifting on their own, with an offhand gesture that would go unnoticed, a slight, casual nudge, almost a caress below the calf, by which I actually raised my passive limbs, until the move came to seem so natural that even to my eyes my legs rose by themselves. Hours of bending, sitting down, until I could touch my toes with my hands, or lying facedown until I was able to sit up on my calves, in short, all the exercises that I had done earlier in Mainz, along with massages. I don't know how much time I spent in front of the mirror, monitoring whether I slid gracefully from the bed into the wheelchair and vice versa. A secret drudgery, nonstop, to delimit my physical incapacity mainly in the eyes of others. Just thinking about it, I wondered why I took such pleasure in being with people, what was the point of such a desire to live that, given my lack of confidence, seemed indecent.

It even made me angry, as though the feeling of being overburdened that I'd seemed to sense in my life came from this bodily exertion. Where does a miner, or a farmer who has hoed the land all day, find the energy to think about fundamental problems? I say this solely from where I was, confined by society to my injury.

That was what I did not want to admit. I had so hated those people who equated me to my wheelchair that I had erased them from my consciousness. I had brutally exposed the spectacle of my paralysis in Mainz, in Homburg, and in the asylum in Munich, the better to ignore it later. But it wasn't like that. The physical servitude had continued even after the repatriation, greater than before, because I returned, with my legs now imprisoned, to the place from which I had twice fled.

That enslavement had cost me immeasurable time: no need to look far, merely the hours I'd spent standing with cardboard tubes around my knees. All that concentration so I would be seen as a normal person and not a poor unfortunate (as disabled individuals were commonly viewed). I studied myself with a Nazi eye.

I had to avoid giving the impression that I dragged my legs at all costs, jerkily lifting one hip at a time, as did the other paralyzed patients I'd seen standing in physiotherapy gyms. Their hands gripping the parallel bars as leverage, they twisted their torso to the side and flung out a rigid leg that fell heavily forward, bringing the pelvis with it so forcefully that only by abruptly counterthrusting their chest backward could they keep their balance.

To try to move more naturally, I got the idea of taking very small steps. I rotated my hips slightly with a continuous motion that, accompanying the leg, would not appear stiff but merely languid.

Even now I recall those walks as a form of madness. I went up and down the house getting in the way with my walker, in constant fear that someone would accidentally bump me. The slightest jolt for which I was not prepared caused me to lose my balance, and I then had to recalculate the walker's distance from my body and a millimetric dose of hip sway to regain my equilibrium. If I was alone, I even lifted myself on my arms to move more quickly, besides helping myself along with my torso. Hold it! I stopped myself: your biceps will get too big and you'll look misshapen. And I continued walking in little steps.

Not a week or two went by before my fever rose again, with the usual excruciating pain. Like a guard relieved of sentry duty, I went back to going around in my wheelchair. But as soon as I recovered, the orthopedists began hammering at me to give up the wheelchair and resume ambulation, as they called that walking on passive legs: "Try again, you can do it. It's only a question of will." Until in '57 in the Riviera, after yet another relapse—after twelve years of alternating these marathons with long bouts of fever due to abscesses that each time required surgical removal of bone fragments expelled from the shattered ischia—I said to hell with this Sisyphean labor and stopped listening to anyone anymore. Of course, mine was a special case because the collapse of the wall in Mainz had crushed the bones of my pelvis. However, I have always considered that obstinacy a comedy worthy of the emperor Vespasian, who wanted to die on his feet—this obstinacy, that is, on the part of modern doctors to make paralyzed people "ambulatory" with the aid of crutches or canes that keep their hands occupied. So that they can't help but achieve that motoric fiction. Still, however long a person may stand while under society's scrutiny, she can't live her life that way.

In fact, I have always had an incomparably greater autonomy in my wheelchair. For one thing, I wasn't forced to think about my body every moment when I was in it, and I did everything much more nimbly: I simply had to check the stability of my little chair to make sure it wouldn't spin away as I leaped out and, with one hop, slipped into the bathtub or jumped behind the wheel of the car or sank into a seat at the movies. Not only that. Even from an aesthetic point of view, it seemed to me that once people got past the first awkwardness, they paid less attention to it. Once they found out I couldn't walk, it was an established fact that wasn't mentioned again. In the long run, my body and with it my physical situation went unnoticed. To the degree that even I myself forgot it; waking up in the morning, I would sometimes get out of bed lost in thought and find myself on the floor.

I'd burst out laughing and clamber back up—easily if I was alone, terribly awkward if anyone were watching me, my limbs suddenly stiff as granite.

For years, the most repulsive thing for me was others' pity, in the form of admiration for my so-called courage. So great was the social humiliation of my condition—I'll skip the hundreds of anecdotes—that for an infinite time I felt paralyzed only in people's awareness. A detail that recurred regularly in my dreams is proof of it. There, I was still uninjured, but wherever I walked or ran, I dragged an empty wheelchair along behind me, sitting in it as soon as I spotted an acquaintance, my legs immediately immobilized.

It's been several years since this sequence reappeared. Now in my dreams I walk freely even if there are people around, and no one pays any attention. Not only that, but sometimes I'm *naturally* paralyzed, in a new dream that occasionally alternates with my nocturnal walks, and repeats periodically and almost identically.

In this dream, one or two loved ones are pushing me in a wheelchair along rocky paths, in a rugged landscape that is always the same. The closest faces of those moving forward with us—columns of people extending back to the horizon—change. Everyone is going in the same direction and I bump along on the rocks, but the effort of those pushing me doesn't make me feel like a burden.

Subsequently I no longer wake up lost in thought in the morning to find myself on the floor.

So then my paralysis had been a source of other people's power, for many years. That's the truth, never mind the physical impediment. The latter had been relative, some training initially, then as much attention as the legs' passivity required, or little more. Exercise is good for anyone; what's more, it's also enjoyable, tones a person up, and is relaxing. Where did that memory of physical drudgery come from, which I'd thought was an illumination? Maybe it was because I was exhausted at the time. It was dawn following one of those nights when I was afraid to sleep for fear my memory would take advantage of it to reshuffle the past on me again. Keeping my mind at bay must have left me in such a state of fatigue that I saw everything in terms of effort, and it didn't seem like I was giving in to an explanation that complied so well to my need for rest after nights of insomnia. At least I was able to sleep for a few hours (it was the end of August).

There had been effort, yes; not the physical kind, however, which I repeat—could be adapted, but enormous moral effort, precisely because I didn't want to be subservient to my body when in fact everything around me tended to lock me into my disability.

In the wake of this truth, my memories now flowed along without obstructing or contradicting one another. They were even too vivid (they disturbed me a little), so much so that I was tempted to tone them down. I certainly didn't need to go searching for revealing episodes: there were any number of choices to pick from.

Especially during the first months of my definitive return to Italy after the war, I'd had to struggle not to lend weight to my humiliations. The fact that I've never been able to think back to that period without an even greater reluctance (if possible) than I experienced in recalling the Lagers confirms it. Each time my mind shrank from the moment when I was dropped off the train of Russian veterans, on a stretcher, in Merano, on December 4 of '45; when I was left there, under the roof of the station platform, to claim my luggage, and found all the goods that I had scraped together by selling good moods in Homburg suddenly gone. Perhaps the recollection of the autonomy of actions and decisions that, even in the direst misery, I'd had in the camps made me feel the limitations of my present situation even more, a regret that tightened my throat. Perhaps this too contributed to the repression of that past, to the painful beginning (I remember it now).

VIII

In January '46 I'd been hospitalized in Bologna. It doesn't matter if your legs are immobilized, I told myself, your conscience fortunately is not. I was determined to play a part in the country's social rehabilitation. I would live a normal life.

I turned to every possible agency, alliances of former internees, partisans' associations, Resistance committees, political parties, Catholic institutions.

I groomed and dressed with care and, sitting nice and straight in my wheelchair, visited every local headquarters, pushed by hand by a friend who was an orderly, a bony, taciturn young man with red hair and a freckled face, in whom I confided.

At first the people who sat across the desk in those offices received me warmly, their expressions moved (so young and so destroyed, their eyes said); as I proffered my skills in exchange for some minimal subsidy as I had done in Mainz, they exchanged moist glances, shaking their heads: "Such fortitude!" they said, nodding, their voices cracking. "We'll keep you in mind, you can be sure of it, and as soon as an opportunity arises, we'll call you," and they said goodbye with the broadest charitable smiles.

But later, when weeks had passed and I went back, the tearful, concerned tones were gone, and only weary faces confronted me: "We told you we would call you," the overburdened voices grunted.

"You know, Vincenzo," I finally said to my orderly friend as I lay huddled in bed in the ward, "it was my mistake. I behaved like a supplicant."

"Don't be discouraged." He put his hand on my shoulder. "On my next day off, we'll try again."

I'd been wrong to keep silent about the most critical topics. Of course, it would be better to reveal them in good time, in a reflective, well-thought-out way. But it was my last card and it was worth playing. I prepared a little speech that was persuasive and concise, and when I thought I'd worded it properly, Vincenzo and I went at it again.

We drove into the city on my friend's motorcycle. I sat in the sidecar, behind which a contraption carrying my wheelchair was attached.

When I was led into the office I'd targeted, I said more or less:

"I can provide useful information, mine is a special case, I voluntarily went to the Lagers as a Fascist, there is a whole sequence of steps in my mental progression that can be helpful, I can be your social guinea pig." But I noticed that my listeners stiffened, their eyes avoided mine, their voices became inquisitorial.

I would tell my story, and each time there would be the same suspicious questions, the same incredulous perplexity. Then the verdict: "You ruined your life chasing after empty words."

"But only because I took that rhetoric seriously," I pleaded ingratiatingly.

"I doubted the rumors about the Lagers and wanted to substantiate them by going there myself. And so I learned from everything I went through."

"And you feel fortunate?" my interrogator of the moment asked.

"In a way, yes," I said, with a modest smile.

"You're not kicking yourself for it?" he said, astounded.

"No," I said, I too taken aback.

"Don't you bitterly regret it?" he said, as his gaze slid over my body in the wheelchair.

"No," I said, with the start of contempt in my eyes. Never mind, I thought, the important thing is to get what I came for. And, modifying my expression, I said: "Even a mistake can teach one to . . ."

"Certainly, we don't doubt that . . . but you must also understand that . . . this is a delicate time, the Nazi-Fascist atrocities are too recent, and having served as a volunteer is no small matter, these are things that must be weighed, examined, there's a special purge commission for this purpose . . . You yourself know that if anything can be done, priority is given to valid deportees."

"But if I hadn't told you, you would never have known."

"Possibly."

So as not to pay the price, I backpedaled. "There's always the fact that a woman's point of view is different from that of a man." By now I was stammering. "A female survivor opens a . . ."

"Go on," the voice cracked, "don't worry, the matter will remain between us, we won't use it against you." Staring sadly at my legs on the footrests of the wheelchair, he added, "You've already paid too high a price, don't give it another thought, go back to the hospital in peace."

"Poor little thing, what a fate!" I heard him sigh as my friend the orderly pushed me away.

"On the other hand," someone replied, "she asked for it."

When I applied for a pension: "Omit your volunteer service," an official who had been moved to pity by my story advised me. "It will be easier for you to acquire invalid status if you're classified as a deportee. Say you were rounded up in Verona and describe the circumstances in detail. As it is, it'll take three or four years before you obtain your pension. If you add to that the problem of your volunteering . . . In general, take my word for it, don't talk about it."

"Be patient," everyone told me, the same old story told to those who are suffering, "little by little you will resign yourself." Some added, "You are really fortunate that your disability has been established. Once you get your pension, you can decide to do as you see fit. You're so young, good heavens, what's a few years of waiting? The procedures are lengthy, it's true, but in the meantime you're cared for, with all expenses paid, what more can you ask for? Think of those who are worse off than you." (All my life I've run into this humanitarian consolation, which holds that seeing others' misfortunes alleviates your own.)

In my gloomy state of melancholy, the delays and red tape with which the paperwork was completed seemed calculated to me, as had the aimless wanderings of the Nazi convoys, whose deportees, crammed into cattle wagons, would be completely depleted by the time they were unloaded at a destination. I was aware that likening the two was paradoxical: in hospitals one was kept warm, fed, given food and water, treated and looked after like a child. But I was afraid that, if I adapted to years of hospitalization, I would inevitably acquire the mind-set of an aid recipient and, when I was finally able to arrange a proper life, that I wouldn't be able to do anything but live off the income from my disability, at most brightening my existence with meaningless diversions, hobbies and so on, to save face.

And so, once again as in Dachau, I had to act quickly if I didn't want the prison of my body to incarcerate my mind as well.

In effect to prove to myself, as well as to others, that I was not branded by my injury, I made it a point of honor to always appear cheerful, strong, serene, "*non doma*" (not crushed), unfazed by my misfortune even when the pain was killing me or when I felt consumed by humiliation. To avoid being pitied, I began feigning an imaginary freedom.

Was it any wonder that I'd lost my connection and couldn't remember my real Germany? And so for years I acted out the defensive fairy tale of mind over matter . . .

All this, however, became apparent later on. For me, at age twenty, ignoring any obstacles was really the only way not to find myself in the role that I feared most, that of the prodigal son who has returned to the fold defeated, an invalid.

There's one last thing that I must also add. In the summer of '46, I was truly overwhelmed with my woes. I was so thirsty for peace and I had so much tension to work through that concentrating on personal relationships suddenly seemed like the most desirable form of relief. Now that I had fallen in love with a young man in whose eyes I didn't see myself as an invalid, I thought it unnecessary to keep trying to convince others. I went along with it only to silence them, to get rid of them—brusquely, it's true, but also with no particular rancor.

I remember one specific situation, still in Bologna, in '46. In early September, news of my upcoming wedding (the date was set for the ninth) had spread. A crowd of visitors started parading past my bed, all day long, not just doctors and other patients in that big orthopedic hospital—soldiers in plaster casts, some wearing neck braces, some on crutches—but people from outside as well. I felt like a monkey in a zoo and I was somewhat amused to note the incredible circumlocutions they used to express their concern about one thing: my presumed inability *coeundi et generandi* (regarding coitus and procreation). Amid congratulations, acclaim for the sainted man (my future husband), the hope that by some miracle I would become pregnant (God is truly great), reflections on platonic love—which is worth even more than carnal love if you can be satisfied with it—they did their very best; absolutely certain that they were pleasing me, they passed the word around for everyone to come and say a kind word.

But the charade began to irritate me, and I sent around my neurological certificate, which indicated that my body showed no contraindications to either normal sexual relations or normal pregnancy.

And then they say that Nazism is over, I laughed to myself, handing my biological guarantees to my eager visitors. They looked at one another, offended, and stopped coming.

It seemed incredible to me, to be marrying a young man, a war survivor like me (he from Russia), a student like me (he studying law), who was offering me a simple, ordinary union between two people who loved each

other reciprocally. One who gave me his love and support with no preten-
tions, no grandiose words, but plainly, with natural authority, a paterfamil-
ias on whom I could finally rely.

Even my laborious walking with him became something normal, as if
it were nothing, where the issues were purely technical.

At times he came to see me in the gym when I was between the parallel bars, completely focused on standing up straight and trying to take my
first steps (still with cardboard tubes on my knees).

He would lean against the bar, standing in front of me, watching me.
After a while, he shook his head. "You're not doing it right."

"What do you mean?" I laughed. "I always check myself in the mirror!"

"That's your mistake," he said, inhaling smoke, his eyes on his cigarette.
"You look like one of those little Chinese girls whose feet are bound."

"I see myself the way others see me, you know," I told him one day. "I
don't want to look like an automaton."

"I wouldn't say that," he said, turning his face to study me better. "You're
pretty well formed, even if your rear end is a bit low," he mused thoughtfully. "Your legs should maybe be a bit longer, but your waist is slender, your
breasts erect, and you have beautiful shoulders, beautiful arms too," he said,
appraising the one close to him with the eye of a connoisseur. "You have an
agile body, so you're right to not rely solely on your arms. But you should
activate the lumbar muscles even more."

We got married without a penny, bread and mortadella our main course
at dinner along with a carafe of wine (I, however, devoured a kilo of sug-
ared almonds on my own).

For years afterward I relied in every way on the animal warmth and
languor of an orderly life as a couple, with clear-cut roles, letting myself
be led by emotional, sexual, trifling appetites.

What with the pregnancy, giving birth, nursing, weaning, and raising
a child, between university exams (him to graduate in law and me in humanities) and working to earn a living (translations, private tutoring, and
grant competitions), in addition to treatments and exercise, outdoor walks,
household chores, and all those little things that fill the days, there was certainly no room for the past.

And then I wondered where the repression of the Lagers had come from and why it had lasted so long. Now the opposite surprised me: After burying it for so long, in deep, extensive layers, how come my Germany came back to me again? Though only in brief glimpses, at intervals. "Purged" . . .

In fact, nearly a lifetime went by, in which only fragmented memories of the camps and hospitals emerged, and always in very specific circumstances—a forced choice on the part of my consciousness—which cluster around only two periods: the years '53–'54 and '60–'61.

That too. Why the devil did my German experience resurface *only* in periods of extreme difficulty, of absolute urgency in my eyes, where what was at stake was my life viewed as an encumbrance (whether my continuing to live was justified), and never when I was making progress during the brief but steady periods of recovery, which quickly comforted me?

The first time my thoughts went back to my Germany was when differences with my husband led us to break up, toward the seventh year of marriage.

I remember that night in '53, early in the year; I no longer recall the date but I can picture the scene in which I spoke of it for the first time. We were already at loggerheads over how to raise the child. "Stop being so controlling," I told him, "you'll make him into a slave." "And you'll turn him into a maladjusted misfit," he shot back. Then his infidelities had started, and between hissed insults ("A Don Juan you are, you're just like my father, a shitty womanizer!") and tears, I'd begged him to spare me that shame, and he, laughing, replied, "You have too much imagination." Or with a frown on his handsome face, he'd come back with, "Pride will kill you," as he lit a cigarette with studied calm.

"You know, Domenico," I began, "I really think we should leave each other."

It was after dinner at the end of a chess game that he had won as usual. With his head lowered, the brown hair falling over his forehead, and his golden eyes narrowed on mine, he listened without interrupting me; his features tightened, and I saw him sharpening his response as he stood up:

"I didn't think you were so prosaic," he said, and walked out.

The next day I made another attempt.

"You want war? You'll have war," he replied, and the same evening he brought home a young colleague, whom I'd accused him of sleeping with, to complete some urgent work (he said) inside, in the study.

I turned to a lawyer, who served him notice of my request for a consensual separation.

"You're not a wife, you're an enemy," he muttered through clenched teeth.

"And you're a coward." I had started murmuring that word as a sigh, I knew it wounded him; an officer in the *bersaglieri*, he'd been decorated for bravery in the field in '42, at age twenty.

He blanched: "I'll knock some sense into you," he said softly, confirming it with his eyes. His gaze lingered on my figure in a wheelchair: "You're pathetic."

"You tried to crush me!" I laughed, struggling to control my rage.

IX

I fell ill with one of my then recurring bone inflammations, osteomyelitis in my right hip. I had persistent shivers from the fever that came in waves and I was (secretly) hurting.

I heard joking and laughter at all hours from in there, in the study, uncertain whether the voices were imaginary. I started slipping noiselessly from the bed to the wheelchair; moving stealthily as a wolf, holding my breath, I made my way down the hallway in the dark, keeping my hands between the front wheels and the walls after each small push I gave myself, to make sure that I was going straight ahead and wouldn't bump into a wall.

I covered what seemed like an infinitely long distance (six meters) from the bedroom to the door of the study. I stationed myself there, heart pounding, listening to the suppressed voices, trying to glimpse a corner of the couch through the keyhole, waiting for the panting silences.

An abrupt sound made me straighten up, terrified that the door might suddenly open. Sometimes I would retreat slowly, taking the same precautions as before; other times I fled blindly down the hall to the bathroom, where I noisily locked myself in. Then I very slowly opened the door a crack and stayed there spying, although the bathroom door slit wasn't aligned with the entryway. The dining room door was ideal, however. I moved my surveillance post. I went into the dining room at night, as always paying attention to the distance between the wheels and the walls, and, quietly, with my eye at the door crack, waited to see them go out on tiptoe, their figures illuminated a moment by the night-light on the landing before an arm pulled the door behind it, erasing them from my view. I remained there a little longer, lurking idly, my mind a blank, nodding at the confirmation until the pain in my bones called me back to my body; and with a crick in my neck, I hurried to inject a sedative. So I told myself. In fact, though I denied it to myself, I took drugs with the excuse that my heart couldn't take the severe pain in my bones. I'd started by ingesting analgesics and went on to injecting sedatives, then opium and pure papaverine, increasingly stronger narcotics with therapeutic names. I had become friends with half a dozen young doctors, chosen because they didn't know one another; I cultivated them separately, careful not to ever let them run into one another at my house. Each of them gave me the prescriptions I needed, thinking he was the only one providing me with them. Then there was the regular flow of those designated to pick up the ampules at the pharmacy for me, friends who also didn't communicate with one another. I got to the point of giving myself four injections a day. The fact that I didn't inject myself intravenously but only subcutaneously may be due to my recollection of the morphine addict screaming in the morgue at the hospital in Mainz, or rather of the foaming at the mouth I experienced the first night without morphine in my blood, in that chamber of death. I was later left, however, with small subcutaneous lumps and nodules on my upper buttocks and on my thighs, which still feel knotty despite plenty of massages.

But to get back to my nocturnal ambushes, the door suddenly opens, what do you expect, as I sit there eavesdropping, dear God, very slowly I turn the wheels backward, oh no! (in a panic), and in my mind's ear I replay the silences I'd heard coming from the study; perhaps I had mistaken the moving of a chair for the sofa's creaking, a rustling of papers for a moan. Stop, listen more carefully, try to make out the sounds. I was not my mother, who had always preferred to ignore human miseries, including being betrayed. I wanted the truth, I would get to the bottom of it, I would ascertain whether I was distorting things or whether I was seeing them as they really were.

In practical terms, I schemed day and night to arrange memorable talks with my suspected rivals, whom I would phone behind Domenico's back and have come to the house when he was at work.

The responses I regularly received were astounding. It wasn't at all true. How could such an outrageous suspicion have occurred to me? I presented facts, displayed evidence, I wept (it was then that I thought of playing the card of the Lagers), I became emotional, and the more I bared myself, the more they covered themselves by being offended. I always ended up begging them to forgive me. I abandoned that route.

Meanwhile, Domenico had fallen into the habit of singing under his breath (off-key) a refrain that was then popular:

A me piaccion gli occhi neri,
a me piaccion gli occhi blu,
ma le gambe, ma le gambe
a me piacciono di più.

"I love dark eyes, I love blue eyes, but legs, legs I love the most." As he repeated *"ma le gambe"* he looked at me and spread his hands slightly.

I locked myself in the bedroom. He came home late at night and I heard him trying the handle. He moved off down the hall whistling that tune.

"You're so transparent," I told him.

"Right," he said, eyes flashing behind the cigarette smoke. "Ridiculous, isn't it?" He smiled thinly. "For better or for worse, thoroughly candid." (Years before I had accused him of this as well.)

Sometimes he would come home as if we had left each other on good terms, which to me seemed like his most subtle cruelty. But if it was me who mildly tried to start a friendly conversation, "a frank clarification," I'd tell him, I felt him slither over the subjects on which he said I wanted to nail him.

"You're so transparent," I repeated (distraught, I could hear my mother's noble tones in my voice).

The evidence of his cheating was never sufficient. I accumulated it hoping for some unspecified clarification. Once it became known that negotiations for a legal separation had begun, several of my rivals—the most scrupulous ones who didn't want to feel responsible for the destruction of a family—came forward spontaneously to confess their affair with my husband. To prove to me that there hadn't been anything serious between them, that it had all been a "tempest in a teapot" that quickly fizzled, they told me the circumstances and manner of their "teapot tempests" along with all the "painful" details, to which I listened avidly as I tried to soothe their remorse; later, after they left, I felt ashamed at having been such a worm as to comfort my husband's lovers.

My husband too was relieved. He had stored up so many offenses against me that the separation, though his fault, was no longer a disgrace he had to wash away.

"The process takes a long time," he said, looking affectionately at my haggard face with its moist eyes and dilated pupils. He pointed it out to me: "Always on the verge of tears, you are, and that vague expression . . ." He didn't suspect that I was taking drugs. He was all for facing pain with stoicism; he even begrudged me aspirin—imagine if he'd known. Just the thought of it made me tremble with fear, and I imposed an elaborate measure of complicity on the friends who helped me.

He'd attempt to stroke my hair and, in the commiserate lucidity of the drug, it seemed to me that everything could be cleared up and I started to tell him . . . because in fact . . .

"No," he cut me short, patiently, raising his open hand in front of me, "no discussion, no bargaining, Lucia. Take it or leave it. If you want me, accept me as I am. Otherwise leave." Then in a tender tone, he added, "You'll see, I'll make you give in," and he stole a glance at me. He smoked constantly, slowly inhaling countless cigarettes that glowed red, until white puffs of smoke came out of his mouth along with the words, rising before his face in a blurry haze that hid his eyes. "The process takes a long time," he repeated, "it can take years. As far as I'm concerned, it's fine that way. If you want to split up before then, you're free to go, no one is holding you back. Just be aware," he added after a pause, with a practiced smile, "that if you abandon the marital roof, you lose your son. Don't say afterward that I didn't warn you."

"You know very well," I replied, "that wrongs have been committed, and even perpetuated, under that marital roof. I have proof of it, confessions, and if . . ."

He shook his head, amused. The law was his profession, and he knew the effect of his words on me. "You lack a legal mentality," he said, as if thinking out loud.

That's the context in which I resurrected the buried German experience for the first time. A time when it seemed to me I needed to make a clean break with my present life. No longer physically fit, however, and with a young son to raise, I couldn't bring myself to decide. Unable to run away as I'd done then, held captive by paralysis, by fever, by drugs, by the betrayals, and by my jealousy, what else could I do but look for a less imprisoned version of myself? It was natural for me to recall the escape from Dachau, in October '44, the previous months having vanished.

Starting from the moment I bolted, I began remembering, in great detail, the events that had led me almost from one end of the Third Reich to the other, from Munich in Bavaria to the collapse of the wall in Mainz am Rhine.

It seemed like the happiest time in my life, when I was free, on my own, with no papers, no identity, nowhere to take shelter, living day by day, never knowing when and how I would eat or where I would sleep wherever I landed next.

Several particulars flowed from my pen that at the time seemed inconsequential: superfluous. For example, I remember quite clearly feeling a bizarre elation at the fact that I was always able to get by during the time I wandered around. I felt invulnerable when, right after a bombing, I would go into a burning house and steal food and clothing, at the risk of being shot on the spot, the fate which awaited *vultures*; that is, looters. Taking advantage of the bombings to ransack homes was the only crime that united Germans and foreigners alike, all of them punished by death, standing in a hole they had to dig themselves at the scene of the crime, their torsos exposed to the penitential rifle blasts, without racial distinction.

I tore up those pages that were oppressive and instead described walks in the snow, through fields or at the edge of a forest, from village to village, hiding from view as soon as I sensed a threat. I could tell from afar the people who could harm me by the way they walked, by their behavior in the fog. I agonized retroactively for the children of the *Osten* and Jews whom I could see clustered behind the barbed wire when I skirted the transit camps in search of shelter, and who, in my distorted memory, stared at me with the dark eyes of my son. Many times I'd caught them rolling around in the trash; out of sight of the adults, they ran wild, erupting into small happy cries, though abruptly settling down if a parent called or appeared. Then they put on a sad, irritable face and started whimpering again. If a Nazi soldier scattered them, they accused one another, scowling. Afterward, as soon as the adults turned their backs, they returned to their games.

Once, three little boys covered in rags, their faces scabby with crusts, were playing a game: peeing into a rubber tube to see who could squirt his stream the farthest. The trick was not to waste all your piss in one go, but to pass the tube from one small penis to another, several times over. They were so engrossed in their competition behind a shed, their faces happy, untroubled, that they hadn't noticed their mothers coming. As mangy and tattered as the boys, the women yelled at them, "Filthy little pigs, worse than animals!"

I realize now that all those nights when I spied on Domenico from behind the dining room door, as my health gradually worsened and I injected the drugs at shorter and shorter intervals, telling myself stories about escape was my way of secretly laughing. I remembered the foreigners who had let me stay in their barracks, the brief, intense friendships, a succession of encounters and isolated bondings, unrelated to one another, linked solely by my wanderings. And I felt free and light.

I even felt like I was producing something useful, making a historic contribution. I had also started reading every possible publication about the Nazi Lagers, and it surprised me that no one had ever written about the escapees, at least three million of them, circulating around in the Third Reich, exchanging information and changing identities at will. We recognized one another by a gesture, a mere hint, and confidences hesitantly seeped out: places to avoid, the fact that the records of such-and-such factory in this-or-that city had been burned. The files of the local Labor Bureau had been blown up. All you had to do was appear at an adjacent Kommandantur and say you came from that factory. Impossible to check. The Nazis were actually relieved that you showed up of your own accord. There were always foreigners with proper papers ready to attest to you. Between one incinerated *Ausweis* and another, I was a Belgian Walloon from Namur and a Lithuanian from Wilno. I had gone to Namur on vacation with my parents since I was a child, and Johann and Stanislaw had talked about the streets and squares of Wilno, being natives there (Stanislaw had even drawn a sketch of his neighborhood, one day when we were lying on the canal bank of IG Farben); so I could hold my own in any eventual interrogation. As the Belgian, I was a cleaning woman (*Putzfrau*) in the stone house behind the BMW camp in Munich, where a contingent of American prisoners was lodged, sleeping on cots with checkered netting, mattresses, sheets and pillowcases. With plenty of provisions, they threw stale bread and half-smoked cigarette butts away. I hated them so much for their prosperity and comforts and the camaraderie they enjoyed as equals with the SS who guarded them—I couldn't help comparing it to the treatment given to the European dregs—that one day I slashed the mattresses and sheets under the tightly tucked covers, and I was forced to flee. Farther on I tagged onto a convoy of Lithuanian farmers, after getting friendly with their interpreter, who had me hired as an errand girl on a farm on the outskirts of Donauwörth, in Swabia. The Germans, however, were quick to realize that I didn't understand a word of what my fellow countrymen said, and when my Lithuanian claim aroused the interest of the local police, I barely had time to slip away, headed for the Rhine.

But my masterstroke had occurred before that, in Munich, Bavaria, when I'd left the transit camp of Dachau (like Jean de Lille). I'd gotten a job with my real name at Siemens, the most humane factory that I came upon in Germany, where *Osten* and Westerners ate at the same canteen and German managers came by to taste. But I'd become overconfident, convinced I was uncatchable, and had stolen stamped sick-leave forms from the factory doctor's office; then, instead of working, I'd go walking around the city (there were no fences at the camp connected with the Siemens facilities). One day I was summoned to the manager's office, however, and I had no choice but to disappear.

I'm summarizing because I've already written about these events in the fictionalized accounts I composed during the years of my marital crisis, stories in which the hardships, the escapes, the terrors had a poignant immateriality, the unmoored precision that drugs can provide. If among those texts, some published and some unpublished, I chose "Thomasbräu" and "Asylum at Dachau" to begin this book, it is because they are the only stories in which, at the time, I retraced the events I'd experienced without adapting them to a narrative thread, but letting them unfold as they'd actually happened. That is, if you don't count the feeling of unmooredness and blunted materiality that no longer seems to characterize those months on the run, but to have been superimposed by me as I recalled them. Just as that kind of sexual anxiety that disturbs the protagonist, especially in "Thomasbräu," doesn't represent reality, but my imagination at that time: it's not the runaway minor but the betrayed woman in her thirties who views the deportees' acts of intercourse as slimy tangles of snails with monstrous antennae.

There's another reason for choosing "Asylum at Dachau," however. It is immediately clear that both the Gascon engineering student and the Italian clerk with the slicked-back hair, though they have different sensibilities, thought only of not being touched by the baseness of the camps, not getting *soiled*. It was important to them to preserve who they were earlier, to forget the Lager as soon as possible. As I too had done later, after the war. The matter affected me. You can tell by how I insist, in the story, on their wanting to remain apart from the others. Unlike those who were not of our class. The Russians, Jean de Lille, didn't feel they were above what they were experiencing. For that reason I never grew tired of bringing them to life: I was trying to recover myself by remembering them. By remembering entire families of Soviet deportees who offered shelter to escapees at the risk of being shot; of little Jeanine, for whom striving to do her utmost was as natural as breathing; of undernourished Benito . . .

But I no longer hoped to find them.

Intolerant of the criteria by which my surroundings judged me and sought to demoralize me, I was nonetheless trapped by them. In my mental confusion, I wasn't even certain of my way of viewing things. I doubted my own feelings, my own memories, I had second thoughts, I didn't dare give myself any credit. As mentioned, I read books about the Lagers and, even knowing that they were written by officials or by internees with "mental capital," as the Nazis called it (the so-called *Akademiker*)—that is, by civilians who had protected themselves within the niche of their preexisting morality, and never as workers, as fugitives, or as those who shared their vulnerability—I distrusted my direct perceptions all the same. Even when describing accounts of escapes and life underground in the Third Reich that had never been written before, I tried to correlate my recollections with the *accurate* memories of authors who had been recommended to me—for example, by Elio Vittorini—as essential models. "You must free yourself from the oppression of memory," he wrote to me in 1957, when—under the constant barrage of the exact same advice from my father and from my uncle in the Pontine Marshes—I'd done nothing but that. Surrounded by the sensitive people with whom I lived, I'd done nothing but put blinders on my brain so as not to look at things realistically: a modicum of aesthetic detachment is essential. Vittorini even found "Thomasbräu," that mild, almost idyllic account with which I timidly faced the past, too encumbered by the oppression of remembrance.

Literary intimidation also prevented me from completely dispelling the fog that surrounded my running, trapped as I was, and taking refuge in Nazi Germany.

In fact, the accounts of those months, from the end of October '44 to the end of January '45—continually relived and re-created in stacks of notebooks—invariably broke off before my reappearance at the Lager in Frankfurt-Höchst, in early February 1945, a story I haven't yet told. A reappearance that deep down had been the purpose of my joining the deportees in Verona: to let my companions know that I hadn't run out on them. There was no conscious resistance on my part to that episode, however, it was just that my memory always exhausted itself on some earlier situation before I could get there. The memories scattered, all by themselves, into a succession of displacements and instantly consumed human contacts, in which thirteen months of brutal confrontation had been touched up and disconnected to seem like nothing more than a few weeks of tragically light adventures, crammed into the void.

Yet those modest memories, set down in endless detail almost for fear that they might get away, gave me respite. Little by little, superimposed on my present imprisonment, they helped me deal with my decisions. I stopped secretly begging the lawyer to hold off on initiating my request for a marital separation. I ended my agonizing tête-à-têtes with my presumed rivals. I abandoned my guard duty behind closed doors.

In the lull after the storm as we awaited the legal ruling, Domenico and I were almost equable. The acrimony, the cruelty had blown over. He devoted every free moment away from work to perfecting my means of locomotion. (I actually think that during those months he went without a lover; I now believe that maybe one reason why he'd cheated on me there at home was to be so in the wrong that he could leave me the child without seeming like he was giving in to my "crazy demand.") He was designing a wheelchair for me that I still use: small, lightweight, and able to be disassembled, it would afford me the greatest agility of movement, yet be stable and comfortable. There wasn't an elevator, cinema, or theater that Domenico entered without measuring the width of the narrowest aisles and the height of each seat or chair from the ground. But the mechanics always raised objections, saying it wasn't feasible, that such a chair wouldn't be steady, and how would I manage with the rear wheels jutting out? He started over, measuring my hips, my back, my legs, and redesigned the model from scratch.

As soon as he saw me sitting quietly, he appeared with his folder of plans under his arm, a sampling of nuts and bolts in his hand, and sat next to me with a sigh of relief. He asked me if I thought one type of screw was better or the other one, if I preferred that such-and-such a support be tubular or flat. And to top it all off, I found him boring.

In the spring of '55 the proceedings were complete. Domenico retained parental authority over our son and I was given qualified custody.

X

As if having to make up for lost time, I rolled up my sleeves. After Domenico left, my home became a real caravanserai. I took in former prisoners, young unmarried mothers, half a dozen cats. In short, the period that I later referred to as "my parenthesis of secondary fronts" began. During those years I did nothing but accrue parentheses: there was "the German parenthesis," then the "marital" one, when Domenico and I got along, "the Italian parenthesis" (said sarcastically), and now this one.

My relationship with my son, who was nearly eight, was good. He didn't mind the mayhem, especially since he added to it himself with all his little neighborhood friends coming and going. And oddly enough, he had never been so diligent and focused about his schoolwork. A precocious reader, he loved history. He collected picture cards sold at newsstands, which he pasted into thick notebooks, by time period. There were Romans, Gauls, Carolingians. If he saw me busy reading, he'd ask, "Where are you? I'm in the Crusades."

"I'm in the First World War," I'd reply, or in the Renaissance, depending on the private lessons I had to prepare for that day.

Every now and then we would invite each other into the centuries in which we found ourselves at that moment. We read the captions behind the pictures, consulted books, enriched our knowledge about the figure with the helmet, or the character with a sword at his side, who eyed us haughtily from the flamboyant image.

By that time I was tutoring university students or exam candidates in classical studies almost exclusively. My subject areas were Italian, Latin, French, and German, along with history and philosophy (in the interim I had also earned a doctorate with a thesis on Kant's reflective judgment). I wrote dissertations for a fee; I remember three in particular, on Sallust, on La Rochefoucauld, and on Unamuno. I made good money.

But I'm digressing again (an inveterate bad habit). The truth is that I maintained an expensive tenor of life so as not to have my son pay the price for my physical privation—which is why I'd also hired a governess for him, in addition to the housekeeper who saw to the household chores and the laundress who came to help the housekeeper (an unmarried pregnant girl). Then there was the beach villa rental for summer vacations, trips and excursions, inducements; I wanted to make up for everything so that the boy wouldn't feel like he was different, the only son of a mother who was an invalid and alone, as too many people reminded him. Poor little thing, they sighed, patting his head.

In fact, I was seized with a frenzy to prove that I could make it. In my feigned detachment, nothing got to me so much as allusions to my son about my being in a wheelchair: "There now, Lorenzo, be a good boy. Don't you see your mother isn't well?" the relatives would say. "Hurry, run! Your mother needs help," an anxious female voice urged if I dropped a pencil, a match. "Pick it up for her, Lorenzo, bending down tires your mother out, don't you see she can't do it?" they said, giving me a smile of pedagogical complicity. As if I had generated a living prosthesis, a creature forced to grow in the shadow of my misfortune. The most tragic thing for me was the fact that words like these were well-intentioned, meant to be thoughtful.

On the other hand, my "defiant way of life" drew a number of eyebrows raised disapprovingly, especially with regard to the dubious individuals I protected. You could tell that what was lacking was the firm hand of a man who would restrain my "intemperances" and keep me *in my place*. Poor Lorenzo, forever the only child of a mother who was not only an invalid and alone but also irresponsible; in short, the same hotheaded, reckless girl who ran away from home when she was eighteen, an "asocial" (as the Nazis had already classified me). And I, to show them that . . .

Later on, I moderated that raging hunger of mine for freedom and joyfulness, my obsession with personally helping the most vilified people at the drop of a hat. Partly because my protégés, used to being mistreated, took me for a gullible fool for taking care of them, even thinking they were doing me a favor by living off me. I also gave up my retaliations.

Yet I remember those years with pleasure. Lorenzo grew up as an outgoing child, always engaged, nice, and sturdy, his laughter effusive. One day I'd caught him too competing with a little friend on the terrace to see who could urinate the farthest—the target was an oleander plant a couple of meters away—and I quickly withdrew so as not to disturb the contest.

In the end, however, I didn't make it. Due to the excessive obligations that I had created for myself, that pace of that life, overloaded with vitality, relationships, work, overwhelmed me, and I began to go adrift.

Fall of 1960. I landed in a home for the disabled, Villa della Pace, at the eleventh kilometer of the Ardeatina, on the outskirts of Rome.

I arrived driving a huge beige Studebaker that I'd bought secondhand and whose resale I was negotiating. I'd purchased it a couple of years earlier, when small-engined cars with the qualifications required by my driver's license didn't yet exist.

I won't describe the sinking feeling I had as I parked among the figures abandoned on wheelchairs or on benches, in the wan sun of late September. Dozens and dozens of disabled war veterans who looked at me as if I were a rare beast. I'd returned to my proper place, to the role of aid recipient that society had assigned me. At age thirty-five, I found myself back where I started; what's more, loaded with debt and sitting on the soft, pale suede seat of an impressive custom-built car.

But my economic difficulties and my argument with charitable assistance were the least of my worries. It was something else that truly depressed me.

There must have been about a hundred residents at this institution, most of them accompanied by a family member, due to the directive that they not be isolated from their environment, and to the savings in staff costs that family assistance afforded the administration. They lived in large cottages grouped around the garden in front of the gate. Looking around, I was so upset at seeing my physical disability multiplied in the patients that for days I shut myself up in my room (a single with bath)

"I can't come to the door," I shouted to anyone who knocked.

If I left the room to go to the dining hall or to have a massage and ran into crippled or maimed individuals, paralytics, those whose limbs trembled from Parkinson's disease, I didn't know how to turn away. I humiliated myself repeating the plaintive litany that many of these disabled people had heard from their healthy relatives: the perpetual "Lucky you, you can walk, good for you, you're doing well," murmured with sidelong glances. The endless discussions about health, intestines, bladders, stomachs, joints, their eyes lit up, engaged, obsessed with their own bodies. I slinked away, pleading commitments I couldn't put off.

But one night when I was gripped by colitis, shivering in the bathroom in my nightshirt, watching for intestinal spasms so I could make it onto the toilet bowl in time without soiling the wheelchair, I suddenly saw myself in the mirror of my mind: there I was, *me of all people*, looking at my comrades in physical humiliation with an aesthetic eye. *I myself* had become that societal eye that had blighted my existence.

I was so crushed that I forgot the rumblings of my bowels (the colitis had passed). I sat there in front of the toilet bowl, doubled over in shame as if before a confessor. I, because I was thankfully spared the incontinence of bodily functions, because of a little hard-earned motility, felt superior to my fellow patients, *arming myself with their disabilities so they could be used against them.* What had happened to me during those years to reduce me to this vulgar aristocratic revulsion from physical contact with those who are dependent and infirm? I sat there like a killer who has mentally slaughtered her subhumans. How easily my class-conscious skin had grown back, like that of a snake.

Finally, I started venturing out. Hadn't I once scuffled for a potato, a turnip? Hadn't I shared slices of bread as thin as hosts with my comrades? Didn't I know that we are always most absorbed by what we lack? And now here I was wrinkling my nose because these new companions, hungry for good health, spoke of nothing else. I was reminded of my volunteer experience in the Lagers, in Frankfurt-Höchst, my initial squeamishness toward the internees due to the overly delicate refinement of my senses. But so great was my shame—shame is clever, it becomes reserve, silence—that I didn't talk about it in "As Long as the Head Lives," written while I was in that home for the disabled.

Besides, it's not even true that they were only focused on their own bodies.

I remember Amedeo, a gaunt Ligurian in a wheelchair, about forty years old, wounded in Africa. Once a metalworker, he had become a skilled watchmaker. He offered to teach his art to anyone who wanted to learn it, and designed models for small presses or other tools that even someone with only one hand could use.

Giovanni, a bachelor from Bologna wounded in Greece, had a form of paresis that was the opposite of mine. Following a laminectomy that had decompressed the medulla, he had recovered movement but not sensation.

He wanted to organize a union for both disabled war veterans and those injured on the job. But he met with a lot of resistance because most of the "war surplus," as he called the residents of Villa della Pace, had a superstitious aversion to politics. They inundated him with questions about subsidies and assistance, which he compiled and forwarded to the relevant entities, but they drew back as soon as he spoke to them about the need to organize.

Vincenzo, from Friuli, was a little younger than me. A partisan in the mountains, he'd been struck by a bullet at age eighteen. His spinal injury was also unique: though depriving him of control over his motor nerves, it had left him the ability to have sex. Always standing upright on metal braces, tall and robust in the midst of our wheelchairs, he was fighting to get an "annual checkup, like they do with engines." He continued his battle over the years, finally leading a mass occupation of a hospital ward in Florence, in '73, which the national press reported cursorily (I myself only managed to publish a ten-line paragraph in a left-wing, extraparliamentary paper).

For my part, I wrote articles with titles like "Guilty of What?" in newsletters for the disabled and promoted debates on social psychology. Insignificant things, but I felt like I was beginning to be myself again.

After the Christmas holidays, which my son had spent skiing with a group of friends in the mountains, Lorenzo joined me at Villa della Pace. He'd left his father, who had reclaimed him when I had my downfall but was now going through a stormy love affair. The boy had refused to move in with his grandparents, either paternal or maternal. I was the only one left.

"I'll come and stay with you." He winked at me: "Tell the management that I'm your attendant," he said, as if he'd come up with a clever ruse.

The predictions had come true: Lorenzo was growing up in the shadow of my misfortune, at the most difficult age, early adolescence.

Every day he rode his bicycle to school, in the center of Rome, covering about thirty kilometers there and back, rain or shine. We lived in the same room with two beds. I dressed and did my exercises when he wasn't there. He seemed untroubled as he went over his lessons with me. We counted the liras for him to see a film, have a drink at the bar, go roller-skating with his friends in the city. But he also painted some dark heads of Christ whose features were red rivulets like clotted blood.

I noticed that Lorenzo sometimes came back to the room as if he were fleeing something. If someone knocked, he locked himself in the bathroom. He would go out but then race back to ask if a schoolmate had phoned him. One day when he'd dialed a number numerous times, he looked at the phone in his hand and chuckled: "Two people can't communicate when they're busy calling each other, it seems." He replaced the receiver.

If one of the patients in the garden called him over, "Come here, you who can walk," with a plaintive insinuation that, even after I'd resigned myself to it, continued to get on my nerves, he just grunted and kept going.

A wheelchair-bound man in his thirties, who must have been injured at more or less the same age that Lorenzo was then, was the most insistent upon beckoning to him, detaining him, touching him. He couldn't watch Lorenzo go by in the garden without asking him to do something for him. Usually, if he didn't feel like he was being waylaid, Lorenzo volunteered to help, rushing over on his own as soon as he thought someone needed anything (with the same easiness as his father). It was that "you who can walk" that irritated him, that made him run off.

One day when he was returning from school, hungry after covering fifteen kilometers on his bike, that same man grabbed hold of his sweater and warned him: "Watch out, it can happen to you too."

At which the boy broke out of his grip and in a shrill voice that occasionally cracked into deeper tones said, "So does that make me a criminal if I can walk? Is it my fault if I'm not crippled?" And the dark eyes in his round face welled with tears.

It was in that jumble of feelings and thoughts that I wrote "As Long as the Head Lives." I recognized myself in the period in Mainz where I had first confronted paralysis. Perhaps, in recounting it, I emphasized my couldn't-care-less attitude of that time because I was seeking a strength that I now needed. And, to buoy myself up, I concocted the cunning, false fable that good always triumphs . . .

School closed at the end of May and Lorenzo went to spend the vacation at his paternal grandparents' farm, on the Gran Sasso plateau, along with a swarm of cousins who gathered there in summer. I didn't want him to start the school year at Villa della Pace again, and I spent my days overcoming old difficulties on paper, almost as if by doing so I could ward off tomorrow. I completed that story in August. But there was nothing on the horizon. I didn't have the money to set up house again. I'd just paid off my debts and sold the Studebaker, and I'd purchased a small DAF 600 with automatic transmission, a recently launched model. Another month passed.

By now it would soon be a year that I'd been living in that home for the disabled, when finally some German friends, whom I had put up in the prosperous days when I had a home, offered me an apartment in the Taunus. Lorenzo wrote from Abruzzo, enthusiastic about the plan (later, however, in that village in the forest, in the snowy silence, surrounded by foreign words, he must certainly have felt lonely). I made arrangements by mail with a local housekeeper to come and clean.

In late September, the boy returned from Gran Sasso, invigorated, tanned, all muscle. We loaded up the DAF 600 and set out for Germany. An electrician friend headed for Hamburg spelled me at the wheel.

On one of his last aimless nights at Villa della Pace, while I chatted with friends in another room, Lorenzo, left alone as usual, read my manuscript. More than anything else, my brief mention of the Höchst factory had intrigued him. So when we were almost at the end of the trip, approaching the turnoff to the Taunus, he suggested that we continue on to Frankfurt instead, before settling in Glashütten, the little village set amid fir trees where we were headed, close to Königstein: "Come on," he said, "we're on the road, let's go to IG Farben!"

"But it's quite a drive." I hesitated. "Won't it be too long?" We were already racing north.

"Were you seriously a worker?" Lorenzo laughed. "With shifts and all? Operating machinery?" he asked, in the deep newfound voice of a young man, still gangly, his face still beardless.

The electrician had been dropped off by then and I was driving. We reached Höchst in the late afternoon. We proceeded at a snail's pace amid the angry honking of drivers irritated by my slow driving. Finally, I found my gate, the one where I used to stamp my card. I stopped the car. I felt a sense of emptiness. My eyes fixed on the details. The brick wall that enclosed the facilities seemed blackened, darker than I remembered it, the housing in front grayer and more barrack-like.

"Why don't you tell me about the work you did? And your fellow workers, did you get along?" Lorenzo encouraged me.

I started telling him about the Russians, about Director Lopp, about the Warsaw prisoners, and I became animated. Then somehow I wound up telling him about the strike too, because he kept asking questions, even when I was ready to be done remembering.

"Do you think you could have pulled it off or not?"

I got flustered, I said yes and then I said no. It depended, maybe he hadn't considered that . . . "Why are you looking at me like that?" I said, noting a hint of sadness in his face.

"But did you think you could succeed?"

"I don't know. But we saw that we could at least try."

"Sure, that much at least," he said hastily, but it was as if he'd missed the essential point. His fourteen-year-old baby face remained saddened.

Now I think that he couldn't stand the idea that our action was doomed to failure, but at the time, as we sat in the car in the twilight opposite my gate at IG Farben, I had the feeling he was wondering where my past had gone to—though, actually, this was what I was wondering, worried that my account might have made my story seem like little more than an impulsive act that had amounted to nothing, one of those myths of the past that every parent crows about and that are of no interest to their children.

"Shall we continue on?"

He nodded, and I pressed the accelerator.

The years get mixed up.

The judicious face of the boy with the dark, impudent eyes, sitting beside me in the car watching for the road signs, turns into the face of the bearded twenty-year-old who, sometimes with glasses and sometimes without, pored over the newspaper and magazine photos rediscovered among my papers during the months when I was searching for my past. One image in particular recurs, from the spring of '68. On top of a ladder, Lorenzo is with his university friends, brandishing chairs to fend off a squad of big men with clubs rushing at them from below. Lorenzo is bent forward, in three-quarters view, his mouth open in a snarl, his face grim and scared.

In other photos he appears in demonstrations, his gaze relentless. But then he's by himself, half a page for him alone, his expression defiant, his fist raised, his determination so different from my own at that same age, on my Siemens card. His is more intimate, more tormented. Now he's clean-shaven, rather pale; when he's focused he speaks in a low, contained voice, the dark, narrowed eyes recalling those of the boy who at Höchst wanted to know about the IG Farben strike.

As we drove through Frankfurt that night, Lorenzo shouted, "Pizzeria!" Pointing to the Italian sign on the ground floor of an old building, he rubbed his palms delightedly over his thighs as his watchful eyes followed my maneuvers to park. When we went in, however, the burst of joy faded at the sight of the poorly dressed immigrants crowded into the room, almost all from the south, their faces guarded, their eyes fiery. They helped me manage the steps in the wheelchair, asking and answering questions. They lived in the barracks, of course, the ones outside the city, in the camp called Pfaffenwiese, on the way to Mainz, yes, that's the one, the old Frankfurt-Höchst Lager that had later been adapted for foreign workers.

XI

Afterward I never looked back on my wartime experiences, until '75. For thirteen years I felt no need to think about them. Thirteen years is a long time, all the more so since, on balance, up until '62 I had actually clarified very little about that entire chapter: episodes of escapes and hospital stays recounted for pages and pages, whereas I'd dedicated just a couple of paragraphs in "As Long as the Head Lives," about twenty lines, to my first nine months in the Lagers. Not even stopping by IG Farben with Lorenzo, after leaving Villa della Pace, had made me want to more evenly balance my memories of that part of the past. Apparently, I was content with having come to terms with the paralysis and satisfied at having finally atoned for my crime of volunteering in the Lagers.

I must say that in '62 I had only one purpose: to have a home again and establish a circumspect way of life, in part so that my son—albeit belatedly—could grow up in a stable environment. To actually realize that goal took me years.

I gradually distanced myself from my social class by creating a vacuum, telling would-be visitors that I did not have time to receive them. "I'm so sorry," I said to avoid them. "Excuse me for taking the liberty of existing," I would add sweetly. No one understood anyway, and the words, intended to be sarcastic, sounded like an amusing witticism. And, *d'emblée*, the usual astonished admiration—"You dress yourself? Shoes too? But how do you manage?"—immediately became less frequent.

I rationed my physical and moral strength by the milligram. And little by little, in part because I had done away with the marathons and in part because I took better care of myself, my health stabilized. The need to earn was less nagging. Lorenzo had come of age; I was doing better.

Consequently I was able to work more calmly: essays, articles, lectures. Then Lorenzo became independent and went to live in Paris, where he did socioeconomic research while writing for an Italian communist newspaper.

In addition, and perhaps most important, the times had changed. A progressive culture had taken hold and opened minds a little; conventions had become somewhat freer everywhere. Young people were no longer subject to the kind of prejudices that had cost me so much energy to neutralize.

This for me was the ultimate confirmation that my memory block had been linked to the struggle against the social pressures that wanted to confine me to the role of invalid. In fact, I fully recovered my past in the Lagers once that struggle was over, with the added triumph of living on my own, with no assistance other than that of an aide who comes for a few hours in the morning to straighten up the house, do my shopping, and above all run work-related errands, at the photocopy shop, post offices, and agencies. (Although there is always someone who asks, "What! You live alone?" in a mournful voice. "What if you were to fall?") And it had not been necessary for me to be despondent, crushed, and deranged for memories of my Germany to reemerge again: all it took was a simple move.

Toward the end of '75 I received an eviction notice from the sixth-floor apartment where I'd lived since I'd finally set up house, after the downfall that had sent me to Villa della Pace with my son. I was a little worried about all the stuff that had accumulated and, to begin with, I took a first crack at clearing out my file cabinets. I happened to come across my worker's card from my time in the Lagers, which I didn't even know I still had. The heavy face in the photo called up my frame of mind back then, later repressed, and I wrote "In the Ch 89." Afterward an apartment in the same building opened up and I moved to the third floor, just three flights down. I completed an editorial assignment I had, but it was clear, at that point, that the episode in Verona would not be long in emerging either. In fact, as soon as my mind was uncluttered, it imposed itself so forcefully that it occupied me entirely. All the repressed events, from prison in Frankfurt and subsequent to that—not just the repatriation and the days in Verona but, perhaps even more intensely, the twelve weeks of constant astonishment at the "normality" of Dachau—appeared before me, sharp and precise, with no difficulty. And I faced the *deviation*.

Now that it was all clear, however—this happened in September—I had a nagging feeling. I wasn't at all relieved, as I had expected to be. I felt almost as though I'd been left empty-handed. Everything added up so well that, for some reason, it didn't convince me. Especially that virtuous ending: freed of physical dependence (so to speak) and suddenly freed of everything, of her social class, of any interior void. Who was I trying to fool? And then too, when did I ever lead a solitary life? Far from it. In reality those were the years when I met and frequented many people, not friends handed down from my milieu, but friends found in Rome, Paris, Berlin.

Oh God, all those months of racking my brain only to wind up with this edifying story of a disabled person who made it despite all the odds— the classic American fairy tale, meritocratic, individualistic, the untarnished heroine who through mistakes and misunderstandings overcomes all adversity, an example and a warning, albeit with the modernly muted epilogue of an actor discreetly leaving the scene—the rhetorical figure of moving down to the lower floors—without any bombastic nineteenth-century theatricality. And on top of it I felt liberated. But from what?

A lifetime of denying others the right to judge me by the yardstick of my paralysis, only to do so myself. They won. I am them.

It may seem strange to you, reader, that I did not get discouraged. For sixteen years now I've known that I'm a social snake, and when I shed one old skin and grow an equally conservative new one it now takes me less time to realize it. I had shed the rainbow-colored, iridescent skin of the complex creature whose memories overflow for hundreds of pages into scattered streams, and had slipped into that of the wounded being, misunderstood at first, then lost (drugged, megalomaniacal), who ultimately redeems herself.

Fine, I said to myself: now I'll pit one skin against the other. I'll dismantle the deus ex machina of the wheelchair with other memories of my problematic image. We'll see if they don't annihilate one another.

And so, six weeks ago, I went leafing through the hundreds of pages in which, for days and nights, in spring's coolness and summer's suffocating heat, shut up in my room (as I am now), I had tried fruitlessly, though less prejudicially, to recompose my life. Thank you, I exclaimed to myself as I reread: I'd left out thousands of episodes to focus only on those that magnified my battle against the pillory of my physical affliction! But there were plenty of them that contradicted this premise. Once again I had only to pick and choose. Starting with Merano, in December '45, after I was let off the train of veterans from Russia.

For a couple of weeks I had been lying in a hotel pressed into service as a transit hospital for wounded veterans, in a small room, waiting for one of my family members—officially informed of my arrival—to show up. And I see standing in the doorway a young man whose green eyes lock onto mine, behind the load of flowers and gift boxes piled up in his arms.

I stared at him, astonished. I would have expected anything except to see before me the last boyfriend I'd had in Rome in '43, before moving to the north with my parents. It was him, his long, almond-shaped eyes, full lips. The Cossack hat on his head accentuated his oriental features that at one time I hadn't noticed, the wide nostrils, broad face.

"I'm Gheorg, don't you recognize me?"

I had started going with him when I was seventeen and we'd stayed together for several months, constantly squabbling because he was anti-Fascist and I was the opposite, but we always went looking for each other and, arms tightly around each other's waist, we would disappear into the Palatine ruins just a short walk from my home (I lived on the Aventine and came up with all sorts of excuses to leave the house). We went on meeting like that, in secret, even after he had formally asked for my hand, as was the custom then.

He was a Romanian count, exiled from his country during the exodus of the members of the aristocracy closest to King Carol, at the time of Codreanu's insurrection, later superseded by Antonescu's coup d'etat. His family had sought refuge in England, and he had come to Italy with a study grant from the Academy of Romania (Antonescu's pro-Nazi regime had kept a concerned eye on the aristocrats in exile). He'd asked me to marry him and stay in Rome with him, as soon as he heard that my father planned to move to the north, where the Fascist government had been reestablished following the liberation of Mussolini at Gran Sasso (late summer of '43). I said yes, if he came with us.

Those had been fretful days; we begged each other, tore each other apart, each accusing the other of not loving them, with tears and exchanges of letters that we delivered by hand, until the moment of separation came and he'd told me, "It will bring you bad luck, I can feel it," and I made horns at him.

I'd erased him from my memory, and only in Frankfurt-Höchst, the following March, a few weeks after my arrival in the Lager, when I'd received the first two letters from my mother and tore up the aerogram allotted to me for the next two weeks, isolated by my companions, shunned by the internees, as I loaded and unloaded the frozen blocks of sulfuric acid—only then did I remember his face lighting up when he saw me, his apprehension for me, the intensity with which he had implored me to stay. I'd bought another aerogram from a companion and written to him in Rome, begging him to come; I was lost and I needed his help. At the end of the same month, March '44, I'd written to him again, saying, if he came, he should bring me a pair of boots, and not to forget *food* (I specified: salami, oil, sugar). Then, one evening, returning from the factory, I thought I saw his figure standing in front of the Lager. For a while I kept waiting for a letter. In the end I buried him again, so deeply that he was the last person whose name I would have thought of that afternoon in Merano.

Seeing him there, agitated as I was at the thought of meeting my father again (the tender feelings for my parents, which I'd had in Homburg when

I'd thought of going to live in the Soviet Union, had vanished into thin air), I felt a surge of affection for that forgotten young man who'd been the first to rush to welcome me.

We cried, laughed, remembered, and we got back together. He slept on a cot next to my bed.

A couple of days later, I asked him (swallowing hard), "Did you ever receive my letters from the Lager?" He said yes with his eyes and, his face red, went to rummage in his suitcase. Meanwhile, he spoke hurriedly, in broken sentences. He seemed to have been waiting nervously for this question.

He had received my aerograms and now handed me his replies, a hundred or so letters that he'd written to me without ever sending them, a stack of pages arranged in a folder, in date order, sequentially numbered, and seeing them so well organized had a curious effect on me. I glanced through them perhaps a bit too negligently and put them on the nightstand.

"I'll read them later," I said with a smile. But out of the corner of my eye I saw that he darkened (in his own way, a shadow). I picked them up again. He immediately put a sonata on the gramophone that he'd brought me, in F-sharp he said. I dove into his whimsical but clear handwriting, the serpentine *s*, the rounded *a*.

In those letters he'd never sent me, he reminded me of our discussions during our last days together, when he'd tried to make me face my inconsistencies, for example, between the accusations I'd made against my parents and my decision to follow them up north. I'd told him (I hadn't remembered it) that my mother had become "rarefied" due to excessive virtue but that at least she was capable of dedication, whereas my father was "arid"; although he seemed so cordial, it was all a smokescreen: he was merely sentimental as cynics always are, just read Dostoyevsky. To some extent I was intrigued by the judgments (facile for that matter) that I had formed when I had no experience whatsoever, which Gheorg had scrupulously preserved in his letters. Yet I was a little uncomfortable, because even now Gheorg's arguments didn't convince me that it had been a venture doomed to perdition, that a thirst for the depths had attracted me, that I had gone to Germany out of nihilism (as I read, he paced around me to see where I was up to, if I would say anything).

That may have even been so, I thought, but it was also significant that

I had not enlisted in a women's auxiliary corps or some other group with a "lust for war," as he wrote, but had gone directly to the Lagers, where there was nothing heroic, no noble death, just the prospect of working in a factory, *"Hilfsarbeiterin"* (laborer) was written on my employment card, so I had gone there to be a worker, hadn't I? Why wouldn't he admit that was what I'd wanted even if the shock had been greater than expected? He himself knew how many offers I'd already had in Rome to be an interpreter, given that I spoke French, Italian, and German equally well. I had even explained to him why I wasn't interested, after I was personally received by Alessandro Pavolini in late September '43, when the new Republican Fascist Party was established. I wanted to leave that elite world, not look down on things anymore. Why did he keep repeating in the letters what he'd already told me a thousand times between one embrace and another, to the point that I remained unresponsive, indifferent.

As I went on reading, I realized that, no, he took my being a worker into account, citing from two of my letters, in which I wrote: "I'm learning what I wanted to know, if you come and be a *worker* with me, you too will understand. *Maybe I'm afraid to find out too much, by myself I'm afraid*, I have no one to turn to except you, who once said you loved me." And: "We lived in Limbo. Don't stay there sheltered, come." He replied that I was discovering what he already knew, which he'd so desperately expressed in our final meetings—violence, cruelty, poverty, injustice—and that it was folly to go looking for them. But at the same time he tormented himself, picturing my life in the camps; he described it to me—very close to what it actually was—and you could tell he lived through it personally day and night. He would make up his mind to come and join me, but, when he got to the offices of the Todt, when the moment came to submit an application to the Nazi officer, he felt faint and turned back; then he'd start writing to me again, during the night or at a table in the bar where he had waited for my irregular appearances, at the time when we were happy together.

And page after page he told me how much he loved me, how he couldn't live without me, and how he couldn't come and join me. At times he resolved to send me the letter he was writing, but he feared the censors, he was already an exile, barely tolerated, what if they were watching him? What if they found these letters? Even without sending them to me, he lived in terror of being discovered, he would abruptly break off a sentence, then resume writing to apologize, he'd heard footsteps outside the door, he'd hidden everything under the mattress . . .

I had already tired of reading but I didn't dare stop, I felt him pacing anxiously around me. I'll read as far as the liberation of Rome, I thought, that way at least when the Americans have come he'll have gotten over his fears. I flicked through the sheets furtively to see the dates, but there were still quite a few pages to go. I was only at the end of April '44 and I had to get to June!

"I must seem ridiculous to you," I heard him murmur finally. He was sitting on the cot beside me, elbows on his knees, pinching the backs of his hands: a gesture of distress that I had also seen him do back when it was clear that we would separate.

"No," I laughed. "But if you'd sent me a parcel of food it would have been better." He didn't find it funny, though; his lips were quivering. I couldn't let him see that his inner drama left me unmoved: "It wasn't your concern," I told him, "I was wrong to write to you, that was quite a demand I made!"

"What are you saying?" he cried as if I'd slapped him.

"Look, Gheorg, now it's as if you had come," I consoled him.

During my absence, he'd obtained a degree in humanities, published essays and poems, and was now a lecturer in contemporary literature at the University of Rome.

"A lifetime ahead of us," he laughed contentedly.

In early January, we went together to Bologna, to the military orthopedic center, which I've already written about, where Gheorg himself had managed to have me assigned, even going to pull some strings at the prefecture in Merano.

To stay with me in Bologna he obtained permission to sleep on a mattress on the floor in the hallway, outside my room. Every night, for months, he went to get it from the storage room in our ward and every morning he rolled it up again and went to put it back. Then in the spring we left each other, for reasons inherent to our relationship itself.

He kept thinking of me exactly the way he'd thought of me before we met again. Hours and hours of new confidences had not affected his judgment. He saw me as a lively, proud girl who doesn't look back; and this quality, which he attributed to a ruminant like me, intrigued him and attracted him sensually. This hurt me because I felt an emotional framework being re-created around me that negated who I was; being with him made me feel as though he loved a different person. And yet we did not leave each other because of a quarrel over the past but over the future. He wanted us to move to the United States as soon as we were married, where he had been offered a three-year term at a college. He described the life that we would have: wide-ranging, well-off, interesting, among cultured people. Whereas I, having just returned to Italy after so much doubting and reflection, was determined to stay.

They were pressing weeks. We didn't leave each other for a moment. In the evening we would go to a shed at the back of the grounds and lie on the straw.

"Forget those vain passions," he said, "or they'll consume you again."

Meticulously, stubbornly, I reconstructed my line of thinking to explain my behavior to him and to derive some direction for myself as well, until he gave up, defeated.

"Here you can't do anything. Are you afraid of happiness? Your mind is still in a Lager. Open your eyes, Lucina, the war is over, the world is ours."

The more he argued, the more I clung to Martine, Grùscenka, Alain, Lulù, the Flemish girl, Louis, Jeanine.

"You're mentally distancing yourself, I can feel it," he said, pulling me to him, while I told myself to deny it. Meanwhile, I thought back to the individuals behind the desks at the partisans' association, at the Resistance committee: "Give me another chance, like at the Ch 89, hire me, please."

"Don't you see that these things sadden you? You're eating yourself up and you want me to just stand by and watch?" Gheorg went on, trying to shake me out of it.

"If you shared in it, it would be different," I murmured.

"My father used to say that fanaticism is a plebeian passion. And you're infected with it," he said. Then, fearful of having offended me, he quickly went back to declaring his love.

"All right, we'll stay in Italy," he finally said one day when we were sitting in the hospital garden, just when I had convinced myself the night before that this relationship was a mistake.

"Gheorg, why are we pointlessly tormenting ourselves? At the end of the day even you always knew that we two would never live together," I said, suddenly drained, unable to hold back tears.

I saw him flush, a tremor on his lips, his eyes moist. He noticed that the back of the wheelchair was too vertical: "I'll tilt it back a little."

He wouldn't give up: "I backed away once, not twice." We were having supper in the ward, in the usual awkward way, he with his soup plate on his knees and I beside him in the bed, the bowl resting on the blanket. He demonstrated to me that I was wrong, that I was driven by a self-destructive instinct. "And then *you* talk about a sense of reality." His green eyes bored into mine. "As you wish, we'll destroy ourselves together," he concluded, as if I were leading him before the firing squad (I thought).

It was I who by then no longer wanted to reason but only caress him, embrace him, seeing his narrow shoulders, the chest of an adolescent, only his legs muscular, robust, and it was he who pulled back. He twisted his full lips, rubbed his fingertips.

At night, even after the shed, Gheorg came into the ward barefoot and we whispered together, or else he would fall asleep sitting up, his head resting on my bed, in the crook of his elbow, his other arm around me. Even on the weekend when my mother was there, he no longer went into the city, to the library or elsewhere as he had before, but remained beside me as if glued there, always finding ways to touch me as he read or studied, holding my hand, resting his elbow against mine on the chair arm, putting his leg next to mine on the footrest of the wheelchair, sitting on the bed propped against my lap. We were bound together by the anguish of leaving each other.

The wedding date, set for March, with the banns already published, had passed. In the evening, at the shed, I felt cold. Staying too long on that straw, aching all over, was hard, the stalks were sharp. Even at twenty-five, Gheorg's mind was too programmed to change. I slowly moved away from him and turned on the flashlight, projecting it around the shed. The tools, pitchforks, shovels, and other things leaning in a corner cast out irregular, toothed, hook-shaped shadows that shrank, lengthened, and twisted depending on the movements of my beam. How ridiculous. In April we split up.

Perhaps I never felt the pointlessness of my experience in the Lagers with anyone as I did with Gheorg (with my father I expected it). Yet God knows how much I vacillated before adjusting to the idea of breaking up with him. But the Lucia whom he loved made it hard for me to breathe, gently obliterating all that I had gone to look for in Germany.

Maybe discovering the impossibility of that union opened the first chink in my memory. But the cost of not repudiating my Germany (losing Gheorg) had been so high that I began to fear it. Shortly afterward I met Domenico.

Besides, there was nothing left to explain, everyone already had a well-formed opinion of what I had gone through, even before I began to speak. They all saw me with the same eyes as Gheorg: the people I shrank from had a high regard for me, but those I preferred were wary of me.

XII

In April '45, my father had managed to escape arrest at the time of the days of reckoning, in the wake of Liberation, by hiding with a lover who had Resistance merits. So he had only been arrested later on, when he turned himself in. The trial had established summarily that, in his duties as undersecretary to the Ministry of Propaganda in the Aviation Division, my father had never performed military actions but only administrative functions. A dossier of documents had made a good impression on the prosecutor. They included public statements in which he deplored the civil war, claims in which he asserted the autonomy of the *repubblichine* forces from Nazi control, and testimonies of partisans whom he had helped to hide and escape.

A month after my return to Italy, he was fully acquitted and went into business. Then he gradually resumed editing a series of publications, first on shows and nightlife, and a few years later on aeronautic propaganda again.

His brother, my uncle the engineer, who, as a high-ranking Fascist Party leader, had presided over the reclamation works in the Pontine Marshes, had also fared well: he had joined Confindustria, the General Confederation of Italian Industry, where he soon attained a high-level post.

Now, it's not as if I wanted to see these two people pilloried in '46: my father truly did deplore the civil war, and had indeed aided the partisans, and my uncle was a highly skilled engineer whose talents it would have been foolish to waste. But what stuck in my craw were the *social circumstances* that enable certain people to pass through the history of their time unscathed, while others find themselves bearing the full weight of it on their backs.

I looked around the military hospital where I'd been admitted, a very large building, perhaps a former monastery, rising on top of a hill from which it towered over the city of Bologna. It was full of men, veterans from all the fronts, bedridden patients even in the corridors and on the landings, except for the big square room on the top floor that only housed about a dozen women, myself included. Among the hundreds of convalescent soldiers, there were about thirty partisans who occupied a ward on the ground floor behind the gym.

More or less the same number of *repubblichini* soldiers filled a ward on the top floor, opposite our door, through which their songs, belted out at the top of their lungs, reached us at times:

> Le donne non ci vogliono più bene
> perché portiamo la camicia nera,
> ci hanno detto che siamo da galera
> ci hanno detto che siamo da catene.

"Women don't love us anymore because we wear black shirts, they say we should be jailed, they say we should be in chains."

Two boys in particular made an impression on me, a sixteen-year-old, on crutches, with one leg amputated up to his thigh, and another, around twenty, in a wheelchair, who, on leaving the gym, invariably stopped in the hallway in front of the open door of the partisans' ward and sang:

> L'amore coi fascisti non conviene
> meglio un vigliacco che non ha bandiera
> uno che salverà la pelle intera,
> uno che non ha sangue nelle vene.

"You shouldn't make love with Fascists, better a coward with no flag who will save his skin, one who has no blood in his veins."

The Resistance volunteers would slam the door in their faces. "Come on out if you dare!" The sixteen-year-old hopped on his only foot, poking a crutch against the closed door that suddenly swung open: "I won't fight with a remnant of a man," a deep voice boomed.

"Lily-livered cowards," the gaunt twenty-year-old in the wheelchair shouted in a shrill, trembling voice.

Then, with the alternating sound of the tapping of crutches and steps, another guy, rosy-faced, eyes bloodshot under long lashes, who'd also had a leg amputated, came out and rushed at the sixteen-year-old. Dropping their crutches, they grappled hand to hand until two orderlies ran to separate them.

The officers, on the other hand, did not come to blows. For one thing, they were not divided: both those of the Liberation army and those of the Republic of Salò were on the first floor, which was reserved for them, near the operating rooms and the administrative offices. They were sorted by rank, not by political stripe. Rooms with a few beds held lieutenants, others captains, while high-ranking officers were given single rooms. Sometimes their raised voices could be heard in the dining room set aside for them, but usually they avoided one another civilly. I had the same feeling I'd had in Germany, that the utmost would be done to keep the social hierarchies intact after so much liberation. Ideological crusades were proclaimed so as to better conceal everything that hadn't changed. At that time I realized that a war isn't enough to banish prejudices, but I didn't understand that a war isn't enough to overthrow a social structure unless the elements of its dissolution are already contained within it. Was that what I was afraid to say, hiding behind the shield of paralysis? Was recognizing that I had been so ingenuous in '46 what was weighing on me?

I spent time with the partisans—they often came up to my room—and in fact I began to find them as deluded as I had been in Dachau.

I remember a strapping young man, from Grappa. He recalled the nights when, together with a few comrades, he would ambush the patrols of Black Brigades, the ones dressed in black with a white skull on their black berets.

Sometimes, as he spoke, he ducked his head, finger on the trigger, his eye on the sights of a nonexistent rifle held against his shoulder, and his vivid complexion would pale. He would then give us a disoriented look.

I especially remember a tall, dark, rigid boy from Imola, eighteen years old, who had fought in the Po Valley. What remained most impressed in his memory were the nights he'd spent on sentry duty at a munitions depot. One day when Luciano, the lookout, was at my bedside with a bearded partisan from Milan, we talked about those nights when he'd stood guard.

His comrades would go out seeking action, hunting soldiers or Nazis who ventured into the area; they chose to leave him behind since he couldn't move swiftly in the dark (they said) and so, as a result, he never learned. The fact is that fear of the Nazi dogs paralyzed him. The first times his buddies had brought him along with them, he'd stayed behind, frozen, as if rooted in the darkness, unable to respond to their calls (bird whistling, frog croaking); whoever went back for him had to shake him a bit before he could speak. But then on sentry duty he'd been even worse (a shiver runs down his back as he tells it). He'd stand there in the cold, in the darkness, staring at the bushes, and no matter which way he spun around, the suspicious rustling seemed to be behind him. He felt like the only exposed target on the entire plain, though his brain told him that in the fog he was only a blur, like the shadows of the woods, and that the precious crates of bullets and hand grenades wrapped in tarpaulins were hidden underground. There, the other guy was taking aim. They would shout Halt! before shooting at him (it might even be one of them) and he would just have time to toss the rifle into the marsh . . .

"Terrific," the short, chubby-faced Milanese partisan with the curly beard bursts out, "great thinking!" Then, abruptly whirling around: "This is what you should have done," he says. Crouched over an imaginary weapon in his hands, he fires a volley of shots into his friend's darkness.

Meanwhile, some soldiers visiting other patients had come over.

"Oh sure," a Russian veteran threw out, "you're dreaming if you think you can react that quickly, buddy. When you've been on sentry duty for a few hours, out in the open, you become insensate."

"Guerrilla action isn't the front, where you don't know why you're fighting," the Milanese replied in a deep voice, "there you have a purpose."

"Your life is your life," the Russian said with a shrug, "with or without a purpose. Fear plays tricks on you when you find yourself standing like an asshole, on lookout duty in the night."

"Someone who shoots at the Russians is of course an asshole, what else would he be?"

"Listen to this blowhard, he thinks he can teach me, who—"

"Who are you calling a blowhard?"

They faced off. The others also jumped in.

"Just look at these eleventh-hour heroes," one of the soldiers said, stepping forward.

"And you, a bunch of sheep."

"Shirkers."

"Nò-duè, nò-duè."

"Ditch that beard, kid, you still stink of mother's milk."

"Fuckers."

Other visitors gathered around, the patients who could get up, coming between them. A gray-haired man, blind in one eye, his other eye sad, kept saying: "Stop it, shame on you!"

"Shame on who? I lost an arm in Libya."

"On all of you, on all of us," he said, hands outstretched before him to quell the altercation.

"Tell it to your precious comrades who are still playing war, not to us. We've had enough of you clowns," the other one said, running a hand across his forehead.

"Fascist."

"Who's a Fascist?" he said, grabbing the Milanese partisan by the pajama collar.

"Anyone who calls the Resistance a bunch of clowns. We liberated you from Fascism."

"Behind the tanks of the Americans."

By then they'd come to blows.

"These cocky bastards," the veteran who'd lost his arm in Libya yelled, "for a few piddly firecrackers fired at—"

"I left half my guts there," the Russian veteran said, shaking his head. "And now they want to put words in my mouth."

"You too, though." I tried to calm him down from my bed. "You treated him like he was boasting!"

He came over to me, his hands joined: "But they want to make me think I was a fool. A real asshole to have served three years at the front and two in captivity! Don't you see?"

"And what did it get you?" The Milanese partisan shook his closed fist at him. "Can you tell me that?"

"I not only lost my youth but I was a fool to boot? Go to hell . . ." he snapped with an irritated gesture.

Two nurses rushed in: "Have you all gone crazy, screaming like that? Do you want the administrators to prohibit visiting? Now go, off with you, all of you."

The men scattered, pushing up a sleeve, adjusting a belt, muttering "Poor Italy," "We'll show you," "Look, we just have to take it."

"You were wrong too, though," I told Vittorio, the Milanese partisan, the following day. "You shouldn't humiliate them . . ."

"Me? Humiliate them?" he said, mouth open in astonishment.

"I know you don't mean to, but that's just why you humiliate them all the more" (I identified with those soldiers). "You know, these are sensitive matters—a man's whole life, you can't toss it out with the trash," I said, unable to find the right words.

"And who tossed it out with the trash, me? Just the opposite! It's you who's okay with seeing them as slaves."

"And what should they be, masters?"

That's the way I was thinking by then, that was what I didn't want to say.

Later those men with whom I had identified were the same ones who paraded in front of my bed, basically scandalized that I would get married in my condition. An infantry sergeant said to me, "And I was mourning the fact that my wife and daughter were buried in a bombing! What if I had found them like this?" he said, pointing to my legs. "It's really true, death isn't the worst thing."

(The only kind memory of the visitors who filed past me is the face of the sentry from the Po Valley who stopped a moment by my bed and said, "You're sad, huh?")

Vittorio had left. Our last talks had been relentless.

"You don't want to understand me," I told him. "This isn't a matter of redressing workers. Don't you see those sixteen-year-olds here at the hospital who get beaten up? Don't those scenes teach you anything? To me they do, because I did it myself in the Lagers, I came to blows and fought with those pitiful wretches, understand? I had hatred in my body. Hatred against the Nazis boomeranged on us," I told him, "and we internees attacked one another. I learned that, you know? That much at least I've learned." I told him about the strike organized by the comrades of IG Farben: "We certainly didn't fight among ourselves there," I said. "With all the effort it took to involve the internees, imagine if we foreign workers had quarreled with one another! We didn't give a damn about what everyone thought before. Whether they were volunteers or deportees, it was all the same to us."

"Exactly, all united against the Nazis," Vittorio said, more affably.

"But because they were in command!"

However, I could never finish what I wanted to say because Vittorio quickly started in with his list of atrocities again: "And how did they command? By exterminating, by the most sinister repression, the suppression of all democratic liberties."

"Of course!" I jeered. "You're preaching to the choir, my dear Vittorio. Anyway, they're not in command anymore."

The next morning he stopped me in the gym and, stroking the curly beard framing his chubby face, unintentionally jovial, said, "So for you the Nazi-Fascists have now been crushed and that's that," he said, gesturing as if washing his hands, his eyes darting over my face. Then, almost without moving his lips, he asked, "Just like that, you would absolve them all?"

"And you want to see them at the bottom of the social ladder?"

And the next time we met: "Even at the bottom, isn't there perhaps some small difference between enemies and comrades?" he asked, holding up the edge of a fingernail and flashing his black eyes at me.

"It doesn't count all that much!" I shrugged. I thought of Schwarzwald and of Lulù in Dachau.

"So you'd leave them where they are? Great!" he said angrily, his voice shrill.

"I look for enemies elsewhere," I said, also fuming.

"Oh really? And how can you do that unless you first recognize comrades?"

"On paper? By a party card? The herd mentality again?" I ask.

"Frankly, I don't follow you. Doesn't the end result count for anything with you? Won't our result be a bit different from that of your Nazi-Fascists?" he said, twisting the curly hair on his chin.

"But it's because the result is different that we don't need people who obey us. Our adversary can be recognized by his actions, by the factual evidence. Why would I need a follower? I'll prove it to you. At IG Farben, for four months I was convinced that the *Meister*, that is, the foreman of the Ch 89, was a Nazi, I looked at him as such, then during the foreigners' strike it was clear that he was in fact on our side. Yet he wore a Nazi badge on his lapel. I had mistaken another *Vorarbeiter* without a badge for a comrade, because, away from the others, he always showed me a clenched fist, winked at me, and didn't harass me at work. And I kept smiling complicitly at him. One day he rubbed up against me and said in my ear, 'Tonight?' still showing me his fist, and I saw that he was holding it like this." I showed Vittorio my fist, thumb stuck between my index and middle fingers. "Beginning to suspect, I nodded yes and asked permission to go to the toilet. I consulted Grùscenka, a Soviet comrade assigned to the latrine, and you can imagine how hard she laughed. The story made the rounds of the Lagers: I had mistaken a proposal to fuck for a communist salute. And from a man who was the section's worst womanizer and who, while not even registered with the party—on the contrary, passing himself off to us as an anti-Nazi—was taking advantage of the deportees' hunger."

"And what's that supposed to prove to me?" Vittorio said. "You think we don't know? Or have you taken to perpetually stating the obvious just to be difficult?" And as if to himself: "I don't get what you're driving at." He went on: "It seems like a trick of yours to stand back. You know, when a person clings to petty distinctions already known to all, reckoned with a thousand times"—he shook his head and looked at me—"when someone begins to resort to sophistry . . ."

"Sophistry?" I hooted. "Don't you have eyes? What's the use of hammering hatred and love into the heads of those who are exploited if they don't see what's subjugating them?"

I thought of my companions in the ward, workers and peasants from Emilia, victims of bombs or machine guns, who were always talking about the miseries they suffered at the hands of the Nazi-Fascists. Yet when my father, a liberal, showed up—he sometimes accompanied my mother on the trips she made from Milan every weekend to visit me—these same comrades were glad to see him:

"Such a wonderful father!" they told me.

He came in smiling, with the handsome demeanor of a former pilot, handed out tips to the nurses, brought cookies and candies to patients whose hand he kissed (as he had also done with Gheorg), snapped their photos. Tall, bald, with a Roman profile and flashing brown eyes, he was a man who sparkled in public, polished and refined when it came to women's topics, while abruptly dismissive when talking about serious issues. Even his voice changed. Confidential and husky at social gatherings or among a few close friends, it became sharp, impatient, almost nasal when he dealt with matters that irritated him, unless he chose to deflect them with a light, somewhat distracted tone.

He was especially exuberant that summer of '46 because he had obtained the funding to rent a nineteenth-century building on a street in central Milan, in whose ground-floor salons he displayed the aquariums he designed to order. He showed me color photos of these underwater worlds he created for the villas of industrialists, for first-run cinemas, for nightspots catering to Rotary Clubs. Genially, he went from bed to bed to show them to my neighbors as well, bending over them as they lay there in their cotton hospital gowns, contemplating the pictures with dumbstruck faces, flattered to listen to such a "true gentleman." With great charm, he pointed out how the plants in those aquariums swayed among stalactites and ravines that seemed to have formed in sunken cities ("miniature Atlantises," he said with a smile), in the midst of which darted precious little exotic fish, red, coral, or silver (I must admit that, among other things, he had real promotional talent).

In that ward in which our food was served in earthenware bowls with the aluminum cutlery of the Lagers, he emphasized the high cost of the fine porcelain with which he had his underwater metropolises constructed. And that unapproachable price aroused reverence in the patients, who seemed to get a boost from it.

Finally, he would return to me: "Such nice companions you have, such darling little women, you're well-off here. So don't do anything foolish again, you hear?" he said, with a sideways look that was stern yet playful, as if to say: I don't want to say it again, you've already paid so much . . .

But wait, am I about to start over again from the beginning? I'm dismayed. You're right, you're right, I tell the literary compartment of my brain, I'll stop right now. Only one more thing (I mentally raise a finger, asking my censor for permission) and then that's it, it'll only take two shakes of a lamb's tail, I promise. Just this one thing, be fair, it's too important.

One Sunday, that '46 in Bologna, I asked my father what inquiries he had made when he learned that I'd been repatriated.

"Inquiries? Why?" he asked distractedly.

"Didn't they telegraph you from Verona that I had arrived on August 2 of '44?" I said hesitantly.

"Yes, I don't remember the date but I think so. It's true, that's right, we were expecting you any day. But excuse me, didn't you write us that you had been captured in a Nazi roundup on the street in Verona?"

"Yes, Papa, but I wrote to you about it six months later."

It was the last time I'd been in touch with my family, in December '44. As I said, after Thomasbräu I had gotten hired at Siemens under my real name, and from there I was able to send home word of myself (I did it mainly for my mother, who, despite her perceptual distance, I sensed was suffering because of me).

"Forgive me, Lucia, I have no memory for dates, you know. I don't know how much time had passed, but a repatriation is not a simple thing, my dear girl, the Germans were exacting, you were out of the hospital, am I right? We knew these things took time. Besides, why dig up the past, sweetheart, you're here now, think about enjoying life. As soon as you're up to it, you'll see, we'll come and pick you up at the hospital and take you for some nice drives, forget this wheelchair, hm? Isn't that better? You'll see, you won't have time to be sad. Let me take care of it. Look at this," he said, taking some new color photos out of his bag, "this little crested fish, flat as a blade, tell me, don't his fins look golden?" And I recognized myself in that little confined creature, caught by the lens with his mouth like a suction cup against the glass.

It was then, I think, that I began to erase my departure from Verona. It had been an imaginary danger, thinking that my father was looking for me. I could easily have gone to work in a factory in Turin or elsewhere. What an error of judgment.

Perhaps that had been the deepest obstacle—for thirty years—to remembering the about-face in Verona, a reluctance to talk about my family. More accurately, I was afraid to reopen the whole question of my relationship with my parents.

What did my paralysis have to do with all those years of self-censorship? Who knows whether the excuse I'd subconsciously been giving myself not to sever relations with my father a second time didn't go back to '46.

XIII

Due to my economic difficulties, by early '60, I was no longer able to pay my rent. Toward June, I asked my father if he could put me up with Lorenzo for a few months until I got back on my feet.

After I'd split up with Domenico, my mother had also separated from my father, amicably. Years earlier she had already resumed her studies when she was certain that her husband was squandering the family assets. With a diploma in French that she had obtained as a young woman in a college in Grenoble, in middle age she had enrolled at university, learning Latin all over again and majoring in languages with the highest honors. Then, after passing the competitive exams, she began teaching. She was now a tenured instructor at a high school in Milan, where she lived. My father had never forgiven her for "rearing up like a suffragette." He referred to her as "Granny the student!" and from then on relations between my parents had deteriorated.

My father had furnished a penthouse apartment in Balduina, in which he let me and my son live during a time when I began to systematically forge contacts with workers and immigrants from the south. I studied the conditions of the *borgatari* in Pietralata and in the huts at Gordiani and I became friends with some of the employees in the gas refineries in San Paolo. When the gas workers went on strike in September, I banded with them from the outside to support their demands (I wrote about it as well).

One day, I invited a group of strikers to my father's house. When he returned from the office in the evening, he greeted them politely and retired to his room. That evening he dined out and, the following morning, he advised me to look for another place to live.

"The reason?" I asked.

"You cannot receive strange men in my house, this is not a—"

"Oh, morality!" I broke in.

"That's right," his lady friend at the time who witnessed the conversation interjected, "when we come home, we never know who we're going to find in this house. And if this continues . . ."

"I see."

I looked in the phone book for some refuge for myself and found the Villa della Pace for disabled war veterans. I called, yes, there were vacancies, and that very same day, early in the afternoon, I loaded what little stuff I needed in the Studebaker and drove off.

"What about me?" my son asked me. He bundled up his things to return to his father.

"You'll see, in a couple of months we'll have a home again, I'll find some loans." I was wrong about that.

Though by then I was no longer angry with my mother, I still didn't communicate with her much, due to the ongoing incompatibility of our ways of life.

"Each of us should do what he must and live in peace," she said, "the rest is just pretext."

It makes me smile to remember the sense of impotence that overcame me as we sat in the living room and drank tea, which for her was a ritual. Sometimes I flew off the handle.

"Swear words too now?" she would observe in her soprano voice. "Do you think you can change the world by shouting and using coarse language?" Lowering her eyelids, she went on softly: "Believe me, Lucia, rudeness has never helped anyone, vulgarity has never alleviated an injustice."

"Of course." I gritted my teeth so as not to raise my voice. "In fact, it creates it. Not what you say, though, but what's in here." I thumped my chest. "That's where the real vulgarity lies, deep and intimate, putting oneself above it all, refusing to see."

"What do you want from me?" my mother would snap at that point. "You want me to become one of those frenzied, immoral, corrupt people the world is full of?" she countered, her voice crystalline, electric. "What do you expect from me? I'm made for finer things. Ugliness doesn't interest me." Then she regained her composure and in a melodious voice added, "Take my word for it, Lucia, everyone in his place," disappointed that I couldn't understand so simple, so obvious a concept.

"What place?" I yelled. "Who assigned it? Can you tell me that? Who!?"

My mother rolled her eyes to the ceiling and, almost incredulous at my blindness, shook her head, her lovely face showing no sign of wrinkles at age fifty: "Such confusion in that little head of yours, Lucia," she said, her fingers lightly sweeping my forehead as she smiled appealingly. "But can it be?" As if startled, she looked at the time: "It's gotten late." She wrapped herself in her Persian lamb coat, pulled on her gloves, and briefly patted the blonde chignon under the pale fur hat; with a gracious nod of pleasure for the tea I'd offered her and a kiss on the forehead, off she went on her elegant high heels.

The separation from her husband had been good for her, in my eyes that is. Although she was now solely dependent on her meager salary as a teacher and was herself unusually frugal, when I came back from Germany with Lorenzo in '62 (after leaving the Villa) she had helped me find a place to live and buy furniture and linens with her ant-like savings. Though her disapproval of my way of life remained unwavering, she kept telling me: "Men can be so hateful at times," her dark eyes riveted. "Don't let them snare you, believe me, pay no attention to them but look and pass on," she recited, sitting straight in her chair, her voice virginal, her beautiful legs crossed.

It definitely makes me smile to think how inexplicable it must have seemed to her to end up with a daughter like me:

Me of all people, she must have thought to herself, astounded, who never deviated from the straight and narrow, either in thought or action. And while for years I didn't dare tell my father what I thought and felt, with her I lost my patience, as if it were easy to depart from one's habitual ways, from one's fictitious world, an imaginary castle that . . .

I thought I had gone over all the issues that I had laid on the altar of my physical affliction. It was late September. If the reader only knew how it felt to see the lovely weather outside through the half-open window, as I sat shut up in a room, at my desk, forever reweaving the same memories.

And drugs? There too I had hidden behind the paralysis when I became addicted to them. And what an effort to detoxify, less violent than that Easter in Mainz, but a hundred times longer: the addiction had lasted for an extended period of time. I began by replacing (in '55) the stronger narcotics with other, milder ones, morphine with tebasolo, opium with nisidina, with the intention of going from ampules to suppositories to tablets. I ingested diradon and noan pills, always checking the proportions of chloromethyl-phenyl-benzodiazepine, of diazepam at 1 or 2H-1 and so on, of all these products. I especially stopped resorting to any additional Valium, which had been a constant supplement to my ampules, suddenly panicked at the thought of the particular docility induced by that drug, which inadvertently leads to a loss of control over the nervous system, to a loss of will. How could I have forgotten that it was the basic component of the truth serum used by the Nazis in Dachau?

It was in that circumstance that my first precise memory of the K-Lager broke through to me. I no longer had to muddle around with the excuse that they were soft drugs, and, whenever I was tempted, I thought of Dachau.

Perhaps the most painful thing, at the time, was to halve the ampules, knowing what it had taken me to procure them, and pour the leftover down the sink with the water running.

So painful that, subsequently, so as not to go through that ordeal again, when I had to undergo surgery, I chose—for a time—to have them operate on me while awake rather than be given narcotics and go back to needing drugs. I thought of it as undergoing torture. If you scream, you betray your comrades. I didn't make a sound and the joy of not having betrayed my comrades generously compensated me for the pain I'd suffered. Now I no longer have these temptations (knock on wood); I haven't for several years, in fact, and I can do without forbidding myself at so dear a price (let them torture me, I won't talk).

Oh God, this parenthesis: "(let them torture me, I won't talk)." I could delete it and pretend I never wrote it, but I certainly thought it. Can it be that my core nobility pursues me so relentlessly? Who is torturing me, who wants to torture me?

And all the rest: I take drugs, I'm unjust, I'm wrong—yet the fault is always attributed elsewhere. What have I done up till now if not imply that the combination of circumstances was such that . . . First I blamed my decline on the struggle related to my physical affliction; then, when that alibi failed, it was the overwhelming battle against my social environment instead. And always this innocence, this ineradicable nobility of intention and genuineness of feeling that are so typical of me. Choleric, fraudulent, muddleheaded, dangerous—but so human, maybe too human. Seemingly a worm but essentially of such refinement, sensitivity, goodness. Wait, I've got it: an inveterately elite worm.

What didn't I seize upon, in this story of my distortions, to assert this candid image of my deepest nature, always striving against all odds, albeit in the blindest error, for the ultimate welfare of all? And then I railed against bourgeois compunction! I simply replaced the lofty tone that I abhorred in my social class with a tone of humility, of one who *also* sees her own shortcomings: a more malleable snakeskin, more current.

It may have been mental fatigue, a lack of confidence that I would ever sort out my repressions—I was lying on the bed again, motionless, my eyes closed—when the thought hit me that this tendency to constantly scrape through was not one of the usual snakeskins to be shed, only more adherent than the others, but my *real* skin. I could go on stirring up my memories until the end of time, I would never find myself wearing any other one.

And then the most appalling suspicion of all came to me: given that I was so perfectly, indeed, so ardently *like them*, to the point of constantly being of a superior order of humanity (even in front of the toilet bowl), who was to say that I had ever been different? What if from the beginning I had always and solely been a snake? I claimed that I had betrayed my Lagers. *What if I hadn't betrayed a single thing?*

What evidence did I have that things in the Lagers had been as I had reconstructed them? Not with regard to facts, because those can be spun any way you want, but deep within me, in my innermost self. My heart winced. Maybe you never really went over to the other side, one among many; maybe you've always been one of those people who looks down on the "humiliated and insulted." Maybe your consciousness didn't make that social leap in '44 that you're so proud of. Your footsteps, yes, but not your consciousness. What you've now discovered in your Lagers is what you wanted to see, you put it there, it didn't really exist: in the deepest corner of your mind *you've always been on this side*, WHAT YOU'RE LOOKING FOR NEVER EXISTED.

But then why did I go and be a worker, I defended myself in a whispered pious voice (that suspicion had the clarity of evidence, of something that is real), why did I get myself deported to Dachau?

Descents into hell, in accordance with the Dantean love of knowledge learned in school. There was no need to drag in the class struggle for that. An artist's curiosity was enough, as Terence said two thousand years ago, *Nihil humani a me alienum puto.* Nothing that is human is alien to me, and since today social unrest was also human, I had entered into it owing to my adventurous nature. The rest was a figment of my imagination to ennoble that episode of the Lagers, making it more important (the better to adorn myself).

No, I rebelled, pitiable, yes, but not to that extent. I'm killing myself to get to the truth, you can't take that away from me, if you deny that even now . . .

Exactly. Now. *Not* then.

Therefore (all the more reason) I was only chasing a fantasy, a delusion of *how I would have wanted to experience* that chapter; I was pursuing a memory produced by my desire. How could I have found any trace of it? That's why the infamous memory gap loosened up as soon as I thought I'd identified it in the rushing torrent of my life. For this reason not one of the scapegoats blamed for my repression held up to verification. That was the only way to explain why my coming and going in Germany had remained a parenthesis: it did not encompass the significance that I attributed to it. I was populating those forgotten acts and gestures with new thoughts that made the recollection so compelling to me now, almost as if I were repaying a debt.

Maybe I hadn't even left Verona of my own free will.

Think whatever you like, reader, that this is a theatrical dramatization, yet another snakeskin sloughed off so as to be reborn more humane and nobler than ever. Now that it's all over, I almost think so too. It may be because it took me a lifetime to try to make my suppressions mean something that I now find this pastime tedious. Who hasn't experienced extreme about-faces, how can you not distrust them? I distrust them and I experienced them!

I must also say that now, as I write these words, the doubt that came to me doesn't seem so critical. It can happen, indeed it's common, inevitable, that the past is viewed through the lens of hindsight. If one then represents it as something grander than the truth, it's not the end of the world. But at the time, five weeks ago, the life I'd been leading for months may have driven me a little crazy: eyes bloodshot and burning, hair uncombed, a bite to eat at the most irregular hours then left untouched. The fact is that that doubt seemed like the failure of my attempt at self-awareness.

I had based the recovery of my memories on a falsehood; therefore that recovery was also unsubstantiated. While I'd thought I finally had my feet on solid ground, I'd been resting them on imaginary terrain. I no longer had any hope of making my subjective self line up with my objective self. What else is paranoia? My social rage in the Lagers was my believing myself to be Napoleon or Henry IV.

It seems incredible but what saved me from the silence of the rationality I was striving for—so that I finally said to myself, if I have to be my own Gestapo, I give up—in short, what unexpectedly saved me (an unhoped-for intervention) was the literary compartment of my brain.

"What are you complaining about?" it asked me, as it usually does, telepathically, to soothe me. "If things are really as you fear, from a compositional point of view you can only rejoice: you don't have to understand the repression—your search fails, and that's that. You even have a nice conclusion: you reveal to the reader that the story of your deviation was a dream in which your imagination enacted one of the most tenacious (and vain) aspirations of all mortals, the eternal human dream of *correcting the past*."

I'll skip my ego's indignation ("*You're* my real snake, I flushed you out etcetera, your depraved sublimations etcetera"), but then again (why deny it?) my ego was tempted too, being ever so docile behind all its theatrical pretensions.

It was such a relief to be able to wrap up not only my wartime Germany but my entire complicated life that I almost followed that poetic diversion. Okay, let's delete the *almost*: I followed it.

I don't think I've ever felt so good. After a restorative two-day slumber, I tended to my fingernails, tinted my hair, smeared anti-wrinkle cream on my pasty face, applied tea compresses to my eyelids. I spruced myself up, straightened out the house, and even took a trip to Spain, invited by a couple of young friends.

For a week we drove around with local hosts, from Toledo to the Escurial, from Madrid to Córdoba and Granada, through La Mancha, with its old windmills profiled against the sky on the ridge of barren hills. I won't be like Don Quixote (I thought), who at the end of his life repudiated his knighthood: I was insane, I was insane, he said, now I'm sensible. I've known for some time who I am: a woman who's always told herself imaginary stories . . .

XIV

When I returned home (to Rome), given that the matter of the narrative was in any case resolved—how I'd tormented myself!—I unexpectedly got the idea that I might also satisfy my curiosity to know whether or not I had experienced the strike at IG Farben, the flight from Verona, and all the rest with the mentality (social rage) with which I had represented them.

It wasn't idle curiosity, I told myself, or a roundabout way of slipping back into the paranoia that I had verged on: it was a technique (there, that's the right word) to exercise my apperception of the external world.

Maybe, depending on the discrepancies I found between how I perceived myself and how I'd actually been, I could calculate the curve of my imagination, and then get into the habit of grading it based on my judgments of reality.

Armed with this new plan, I took the car and went out. Obviously, I needed something more than a single certificate, more than one document, mere guarantees of facts that can easily be manipulated. I needed a tangible sign of my interior shifts, a graph plotting my thinking in '44. The letters! That was my proof: the letters that I had written from IG Farben. They couldn't contain much, given the censorship and the fact that they were written to my parents. But if there was the slightest trace of the rage I now saw . . . stop! don't get ahead of yourself, find them first. However (my ego and the literary compartment of my brain secretly kept telling me), if I found the trace I was looking for, I would never again let myself be constrained by my snake. Now I understood that it was him, with his classist coils, who had almost convinced me that we were one soul, that my consciousness had never really been with the other side. You can squirm all you want, he taunted, tightening his grip, end up in the K-Lagers or nursing homes, it makes no difference, wherever you go, I am and will remain the social locus of your spirit.

You've revealed yourself! I hissed back at him. I quivered with emotion; you feel threatened, I said, trying to hypnotize him in turn. We are no longer in the same skin, all that shedding was not in vain, you were forced to come out to smother me, to silence me, and so you gave yourself away. Now I know what I must look for in my IG Farben letters, not just my social rage, but your disguises. Watch out, I'll flush you out no matter what, even if it means admitting that I made it all up.

I'll skip the initial attempts. Those letters from Höchst seemed to have vanished into thin air. To put it briefly, in one of my father's filing cabinets I found a slim folder containing the letters, arranged by date, that my mother had written to me at the Pfaffenwiese camp when I worked at IG Farben.

How did they get here? I'd kept them stowed in the inside pocket of the duffel bag that I had abandoned on the ground in Verona. How could my father have gotten hold of them? Of course, someone must have picked up the bag and found the letters, which must have been returned to the sender indicated on the back of the envelopes. An anonymous way of informing the sender that I'd been captured. Maybe it was someone who had witnessed the scene of the roundup from behind the closed shutters of a window. So the scene was accurate (otherwise how could these letters have gotten here?): If I had simply been rounded up, why would I have thrown away the bag with my documents? They would have been useful to me, they would have liberated me! The person who found the bag would have sent them back along with the letters. I flip through the folder, but all I find is my last time card from IG Farben, the one I had to punch when entering and leaving the factory. My first foreign worker's passport with the Frankfurt prison stamp isn't there. Neither is the discharge certificate from the hospital with the diagnosis of the reason for my admission: poisoning due to attempted suicide. My father must have torn them up. So he knew everything about me, at the time of that conversation in Bologna in '46 when I'd asked him if he'd had them search for me in August '44; that's why he was so evasive, as if he couldn't remember the details.

I stare at those letters as if they were relics: they prove to me that at least on one occasion I broke away from my classist snake, discarding my social identity along with that duffel bag, so I wouldn't be protected by it any longer.

I took the folder with me and hurried home.

My mother's letters, on gray-blue linen stationery, are all stamped by the censors, with pen strokes here and there. The writing is large and distinct, the lines spaced. Her feelings are patent and proud, the phrasing lofty:

. . . remember never to do anything either in public or in private against your dignity as a girl and as an Italian, nor allow others to do so, to do anything against your dignity, that is. (April 1, 1944)

I wonder whether this interlude of yours wasn't fated (since you certainly sought this fate). To learn about people and things and nations. I only pray that the Almighty sustain you and make you a serene observer. (April 27, 1944)

With respect to the reconstruction of my time at Höchst, recounted in "In the Ch 89," I discover two repressions that I attribute to my mental snake, and which I intend to go back and reexamine more deliberately.

One concerns my correspondence. It isn't true, as I said in "In the Ch 89," that in March I stopped writing to my parents once and for all. I had resumed in early April, then stopped immediately afterward. In early May I'd written again, with another interruption toward the end of that month (the time of the strike, prison, and suicide attempt), and a new exchange of letters from the hospital, starting June 20, as shown by an appeal from my mother. I am reconstructing this writing with its fits and starts from salutations like "My dear silent daughter," and from pleas such as "Let us hear from you, your mother is begging you."

The other repression regards my intention to relocate to the Collis Metall Werke in Mannheim. From my mother's letters it appears that, in early April, I'd asked her to procure a recommendation for me that would enable me to obtain a reassignment (it was the period of time when I was avoiding the comrades who had treated me as a "spy" and as a "*provò*," provocateur).

I can't remember the reason why I wanted to go to that factory and not another. In any case, I had completely forgotten the whole episode. At first, my mother had made another attempt to ask why I didn't request repatriation from the Italian consul instead, then why I didn't at least ask to be hired as an interpreter rather than as a worker; ultimately she'd suggested the names of senior officials to whom I might turn, to support my request for transfer. It seems I wrote to one of them and obtained what I wanted: the manager of the Collis Metall Werke had had me summoned but I turned the opportunity down (most likely when I'd linked up with Grùscenka and the Poles and reconciled with Martine). My mother was confused by my impulses.

Mainly she portrayed her days to me in great detail. Now I understand that she was trying to share their quietude with me, in part to raise my spirits and make me feel close to her, but I also know that back then her accounts had a chilling effect on me, and her anguish for her daughter and for "human suffering" sounded abstract to me. She spoke of her early-afternoon walks along Lake Como, her tone relaxed. In between the depictions of boat tours in Varenna, concerts, afternoon teas, and a visit to Villa Monastero—whose "paths and terraces and loggias and stairways" she described to me, noting the "marvelous view" they afforded—her anxieties for me cropped up in these terms:

> You say you're hungry and your work is exhausting and arduous. Can't you find something else to do? (May 5, 1944)

> You know, I don't understand why you don't find more intelligent work than that of a *femme de peine*. (May 10, 1944)

I must have responded with harsh words, because on May 15 she wrote:

> Mothers understand that life often makes us speak and act angrily, in part due to a suppressed intolerance of life itself, too often onerous and *désespérante*. We'd like to overcome all opposition and we can't, so we rebel however and whenever it occurs. Yesterday we had a nice excursion . . .

And she spoke about the beautiful vistas to end on a hopeful note: "We'll go back again together when you return."

The following day she expressed concern about my health:

> You wrote that you're starving and meanwhile you're gaining weight. It's the bread that's fattening.

And the day after she explained:

> It's the bread that makes your skin break out. If you ate more meat and more fruit instead, you'd feel better.

On May 19 she worried:

> You write that you won't return ahead of time, because you want to "acquire social experience." But don't you think six months are sufficient for that?

On May 20 she was distressed:

My dear little *pupetta*, I keep thinking about your hands since I know
you're not working as an interpreter and I'm worried about them. How is
it that they still haven't healed? Didn't you get the cream I sent you? Show
that not everyone is a traitor. Live in accordance with your own ideals. So
many illusions and so much presumption in us poor atoms tossed about
by the tempestuous winds of war. And Wiechert is right: start living a
simple, solitary life among the fields and woods, gardening and reading
books. The rest is vain agitation, pointless experience.

By then she no longer wrote a couple of times a week, as she had the
first few months, but every day; she lived in a state of insomnia, and implored me to come back: "It's your mother who is begging you." She'd sent
me one parcel after another (all arrived too late), and she harbored hopes
that my father would forgive me: one night, hearing her crying, he'd allowed her to speak about me. On another evening "Papa" had let her read
one of my letters aloud to him and had listened "with understanding." She
kept praising him to me, a man who lived for his family, a hard worker,
generous ("What would we do without him?"). Now I realize that she had
assumed the role of mediator, and was performing with me the same kind
of conciliation toward my father that she performed with him toward me.
At the time, however, I thought she had lost all critical judgment if she could
be grateful to a man who even disapproved of her maternal love. At least
in that regard, when I was back at home, I'd heard her exclaim, "Your father
is a dear man, kind and amiable, but so vacuous at times."

I probably felt she was insecure and I must have wanted to bolster her,
because the letters show that I reassured her of my affection each time, and
expressed my admiration for her "pureness of heart," her "elegant way of
dressing," and she replied that she'd told "Papa" how much I appreciated
her. Finally, it appears that I alluded to vague persecutions but had to then
add that I was "strong," because she wrote back that she'd been quite
alarmed but was glad that I was "well-liked, respected by everyone," and
she immediately explained the importance of dignity. Now her writing was
more agitated, jerky, the lines closer together; this reminder of the rules

was now peremptory. After she learned that I'd been in prison, she wrote to me on June 28 (her last letter):

> I thought that everything was settled and then that terrible misfortune happens to you and you go to the hospital. When will your trials end? Remember, my dear daughter, that I want nothing more than your physical, moral, social, and judicial well-being. You must not do anything against the laws, usages, and customs for any reason. Don't smoke. Don't give in to instinct. Exchange what I sent you, if you receive it, for food, but do so openly. Remember the words of Manzoni: "Never say a word that applauds vice and mocks virtue." And obey my advice, I beg you. No one will ever love you more selflessly than your mother.

I reassemble the letters and am about to put them back in the folder when I see an envelope sticking out from the bottom of the cover flap, which I hadn't noticed. I pull it out, feel it, it's bumpy. I open it and find strange strips of paper covered with my dense, cramped writing, a spattering of marks crammed all around the pages (the scraps that remain), and four aerograms written in pencil, the words crowded together there too, as if there was never enough room to write.

Those irregular cut-up scraps are what remain of my letters from Höchst. As I read, I am unable to come up with an explanation for those cuttings. I seem to think (maybe I'm wrong) that censorship at the time was limited to drawing black lines through forbidden phrases and did not resort to scissors, let alone take the trouble to put together the saved fragments with Scotch tape. What on earth could I have written if even the preserved passages were an indictment? Why hadn't they also censored snippets like these (undated among the clippings)?

> I saw photographs of young German girls in a German magazine, volunteers employed as postal clerks or in other labor service jobs. Heroines. I felt bad. And to think that I would be terribly ashamed to be pictured there. [snip] How can they smile so impudently and confidently in those pages? So much rhetoric.

[snip] on this point: poor people, when they can, spend it all on food. Mama who is astonished and looks down on "instincts" doesn't know what it is to live on rutabagas.

[snip] politically as well, even the letters from [censored] seem false and rhetorical to me.

And I confess: I hide the fact of having volunteered out of patriotism even from the Germans, from the SS. I'm ashamed of it. I'm telling you the truth, I'm ashamed of that. Oh, not of having done it: indeed I can't even believe I was so serious, so steadfast in my impulses, *despite having thought it all through*. But no one can believe and understand it. A little like Papa [censored]. So I put up with it and keep quiet. I tell people: compulsory labor service for declared Fascists. But I'm ashamed of having been a declared Fascist. Genuinely.

On a scrap where the ink is diluted, as if stained by water (my tears or my mother's?), I read a clear affirmation: "I don't want to have an *individual* life or opinions anymore." Further down, between strokes of the censor's pen, this little phrase appears:

The Ighé [I meant the IG Farben] is independent and the *Arbeitsfront* bows to it.

So I had already sensed at Höchst the discovery, which I thought I had only made in Dachau, of the Nazi Party's subordination to the economic power (of capitalism).

In a fragment that was obscure, too cut-up, I finally realized that I was replying to the letter in which my mother had written me that, other than a life in harmony with nature and among books, "the rest is vain agitation, pointless experience." I copy it, again without piecing together the snippets:

The rest is vain agitation, true. But not pointless experience. That is, *vain* [censored] *would and should achieve* the intended purpose: yes. But not

[snip] of the individual who experiences it. In fact, the more he [censored] experience, the *truer* and more considerate of others [snip] he will emerge from it.

The letters are postmarked from Frankfurt and not from the Lager; a nurse must have mailed them for me. In one of them I read:

[censored] a society that I *had understood differently* at the time of my blissful, untroubled studies. I'm in the hospital [censored]. Like in the Lager, like in prison.

There is another scissored scrap that seems to be on different paper from that of the camp. I read the fragment of a sentence:

rumors about my alleged spying activities for which I had been imprisoned [I note the historical past tense].

I had probably already intuited that the class struggle was the most forbidden topic, since, while I said too much about my political opinions (on Fascism and Nazism), I was careful not to mention our failed strike. At the time we workers didn't know that the Nazis had been preparing for a mass uprising of foreign workers since '42 by developing a plan called Operation Valkyrie, but even I with my individualistic upbringing had grasped the fact that, for me personally, rebellion could be overlooked, whereas if there were even a remote hint of a class action in concert with my comrades I was done for.

In another letter I describe vomiting, blood transfusions, hemorrhaging for six weeks. I write that I have a fever and am urinating blood as a result of the hardships I've undergone (I don't mention the attempted suicide). I announce that "I will be officially repatriated." Perhaps a few days later (the postmarks are illegible and I did not write the dates), I report:

The day before yesterday the consul in Frankfurt actually came in person with another man (his deputy) to visit me. He wants to have me return home and I am totally in agreement.

But perhaps the letter that strikes me the most is the one where I ask, "Do you mind if I come back?" Adding:

> You'll see, when I return you'll tell me: "Well? You look fine. Where's all the suffering you say you witnessed and endured?"

The scraps end there. Missing is most of the information provided in my mother's letters, which must have gotten lost somehow, about my hunger, about the Collis Metall Werke, about my work as a *femme de peine*, about the lesions on my hands, which had actually lasted much longer than I remembered (another repression to bolster the memory of being much stronger than I was, physically as well). But there *is*, in these mutilated sentences, the social rage those letters hadn't been aware of. Reading them, it appeared that I was speaking and acting "angrily" because of my rebellious nature. The only revolt my mother had been fervent about was the famous crusade for washbasins (I had told her about that too!), "in rightful defense of decency," as she had commented.

XV

So, not only were the events true, but I also found everything I was looking for. I uncovered your most secret hiding place (I'm talking to my snake), now it's I who will stifle you.

It was all true, I keep telling myself. It was even more true than I'd remembered because the exchange of letters represents an umbilical cord with the family that was not abruptly severed, and therefore the attempted suicide and the about-face in Verona appear less like the rash actions of a minor, prone to extreme emotions, than like virtually the last resort of a person acknowledging the state of things after having tried in vain to change them. There is an inaccessible divinity, a father awaiting the unconditional surrender of a daughter who dared to violate his law; there are the unbending principles of "laws, usages, and customs"; there is the frightened solitude of a girl who, from the depths of a Lager, expresses her convictions, declares her new political positions (even from those few snippets of words you can see that she persists in it, keeps returning to it), while at the same time pitying her mother's vain anguish and reassuring her, "Don't worry, I'm strong!" But bounced like a ball between her mother's "finer things" and the filthy spoon of the lice-ridden man at the Lager's canteen, that girl had been a lot less "strong" than I remembered her. No wonder I had omitted, in my reconstruction, the steady trickle of my sporadic correspondence. The fact that I constantly went back to writing showed that, in my heart, during those first six months of my volunteer experience, there had not been as clean a break with my environment as I wanted to believe. That's where my classist snake had lurked: in the recesses of my feelings that resisted making an *absolute* leap to the other side.

Never mind that it may not have been easy; Dostoyevsky said that reality justifies everything, but that doesn't change a thing. So don't interrupt me (to my snake). Here's the proof: if that girl preferred to die, seek asylum in a K-Lager, and disappear out of the country after being paralyzed, it means that, even when she was well, she had lost all hope of being able to continue the social struggle once she found herself back with her family. As a result, from the moment she returned to Italy on a stretcher, she was subconsciously resigned to giving up. She made the last wrench away from her surroundings with Gheorg the poet. But that split convinced her once and for all of the impossibility of reconciling private affections and the collective struggle. By then she was snared by the dissociation cultivated by those who do not struggle; namely, that fighting for social justice was incompatible with personal happiness. She was *committed* to finding fulfillment in the private sphere (with Domenico).

Added to that was the fact that everyone around her after the war—just like her father, though for opposite reasons—expected her to regret her volunteer work in the Third Reich. But she'd already answered those accusations in her letters from Höchst, when she was ashamed of having been a Fascist but not of having left home; in fact, she couldn't "even believe" she'd been "so serious, so steadfast" in her impulses as to enlist for the Lagers. The condemnation of those who had been part of the Resistance rekindled all the unpleasant insults, the mockery she'd experienced at Höchst, the arguments with her friend-enemy in the cattle car, the beating from the red triangles in the Dachau toilet. But it was there, in Dachau, that the snake had unquestionably settled in, when Lucia had chosen a solitary path of rebellion, which lasted thirty years . . . She'd fled from Verona but also from Dachau: from her privileged status but also from the fate common to those on the other side, who have no means of getting out, who lack the psychological resources that stemmed from her class and allowed her to address the guards uncaringly. You're shriveling up, huh? (to my snake).

That girl, later woman, saw the ambiguity of her social consciousness as the objective impossibility of sharing what she had learned with anyone; consequently, as luck would have it, she forgot the actions by which she had personally gone to the other side. Rooted for half a lifetime on a pillar of silence, like an ancient anchorite . . .

And it never occurred to me (odd, don't you think?) that *this silence*, which I had imposed on myself and which I attributed to social pressure, could *actually be ascribed to me*.

It isn't true, I was well aware of it—even now I'm lying. The proof is that in '54, referring to my escape from the K-Lager, I wrote in "Asylum at Dachau": "I didn't make it." A judgment that was also appropriate later on. So I knew it even while my memory was silent regarding IG Farben, the repatriation, the redeparture from Verona, and being interned as an asocial, a black triangle. I knew it when I went back to Germany in the fall of '54, one of the many events that I have not written about here (I couldn't recount everything). But I can't omit that: I wandered along the Rhine for a couple of months, with stops in Bonn and Cologne, never thinking of going to Frankfurt-Höchst though I spent several days in Mainz, thirty kilometers from my first Lager. I was convinced I'd gone back there to see Schwester Vincentia, as I'd promised nine years earlier in August '45 when I left for Homburg with the Russians. I kept repeating that I'd been right to live.

"But of course, I believe you," she reassured me in the gruff tone her voice took on when she was sad. "Be at peace, Luzi, you were right."

But I'm afraid I went there mainly to restock my supply of drugs from the various doctors at the university clinic where I'd been hospitalized at the end of the war, counting on a certain popularity that I hoped would carry over from my earlier stay in Pavilion VIII. I went around discreetly showing one and the other my bone X-rays, which I had brought with me to induce them to compassion, and to obtain the precious prescriptions I needed to buy the ampules at the pharmacy. I told them about the Lagers to move them even more.

Sometimes when you go astray and touch bottom, you finally come out on the other side. And I had started to recover. But what I meant to say now is that deep inside I was secretly aware that it was I who had failed. Simply because the class leap in Dachau had been so extreme, the terror of it so violent, that it drove me to take refuge in oblivion. Actually acknowledging it, however? Never! The lady couldn't admit to her failures, she made others pay for them. The lady understood human frailties so she relativized everything so as not to really side with those beneath her, with whom she declared herself to be so sympathetic. She felt different from the people of her bourgeois class solely because she criticized their *conformist* lifestyle no matter how they were defined (right or left), while continuing in fact— though with her fruitless reservations—to live like them herself.

You know, snake, it's not that I'm now shocked by my small-mindedness. I know that human beings' need to find significance is such that sometimes they seek it even in crime (I had already seen that in Dachau), which wasn't even my pathetic case. Still, it gives me no pleasure, even academically since I can't do anything about it, to ascertain that I spent half my life playing hide-and-seek with myself.

That's how you want it? So be it. That's how I reacted for thirty years. And we became one and the same, my snake. Even when I finally recognized you, at Villa della Pace, and cried to myself, "I'm a snake," even then I ignored you coiled up there where you had firmly lodged yourself: in my rancor toward all those who had doomed me and pushed me into your coils.

You want proof? See "As Long as the Head Lives." In the story where I shed my neo-racism toward my disabled brothers, I accepted as my own the judgment that had devastated me after the war, by writing, Yes, that's right, I went to the Lagers *because* I was a Fascist, and, oh, the Soviet captain, though from a country that had seen a revolution from below, did not reject me for it; indeed, he *genuinely* took pity on me and had effectively helped me without hiding behind slippery words. That was enough for me.

Look, my poor snake, I haven't lost heart because of that. Gone are the days when feeling like a worm demoralized and depressed me even more. I'll tell you my one last thought: I am no worse than the others. I am like them (those under your control, I mean), but a bit more rigorous.

At least I was spared one thing in this seesawing back-and-forth, and I kiss the ground in gratitude: I never bought a social conscience with the small change of an ideological label, just as at one time people bought indulgences to get to paradise at a lesser cost.

But that didn't spare me from also becoming your prey, albeit in a more abstruse and arduous way because you left me nothing to stand on, no matter where I turned. Where did you get the slimy nerve to do such an abominable thing? Just at the time when I'd come closest to escaping from you forever, when I went to the Lagers *of my own accord*.

And now, my dear enemy, I will crush that reptilian head of yours with the decisive proof (thank God for my mother's letters, which provided it). Doesn't the complete absence of the Collis Metall Werke episode tell you something? Only at this moment does the visual image I had of it ten months later materialize before me: it was during the time I was in hiding when, going back toward Höchst, I passed through Mannheim and that underground factory was shown to me from outside. So, before I discovered you and convinced myself that I had always, solely, been on your side, you forked tongue, you had attempted an opposite maneuver to make me believe that, in the Third Reich, I was wholly on the side of the oppressed, fully with them. So that I wouldn't look for you where you had so cleverly, insidiously coiled up and retreated, there, in the mental reservation with which I had thought to decamp, not entirely because I refused to go back to Italy, but in part, yes, when I had entertained the plan to get myself transferred to the Collis Metall Werke. Most likely I intended to introduce myself to my new comrades in Mannheim as a deportee, without having to deal with being a volunteer Fascist student. But how would I do it? By securing that transfer with a recommendation from above; that is, by taking advantage of the social status of my origins. I had later become aware of the contradiction, for one thing because my relations with my fellow Lager mates had improved, but this oscillation had existed: I wanted to be a worker, while letting people know who I was, thereby deep down laying the ground for the consideration due to my bourgeois circumstances. The fear I subsequently had of reverting to that temptation—using class privilege to save myself from the fate of vulnerable commoners—and wanting to throw away my papers so as to put myself in a similarly helpless position, is even more understandable. But, in this light, the fact that after Dachau and Thomasbräu I got myself hired at Siemens in Munich, again using my real name, is no longer just the boldness of a nineteen-year-old carried away by her impregnability: it's you popping up again, Mr. Snake, as though I was unconsciously holding on to the possibility of resorting to high places.

Then I'd once again shut off that means of salvation—though hastily, almost as if I didn't trust myself anymore—by stealing and falsifying doctors' notes at the factory, a crime that was summarily punished. And when I disappeared, after three weeks at Siemens, I had once more discarded my name (and my class) by sending the factory ID card with my true identity to my mother.

So I was inured against you because in any case, you see, choices do in fact help, but then I didn't know you as I do today. Now I'm much more alerted to you. I am well aware that our grappling isn't over (by now this is how it is, I too have my coils around you). But you also know that, despite your deceitful tricks, you had not completely beaten me when I'd escaped from Dachau: love for my comrades still led me back to Höchst, to the place where I had joined their struggle. You know very well that later on, over the course of my life, my excesses and confusions were the results of your poison, true, but they were also the cries by which I called out to them, those lost comrades, as I remained atop the pillar of silence where I unknowingly kept them within me.

And now I am fully aware (you know that, right?), also knowing the aftermath, as I return to the place where my steps led me on that night thirty-two years ago to find my IG Farben comrades at Höchst.

It's February 7, 1945, the Americans are deployed beyond Worms, I have to hurry if I want to be in time to reach my old Lager, the unconscious destination of my about-face in Verona that now seems to have been predestined from the start.

I slept in Mannheim, in a barrack with internees working at the Collis Metall Werke underground factory where I had once thought of being transferred, from the outside a snow-covered hill with bunker-type access. I waited all day for a chance to jump between two carriages of a train bound for Frankfurt. I finally did it when it was twilight and, hanging on to a bumper, my hands and face stung by frost, I reached Höchst. I started walking to Mainz at night; the dry air seemed almost warm after the trip on the bumpers. In the total darkness I made out my barracks: Pfaffenwiese 300, Ledigenheim Lager.

I crawl along the ground and lift the lowest strand of the barbed wire fence. I'm hesitant to press my index finger on the sharp metal points that are not charged by the electric current. I'll see my IG Farben comrades again. I slip along the wooden barracks and I'm just at my dorm when I see a girl come out:

"Carla, is it you?"

"Lucia!"

We look at each other wordlessly, like ghosts in the darkness of that February night.

"Didn't they repatriate you?" she asks.

"Then they deported me to Dachau and I escaped."

"You shouldn't have come back here, it's worse than before."

"What about you, Carla?"

"They released me after the strike, Luigi too. We're still together as before, but we're holding our breath. We're waiting for the war to end."

Carla has lost weight. I can't make out colors but she no longer seems like the big rosy girl she used to be. Her voice is drawn.

"You've changed," I say.

"You too. How did you get in?"

I tell her quickly.

"Please, don't come to us. The war is almost over. We don't need any new trouble right now."

"And the others?" I ask.

"The jinx is gone. If it's Martine and Grùscenka you want to know about, zilch. Didn't you find them in Dachau? Pina is seeing a Russian guy, Jacqueline is in the *Krankenrevier* (the camp infirmary); she sprayed acid in her eyes so she wouldn't have to work but she used the wrong dose and she's going blind. But, look, I don't want to linger with you, they might see us. Go on, clear out, don't get me in trouble just now." She starts to return to the barrack and says, "You scare me, you know, you look like a felon." She closes the door behind her.

I lean against the wooden wall. I'll go to the Russians, maybe they'll take me in. A felon, I repeat to myself, and it wrings my heart. My mind suddenly finds solace with the Flemish girl and Lulù (help me, you two, from up there):

Two days before I escaped from Dachau, they had scuffled with two political internees during evening roll call.

"Murderer," a red triangle shouted at Lulù, "you turned in our comrades."

"You bet, ladies," Lulù replied. "*Mais oui, mesdames, mesdames,*" she repeated, "*mesdames.*"

"And you, fucking the oppressors!" the political internees threw at the Flemish girl. "Aren't you ashamed of yourself?"

That night I'd heard a commotion behind the barrack in the K-Lager. I glued my face to the windowpane. I glimpsed Lulù from behind, kneeling with her head in the pants of an SS soldier who, standing in front of her, was kicking her and yelling, trying to wrench her head. The Flemish girl appeared, raising a clenched fist to the soldier and screaming, "Filthy Hitler, filthy Hitler."

The soldier had put two fingers in his mouth (I imagine), because three long whistles pierced the darkness. Lulù had broken away.

"I bit a Nazi dick," her raucous slit of a mouth crowed triumphantly to the Flemish girl, who was still waving her fist, and, dragging her by the hand, she ran and hid in the barrack.

The soldiers had come with leaden steps. They'd seized both of them. The Flemish girl looked at me, white as a sheet, her voice expressionless: "Tell what they did to me," she mumbled.

"Tell what I did instead," Lulù shouted, her hand raised to the sky.

Two machine-gun bursts exploded near the fence. Two days later I fled from that Lager and now I whisper, "Help me, you two," as I move away from the wall of my longed-for barrack at Frankfurt-Höchst; I'll go to the

Russians, they weren't programmed for individualism, they won't reject me. I lie on the ground and crawl to the fence on all fours.

"Halt!" A male voice, German. I lie still, as I've seen cockroaches do when playing dead. Cockroaches can think. But the steps move closer, a foot pokes me. I steal a peek from between lowered lids; the eye of a gun barrel is staring at me.

"Stand up, let's go."

With the rifle prodding my back, I walk to the *Lagerführer*'s office. Some phone calls are made. A kick shoves me into a corner.

At some point, I don't know when, my former *Lagerführer* comes in; tall, imposing, wearing boots, he slams the door angrily. But as soon as he sees me he's stunned. His face relaxes. A smile plays on his lips. He sends the guards away with a slight wave of his fingers.

"You are Lucia M.," he says (but his tone is questioning).

"No."

"You are Lucia M.," he says, more and more impressed. "You are Lucia M.," he yells, suddenly enraged. But he controls himself: "What are you doing here?" he asks softly. I don't answer, curled up on the floor in my corner.

He calls the guards with a shout: "Search her. Her documents."

Two men pat me down thoroughly: "No documents."

"Perfect." The *Lagerführer* smiles, and sends the guards away again. I am now standing against the wall. The boots approach slowly, until the voice roars with unimaginable fury, the purple face inches away from my eyes.

"You," he spits, "the daughter of a Fascist undersecretary, repatriated and treated with all due consideration, have the effrontery to turn up here again and show that slutty face of yours?" A slap. "Whore." Another slap. "What have you been doing all these months?" A kick to the shins. "Answer me!" Another kick. "I said, answer me!" And on and on. "Filthy whore," he shakes me, "traitor," he grabs me by the shoulders and jostles me, "twenty years old, is it possible you can be such a traitor at twenty years old, filthy shameless tramp." I stare at him, my eyes boring into his face, concentrating on leaning against the wall so I won't lose its support and collapse (I must have thought that if I broke off eye contact with him I'd be lost). "But I'll kill you, see," he snarls as I go on staring at him. It's over if I faint. And from deep down in my diaphragm, my voice involuntarily hurls the word *"Feige"* (coward) at him. Like a conditioned reflex I go on repeating it as if that word were keeping me alive.

Herr Barek, the *Lagerführer* (a German Czechoslovakian), is panting. He sits behind his desk and I slump to the floor (don't faint).

"That's why we lost the war," he mumbles, "because of worthless trash like you." And as he says it, he doesn't know that thirty-two years later I still won't remember him with hatred because he at least admitted that we made him lose the war (it's the only acknowledgment I've ever had).

"I could crush you between two fingers," he continues, "like a flea, but it would be slim consolation. I'll have you sent to Dachau—no." His eyes light up. "Better yet, to a brothel for the *Strafbataillonen*." He gives a shout and the guards arrive: "In the guardhouse," he says, "and tomorrow morning," he instructs by gestures: two wrists crossed, to specify handcuffs, then a hand chop into the crook of his elbow, to indicate the brothel.

In the guardhouse, a small room of about two by three meters, I find a woman huddled up in a corner. I take a closer look: it's Lidja, a beautiful Russian girl I was friendly with at the time of the strike.

"What are you doing here?" I whisper in Russian.

She tells me that she was caught outside the fence, where she'd gone to pick up some bread from a friend. I tell her my situation.

"Poor you," she sighs. "I'm getting off with one night in lockup, it's the maximum penalty for a crime like mine, but you're screwed."

"Quiet!" the guard, an elderly man, orders us every so often in an exasperated voice.

Meanwhile, Lidja fingers my coat, my dress, my shoes, all expensive stuff because it's the best of what I robbed from the bombed-out apartments. Like Louis, I chose wisely. I took only what I could wear. On my wrist I have the little watch he'd given me and around my neck a slim gold chain that I snatched from a body, like the Jewish *Sonderkommandos* did at Auschwitz.

Lidja has an idea.

"Listen," she whispers in my ear, "give the guard your watch. Tell him you don't need it anyway because you're going to end up gassed in Dachau. In return ask him to give us a blanket for tonight because we feel cold." I look at her doubtfully. "Do what I tell you," she insists.

Things go as Lidja predicted. The guard gives me a pitying look, pockets the wristwatch, and tosses us a blanket.

Once we're wrapped tightly under the cover, Lidja gives me instructions: "Take off all your good things, including your socks and panties, which I don't have, and put on my rags. I'll put on all the good stuff. But slowly, so the guard won't notice too much movement under the blanket. Okay?"

"Why not?" I whisper.

"Good girl," Lidja says excitedly. "Then I'll say that I have an upset stomach and can't hold it in. When he hears my voice, he won't prevent me from using the toilet. He knows I won't run away, he himself is releasing me tomorrow morning. Instead you'll go to the toilet, wearing my rags. Do you get it?"

"Lidja, they'll punish you."

"For what? What did I know? He took the wristwatch, you can tell it's a woman's watch, he can't deny it. If they accuse me, I'll report him. He'll have to say that you gave it to him. And the same goes for me. And if I didn't go to the toilet after all, it was because I blacked out. I'll have to go in your elegant panties, what a pity, to prove to him that I wasn't lying. How could I ever have imagined that you would take advantage of the situation? That devious Italian, I'll say, instead of reviving me . . . What a bunch of traitors, you Nazis fell for it, trusting them as an ally! Don't worry, Lucia, words won't fail me."

"You're doing this for me."

"Hurry up, give me those good things, I've been dreaming about them for years."

An hour later I had changed into Lidja's coverall and clogs, with her scarf wound around my neck, tied under the chin like a Russian peasant girl.

"Ohhh," Lidja starts moaning with shrill cries and I writhe as though having a colic attack. She makes a rude spluttering noise with her mouth: "I can't hold it, I can't hold it," and I bend over double.

"Don't stink up the guardhouse, you shitty Bolshevik, get to the latrines, go on," the guard says, losing his patience.

And meekly clutching my belly and taking tight little steps as if to hold it in, I hurry out, go through the gate, straighten up and make a run for it. By the time he looks for me, sounds the alarm, and they unleash the dogs, I'm far away! Racing like mad.

Lidja was arrested as my accomplice and sent to Dachau. But as soon as they loaded her into the freight car, she jumped from the moving train and crawled to a bush with a fractured femur. She hid in a hayloft, living on chestnuts, tubers, and snails for three weeks, until the Americans arrived. I met up with her again in the transit camp in Homburg, in the Saar, when I arrived in a wheelchair with my Russian captain, six months later. She was completely healed and was dancing the Cossack, her beautiful face proud, her voice effusive: "See your gold chain? Spoils of war!" And she still laughed about the trick we'd played on the guard (she wanted to make me smile because it hurt her to see me in a wheelchair).

But I didn't yet know any of this when I fled in her rags from the guard-house of my old Lager at Höchst, crying from the pain of the *Lagerführer's* blows, which the running aggravated. At the same time, like Lulù, I felt triumphant: finally, I thought (laughing through my tears), I myself, personally, have also been beaten. Now I'm truly like the others, thrashed, spat upon, just like them, I won't revert back to my social class, and I ran and ran toward Mainz.

Rome, November 1977

TRANSLATOR'S NOTES

37 *"Arriva la banda . . ."*: "Here comes the band, here comes the band of good-for-nothing scoundrels with the Duce as ringleader, the black shirts are all here . . ."

172 "experience human affairs sufficiently . . .": From the free-verse poem "On the Death of Carlo Imbonati" (1806).

176 Ph 32: Though the terms *Ch 89* and *Ph 32* are not explained in the novel, presumably they are factory shops within the Chemical (*Chemische*) and Pharmaceutical (*Pharmazeutisch*) divisions of IG Farben.

176 *"badogliani"*: A reference to the Badogli partisans and the government of Pietro Badoglio. On September 8, 1943, Italy, formerly an ally of Germany, surrendered to the Allies (under the Badoglio government) and Italian troops ceased fighting; the fall of Mussolini had occurred in July.

182 *maquisards*: The Maquis were rural guerrilla bands of French Resistance fighters, called *maquisards*, during the Occupation of France in World War II.

184 Pétainists: After French marshal Philippe Pétain, chief of state of Vichy France, from 1940 to 1944.

184 the Iron Cross: A German military medal dating back to the nineteenth century. During the 1930s, the Nazi regime in Germany superimposed a swastika on it, turning it into a Nazi symbol.

185 KG: *Kriegsgefangenen*, prisoners of war.

185 *Volksdeutschen*: Ethnic Germans (excluding those of Jewish origin) living outside of Germany; they were considered German regardless of the fact that they did not hold German or Austrian citizenship. By contrast, *Reichsdeutschen*, or Imperial Germans, were German citizens living within Germany.

187 Nice and Savoy: A reference to Italian irredentism in Savoy. In November 1942, in conjunction with the German occupation of most of Vichy France, Italian forces took control of Grenoble, Nice, the Rhône River delta, and nearly all of Savoy.

190 *Sicherheitsdienst*: The *Sicherheitsdienst des Reichsführers* (SS or SD) was the intelligence agency of the SS and the Nazi Party.

191 "Piazza Venezia": Mussolini talked to the crowds from the balcony of Palazzo Venezia, overlooking Piazza Venezia.

197 "the Na 14": Here, "Na" stands for the element sodium, used in the process to produce a synthetic rubber substitute for the war effort.

223 *repubblichini*: The name given to supporters of the RSI, the Fascist Italian Social Republic (Repubblica Sociale Italiana), formed as a puppet state in northern Italy with Mussolini as its leader.

237 black triangle: The black triangle badge marked prisoners in Nazi concentration camps as "asocial" (*arbeitsscheu*); such individuals were considered a threat to the values of the Third Reich.

242 *Strafbataillonen*: Penal battalions in the Wehrmacht during World War II were brigades made up of military and civilian criminals; those sentenced to these units were usually made to undertake dangerous, high-casualty missions.

249 "*über alles auf der Welt*": From the first line of the German national anthem: "Germany, Germany above all else, above all else in the world."

250 "put himself out . . . for the sake of his art": Fyodor Dostoyevsky, *The House of the Dead*, trans. David McDuff (New York: Penguin, 1985), 244.

252 *Hochdeutsch*: Standard German.

256 "Work sets you free": The slogan "*Arbeit macht frei*" appeared on the entrance to Auschwitz and other labor camps.

275 "*non doma*": The phrase is from Garibaldi's hymn: "*Bastone Tedesco l'Italia non doma*": the German truncheon will not subjugate/crush Italy.

279 *bersaglieri*: The rifle regiment of the Italian army.

281 "*A me piaccion gli occhi neri . . .*": From the song "Ma le gambe," lyrics by Alfredo Bracchi, 1938.

303 the Todt: The Todt Organization, named for its founder, Fritz Todt, was a German engineering group in the Third Reich known for using forced labor.

307 Resistance merits: Surviving partisans were awarded gold medals as representatives of the Resistance.

308 *"Le donne non ci vogliono . . . uno che non ha sangue nelle vene"*: A Fascist song whose text was written in 1944 by Mario Castellacci.

317 Balduina . . . *borgatari* . . . San Paolo: Balduina is a modern suburb of Rome. A *borgataro* is an inhabitant of a Roman working-class suburb. Italgas is one of the gas refineries in San Paolo.

319 "look and pass on": The reference is to a line from Dante's *Commedia*: *"Non ragioniam di lor, ma guarda e passa"* (Inf. III, 51), "Let us not talk of them, but look and pass on."

322 "humiliated and insulted": A reference to a novel by Fyodor Dostoyevsky, first published in 1861, known in English by various titles: *Humiliated and Insulted*, *The Insulted and Humiliated*, *The Insulted and the Injured*, or *Injury and Insult*.

323 Henry IV: A reference to Luigi Pirandello's 1922 play *Enrico IV*, about an Italian aristocrat who falls off his horse while playing the role of Henry IV during Carnevale and who, when he comes to, believes himself to actually be Henry.

330 "'Never say a word that applauds vice and mocks virtue'": From "On the Death of Carlo Imbonati."

331 *"Arbeitsfront"*: Labor Front.

335 an ancient anchorite: The reference is likely to stylites, or "pillar dwellers," solitary Christian ascetics who lived on pillars, preaching, fasting, and praying, in the belief that bodily mortification would ensure the salvation of their souls.

342 *Sonderkommandos*: *Sonderkommandos* were units composed of Nazi death camp prisoners, mainly Jews, who during the Holocaust were forced to assist with the disposal of gas chamber victims.